TAKE
A
NUMBER

AMY DAWS

Published by: Amy Daws, LLC
ISBN 978-1-944565-65-7

Proofing: Julia Griffis and Lydia Rella
Editing: Jenny Sims with Editing4Indies
Formatting:Champagne Book Design
Cover Design: Amy Daws

CONNECT WITH AMY DAWS

To be notified of my upcoming releases, sales, and giveaways, signup for my newsletter!

And if you like to talk bookish things with other book lovers, join my Facebook reader group.
www.facebook.com/groups/AmyDawsLondonLovers

Or follow me on social media!
www.facebook.com/amydawsauthor
www.twitter.com/amydawsauthor
instagram.com/amydawsauthor

CHAPTER 1

Dean

The bell above the door jingles as the familiar scent of fried dough permeates my nose. I glance around the quaint bakery peppered with regulars and find Norah behind the glass display case.

She purses her lips when she sees me coming. "You were just here last night, Moser. Aren't you worried about ruining that supposed six-pack you're always bragging about?"

"Norah, have you been thinking about me naked *again?*" A knowing smile spreads across my face. "You really should see a therapist about your obsession with me. My friend Lynsey has her own practice now…you could give her a call."

Her cheeks flush a rosy hue that I've become addicted to bringing out in her, but she maintains her poker face as she fiddles with her bandana over her shoulder-length blond hair. "Dean, did you know that narcissist spelled backward is douchebag?"

"I had no idea!" My lips part in mock surprise. "The alphabet must have changed since last time I checked." She can always dish it out just as well as she can take my overtly flirting ways.

"Hey, if you can make shit up, so can I." She fails to hide her smirk as she lowers her gaze back to her large tray of colorful donuts and begins arranging them in a precise order.

I adjust my glasses and smile fondly. I love it when Norah is in a feisty mood. My first clue should have been her bandana, featuring Heart, a popular band from the eighties. I come into Rise and Shine Bakery enough to know that when Norah is wearing her classic rock bandanas, she's not to be messed with.

Except for the fact that messing with her is always the highlight of my week.

Most women don't fight back the way Norah does. Most women fall for my charms and trip over themselves to flirt with me. I may be bearded, but I'm not the typical knuckle-dragging, small-town Colorado guy who wears flannel and drones on and on about camping and ice fishing. I appreciate the finer things in life, like travel, nice clothing, IPA beer, and artfully constructed charcuterie boards.

Real men can taste the subtle nuances between a one-year aged cheddar and a five-year aged cheddar.

I should print that on a T-shirt.

My point is, the ladies of Boulder, Colorado, dig me. They appreciate my expensive shoes and tailored dress shirts. And they practically salivate over the story of my self-educated brilliance and the wealth I've made in the stock market as a result.

But not the stunning Norah Donahue, who makes the best croissant and donut combination I've ever tasted. She mocks my worldly charms.

I fucking love it.

I lean against the glass case and sigh heavily. "Norah, Norah, Norah, if you want to see me naked, all you have to do is ask." I make a move to undo the top button of my dress shirt.

"Oh, trust me, I know," she groans, her blue eyes meet mine with a challenge. "You've made your availability abundantly clear to the entire state of Colorado, Dean Moser. But no shirt, no service. That's company policy."

I clutch my fist to my chest, wounded. "Is this how you treat your best customer?" My eyes dance over every feature on her face—mostly because it's all that's visible since she's determined to wear an ugly baker's muumuu to work every day. Thankfully, her face is striking enough to distract me from her questionable fashion sense.

Norah's features have a Nordic look to them—fair hair, blue eyes, high cheekbones, and a sloped nose that curves up at the tip to humanize her a bit. Her pale complexion contrasts stunningly with her full, peach lips that my eyes always seem to zero in on. Her top lip is deliciously larger than the bottom, and I've fantasized multiple times what it would be like to kiss them.

In short, Norah is gorgeous, and she couldn't care less.

"You would be my best customer if you didn't make it your life's mission to get on my nerves."

My brows lift. "I wouldn't get on your nerves if you'd finally let me see what's under that biohazard suit you wear to work every day."

Her jaw drops, and she pulls away from the donut case, dropping her empty tray on the counter with a loud clack. "You are the king of too far, Moser. Please God, why did I ever think it'd be wise to let you become an investor in my second bakery?"

I huff out an incredulous noise. "Well, normally, I try not to mix business with pleasure, but something tells me you'd be worth it." I hit her with a stunning smile that she does not reciprocate, and damn if it doesn't make me smile even more.

She crosses her arms over her chest and glowers at me. "I'm a fool because I'd hoped we could have the Luke and Lorelai flirty diner relationship before they decided to date. Everyone knows the show went downhill once they started to hook up."

"Did someone just make a *Gilmore Girls* reference?" a familiar voice chimes in from behind me, and I look over my shoulder to see Kate standing there in all her wild, red-haired glory. "You guys can't make *Gilmore Girls* references without me. I'm president of the Boulder fan club, and I could have you drawn and quartered for that."

I roll my eyes at my best friend's insanity. "I don't know what you guys are talking about."

Kate cuts me a punishing scowl. "Dean, don't make me junk punch you. I've done it before."

I shift and turn my groin away because the girl is a loose cannon. She used to sneak into a tire shop waiting room to write her mommy porn books before she fell in love with one of the mechanics there—so a punch to the balls is not out of the realm of possibility.

"Of course he has no idea what *Gilmore Girls* is," Norah snaps, turning her gaze from me to Kate, "because if he'd watched that show, he might have something mildly clever to say to me when he rolls in here every day."

"Too right, Norah," Kate chirps, jutting out her chin in solidarity. "I mean…Dean is far from Luke Danes."

"So far!"

"He's not even worthy of being compared to the actual Dean from the show who was a wimpy asshat at the best of times."

Norah's eyes widen, and her hands lift. "Stop right there."

"What?" Kate replies, her brows furrowing in confusion.

Norah points at her chest. "I'm Team Dean."

"Norah, no!" Kate gasps, her eyes wide with horror.

"I've always been Team Dean!"

"What kind of idiot is Team Dean?" Kate exclaims with disgust, and when Norah looks like she's about to lunge across the counter to choke Kate out, Kate quickly holds up her hands and backtracks. "Sorry, my emotions got the best of me for a moment, and we aren't close enough to be calling each other idiots…no one's an idiot here…except for DEAN!" she growls, ramping up all over again. "I mean, after season one, he's a home-wrecking idiot with no life goals."

"He was Rory's first love!" Norah splays her hands across the counter and leans closer to Kate.

Kate shrugs and crosses her arms while smugly replying, "We all make mistakes when we're young."

Norah exhales like a bull getting ready to charge. "And let me guess…you're Team Jess."

"Um…duh, Norah. I'm a romance novelist. Books are my life. Of course I want the book nerd to end up with another book nerd. That is basically porn in my world."

A slow smile spreads across my face as I sit back and watch my best friend go back and forth with Norah over a television show. I can't stop the dirtiness of my imagination as it forms a fantasy of Kate and Norah having a pillow fight over who should be in love with who. Before my mind goes too far, a shrill voice breaks into my pillow dreams.

"Jess is a drifter who doesn't know what he wants…at least Dean took some risks for Rory."

Kate shakes her head in disgust. "I can't believe you never told me you were Team Home-wrecker Dean."

"I can't believe you never told me you were Team Zero Ambition Jess. You were one of my favorite customers." Norah blinks back her shock like someone's just told her Santa Claus doesn't exist.

"Feeling's mutual, Norah. I mean…Jesus. I'd be Team Tristan before I'd be Team Dean. I'd be Team *Kirk* before Team Dean."

"Now you're just being ridiculous," Norah growls, and the two go silent as they stare each other down for a long, pregnant pause.

Kate's the first one to crack. "Can I still take a number for a fresh croinut? What's the flavor of the day?"

"It's birthday explosion, and I don't own the machine," Norah snaps back, which breaks the tension as she stutters, "Well, actually I do own the machine because I own the bakery…I just…was saying that for dramatic effect."

Kate breathes a sigh of relief and reaches down to pull a number out of the red ticket machine on the counter. "Oh, thank God because I love birthday explosion, and I've been thinking about a croinut all morning. Tire Depot's Danishes don't hold a candle to your baked goods."

"Aw, you're too sweet," Norah replies, looking touched. "I know how much you love those Danishes."

"Mostly just because they're free, and I'm cheap," Kate says with an awkward laugh. "Seriously, if your bakery was complimentary, I'd do all my writing here."

Norah nods her head awkwardly. "Well, then I'd have no bakery because I'd have no money."

"Right!" Kate barks out a laugh. "Maybe you should start doing oil changes here."

"That would kinda get in the way of my bakery."

"Obviously!"

The two grin at each other for a second, and then Kate says, "I'm gonna go grab a booth. Later, Norah. See you at the next Gilmore meeting."

"Nice seeing you again, Kate."

Kate turns to leave, and Norah busies herself back at the glass display case, rearranging the donuts that don't require patrons to take a number.

My voice is low and strange when I state, "I have no clue what either of you was talking about, but is it odd that I am slightly turned on from watching what just unfolded here?"

"Moser!" Norah snaps, and I quickly take a number and rush over to join Kate at the booth.

Moments later, I'm seated across from my two friends, Kate and Lynsey, who are currently tits deep in wedding plans for Kate. Kate even has some sort of wedding binder spread open as they work through decorations and shit. Before the wedding talk, they discussed Lynsey's sex life and how hard it is to bone your husband when you have a one-year-old who won't sleep at night.

I glance over at Julianna, who's seated in a high chair beside us with eight pounds of pink frosting smeared all over her face.

She's one now and looks like she's about to slip into a diabetic coma any second.

When the fuck did my two closest friends become grown-ups?

It feels like yesterday I was rolling a keg of beer into Kate's house to celebrate the completion of her smutty bed-n-breakfast series. Kate, Lynsey, and I were all neighbors making the city of Boulder our bitch. Now Kate lives in the tiny town of Jamestown with Miles, the mechanic she met at Tire Depot who smokes licorice like cigarettes, and all they do is talk about their rustic-themed wedding coming up. And Lynsey's married to the doctor who knocked her up, and their brown-eyed little cutie is old enough to eat donuts like a well-seasoned trucker.

Jules's eyes begin to close, and her head slowly descends to the table. "Is she okay, Lyns?" I ask, pointing at the bizarre sight.

"She's fine," Lynsey replies, waving me off as she asks Kate for the eighty-seventh time how many Mason jars she needs to paint for the centerpieces.

"She doesn't look fine," I add as Julianna's forehead rests on the table.

Lynsey stops talking long enough to pull Julianna's head up. She holds her hand in front of her mouth and nods. "She's breathing, she's fine. It's just a sugar crash. It happens."

My head jerks back because Julianna's eyes are slightly rolled back into her head, and that does not look normal. Suddenly, Julianna comes to. "Mo dony!" she bellows, and her tiny finger reaches out to press down on a stray sprinkle on the table. She puts the sweet into her mouth before lowering her head and falling fast asleep again.

Fuck me, that was a disturbing sight. I've never been gladder not to have kids.

There are a lot of disturbing sights as of late. Like Kate staying in on a Friday night instead of coming down to Pearl Street Pub to have a beer with me. Or Lynsey having a ribbon cutting at her new family practice she opened with Dr. Dick.

He has a real name.

Josh something.

He's okay, I guess. Both Miles and Josh are decent guys, and the girls are madly in love with them, so I guess they're happy. But those two little smokies have officially taken away my wing women, and because of that, they must be my mortal enemies.

Clearly, I'm bitter.

My two best friends have completely different lives, and I'm here doing what I do best—trying to figure out how big Norah's tits are beneath that ridiculous uniform she wears and avoiding all conversation concerning weddings and babies.

"Dean, did you hear me?" Kate asks, and I pull my gaze away from Norah as she artfully glazes a fresh batch of croinuts. She always looks so technical when she does that, like a scientist performing an experiment, and it's soothing to watch. And every once in a while, she catches me staring, and her cheeks and neck begin to flush, and she gets this faint sheen of sweat on her face. It drives me fucking *wild*.

Kate's voice cuts into my reverie again. "I said I'm going to murder you if you bring some random college girl to my wedding in a few weeks."

"Murder seems a bit excessive," I mumble under my breath and take a sip of my coffee. *Damn, Norah makes a good cup of coffee.*

"It's not an overreaction," Lynsey interjects, reaching out and grabbing my hand from where it's resting on the table. "I still can't forget the Lila disaster that happened a few weeks ago. I'm a therapist, and I think I need therapy to recover."

"Her name was Lala, and you're both being dramatic." At least, I think that was her name. I jerk my hand away, her gentle touch a harsh contrast to my irritation. "It wasn't that big of a deal."

"She lit my tiki bar on fire, Dean," Lynsey exclaims, and I swear her eyes well with tears because she's obsessed with that

8

stupid thing. "Lola or Layla or whatever her name is was so sloppy drunk she caught her hair on fire, which caught my tiki bar on fire, which resulted in the neighbors calling the fire department."

"Your neighbors were overreacting. Nobody was in real danger…well, except for Lala. But your doctor husband said her hair will grow back, and there were no serious burns. Don't make it bigger than it was."

"Dean," Kate chastises. "Listen to yourself."

"I am listening to myself. I replaced Lynsey's tiki bar, so what more do you two want from me?"

"It's not about the tiki bar," Kate blurts, her eyes wide and fierce on mine. "It's about the fact that you brought an underage girl to Lynsey's house for margarita night."

"I wanted to bring a date, and she told me she was twenty-one," I snap, frustration vibrating through my limbs. "I didn't think I needed to check her ID—at least she was over eighteen."

Both Kate and Lynsey gape at me, and I wonder when the fuck I started hanging out with such prudes. Kate writes erotic romance novels, and Lynsey got knocked up by a one-night stand. Surely, bringing a younger woman around isn't that damn shocking for this group.

Kate exhales heavily. "Dean, I'm not even going to address the fact that you're thirty-one to that girl's twenty because I write romance for a living, and I'd be a fool to say that an age gap can't be super-hot. But that girl had nothing going on upstairs. She thought Ebola was a country."

I cringe as I recall her arguing fervently with Josh, *the doctor*, on that particular subject. He had to get out his phone and show her that Ebola was a virus, and even then, she got out her own phone to pull up a map. It was seriously uncomfortable.

"I didn't realize there was an IQ prerequisite in order to hang out with all of you," I reply flippantly, knowing I sound more childish than the child sleeping next to me.

Lynsey gets a sad look on her face and glances at sleeping

Julianna. "Are you even happy with the women you're dating, though? You don't seem happy. You seem…bored."

"What does it matter?" I snap, seriously wishing I was anywhere but here. "It's not like I'm marrying these girls."

I glance out the window at the people milling around Pearl Street, dining and shopping. Kate, Lyns, and I used to own this town. We'd be down here multiple nights a week having so many laughs our stomachs would be sore the next day.

Now, things have changed.

They've changed.

They aren't the fun and wild girls I used to pull pranks on. I miss dropping into Tire Depot to give Kate shit about writing sex scenes in a waiting room. I miss buying Lynsey overpriced charcuterie boards and watching her clumsy ass trip in front of guys. The past year has started to feel…lonely. Which is not something I cope with very well.

Case in point: Lala.

Kate's eyes find mine again. "We're worried about you, Dean. The girls you're dating keep getting younger and younger, and none of them have any substance. You're floundering, man," Kate adds, her voice taking on a serious tone I do not like. "This is a *peen-tervention*."

"A what? Jesus, would you listen to yourself? I don't need a *peen*-tervention…which, by the way, is not a thing. You two don't need to worry about me." I mindlessly brush away the scattered remains of our croinuts. "Business has never been better. My hedge fund company is up and running now, and I have six solid investors from Max's referrals. Plus, I'm investing in Norah's Denver bakery, which I know will be great. I'm at the top of my game."

"We're not talking about your professional life, Dean," Kate says, her eyes bending with sympathy. "You've always been great with your work. We're talking about your peen."

What the fuck is going on here? Kate's my funny friend. She's the one who doesn't take life seriously and threatens nut punches. Why is she looking at me like I have a terminal illness right now while calling my dick a peen? How many croinuts did she eat?

She licks her lips and leans across the table. "I just feel like ever since Lynsey had the baby and I got engaged, you've been hooking up with girls who are nowhere near your level. You're a self-taught genius, Dean. You're attractive, charismatic—"

"Generous," Lynsey adds with a sad smile that instantly transports me to the days she was pregnant and living with me before Josh was allowed in the picture.

It's crazy to think how different my life is with these two in it. They are literal pains in my ass seven days a week, but even when they're annoying the shit out of me, I have a soft spot for them both. There's nothing I wouldn't do for them.

They're kind of like the siblings I never had.

If having inappropriate thoughts about your sisters was okay.

Which *obviously*…it's not.

"Are you and your peen depressed maybe?" Kate asks with a sadness to her eyes that is at odds with her ridiculous words.

"God, my peen is *not* depressed." I adjust my glasses and exhale heavily while briefly wondering if a plastic fork could impale me enough to have to leave for the emergency room. "I'll just quit bringing dates around. Problem solved."

"That's not what we want," Kate replies with a shake of her head. "I'd just like to see you with a girl who you could actually have a conversation with. We have a lot of events coming up with the wedding, and I'd die of shock if you had someone beside you who wasn't a throwaway girl. Lynsey and I have been brainstorming about who we could set your peen up with, haven't we, Lynsey?"

I roll my eyes as they start rambling names and turn my attention back to Norah, who's a lot more fun to watch than these two whack jobs trying to set my dick up on a blind date.

My brows furrow when I see Norah's abandoned her croinut

decorating and is now deep in a conversation with an older woman at the end of the counter. The woman gesticulates wildly, and my body tightens at the cornered look on Norah's face.

Norah suddenly rips off her bandana and shakes her head, her blond hair wild around her face. The woman tries to show her something on her phone, and Norah jerks away and refuses to look at it. When the woman tries again, Norah lets out an exasperated noise and turns to storm out of the bakery through the back exit.

CHAPTER 2

Norah

"I want grandbabies, Norah. Not Cronuts!" my mother chastises in a tight, crisp voice while delicately fingering her short, silver hair gelled into spikes. I glance around at my customers to see if anyone has overheard this madness, and to my horror, Dean is staring at me... arguing...in my bakery...*with my mother.* She steps into my sightline, her nostrils flared. "I've been planning this thirty-fifth wedding anniversary party for weeks, and it would mean a lot to see you with a man before I'm dead in the ground."

"Mom, I make *croinuts*, not Cronuts," I correct, ignoring her comment about her untimely demise because Elaine Donahue is as fit as a fiddle. Honestly, I think she could beat me in a 5K race right this second. She's one of those power-walking, essential-oil-smearing, herbal-tea-drinking fifty-somethings who manage to make silver hair and yoga pants look unbelievably stylish. She's practically a Jamie Lee Curtis clone with shredded triceps to prove it—it's no wonder she still has never sampled any of my baked goods.

Don't get me wrong, she's not an unsupportive momster. She buys a box of croinuts for my dad's law office every week, but perish the thought she'd ever taste her daughter's creations and lose her twenty percent body fat.

I exhale heavily, and despite myself, I decide to educate her on my business I've worked a decade perfecting. "Cronuts have been done before. They're trademarked and take hours to make. Mine are called *croinuts*. They're still a donut-croissant hybrid, but my recipe only requires twenty minutes from dough to dish. My patented recipe alone is worth a pretty penny. That, coupled with the fun concept of customers taking a number to place their order, makes Rise and Shine a fun, original idea for a bakery. Business has gone up three hundred percent since I started the number machine. On average, we sell five hundred croinuts per day. It's fun. It's unique. And it's why I'm opening a second location and getting ready to launch a national franchise. My business is a big deal, Mother." I exhale heavily, feeling like I just hammered her with my business portfolio, but the look on her face makes me realize it's fallen on deaf ears.

"Croinuts, Cronuts. Potato, potahto," she scoffs, waving me off like I'm talking about the weather. "Just let Nathaniel be your date to our anniversary party on Friday. He'll look so nice in the photos, and my Rusty Hinges aqua aerobics group can finally stop asking me if you're seeing somebody." She leans in and lowers her voice to add, "Nathaniel's teeth look *so* much better after he got those adult braces. Let me show you."

She reaches in her purse for her phone, and I immediately back up, pulling off my bandana and shaking my hair out. I'm normally very anal about the cleanliness of my bakery and require a hair net or head wrap on my employees at all times. But my mother shoving a childhood acquaintance in my face like he's her last great hope to be a grandmother has me losing my damn mind.

Nathaniel is the son of my parents' best friends, and the four of them have been trying to push the two of us together since we were teenagers. When Nate went off to college on the West Coast, I thought I'd seen the last of him. But for weeks, my mother has been talking about his return to Boulder to take over his father's

CPA business, and it's like she can hear wedding bells even though I haven't seen the man in a decade.

"You could do a lot worse, pumpkin." My mother attempts to shove her phone in my face again, and before I spew my anger all over her and make a scene in front of my customers, I turn on my heel and storm down the back hallway to the rear exit.

Most of my conversations with my mother go like this. She meddles and tries to matchmake me until I explode, then she leaves. My father calls and guilts me into apologizing, and the pattern starts all over when another man she thinks would be perfect for me pops up. This has repeated since the moment I was old enough to start procreating appropriately.

The warm September air hits my face as I burst into the back alley. I really wish my mother could have had more children. She could then spread out her matchmaking, or at least, I'd have someone to commiserate with. But all she focuses on these days is my love life. It's like she has my fertility clock set on her Apple watch or something. But Nate? God, I cannot go on a date with Nate. I haven't seen him since we were teens, and well…we parted on pretty awkward terms.

My eyes land on the dumpsters behind the door, and my temper spikes even higher. "Rachael told me Zander cleaned up back here," I growl under my breath and shove my bandana into my pocket as I bend over to collect the overflowing garbage. Rachael is my right-hand at the bakery, and both she and Zander know very well about my policy: the back of our business looks as good as our front—alley included.

I hear the door open behind me, and without looking back, I state through clenched teeth, "Mom…I'm not looking at that picture of Nate. I don't care how good his teeth look now." I toss an empty cream carton into the trash that smells so putrid my stomach churns.

"Who the fuck is Nate, and do I need to kick his ass?" a deep voice asks, and my stomach twirls all over again for a very different reason. I slowly turn around to see Dean standing in the alley, looking all…Dean-like.

"What are you doing back here?" I ask, my voice still breathy with adrenaline as I take in his appearance more fully.

He smirks and props himself along the rustic brick wall, looking like a damn J. Crew model. Dean's one of those annoying fashionable guys who manage to make the metro-style look masculine. His glossy chocolate-brown hair and perfectly trimmed beard are always flawless. He usually comes into the bakery wearing crazy tight slacks and slick blazers with a unique dress shirt underneath. But today, he's sporting a more casual look of designer (and super-tight) jeans cuffed over expensive-looking leather boots, and a fitted button-down without a single wrinkle. He looks hot.

Damn him.

He gestures toward the bakery with a sheepish look on his face. "You looked like you were getting ready to assault a senior citizen back there." He holds his hands up in surrender. "I don't usually make a habit of kicking asses of women with gray hair, but I could probably handle this 'perfect teeth guy.'"

I roll my eyes and attempt to straighten my hair because I must look like a lunatic compared to his perfectly put-together self. "That was my mother making my life miserable. It's kind of her specialty."

Dean winces behind his dark-framed glasses. "I have one of those mothers myself. They can be a pain sometimes."

"To say the least," I murmur under my breath.

Dean crosses his arms over his broad chest and narrows his cocoa eyes at me. "I'm a great listener if you want to talk about it. I don't know if that's something Luke Danes would do for Lorelai Gilmore, but it's something Dean Moser does with his friends quite regularly."

I huff out a laugh as I stare back at him, waiting for the punchline—but I see he's serious right now, which is…surprising. "Are we close enough to commiserate about family drama?"

He tilts his head and squints his eyes at the bright sunlight overhead. "I'd say we've been on the friend track for a while now, so I vote yes."

I shake my head at that notion. Dean has been coming into my bakery for years with his computer and Clark Kent glasses to do whatever the hell he does on that laptop of his. Our interactions had been pretty surface level until my franchise developer, Max, officially introduced us sometime last year. Max told me his good friend Dean was a stock market savant with a new hedge fund company, and he was looking to diversify his wealth. And because I was looking for a financial backer to help start my second bakery in Denver, Dean was the perfect person for me to get to know better.

Now, Dean Moser is officially a silent investor in Rise and Shine Bakery-Denver. And ever since we signed on the dotted line, Dean's been happily chatting my ear off at the bakery nearly every single week. His flirting is far from silent, but I've watched Dean in the bakery enough to know that's just how he communicates with his friends. And I'd be lying if I didn't say he was easy on the eyes and our exchanges every week gave a little extra pep to my step.

Regardless of our growing friendship, business relationship, or innocent flirting, Dean's investment is crucial. Max says once we get my second location off the ground, I'll have the cash flow to launch my franchise plan and go national and possibly, international—a pipe dream goal.

Goals. I have goals. Goals my mother cannot seem to understand. "Friends or not, you don't need to hear about my problems, Dean."

"I wouldn't have asked if I didn't want to know."

My brows lift. "But you're an investor in my franchise."

"Silent investor," Dean corrects.

"Still an investor. It would be unprofessional to talk about this."

"Come on, Norah," Dean groans and runs a hand through his hair. "You were on my party bus last year and watched me chug an IPA beer and give Kate a Magic Mike lap dance. I'd say our professional boundaries are irrelevant at this point."

"Who gets a party bus when you turn thirty, by the way?" I reply with a laugh. Seriously, I turned thirty and let myself binge Netflix for the day like a winner. When Max dragged me onto that bus to get to know Dean, I was beginning to have serious doubts about who I was thinking about going into business with.

Dean shoots me a dirty smile. "Boys who never want to grow up."

I exhale heavily. "And this is the person who can help me with my momma drama?"

He licks his lips and tips his head to the side. "Most people solve their problems by simply voicing them out loud. So maybe just view me as a sounding board."

"You want me to voice what's going on?"

"Yeah…why not?"

"Because I'm in a dirty alley with a man who too often voices *all* of his thoughts…most of which are dirty."

"You make a good point," Dean replies with a wink. "But I promise, I'm not thinking anything sexual right now. You're a nun in my eyes…so just say it. You'll feel better."

My head is shaking back and forth, but before I can stop myself, I exhale the heaviness in my chest and start talking. "My mother wants me to bring Nate to their thirty-fifth wedding anniversary party in a couple of days, and I'd rather eat the curdled cream out of the bottom of that carton I just tossed than give her the satisfaction of dating the man she's wanted me to be with since I was a teenager."

With a slow nod, Dean gestures for me to continue.

"Honestly, she makes me crazy. All she cares about is my love life and becoming a grandmother. She's never taken an interest in my bakery or my career aspirations. She's never remotely cared what I'm passionate about. All she cares about are her expectations for me. Expectations I am clearly not living up to."

"So, is this Nate guy really that bad?"

I cringe and shake out my shoulders. "It doesn't matter. I haven't seen him in years. The truth is, I don't want to take him as a date because I don't want to date anybody. I don't care about my love life or getting married or having babies. I want to birth bakeries, Dean. Lots and lots of bakeries with lots and lots of croinuts. And I want my franchise to blow up so much that I can live in Paris for a while and come up with a brand-new recipe while sampling other people's baked goods and get a really fat ass that my mother would hate."

Dean's deep laughter breaks through my ranting. "I think you'd look fantastic with a fat ass."

"So do I," I reply excitedly, just picturing myself walking the streets of France with a fresh croissant in my pie hole. "I just need her to get off my back until the Denver location is open. I can't handle the stress of that and her. It's too much. There's going to be bloodshed."

Dean nods thoughtfully as he ponders my predicament. "Don't hate me, but why not just take this Nate guy to the anniversary party? Surely, he's not going to think you'll want to marry him afterward. Take him to that one event and then ghost him. Your mother wouldn't have to know."

I shake my head. "Oh, she'd know. Nate's parents are my parents' best friends. They'll talk. Then my mother will secretly invite him over for dinner without telling me and then invite me over with an obnoxious *surprise* and a patronizing smile. I'll be miserable because my mother will make passive-aggressive comments about why I never called him after the party, and then I will lose my temper, flip the table, and accidentally catch the house on fire."

"I'm gonna go out on a limb and say you might be a bit of a pessimist," Dean deadpans.

I narrow my eyes at him. "You give my mother an inch, and she'll take 5K. I can't take Nate to their party. It's asking for drama, and I have enough of that with the Denver bakery right now."

Dean shoots me a knowing look because he knows firsthand how the construction has been a mess over there. As a silent investor, he's updated regularly on the progress, and it's been setback after setback even though we're opening in a month. We purchased an old building to stay on brand with the charm of my flagship bakery here in Boulder, and the renovations ended up more in-depth than initially estimated. If my contractor doesn't get his shit together, I'm going to be serving cold croinuts at my grand opening because I'll have to bake them here in Boulder. Talk about a horrible start to my career as a franchiser.

I pin Dean with a serious look. "My focus needs to be entirely on my business right now."

"I can respect that." Dean nods in agreement. "In fact, your ambition is pretty damn sexy."

I roll my eyes. "Don't start flirting again, Moser. I'm a nun, remember?"

Dean holds his hands up. "Sorry, sorry. I didn't mean it. Actually, I empathize with everything you're saying. You and I have very similar views on business, and I, too, have zero desire to ever settle down."

My brows lift curiously. "What's your damage?"

Dean shakes his head dismissively. "No damage. It's just not for me. Kate and Lynsey are on those paths full steam ahead right now, and I am doing everything I can to hop off their train. And apparently, I'm doing too good of a job because they're pissed I'm not dating more serious girls. Girls they can have an actual conversation with. But let me tell you, Norah, they don't have to be bright to be good at…" Dean gestures to his groin, and I cringe with disgust.

"God, you're a pig." I turn away, wondering what the hell is wrong with me for confiding in a terminal bachelor. I glance at him over my shoulder. "You look so put together and professional, and then you open your mouth and ruin everything."

Dean's smile grows. "Some people find it charming."

"You were so normal when I first met you." I shake my head.

"That's because there are two sides to me. Business Dean and Dark Passenger Dean. Now that we're friends, I let my true self come out."

"Lucky me," I grumble and drop down onto the bench by the door. I hunch over and run my hands through my hair. "What am I going to do, Dean? Seriously. My mother won't let this Nate thing go. She's going to involve my dad, and my dad is going to make me feel guilty like he always does."

Dean takes the seat next to me. "Maybe you could take a different date to their party."

I jerk my head to look over at him. "How does that help me? I just told you I don't want to date anyone. I have too much going on."

"I mean not a real date—just someone who'll get your mother off your back. A fake date."

"What, like hire a male hooker?" My mouth goes dry at the thought.

"Jesus, not a hooker!" Dean laughs with genuine amusement that I feel in my belly. "I can't even picture you with a hooker. Your OCD would kick into overdrive around a man who has sex for money."

My face falls. "What makes you think I have OCD?"

Dean flinches like he's revealed too much. "I've seen you in the bakery for years now, Norah. You have these tics."

"Tics?" I ask, feeling exposed. "At what point did you become a level ten stalker?"

"Are you saying you've never noticed me?" He pins me with a challenging look that gives me a jolt of energy. "I come to Rise and Shine a lot...I'm certain you at least know how I take my coffee."

I roll my eyes defensively while inside saying cream and two sugars. But I know several of my other regulars' coffee preferences too. It doesn't *mean* anything.

Dean sighs and tilts his head, his eyes roaming deliberately over my face like he's reading my mind. His close inspection causes my cheeks to flush, and suddenly, it's a lot warmer in this alley than it was a few seconds ago.

Dean licks his lips with determination. "I'm not too shy to admit that I've noticed you measuring everything three times."

"That's just to be precise. Any good baker measures multiple times. I have that included in my franchise manual."

"I didn't first notice it in your manual. I noticed it by watching you. You're a perfectionist, Norah. Your bakery is impeccable, and your business model for the franchise is a great example of that high level of care—your brand story alone is a work of art."

My body flushes from his praise. Who knew having a stalker could be so…flattering? "Well, I want Rise and Shine to be successful. I came up with this idea when I was a teenager, and it still surprises me that I'm taking this next step."

"I know. God, I wish you could understand that I'm complimenting you. Seriously, I've reviewed franchise folders from different restaurants and bakeries, and none have come close to being as marketable as yours. You were the easiest investment I've ever made, and that's coming from someone who's spent his entire adult life investing in the stock market."

My lips part as Dean showers me with all the affirmations I could ever want in life. It's overwhelming, actually, and I hate that I have to quickly swipe at my upper lip, hoping he doesn't notice how much his compliments have affected me. Dean really does have two sides to him, and this one is *highly* appealing. If only my mother could hear everything he just said. Maybe then she'd see my bakery isn't just a bakery, and that I've spent years of blood, sweat, and tears to turn my dream into a reality.

"Back to my original point…why don't you take a guy friend

to this thing? Someone your mom doesn't know who can be your date for the night?" He must think I have tons of those lying around.

"I don't have guy friends. I barely have girlfriends. Rachael is probably my closest friend, and that's only because she works for me. She probably doesn't even like me. I'm sure you'll be shocked to hear this, but I'm a really bossy boss." I sound mopey. Anything to do with my social life always makes me mopey.

Dean nudges me with his shoulder. "I'm sure Rachael likes you, Norah. You're impossible not to like."

My chest swells at the comment he threw out like it was nothing. I've never been very good at the friend thing. In fact, one might say I was terrible at it. In high school, I had a custom cookie business that was so successful I found myself baking on weekends instead of going to parties. My twenties were even worse once I finished culinary school and opened the bakery.

"I suppose I could take Rachael and tell my mother I'm a lesbian," I murmur, mildly tickled at the image that idea conjures in my head. Although knowing my mother, she'll just bust out adoption books or sperm donor catalogs.

Dean laughs. "Surely, you know one guy who's willing to go with you to a party."

"I know you, Dean." I huff, and then my eyes widen as an idea takes root in my mind. "I know *you*."

"You can't be serious," Dean replies with a nervous laugh.

"I am," I exclaim and turn to grab his arm excitedly. "Seriously, Dean, this is perfect. We can say we met through the bakery, and you're an investor, and we just started dating. You can say all those wonderful things you just said about my business model to my mother, to my mother's friends, and to everybody at the party. It'll be great! It'll be like a campaign tour for Rise and Shine Bakery. Maybe then my mother will see this isn't just a lemonade stand I'm running; I'm a legitimate entrepreneur. And since you don't want a girlfriend and I don't want a boyfriend, neither of us will have any expectations. It's perfect!"

Dean stands and fidgets with his glasses nervously. "Did you forget I'm a sexist womanizer? I objectify you on a regular basis."

I roll my eyes dismissively. "I've been ignoring that side of you for months now; it's like an annoying breeze. It's fine. And at the party, you can be the Business Dean you just told me about. This is perfect. I know you can do this."

"Oh. I'm certain I could do this, but why would I want to? What's in it for me, exactly?" he asks, crossing his arms over his chest and eyeing me warily.

I swallow the lump in my throat and stand to face him eye to eye. "What did you have in mind?"

His brows lift, and he glances at my smock.

"Not that." I shove him away. "That is not an option."

He laughs heartily. "I'm sorry, it was a joke…mostly."

"I'm not joking about any of this, Dean. If you're with me at that party, I'll owe you one. A big one." I take a step closer, and his dark eyes zero in on my lips, causing my body to instantly heat. This happens a lot when Dean's eyes are on me. It doesn't mean anything, though. It's just a natural hormonal reaction to being the object of an attractive man's gaze. Ignoring the bead of sweat collecting on my upper lip, I offer, "You could have free croinuts for the rest of the year. Or I could reserve a booth for you every day. I know you have your co-working space down the street, but you spend enough time at the bakery, you deserve your own table. Or maybe I can name a croinut after you at the new Denver location. Wouldn't that be cool? You could pick the flavor. I see you as a maple glaze and bacon variety, but I could do whatever you like. These are your terms. We can look at this like another business transaction. I will do anything to get my mother off my back."

Dean runs both hands through his beard as he thinks long and hard. "Are you really willing to do anything?"

"Well…mostly," I reply nervously when I see a strange glint in his eye. "I do have limits."

A dirty smile spreads across his face. "That's what safe words are for, sugar tits."

"Never mind. This is a horrible idea," I snap and turn to head back into the bakery.

Dean laughs and grabs me around the waist. His firm hands send a spasm of electricity through my body as he turns me back to face him. "Norah, I'm joking. Jesus…you need to relax a little. Of course I'll help you. We're friends, right?"

His eyes fixate on me for a moment, and I'm literally standing in the alley in his arms. I jerk out of his embrace before I get embarrassingly sweaty. "Just friends, yes. But I'm looking at this as a business transaction, so it's not a friendly favor. I want to find an appropriate way to pay you back sometime. Extra emphasis on appropriate."

He nods. "Got it, boss."

"And I have one more condition."

Dean inhales knowingly. "It wouldn't be you if you didn't have conditions."

I quirk a brow at him. "Call me sugar tits ever again, and I get to flatten your nuts with a rolling pin."

Dean flashes me a grin. "Fair enough."

I reach out for a handshake. "Clearly, my mother has made me insane for going to these extremes, but I'll do whatever it takes to get her to quit trying to set me up."

Dean takes my hand in his. "You're kind of hot when you're angry, Norah."

I roll my eyes and pull my hand away before my body overheats again. "I'm already regretting this."

CHAPTER 3

Dean

The next day, I'm on my way to Norah's apartment for a home-cooked dinner and discussion of the "ground rules" for our business transaction. Or at least, that's what her bossy text message said last night. She clearly had an anxiety flare-up after I left yesterday because she sent several messages freaking out about everything that could go wrong at her parents' party and came up with the genius idea of a list of rules. Knowing Norah, she'll probably have a binder and a notary on hand for our signatures.

I can't wait.

I've never seen Norah's apartment, so I'm intrigued to see her outside of the bakery. And out of that stupid smock. The night she came to my thirtieth birthday party was one of the only times I've seen her dressed up. I still can't get the images of her in that red tank top out of my mind. It was simple but effective.

Being Norah's fake date may have been my best idea yet.

And the craziest part is, it wasn't my idea. I didn't see that coming from her. Especially since she's such an introvert. Boulder is a small town, and I never see her out and about. And considering Norah lives above her bakery on downtown Pearl Street that's chock-full of bars and restaurants, it's safe to assume Norah is a homebody.

The sun is beginning to set as I park in front of the bakery. Norah's place is prime real estate with lots of foot traffic from tourists and locals. Plus, her building is historical, which adds tons of character to her bakery. The second location will be very similar once the contractors have completed the restoration process. What's better is, there are few specialized bakeries like it in Denver, so the residents won't know what hit them. Norah's croinuts are unbelievable and addictive. Although I'm still not one hundred percent sure my addiction isn't to Norah more than to her croinuts.

I walk around the building and find the green side door Norah detailed in her text. I press the button labeled Donahue and wait patiently.

"Yes?" Norah's voice echoes over the intercom.

"Hi, this is Dean Moser, your well-hung hooker for the night."

A silent pause on the other end has me briefly regretting my joke, but she must forgive me because I hear the lock open without a word. As soon as I begin climbing the tall staircase, the delicious scent of meat hits my nose and makes my stomach growl.

The apartment door at the top of the stairs opens, and Norah emerges, looking frazzled. "I'm just finishing the béarnaise sauce, come on in."

She turns, and her bare feet pad down the long hallway inside her apartment. I follow, taking in her frayed jeans and white tee that's knotted in the back, revealing a sliver of pale skin just above her checkered apron. Her casual look is completely at odds with my plaid slacks, T-shirt, and sky-blue suit coat I wore to what she described as a business meeting.

Regardless, my stomach likes what it smells as I turn the corner into her bright kitchen with whitewashed walls, white cabinets, and a large cream marble slab over an island containing the sink.

"I hope you eat red meat," she says as she stirs something over the commercial-grade stove.

"I am a carnivore." I slip off my jacket while checking out Norah's ass in those tight jeans.

"Extra-large from what I hear," she says, glancing over her shoulder and catching me before I raise my gaze to hers.

I can't help it. Norah has curves that must be appreciated. I'm an ass man, and Norah's might be the best I've seen. It's a travesty she hides her curves under those aprons.

Shaking the image of her in nothing but an apron out of my head, I mosey into her attached living room that has a bank of windows overlooking Pearl Street. I glance down to see the streetlights have come on and people appear to be heading out for the night. "How long have you lived here?"

A sizzle escapes the stove as Norah replies, "Since I bought the bakery so…eight years, I guess?"

I nod, and my brow furrows. "You were how old when you opened Rise and Shine?"

She glances over her shoulder. "Are you trying to guess my age, Moser?"

"No, I'm trying to figure out how a young twentysomething could afford a bakery and an apartment on Pearl Street. This is a hot location."

She nods and turns back to the stove. "I was twenty-two, which makes me thirty now if you must know. And I had my dad co-sign a business loan for me." She turns to look at me. "I assume you didn't have to take out a loan to invest in Rise and Shine-Denver?"

I ignore that question and turn the corner to peer into a set of frosted sliding doors. They lead into a bedroom with a perfectly made white bed covered in white throw pillows. A large black and white photo of the Eiffel Tower covers the far wall.

"Have you been to Paris before?" I ask as I head back into the kitchen and take a seat at the marble island.

"Not yet." There's a wistful note to her voice as she pours a creamy sauce into a glass gravy boat. "It's at the top of my list, though."

"Why Paris? Why not Thailand or Brazil or South Africa?"

She pins me with a dubious look. "Do you really have to ask a baker that question? Paris is known for its pastries and desserts. It's like a mecca for a baker. Plus, my friend Chelle from culinary school lives there, and she's always sending me photos of Parisian bakeries, and it's just…so inspiring. A lot more inspiring than good ole Boulder, Colorado. I would *love* to move there someday."

I nod and smile as she pushes a bottle of red wine and two glasses toward me, silently bidding me to open it and pour. I do as I'm told as she plates what looks like a filet steak with broccolini and some type of fancy potato. "Looks like you're a decent cook too."

Her blue eyes swerve up to meet mine. "You haven't tasted it yet. It could taste like poison."

I huff out an incredulous laugh. "My nose rarely leads me astray."

She adds a garnish of some crispy herbs and uses a rag to wipe the edges of the plates where the béarnaise sauce went astray.

I lean down to catch her eyes and break through her serious concentration. "Is it perfect yet?"

Her eyes narrow. "Presentation is key to pulling in all of your senses when you eat."

My brows lift. "I must have missed that in the Rise and Shine brand philosophy."

"It's not a me thing. It's a food thing." She straightens and removes the apron from around her waist. I take the opportunity to drift over her hourglass figure before looking at the presentation she's slid in front of me.

"You smelled the food when you walked in, right?" she asks, pinning me with a look.

"Yes."

"And you heard the sizzling of the sauce on the stove?"

"Yes."

She grabs a spoon and dips it into the gravy boat. "You've seen my presentation, which means there's only one thing left." She offers the spoon to me, and I open my mouth and taste the deliciousness of that sauce.

My eyes close, and I let out a deep groan. "That tastes incredible."

"Because I've engaged your senses." I open my eyes to find she's watching me. "Now dig in before it gets cold. Cold food is not a sense I want you to experience."

I can't hide my grin as she joins me with her plate, and I pass her a glass of wine. I attempt to make small talk as we eat, but it's nearly impossible when you're tasting the best steak of your life. By the end, I'm debating whether to lick my damn plate. It's that good.

"You can bake and cook. It's too bad you never want to get married because you really would make someone an excellent wife."

She rolls her eyes. "Every woman's dream come true, right? To cook for her man. What more could she want out of life?"

A sheepish look masks my features. "Alright, I get it. You hate men."

"I do not hate men," she corrects, looking affronted. "I just hate the expectation that since my career is a traditionally feminine activity, it must mean I want to be a wife and mother. There's a lot more to life than that."

"Like?" I prod, my curiosity piqued over all things Norah.

She turns to face me, her blue eyes alight with determination. "For me, it's obviously my business. It takes up a lot of my time, and I love it, so why would I let a relationship distract me?"

"Completely agree."

"And if my dream to live in another country comes to fruition someday, having kids will make that exceedingly more complicated."

"I hear you there," I reply with a cringe. "Lynsey's life with

Julianna is practically unrecognizable to what her life was before. But surprisingly, she's still managed to open a practice with her husband."

Norah nods thoughtfully. "Some women can do it all. And maybe with the right partner, it could work, but good luck finding that. I've had a few boyfriends, and none of them could get over the baker's hours."

"Baker's hours?"

"When I first opened the bakery, my croinut batches took three days to make. It was brutal. I was up at two every morning to get them going so they'd be ready for the morning crowds. Try being intimate when your alarm clock goes off at one a.m. I was in bed by six for most of my twenties."

I inwardly cringe because her waking time is about the time that I'm getting ready to score. And her bedtime is when I'm usually working out and getting primed for the night. Her twenties sounded miserable.

"When did you ever let loose and have fun, Norah?"

She expels a bitter laugh. "Baking is fun. And it got hella more fun when I perfected the twenty-minute croinut and got to sleep normal hours again."

I level her with a look because while yes, her "take a number, twenty-minute dough to dish" routine is a huge part of what makes her franchise so marketable, her "fun" she's talking about is still all about work. "Whatever you say."

"I'm serious. Baking is fun. And cooking is fun." She stands and grabs both of our plates, but I rest my hand on top of hers to stop her in her tracks.

"You cooked. I clean."

She shakes her head stiffly. "I'm particular about my dishes."

My brow furrows. Jesus, this girl is worse off than I thought. I rise to my feet, towering over her meager five-foot-five frame and grab onto her shoulders. "Sit."

I gently press her back into her seat and grab our plates off the counter. I set about rinsing the dishes, which don't consist of much. The girl cooks clean. Every dish she used except her saucepan and whisk is already loaded into the dishwasher.

She winces when I bend over to load the plates. "Just…make sure they're all facing to the left. When you face them toward each other, the water doesn't get up between them."

"Norah…do you do drugs?"

Her eyes widen. "No."

"You should start," I reply and load the dishes, ignoring her tiny murmurs of displeasure. I start the dishwasher so she can't go back and redo what I've done. "Now, let's go over these rules of yours before you have a nervous breakdown over the fact that I barely rinsed the plates before I loaded them."

She rolls her eyes and slips off her stool to grab a yellow legal pad and a Sharpie out of a drawer next to her fridge. I use the opportunity to pour us both more wine. We're going to need this.

"Okay, rule number one. No public displays of affection." She writes down in perfect, kindergarten-teacher print NO PDA. "My mom will be watching me like a hawk, and if you're touching me a lot, it'll be obvious that this is totally fake."

"Okay…what about hand-holding?" I ask, tilting my head curiously at her. "You think your family is going to buy that I'm your date if I can't hold your hand?"

Rubbing her lips together, she nods. "I see what you're saying. Okay, maybe hand-holding, but just the friendly kind. Not the waffling kind. That's way too intimate."

"I'm going to need a demonstration."

She grumbles under her breath, clearly annoyed.

I love it.

She reaches down and cups my hand on my lap, flattening her palm to my palm and folding her fingers around the outside of mine. Her fingers are chilly and a stark contrast to my constant heat.

"Like this."

I nod and stare down at her pale hand in mine. "And what is…waffling?" I ask, trying to keep a straight face.

"This." She lifts my hand between us and interlaces her fingers with mine. Instantly, a warmth creeps through my body as her face flushes with color. Her eyes move from our hands to my eyes, and I see her swallow as she stares at my lips. "We can't do this. This will be too much," she croaks, her voice thick in her throat.

I nod, my eyes dropping to her lips, wondering what they taste like. "If you say so."

She inhales deeply and holds her breath in her shoulders for a moment before shaking her head and abruptly dropping my hand. With trembling fingers, she clutches the marker and writes FRIENDSHIP HOLD on the list.

She continues staring at the notebook when she mutters, "And don't do that staring thing you do sometimes."

"Staring thing?"

She rolls her eyes and continues looking straight ahead. "You stare at me in the bakery sometimes, and it's unnerving. Just… don't do that."

I inwardly cringe over being called out so blatantly on something I thought we were both enjoying. It's a bit of a gut-check moment I need because all of this is fake. And Norah isn't the type of girl to turn a fake thing into a fun thing, so I need to get a fucking grip. "Fair enough…I shall try to stop gazing at your immense beauty."

She fights back a smirk and writes NO STARING. It's highly emasculating, so I bark out the next rule. "No bossing me around at this thing."

Her curious eyes lift, causing me to shift in my seat. "I don't want your father to think I'm some sort of doormat. If I decide I want whiskey with my cake, you need to let me do that."

"There will be a dessert wine—"

"Don't care," I cut her off. "If I decide I want white wine with steak or red wine with fish, you will let me be."

Her nose wrinkles with disgust. "Why would you—?"

"Norah, it's a guy thing. You don't need to control every aspect of me, even if I am your fake date. This will be good for you."

She exhales heavily like I just told her my rule was that we had to run naked through the party together.

"And while we're at it," I continue while I have her somewhat disarmed, "you can't talk business."

"What?" she exclaims, her blue eyes wide and accusing. "Dean, that's the whole point of you being my date—to talk up my business. To show my mother that what I'm doing is important and impressive and…admirable."

"I will brag about your business prowess. You will not. You will be the dutiful, sweet daughter who brought a date to the anniversary party like her mother wanted. I'll handle your image with your mother and her friends. Don't you worry. Plus, it's going to be ten times more accepted coming from me, the new guy, than you…the disgruntled daughter."

"I didn't think I was disgruntled," she murmurs glumly and begins to doodle on the legal pad.

I reach out and touch her leg, feeling her jerk beneath my touch. "I don't mean anything by it, Norah. I just want them to hear me, and if you're too busy pushing your mother's buttons, it'll fall on deaf ears."

Her face softens, and she nods before writing the last two rules. "This looks good. Just one more big, major rule. This might be the most obvious, but it's also the most sacred."

"I can't wait to hear this."

"No kissing." Her cheeks deepen in color again as she focuses really hard on writing down this rule with apparently perfect penmanship. "I'm sure that was a given but better to have it all written out so we know what to expect. We absolutely cannot kiss. It will complicate everything."

I sit back in the stool and watch her finish the list with a flourish at the bottom. She turns to me, and I smile. "What?

We're not signing in blood? Spewing bodily fluids into our palms and shaking hands?"

She rolls her eyes. "I like lists, Dean."

"I'm gathering that, Norah." I smile fondly at her. She's cute when she's flustered and trying not to be. "Well, if that's everything, I guess I just need to know when to pick you up tomorrow."

"The party starts at seven...so...six thirty? I don't like to be late."

My smile grows. "I'll be here at six fifteen."

She nods appreciatively, and we both stand, our bodies touching as we move away from the stools and walk down the hall.

As I turn to head down the stairs, Norah calls out. "Hey, Moser."

I pause and turn to look at her.

"You ever done anything like this before?"

My brows lift. "Fake dated someone to get their mother off their ass? No, can't say that I have."

She fumbles with her fingers. "You think it'll work?"

"Hell if I know," I reply with a laugh. "But it'll be damn fun finding out."

CHAPTER 4

Norah

"**Y**our hair looks amazing," Rachael exclaims with one last coat of hairspray before turning me on my vanity stool to look in the mirror. "I'm a master with braids."

My eyes widen as I take in the finished product. "Rachael, this is so, so cute." I touch the loose Dutch braid across the top of my head. It sweeps down behind my ear like a headband and flows beautifully into short, loose beach waves. "I look like the mother of dragons from Game of Thrones."

Rachael lets out a deep laugh, her brown skin glowing in the vanity light. "I was going for backyard chic, but leave it to you to go medieval on me."

I exhale with relief because my mother called last night to ask if I was getting my hair professionally styled for the party tonight. I knew it was one of her passive-aggressive digs because she's hated my hair ever since I cut off eight inches last year. But dang, Rachael is better than a salon.

I stand and wrap my arms around her neck. "You really are a great friend."

"Whoa, we're hugging friends now?" she asks with a stiff voice.

I pull back nervously. "We *are* friends, right?" Ugh, I sound so stupid. Ever since my social life conversation with Dean, I've been feeling insecure about all my relationships.

Rachael's chocolate eyes widen. "Yes, we're friends, you fool. But you know I hate hugs."

I shake my head from side to side. "Duh. Obviously, I know that. I'm just…I'm nervous, Rachael. Dean and I didn't cover hugging on my list of rules, so I feel seriously unprepared."

A knowing smile spreads across her face. "You like him."

"I don't like him," I snap and turn to face the floor-length mirror to smooth out the wrinkles on my blush-pink floral mini dress. "I mean, yes, he's cute. But he's so cocky."

"Which can be hot," Rachael interjects.

"Okay, sometimes his cockiness is hot." I wince. God, I really hate even saying that out loud, but it's undeniable. Dean has this boyish magnetic charm and an uncanny ability to make a person feel totally at ease, blurring the lines between professional and personal. He's just a carefree guy who doesn't take life too seriously. "But that arrogance is only hot if I was interested…*which I'm not.*"

She rolls her eyes. "I thought once you promoted me to manager last year, you'd get more of a social life."

"I've been social," I argue limply because it's a total lie. "I went to that franchise mastermind conference six months ago. That was very social."

"That does not even come close to counting because it was still for work." She hits me with a look of unmitigated disappointment. "And tonight, you had an opportunity to bring a real date, and you found yourself a fake one just to prevent having any sort of fun. Who does that?"

"Fun?" I bark out a laugh. "At my parents' house? Unlikely." I lean into the mirror and slather on a pale pink gloss that smells like cake batter.

Rachael moves to stand behind me, her giant ball of twisted braids piled on top of her head as she towers over me with all her statuesque bronze glory. She narrows her eyes at me. "I vote you still treat this like a date and have a good time. You work hard, and you deserve to have some fun with a man who you can…" She grabs my hips and swivels me side to side.

"Stop!" I squeak and fight back a nervous giggle as the image of Dean's naked body hovering over me pummels me out of nowhere. I twist to face her and lose all humor. "I showed you the rules. There will be no hip action."

She shakes her head sadly. "When was the last time you had any hip action?"

I squint and look up at the ceiling like it's going to remind me somehow. "Well, Barrett and I broke up a few years ago, but we had that one random hookup last year."

Rachael presses her hands to her temples, her jaw dropped. "How can you go a year without it?"

"I take care of myself, thank you very much." My eyes flit over the bathroom drawer that contains all I'll ever need in that department. Frankly, that drawer is ten times more fun than Barrett ever was.

She rests her hands on my shoulders. "Battery-operated toys cannot replace the natural power of a good dickin.'"

I bark out a laugh that gets caught in my throat, causing an uncomfortable cough attack when suddenly the buzzer on my door sounds off.

Rachael quirks a brow. "And he's punctual…already a match made in heaven."

"Go let him in, please," I choke out and then scurry over to clear the mess spread all over my bathroom counter.

Rachael saunters away without a care in the world, and I immediately regret every decision about this night. I could have told my parents I wasn't feeling well. Or scheduled an important business meeting that couldn't be missed. Why can't there be another franchiser conference somewhere right now? At least if I were there, I'd be excited and energized.

Not nauseous and wondering if the flips in my stomach are nerves or the urge to poo.

By the time I locate my jean jacket, I hear Dean's low voice wafting down the hallway as he chats with Rachael. I do a quick peek around the corner, and I swear my nails dig into the plaster on the wall when my eyes land on him.

Dean looks…*hot.*

And annoyingly, no embarrassing lip sweat in sight.

He's trimmed his dark beard so it's just this thin layer of stubble that exudes sex appeal. He's got on black slacks with brown loafers and no socks—*seriously, how does he pull that off?* And his perfectly tailored white button-down is peppered with black, tiny anchors, the top two buttons undone.

He looks effortlessly casual, like he listens to yacht rock on his imaginary sailboat. *Nothing about me is casual or yacht rock smooth.*

My body temp rises to a level that has me double-checking my deodorant as I swallow the lump in my throat and glance at myself in the hallway mirror. Bright red flesh stares back at me. Stupid fair skin. It shows literally every feeling I ever have.

Why can't I be yacht rock smooth?

"Norah, stop freaking out and get your ass out here," Rachael bellows, and suddenly, I'm no longer nervous. I just want to punch my friend in her pretty face.

Hesitantly, I emerge from around the corner and make my way toward them. I shoot an awkward smile to Dean and notice he's not wearing his dark-framed glasses tonight. His brown eyes really pop now, looking less cocoa and more caramel.

"Wh-what's up, Moser?" I stutter dumbly and fidget with my jacket.

"Norah, you look better than a strawberry cream croinut," Dean says without skipping a beat. His eyes move down my body, and I feel like I could pee a little.

I clear my throat and point at the door. "Let's get this over with, okay?"

Dean beams smugly. "Everything I've ever wanted to hear from a woman."

Rachael laughs. "Try to remind her to have some fun, Dean."

"I'll give it the old college try."

Dean winks at me, and I ignore the rush of butterflies in my stomach. He's always been hot; this isn't new information. My tummy flips are just nerves. Tonight is a business deal and nothing more. I can do this.

My parents live on the edge of suburbia Boulder. They built the house when I was in high school, and I remember drooling when my mother put a double oven in the kitchen. For as long as I can remember, my mother stayed at home, and my father worked long hours at his law office. Growing up, my mom was the one who taught me to bake and cook and do all the homemaker things. It's ironic that she never wanted me to make a career out of it.

These were the pointless thoughts I rambled to Dean as he drove us to the party. I don't think I stopped talking long enough to breathe because by the time he ushers me toward the gated entrance to my parents' backyard, I feel faint.

"Are you sure we should be doing this?" I ask, turning to face him and wiping my sweaty palms off on my dress. "We could just get out of here and get drunk instead."

Dean's eyes dance with amusement. "Do you ever relax enough to get drunk, Norah?"

My brow furrows. "I've been drunk before…I think."

Dean shakes his head and opens the gate. "It's going to be fine. Let's go have some fun."

"Everyone keeps telling me to have fun," I hiss, my hands clenching into fists by my sides. "What part of a bougie backyard barbecue with a bunch of sixty-year-old yuppies sounds fun?"

Dean's shoulders shake with laughter, and the scent of his cologne engulfs me as he leans in to whisper in my ear. "Norah, you look seriously beautiful tonight. Please try to relax."

I swallow the lump in my throat and ignore the shivers running down my neck from his hot breath on my flesh. He gestures for me to walk ahead, and my errant butterflies disappear because my parents' backyard looks like it's hosting a large wedding, not the intimate party for their close friends my mother described.

"She got a live band?" I croak in amazement as I recognize a cover song from Bryan Adams. My brows lift with amazement. My mother may be uptight, but she's also the one who passed along the love of seventies and eighties power ballads, so this is actually pretty impressive.

However, the moment I see she's hired servers in bow ties, who are probably sweating their asses off in this eighty-degree weather, her cool factor is blown to smithereens.

Dean rests his hand on the small of my back. "No back touches," I hiss into his ear as goose bumps erupt up my spine. My body is seriously betraying me tonight, and I don't need him getting handsy, making me even more of a mess than I already am.

"Sorry, I was only leaning in to ask if your mother knew I was coming?"

My eyes fly wide, and I whirl around to face him. "Oh my God, I was going to text her and completely forgot."

Dean smiles while glancing over my shoulder. "I wondered because the woman coming toward us who has your eyes is currently staring at me like I have two heads."

"Norah!" My mother's voice peals from behind me, and I turn too quickly on my heel and damn near face-plant.

Dean's warm hands engulf my waist to help stabilize me as she approaches.

"Hi, Mom. Happy Anniversary." I pull out of Dean's embrace and lean in to give her a tense hug.

"Who is this, pumpkin? Your Uber driver?"

I jerk back. "No, Mom. This is Dean."

"Who is Dean?" she asks, her eyes widening like she's going to cast a spell on me.

"Dean is my date." I plaster on a smile and think I hear my teeth crack. "Dean, this is my mother, Elaine Donahue."

My mother's jaw flaps open and closed repeatedly like those ridiculous talking bass fish that pop out from the walls. "I...I didn't know you were bringing anyone. You never—"

"Surprise!" I shoot her another toothy smile.

Dean reaches his hand out to my mother. "Mrs. Donahue, best wishes to you on your anniversary. Thirty-five years is incredible. We could all be so lucky."

My mother wavers for a moment at a rare loss for words, and thankfully my father arrives to save her just in time. "Pumpkin, you look splendid." He pulls me in for a hug, and I swear I feel him forcing me to exhale. "Who is this young man with you tonight?"

"Dean Moser, sir." Dean reaches out and shakes my father's hand. "Congratulations on your anniversary."

"Thank you very much. My name is Jeffrey, but please, call me Jeff." My dad reaches around and claps Dean on the back. "You're a brave soul for coming to a gathering like this. These people will eat you alive."

Dean laughs with ease and gestures toward me. "That's why I brought a bodyguard. Have you seen your daughter's triceps? Who knew making all those croinuts would give her arms like the Incredible Hulk?"

My dad barks out a laugh, and the two of them shoot the breeze like they've known each other for years. It's a bizarre sight because this is the first time I've introduced my parents to a man. I knew bringing guys around my mom would only encourage her. Seriously, I could introduce her to a crack addict, and she'd still ask me if the guy wanted kids someday.

But my dad…I didn't really expect him to be so warm and welcoming to Dean. Suddenly, my belly is riddled with guilt because if I didn't know any better, I'd think those two have the start of a bromance happening.

And Dean…he's so at ease with all of this. Not a care in the world. Meanwhile, I'm having a nervous breakdown.

"I don't understand why you didn't tell me you were bringing a date," my mother states, interrupting my dad as her eyes rove over Dean like he's some sort of abstract art exhibit she can't quite make sense of.

"It's a party, Mom." I force out a laugh and murmur quietly in her direction, "And you seemed like a date was sort of required."

"You didn't RSVP, though."

My father cuts my mother off as he steps forward and claps Dean on the back. "Son, I sincerely hope you like hard liquor. I find it helps in situations like this." He ushers Dean away despite my wide, pleading eyes.

"Seriously, Norah. What is going on here?" my mother seethes, losing all that fake kindness her voice had earlier as she grabs my arm in a death grip. "I haven't seen you with a date since…well…ever."

"You wanted me to bring a date, Mom," I reply and gently extract myself from her vise grip. "You explicitly told me so multiple times."

"Yes, but I didn't want you to bring just any man. I wanted you to bring Nathaniel. He's perfect for you." She fingers her silver, gelled hair delicately while shooting a fake smile out to her party guests milling about.

"Well, beggars can't be choosers." I reach out to swipe a flute of champagne off a passing server's tray, and the young man reaches out and grabs my hand.

"That's a used champagne, ma'am," he stammers nervously while extracting the glass from me.

"Used?" I glance down and see red lip prints on the edge

of the glass. "Oh my God, gross. Why would you pass out used champagne?"

"I'm just taking the glass away to be washed." He eyes me up and down like I'm in the middle of a psychotic break and then points to the area beside me. "The fresh glasses are behind you."

"Get a grip, Norah!" my mother hisses and swipes a flute from the ridiculous champagne tower backlit with white twinkle lights.

She hands it over to me, and I murmur an apology to the man before taking a fortifying sip. "Sorry, Mom, but you're stressing me out."

My mother demurely sips from her flute. "I just wish you had told me you were bringing someone because…"

"Because what?"

I turn to my mother as she speaks to me out of the side of her mouth. "I invited Nathaniel, and he said he was really looking forward to seeing you." She squeals the last bit like she's some sort of high school gal pal who just passed me a note from the boy I've had a crush on.

"Mother!" I'm shocked. "Why would you invite him?"

Her smile falters as she turns to face me with wide, warning eyes. "Because Jim and Carol are our dearest friends and their son just moved back to town, and it won't kill you to talk to him. Who is this Dean person anyway? You never hinted you were seeing anyone."

My brow furrows, and I open my mouth to reply but then remember the rule about not bringing up work. "I'm…um…I met him at the bakery."

Her face softens a bit. "How long have you been dating?"

"Not long," I reply instantly, and her expression deflates, so I quickly add, "which is why I wasn't sure I should bring him tonight. It's early in our relationship, but he practically insisted. He really wanted to meet you guys."

My mother's eyes twinkle with hope that kills me a little

inside because this is all a big, fat lie. "Well, he's very polished. What does he do for a living?"

I force a proud smile. "Financing and investing. He's a broker for a handful of wealthy people here in Boulder. And he's a primary investor in my Denver location." That's not technically breaking the rules because it's still referring to Dean's work, not mine.

My mother's chest puffs out. "A businessman, how impressive."

I want to roll my eyes because if a man runs a business, it's impressive. If I do, it distracts me from getting married and having babies. I square my shoulders and add, "Dean is very impressive, Mother. I'd love for you to get to know him. We should go find him and Dad."

My mother grasps my arm in her cool hand and leads me slowly into the party toward the bar where Dad and Dean are currently talking. "But this is a sticky situation, pumpkin, because I gave Nathaniel the impression that you needed an escort tonight."

"An escort?" My voice rises sharply. "What am I? A prized heifer at the county fair?"

"Would you stop? It won't kill you to be nice to him. He won't arrive until later because of some West Coast conference call."

I blink my eyes rapidly. "Mom, I can't have two dates tonight. You have to fix this."

"Relax, Norah, it'll work itself out."

"Jeffrey," my mom coos, turning her attention to my dad. "I think you owe me a dance. It is our anniversary, after all."

"It would be my pleasure, wife." My dad takes a sip of his whiskey and lifts his brows knowingly to Dean before whisking my mother off to the checkered dance floor in front of the band.

"This is a disaster," I groan and turn to prop my elbows on the bar. "Can I get another champagne, please?"

Dean sidles up next to me as the bartender fills my glass. "What's up, sugar? I think your dad likes me."

I pin him with a warning look. "If you add tits to the end of that sugar, your balls must have a death wish."

"Why so cheery?" Dean asks, hunching over the bar to sip his brown liquor out of a rocks glass. "Did your mother give you a puppy *again*? That Elaine."

"My mother invited Nathaniel here tonight," I state flatly.

"The perfect teeth guy?"

"Yes."

"So, what's the big deal?"

I pin him with an accusing look. "She gave him the impression I was here for him. Like I was some lonely sack who couldn't get a date even if I wanted to. Jesus, this is embarrassing."

"Relax." Dean turns to face the party and rests his elbows behind him like he doesn't have a care in the world. "We'll just have to break some of your rules."

"What do you mean?" I grab a nut from the bowl on the bar and chew on it nervously.

"Well, if you want this guy to steer clear, then a little PDA might be in order."

"What kind of PDA?" If he says kissing, I'll spontaneously combust.

Dean seems to read my mind and rolls his eyes. "Relax, sugar cake, I mean a little…affection. Maybe we dance. Maybe I put my arms around your waist or play with your hair a little. Or maybe we get practically pornographic, and I waffle your fingers." He laughs casually. "Something to show your mother this Nate guy doesn't have a chance."

I nod thoughtfully as I process what Dean's just said. He mentioned touching me so casually like it's no big deal. I suppose it isn't since he seems to flirt with anything that walks. But I've been out of the game for a while now, and I can count on one hand the number of people I've been affectionate with, and even those were years ago. Is this really something I can pull off?

"Norah, drink the rest of that champagne. It's going to be fine."

I close my eyes, letting his words sink in while feeling anything but fine. "Okay, just promise you won't try to kiss me. I'm barely holding it together as it is, and if I have to worry about you breaking the ultimate rule, I won't survive this night." I tip the rest of the champagne into my mouth.

"Relax, I won't tongue thrust you in front of all your parents' friends. I'm a mountain manwhore, but I draw the line at lip raping."

I huff out an incredulous laugh at that strange phrase and then hear the music shift to the song, "I Want To Know What Love Is." "Oh, I love this song." I sigh wistfully.

Dean's lips twitch as he fights back a smile. "Really? This is what does it for you?"

My head jerks back. "Yes, I think Foreigner is highly underrated. Lesser bands have been inducted into the Rock and Roll Hall of Fame. It's a crime that these guys aren't."

I feel Dean watching me, but I don't want to look. I'm sure he thinks I'm a nut job.

"I've never seen you wear a Foreigner bandana."

My brow furrows, shocked that he would notice something like that. "Yeah, so?"

"Never mind. Come on, let's dance."

He grabs the flute of champagne out of my hand and leads me onto the dance floor where several couples have joined my parents. I force a smile at my dad, who I swear knows something weird is up with Dean and me, but he's too sweet to ever say.

Dean's hand snakes tightly around my waist as he pulls me in so our bodies are flush. My head reaches just below his chin in my wedge heels, and I lift my hand to rest it on his shoulder.

Jesus, his body is hard under these clothes. He's bragged about his abs before, but even his pecs are impressive masses based on what I feel beneath the thin fabric of his shirt. When he grasps my free hand and holds it up against his other pec, all I can think about is how sweaty my palms are right now.

I glance up to see his smile looking completely at ease. "How is this so easy for you?" I ask, briefly dropping my head to his chest and exhaling heavily. "My palms are sweaty...my heart is in my throat. I feel like everyone at this party can tell this isn't natural for me."

Dean shrugs casually. "I hang out with a lot of women."

I roll my eyes and look away, trying to catch a breath of fresh air that doesn't have Dean's seriously delicious-smelling scent. I bet he wears a really expensive cologne. "I don't need to hear about your conquests, Dean."

"I'm not talking about my conquests." He squeezes my hand so I look back at him. "I'm talking about Kate and Lynsey. They've been my best friends for years, so hanging out with women like this is no big deal."

I nod. "Ah yes, your sister wives."

Dean frowns at that remark. "If they were my sister wives, doesn't that mean I should be getting laid?"

I balk. "Don't tell me you're not getting laid."

He shoots me a dirty smile. "Oh, I'm getting laid...but not by them."

"So, you're cheating on your sister wives."

"They're my closest friends, Norah, and I'd have to be in a relationship with them to cheat except I'm not a cheater." Dean tightens his grip on my waist, and I swear I see a flicker of hurt in his eyes. "What exactly are you insinuating?"

I lift my hand in surrender, horrified that I could be coming off like a creepy, jealous fake girlfriend. "Sorry, nothing. I'm just curious about how you met them." I exhale a shaky breath and try to get a grip. Being this close to Dean, in his arms, wrapped up in his scent, it's...confusing. It feels briefly like a real date, but it's not, no matter how good his hands feel on my sides. This is just two friends talking.

Dean inhales deeply. "They were my neighbors, and they were fun. That's pretty much it. Plus, Kate's one of those girls who if she wants you to be her friend, you will be. End of discussion."

His jaw seems tight when he says that, so I pry a little further. "So, you never dated either of them?"

"Define dated."

"Oh jeez, this is worse than I thought," I reply with a groan.

Dean's chest vibrates with laughter. "I haven't slept with either of them if that's what you're tiptoeing around."

My brows furrow. "Sooo, what then exactly?"

He licks his lips and rubs them together for a moment. "Lynsey and I dated for a time. We realized pretty quickly we were better off as friends…and Kate…" His voice trails off as he looks away.

"What about Kate?"

I follow his gaze; he's watching my parents with great fascination. "God, your parents are legitimately in love, aren't they?"

I shake his shoulder to redirect his attention. "What about Kate?"

He levels me with an unamused look. "Kate's more complicated."

"How so?" I ask, my mind drifting to all sorts of scenarios. "Are you…into her?"

"No…not anymore."

My eyes widen.

"Don't look at me like that." Suddenly, he pushes me out from his grasp into a surprisingly effortless spin and pulls me back, tight into his body, and I have to tell my heart rate to settle down. "I had feelings for her at one point. They weren't reciprocated. End of story."

My jaw drops. "Dean Moser rejected by a female. Alert the presses."

He scoffs. "You reject me every day."

"That's not real." I pin him with a knowing look. "I know you're not truly into me. You're just a big flirt."

His brow furrows, but he lets it go. "If you saw my current text chain with Kate and Lynsey right now, you wouldn't have any doubts that they're more like annoying sisters than sister wives."

"What's going on?" His reaction about his friends is so unlike him and has my interest in their relationship piqued.

His jaw tightens as he grumbles out a frustrated sound. "They're trying to set me up. They keep texting me pictures of girls like I'm on some horrible episode of Boulder Bachelor. You think your mom is bad? Try fighting off Kate and Lynsey after they've had a few tropical drinks. There's usually wrestling and bloodshed involved."

I can't help but laugh at that image. "Why do they want to set you up so much? I wouldn't take you as a man who sleeps alone often."

Dean's eyes flicker down to me, clearly shocked that I said something so bold. I'm a little shocked too. I'm more curious about Dean's personal life than I care to admit out loud, but I don't need him to know that.

Heat rises in my cheeks, so I stammer out, "I ju-just mean if you're finding women desperate enough to beg you to be their fake date, surely you wouldn't have any issues finding a real one."

He hits me with a look that says, *stop feeling sorry for yourself.* "It's not that I can't find a date. They just don't like the kind of women they've been seeing me with lately."

My nose wrinkles. "What kind of women are you hanging out with?"

He spins me again, catching me off guard as he pulls me back into him with my back pressed to his chest as he whispers in my ear. "It doesn't matter. If Kate and Lynsey don't like them, they make my life miserable."

He swirls me to face him again, and I notice his attention is distracted by my parents dancing near us. He squeezes my side and chin nods to them. "Look at them. They're actually talking to each other and laughing. You paint a pretty grim picture of your mom, but your dad looks no worse for the wear."

I sigh heavily. "Yeah, he's always doted on her. He's never minded that she's uptight and tense about everything. A bit of an enabler if you ask me."

Dean huffs out a laugh. "Well, at least they actually speak to each other."

My brow furrows. "Are your parents not like that?"

Dean shakes his head like this conversation is taking a turn he doesn't want it to take. "No…my parents are divorced, thank God."

"Was it pretty bad when they were together?" I pry further, noting that Dean suddenly tenses beneath my hand.

He looks away, his jaw muscle ticking beneath his stubble as he thinks for a moment. "My parents could barely be in the same room with each other. And when they did talk, it was usually screaming horrible, vile things about each other that no child should ever have to hear about a parent. I was twelve when they finally split up, but I saw enough to know marriage is a great way to ruin a relationship. Frankly, to have a thirty-fifth wedding anniversary seems…I don't know…too good to be true, perhaps? Is that image your parents are putting out right now real? Do you truly think they are still in love?"

My face twists as his question triggers a horrifying memory.

"What?" Dean asks, his brow furrowing in confusion. "What's with that face?"

I groan and press my forehead into his hard chest. "Don't make me tell this story. I'm scarred for life."

His hand squeezes tightly around my waist, his thumb digging into my hip. "Now you have to tell me."

I lick my lip and tilt my chin up to whisper in his ear. "Last summer, I came home to borrow my mom's porcelain soufflé dishes."

"Naturally," Dean deadpans.

"Anyway, I let myself in with my key, and I caught them." An uncontrollable shudder runs through me as a horrific image of them reemerges in my head.

"Caught them?" Dean asks like he can't begin to imagine what I mean.

"I caught them," I repeat dramatically for emphasis because surely, Dean isn't this dense.

"What are you talking about?"

"They were boning in my dad's recliner, Dean," I exclaim, and Dean quickly claps his hand over my mouth and shushes me as both of us erupt into uncontrollable giggles.

Dean releases his hand and wraps his arms around my waist, his entire body vibrating with silent laughter as he hugs me to him and whispers, "Seriously? A recliner?"

"His recliner." I clasp my hands together behind his neck and do my best to contain my laughter, but it's no use. I giggle even more into his chest because I can't think of a less sexy piece of furniture to have sex on. I tilt up to add quietly into his ear, "The worst part is that it was one of those automatic ones, and my mother's leg must have been bumping the remote because while she was on top of him, it was reclining backward."

Dean jerks back to gaze down at me, his entire face lit up with amusement. "How long were you watching, you pervert?"

"Shut up!" I squeeze his neck in warning. "I was frozen in shock for like five seconds. It was enough to hear the sound of the motor or whatever…I'm scarred for life now. I'll never be able to sit in a recliner again."

Dean laughs and pulls me a little closer as we both try to catch our breath. "Nothing says true love like a power recliner."

I sigh and glance over at my parents again. They are pretty damn cute, even if my mother is a pain in my ass.

The next couple of hours fly by, and despite my earlier thoughts, I'm actually having a good time. Dean smiles perfectly in all the photos and visits with everyone so easily. He even convinces one of my mother's friends to host their weekly book club meetings at the bakery. My mother is in that damn club and has never once suggested that to them. Even my father was impressed by Dean's predictions about my franchise expansion. It was exactly what I was hoping for tonight. In fact, the night has been going so smoothly I sort of forget this is all supposed to be fake. Having Dean by my side feels natural.

Dean is just dragging me back out to the dance floor for one of my favorite Heart cover songs when my mother's voice peals from behind me. "Norah, look who's finally here."

My hand tightens around Dean's, and I desperately want to turtle shell my way out of this meet and greet and run for the hills. Dean gives my hand an encouraging squeeze, and I exhale heavily. This is why he's here. This is what we've been breaking all the rules for all night long. I can do this.

I release Dean's hand and turn to face the music. "Nate, how are…?" My voice gets caught in my throat as I take in the sight before me.

The man standing with my mother beneath an obscene amount of twinkle lights isn't the Nate Hawthorne I was expecting to see. *Not even close.*

Childhood Nathaniel was scrawny and constantly had food in his teeth. He thought showering was bad for the environment and didn't go anywhere without his French horn.

This guy in front of me…is hot! He's all fair-haired and tan with seriously broad shoulders that look like they're going to rip out of that black suit coat any second.

And he's tall. He wasn't this muscular and tall in high school, right? There's no way. I would have remembered that. My mother mentioned he got adult braces, but she failed to mention the rest of his transformation, which is remarkable. Honestly, he's what Rachael and I would call a *"Main-Event-Nut."*

You see, back before I perfected my croinuts recipe, Rise and Shine specialized in more traditional gourmet donuts. Our cases were chock-full of beautiful, colorful donuts we started making at three a.m. every day. And naturally, some donuts were prettier than others. So, Rachael and I came up with a sorting system. The best-looking 'nuts would go front and center. We called them the "Main-Event-Nuts." The "So-So-Nuts" would go behind them. And the donuts in our first batch of the day before our coffee kicked in was called the "Butt-Nuts" and shoved in the back where nobody could see them.

Before this moment, I would have slotted childhood Nate in the "Butt-Nut" category. Quality and taste are great but not quite polished enough to be a headliner.

The man standing before me right now, though, is very much a "Main-Event-Nut."

Color me surprised. *And horrifyingly shallow.* I seriously need to read more.

Nate flashes a pearly white, and yes, definitely very straight-toothed smile at me. "Norah Donahue, you're a sight for sore eyes."

I laugh and feel a flush come over me as I tug on the thin straps of my dress. "Back at you, Nate. California clearly agreed with you." I clear my throat because my voice sounds all stupid and breathy.

"California was good, but I've missed Boulder," he replies with ease. "It's got that small-town feel that no LA neighborhood could ever achieve."

My eyes lower to his protruding pecs under his lapels. "I hear ya there…where are you living?"

"I'm still on the hunt for a nice piece of property to invest in, so I'm staying with Mom and Dad for now. I want something close to the firm." His blue eyes twinkle with that sweet kindness he always had. "Makes it easier to be a workaholic that way."

"Oh, yes. I live above my bakery, so I can understand that desire. My mom mentioned you were taking over for your father. How's that going?"

He smiles knowingly. "About as well as can be expected, considering the old man doesn't want to retire, but my mother is forcing him."

Just then, my father and Nate's parents join us on the side of the dance floor. My mom grabs Nate's mom's arm and says, "Carol, I wish you could force Jeffrey to retire too. We're all supposed to retire together."

"I've still got a few years left in me," my dad says and shoots me a quick wink. "I'm not as elderly as Jimmy here." They all erupt into laughter as Jim mean-mugs my dad.

"How's your little bakery doing?" Nate asks, and our parents all focus back on me.

Just then, Dean's arms snake around my waist from behind me. "Not so little anymore," Dean says, his chest vibrating against my back as he speaks.

Nate's eyes move from me to Dean. "I'm sorry, I don't believe we've been introduced."

"This is Norah's friend Dean," my mom rushes out quickly, glancing nervously at Jim and Carol. "He was kind enough to come along with her tonight."

"As her date." Dean moves to stand beside me, his left hand drifting down my waist as his thumbs skate over my hip in a possessive move that does strange things to my body. "And I'm actually an investor in her second bakery opening up in Denver soon. I know a good thing when I see it." Dean shoots a wink to Nate, and Nate's eyes widen.

"Wow, two bakeries? Good for you, Norah."

"And a national franchise to launch very soon," Dean adds with a smug tone I want to kiss.

Whoa, where did that thought come from?

I shake off the image of my lips on Dean because…what the hell? I guess it's natural to feel attracted to someone who knows your work and praises you to other people. But I've never been *that* girl. I don't need a romantic interest in my life to tell me I did a good job. My parents' approval is another story because I need to retrain their brains to see other successes in life besides marriage and babies.

But a man's praise turning me on? Never. Not needed. Not happening. No way. This warm feeling in my body after hearing Dean's praise must be from the champagne.

My mom's voice cuts in next. "Oh, I can't keep up with

Norah's bakery. I don't understand all this franchise business she's doing. I thought one bakery would keep her busy enough. Who wants all that responsibility of multiple locations? It just seems like a lot of work to me. And so much travel."

Nate's dad nods. "I'm just grateful I have a son to take over my firm. It's nice to keep things small and in the family."

My brow furrows at that remark.

"Then again," Dean chimes in, "if you have a creative vision, a great work ethic, *and* an entrepreneurial spirit like Norah here, you're a triple threat, and the sky's the limit." He offers a cool smile to the group like he's chatting about the weather. "I wouldn't have invested half a million dollars if I didn't believe in Norah. And I do a lot of investing for very wealthy clients. I've told every single one of them about Norah's upcoming franchise opportunities. It has incredible investment potential."

My jaw drops, and I look at Dean, and whisper, "Is that true?"

He frowns down at me. "Of course it's true."

Wow, I didn't know. Max never said a word. I wonder if it was Max's idea or Dean's?

"Max isn't the only one invested in your success," Dean adds, clearly reading my thoughts.

"More business talk that goes right over my head." My mother peals out a laugh before casually extracting herself from the group.

Nate quickly changes the subject and begins discussing the changes he's making to his dad's CPA firm.

Suddenly, my mom comes up behind me and grabs my arm to pull me aside. Her voice is barely a whisper when she says, "Norah, you should take Nathaniel inside to catch up."

My lips part, and I glance over my shoulder to check on Dean, who's politely listening to Nate drone on. I look at my mother's wide, beady eyes. "Mom, that'd be really inappropriate. I'm here with Dean."

She waves her hand with a scoff. "Oh Norah, please. Dean is obviously just some business partner. Leave him with us and go inside to visit with Nate." She straightens a strap on my dress like she's prepping me for my wedding night. "You two look *so* great together. Didn't I tell you he's much more handsome now? I can already picture little blond grandbabies!"

"Mom," I hiss, my brows furrowing with annoyance. "This isn't happening. Dean isn't only a business partner...he's my..." I pause as I try to figure out what to say to get her to back the hell off this Nate thing. "Dean's my *boyfriend*."

All good humor disappears from her face and hits me with a menacing glower. "Norah Renee Donahue, you brought that Dean person here to spite me. I know how you operate. This is like that time you told me you needed money for a prom dress, and I found out later you spent it on a baking class at the community college and borrowed a used dress from Abby Thompson. Now I want you to stop being rude and take Nathaniel inside. He might be your only chance at a real future."

My entire body tenses with an anger I rarely, *very, very rarely,* tap into. In fact, the last time I remember my temper spiking this fast and this hard was when the appliance company shipped the wrong commercial oven to the Denver location and tried to stick me with a restocking fee.

There was bloodshed then.

And there will be bloodshed now.

I bite my lip hard because I know nothing I can say right now will make my mother see that a future isn't just romance and marriage and babies. She won't hear that. She doesn't want to hear that. She wants her only daughter to make her a grandmother with Nathaniel Hawthorne, and she's going to live her senior years out in disappointment because that's never going to happen.

But instead of saying all of that. Instead of repeating myself for the hundredth time in the past week...I decide to do something wildly out of character.

I turn on my heel, grab Dean by the elbow, whirl him around to face me...and kiss the daylights out of him.

CHAPTER 5

Dean

Holy fucking croinuts! Norah grabs my face and yanks my mouth down to meet hers. Her lips are hard against mine, and her entire body is ramrod straight as I grab onto her sides for support and attempt to recover from the sudden assault that I did not *see* coming.

Is Norah actually fucking kissing me right now? *Holy shit!*

This is a moment I've been fantasizing about for…well, probably years. Ever since I walked out of my rented co-working space and stumbled upon her bakery and decided to take a number and wait for the croinut of the day. After that, I went back nearly daily, claiming my appreciation for the croinuts, but secretly, I appreciated the sight of Norah artfully glazing her creations.

Normally, I'm the kind of man who sees what I want and takes it. I've never shied away from asking a woman out. But as I watched Norah in her bakery, I realized quickly that she was not the kind of woman I could date and discard. She's the marrying type…which makes it really fucking ironic that I just now found out she's not into the whole marriage and babies lifestyle.

And knowing that makes the fact that I'm finally tasting Norah's lips even more fucking epic. She tastes sweet, like cake batter and vanilla, and I'm pretty sure her lips are soft, but they're not currently moving, so it's kind of hard to tell.

Well hell, if we're doing this, we might as well really do this.

My hands steal around Norah's waist and dip low on her back, maybe a little too low for this type of crowd, but fuck, Norah started it, and I'm damn well going to finish it. I pull her pelvis into mine in an attempt to soften her against me, and she reacts perfectly, her tits crushing into my chest as her body bows backward, allowing me to take complete control of this gift she's giving me.

Norah melts beneath me, and I have to hold on tight to keep her upright as her lips soften and part, allowing my tongue to do a gentle sweep between her lips. She tastes like champagne, and she's now soft and pliant, giving me a full embrace of that plump upper lip I'm slightly obsessed with.

Okay, majorly obsessed with.

A quiet groan vibrates in my chest as I turn my head and deepen the kiss, massaging her tongue with mine as she squeaks out a soft cry. Her hands move from my jaw to my hair, and her fingers skate through my strands like they've done it a thousand times before.

I've fantasized about kissing Norah Donahue countless times, but this moment right here…exceeds all of those dirty thoughts.

A distant throat clearing interrupts our most likely indecent public display, and I force myself to pull away because *from little acorns, mighty oaks do grow.* And I do not need to pop a boner in front of Norah's parents.

My eyes crack open and attempt to blink away the shock of what just transpired. Norah pulls back, still holding my head, her chest heaving with deep breaths and her lips red and swollen as she stares at me with wide blue eyes.

"I thought you said no kissing," I croak softly, my voice deep and in a weird, raspy tone.

"I might have lost my temper." She exhales a shaky breath, her nostrils flaring with life. "So much for those rules, I guess."

The corner of my mouth pulls up into a smile before I painfully turn away from her to see it's Norah's father who was the throat clearer. He's eyeing me like he doesn't like me as much as he did five minutes ago. I can't blame the guy.

I cough into my fist, and murmur, "I think it might be time for us to go, sugar lips."

"I think you're right," Norah replies, detaching herself from me and turning to face her parents and their friends with a sheepish look. "Happy Anniversary, Mom and Dad. I'm afraid my *boyfriend* and I have to be going now."

My body tenses at that label. When the fuck did we go from a fake date to a fake relationship? If I wake up engaged tomorrow, I might regret this favor for a friend.

Elaine shoots her daughter a murderous glare while her dad appears to be fighting back a smile. Norah then waffles her fingers through mine and practically drags me behind her through the party, out of the backyard and into the dark night full of a million more possibilities that I hadn't considered before.

When we're in the safety of my car, Norah exhales heavily. "Oh my God, my lip is sweating." She jerks down the visor and eyes herself in the mirror before dabbing at the skin above her lip. "I have disgusting lip sweat."

I start the car and pull out of the parking spot. "That's not normally where I make women wet."

"Shut up, Dean," Norah snaps, pressing her hands to her flushed cheeks. "I just…I lost my mind in there."

"You did skip a couple of steps."

"I just tongued you in front of my parents and their friends… and Nate!" She bows her head and runs her fingers through her hair. "What was I thinking?"

"Nate's a douche."

"He's not a douche," she bites back crisply. "He was very nice. Nicer than I expected. And oh my God, he looks nothing like what he looked like when we were kids."

"You want me to take you back so you can tongue rape him too?" I snap, my tone harsher than I intended, but the idea of her kissing that douche wagon makes my hands tighten around the steering wheel.

Norah shakes her head dismissively. "No, God. I'm just saying…he wasn't as bad as I remembered. I don't remember him being that tall. And he must be taking anabolic steroids because I know he didn't have those muscles in high school."

"Norah, would you please stop talking about your childhood crush right after you just kissed the life out of me?" I want to kiss her again just to make her shut up and forget he was ever there.

Norah's head snaps to look at me, but I refuse to look back. Her commentary about Nate Douche Wagon is irritating me for some ridiculous reason. Am I acting like a jealous boyfriend? Jesus, I need to get a fucking grip. This is all a ruse. I know that. But what the fuck was that kiss about? And why the hell are my slacks really fucking tight in the crotch right now?

"I never had a crush on Nate," she says softly, and I hear her inhale sharply before she adds, "Did I really kiss the life out of you?"

I glance over at her, and my body tenses as the blue hue of the dashboard illuminates her features, making her look good enough to fucking eat. I swallow the lump in my throat and shift in my seat. *This is going to be a problem.*

"That was…a really good kiss. Even if it was ill-planned. What the hell made you go off script like that?"

Norah growls and balls her hands into fists on her lap. "She was just being her normal self, and then she accused me of bringing you to spite her, like the idea of you wanting to date me is unbelievable. Ugh! She always does this. She always sees right through me. When I was a kid, she could tell whenever I was lying to her. Her mother's intuition is completely insane. I think she's a freaking witch. A demon witch who can read people's minds."

"Norah, take a breath."

She does as I say and then crosses her arms over her chest, making it hard to avert my eyes back to the road. "God, I told her you were my boyfriend, and to prove it, I kissed you in front of all those people. I charged you like a bull in front of Nate."

"I actually liked that part."

"I wasn't thinking," she rushes out. "My mother is going to be so pissed at me."

"Why would she be pissed at you for kissing your boyfriend?"

"'Cuz she knows you aren't real."

"She doesn't know. She thinks she knows."

Norah nods thoughtfully, and the car goes quiet for a long moment. When I glance over, I see she's chewing on her lip and looking dejected. I fucking hate it. Norah is my friend now whether she likes it or not, and I can't leave her high and dry. We can fix this.

I exhale heavily and decide to drop an idea that's been stewing in my mind ever since we started dancing earlier tonight. Actually, this idea occurred to me when she first asked me to be her fake date in the alley, but I wasn't sure it would work. With tonight's sudden change of events, it might be our best option.

"What if we stay together in this fake relationship for a few weeks...pretending obviously...but we do it long enough for you to be my fake date to Kate's wedding?"

I glance over to see Norah's reaction, and she's staring at me like I've spoken in tongues. "Are you being funny?"

"No," I reply with a bitter laugh. "Hear me out. You told me you'd owe me one for helping you tonight...well, I need a date for Kate's wedding, and you need to prove your mother wrong so she stops riding you about Douche Nozzle Nate. So...we stay together. It's only three weeks...I can totally be your fake boyfriend for that long."

The word is foreign and strange on my tongue because I can't remember the last time I was someone's boyfriend, let alone dated the same person for three weeks straight. I've been doing casual flings for a long damn time now. But hell, being a fake boyfriend can't be that hard.

"How do you honestly expect us to pull this off?"

I shrug. "We tell everyone we've been dating in secret because of our business connection, and it's now become serious. I'll play the dutiful boyfriend one more time for your parents. We can do dinner or something. I'm pretty sure your dad likes me, though after I slipped you the tongue in front of him, he might like me a bit less, but I can handle him. Otherwise, if I disappear now, your mother will know she was right. But if you double down and we go to Kate's wedding together, maybe she'll shut up about this guy and leave you alone."

Norah huffs out an incredulous laugh. "What about your social life? Don't you go out every weekend? Are you going to keep sleeping with other women while we're in this fake relationship? That would make me look really stupid."

I roll my eyes. "I can keep it in my pants for three weeks, sugar lips."

Norah gapes at me for a long while, and then finally says, "Why would you do this for me?"

I exhale heavily to drop her with the real truth. The selfish truth. "So earlier I told you Kate and Lynsey are trying to set me up, right? Well, it's because they think I'm depressed or that my penis is depressed or some shit. They called it a peen-tervention… which is not a thing." My neck cramps as my muscles begin to tense with annoyance. "It's ridiculous and annoying, and Kate thinks I'm going to ruin her wedding if I don't bring a nice girl—not that I've been dating not nice girls…they've just been…a little young? It's all so fucking stupid, and it's making me question my taste in friends, but the truth is, I don't want Kate to worry about me on her wedding day. I don't want her to think about me on her wedding day. I want to look like I'm having the best time ever because, despite the fact I had feelings for her and they weren't reciprocated, I'm good. I'm over her, for real."

"Jesus, Dean, are you nervous right now?" Norah asks, and I hear fucking laughter in her voice. "I don't think I've ever seen you nervous."

"I'm not nervous. It's just, their concern bugs me. Kate deserves to have the perfect day, and if you and I are together, I think that's about as perfect as I can get. It'll totally put her mind at ease."

The car goes quiet for a while, and I briefly wonder if I sound like I'm pining for Kate. Which, I'm not. But fuck, I don't like being pitied by my friends. And I had fun with Norah tonight, so being in a fake relationship with her for a few weeks won't be a hardship. In fact, the thought of being tied to her for a couple of weeks doesn't even make me feel cagey like it has when other women have brought up the relationship thing. It's probably because I know it's going to be a fake arrangement. Definitely.

And actually, maybe it'll be the break I need from fooling around with random women to figure out why the fuck I have been so out of whack lately. As much as I hate to admit it, Kate and Lynsey weren't wrong in that assessment.

Norah's quiet voice breaks the silence. "Wouldn't you feel weird lying to your friends?"

I shrug dismissively. "It's not really a lie. I mean, we can even be official on social media. Just because we both know it's going to end after Kate's wedding doesn't make it any less true."

I glance over to see Norah chewing nervously on her lip. "So, does that mean more dates?"

"Not necessarily," I reply with a shrug. "I mean, if something comes up, great. We can be there for each other. But I'm guessing our daily lives won't be impacted from now until Kate's wedding."

Norah clears her throat and tugs at the hem of her dress. "I feel horrible that you're jumping through all these hoops because I lost my temper and called you my *boyfriend*."

I exhale heavily, still not quite used to the sound of that. "You're my friend, and this is the kind of shit I do for friends. Hell, I offered to be Lynsey's baby daddy if Dr. Dick didn't get his head out of his ass. Faking a relationship with you for three weeks will be nothing compared to almost becoming a father."

Norah barks out a nervous laugh, and I look over to see she's staring straight ahead, shaking her head back and forth in disbelief. "I think I had you pegged wrong, Moser."

"Let's not make this a big, emotional thing. You and I can go steady for a few weeks so you can stick it to your mother. And that Nate Douche Stick guy can go find some other tree to pee on."

"Nice," Norah replies flatly.

I shrug. "You know what I mean. You wanted to get out of seeing him because he's clearly the worst, right?"

"Yeah, but I mean…he wasn't as bad as I was expecting."

I glance at her before returning my eyes to the road, agitation coursing through me at her comment. "Did you miss the part where he called your bakery *little*? And he barely let you say two words about it before he started going on and on about a fucking CPA firm. Like seriously, who the fuck cares about a place that does taxes for a living? I felt myself slowly dying while listening to him. Your kiss brought me back to life."

Norah giggles, clearly pleased with my analogy. "I didn't think he seemed so bad, but it doesn't matter. I don't want a relationship right now."

"Right now," I repeat curiously. Our discussions before made it seem like she never wanted a relationship. Did that fucking smug, D-list Ken doll really turn her head that much?

"If ever," Norah adds flippantly. "I don't know. I drank too much champagne tonight."

My eyes narrow as I turn down Pearl Street and approach Norah's apartment. "Well, think about it. I don't want you making any decisions before making one of your precious pros and cons sheets."

She frowns at me, and I can't help but smile because I bet that's exactly what she plans to do tonight after I drop her off.

I park the car in front of her building, and she turns to face me, her eyes blinking rapidly as she appears to be processing a lot.

"Thank you for doing this, Dean. I know it was kind of a mess at the end there, but it was fun for a while, which was…unexpected."

I shoot her a wink. "Fun looks good on you, Norah. And hey, we made it out of there alive at least."

"Very alive," Norah adds, a smile growing on her face. "Actually, I feel more alive right now than I have in a very long time." She smiles sweetly, and suddenly, this feels like a real date, and I get the overwhelming urge to kiss those soft lips again.

I lift my arm to rest on the seat behind her. "You know, Norah."

"Yes?"

"If you wanted to feel alive again, all you have to do is ask." I lean in a little closer and waggle my brows suggestively at her.

"Stop," she says and gently shoves me away. "The king of too-far strikes again."

I hold my hands up in surrender. "You can't blame me for trying. That kiss awakened my dark passenger."

A girlie smile spreads across her face that I seriously want to kiss. *This is going to be a problem.*

"Well, it's late. I should go inside." She smiles and hesitates for a second before leaning in and kissing me softly on the cheek. Her sweet scent engulfs me, and I want to take a fucking bath in it right then and there. "See you at the bakery on Monday?"

I nod. "I'll take a number."

She huffs out a soft laugh and says good night while sliding out of the car.

As she unlocks her building door, I roll down my window and call out, "Just be sure to put *paying back Dean* in the pro column. I think we'd have fun at that wedding together."

"Duly noted."

I shoot her a wink. "Sleep well, sugar lips."

The look on her face as I drive away isn't one that looks like she wants to flatten my balls. Not at all. I think Norah likes being called sugar lips. In fact, with the right encouragement, I think she could get used to the sound of it.

CHAPTER 6

Dean

Kate: Bachelorette party this weekend in Aspen is now a couples thing. A suitable date is required. Consider this as a test run for the big day.

Kate: Have you selected one of our girls yet?

Me: Go away.

Kate: DEAN...Lynsey and I know what's best for you! Submit to our love!

I pause as I reread the crazy-town texts I received this weekend from Kate while sitting in my favorite booth at Rise and Shine Bakery. I swear to God, Kate must be some sort of evil witch like Norah's mother because it's way too coincidental that she's making changes like this to our Aspen trip right after I offer to be Norah's fake boyfriend for the next few weeks.

Speaking of which, I haven't heard from Norah all weekend, and it's making me fucking nuts. She kissed me, I offered to go steady with her, and then crickets. I'm not used to this type of delayed gratification. In fact, I jacked off three times this weekend just to release some of the tension. How long does it take to make a fucking pros and cons list?

If it were up to me, Norah and I would be Facebook official

already because the text messages I'm getting from Kate and Lynsey are getting more and more erratic.

Lynsey: I know Kate is coming on a little strong, but I do really think you'll like Natasha. Her family is equestrians! Me: Horses, Lyns? Seriously?

How do they know so many single women in Boulder?

I glance at the clock on my phone. Rachael said Norah had a meeting with Max and would be in around ten. It's now 10:10. Where the hell is she? If I have to find a different girl to take to Aspen, I'm going to need to get my ass in gear, or I'll be stuck with one of Kate's picks. And I wouldn't touch any of her recommendations with a ten-foot boner.

"Your friend Kate needs medication," Max states, jerking my focus away from my phone as he slides into the booth across from me.

I glance around and deflate when I see there's still no sign of Norah. "Where did you come from?" I ask, trying to play it cool.

Max frowns at me. "My office, why?"

I shake my head, realizing I'm being an obsessive tool. "With Norah?"

Max's frown lines deepen. "Yes, how did you know that?"

"Rachael mentioned it," I reply and realize I sound fucking nuts because she's probably just stuck in traffic. I close my laptop and push it aside to give Max my full attention. "What's going on with Kate?"

He flattens his palms on the table and exhales heavily. "You knew she booked one of my rental properties in Aspen for this weekend, right?"

"Yeah, for her bachelorette party."

"Yes, well, apparently now she said it's going to be a joint bachelor and bachelorette party with all couples, so she needs a nicer place."

"She mentioned she might do that," I grumble. "Their bridal parties are kind of unique. Miles is having his best friend, Sam, and his sister, Maggie, stand on his side, and Kate is having me and Lynsey stand on her side."

"Do you have to wear a dress?" Max chuckles and winks at me.

"Not as long as I don't piss Kate off," I reply, only halfway kidding. "Everything about this wedding is unique, so I'm not surprised she's shifting the bachelorette party into a joint thing. Surely, it's not a big deal, though. You have several properties in Aspen, right?"

"It's apparently a very big deal to Kate because none of my rental properties are good enough, so she asked if she could have my personal property instead."

I bark out a laugh. "That sounds like Kate."

"She didn't really ask. She just…told me."

I nod slowly.

"Like I was a child."

I press my lips together. "Hurts, doesn't it?"

"Yes! Does she have testicles in those yoga pants she's always wearing?" He rakes his hand over his short blond hair, and his lips puff out with a heavy exhale.

I have to fight back a laugh. Kate's pen name is Mercedes Lee Loveletter, and she uses it as her alter ego all the time. It's amusing to watch people get Loveletter'd. I lean forward and hit him with a knowing look. "She doesn't need balls, Max. She has a super vagina that writes dirty books and crushes any balls that don't submit to her." I sit back and lift my coffee to my lips. "I assume you caved, right?"

"I don't think I could say no if I wanted to. Now she's inviting me and told me to bring a date. Can you believe the nerve? She invited *me* to my own place this weekend."

I laugh at that. "She is a woman who gets what she wants. Don't worry about it. I'll be there. It'll be fun."

Max takes a sip of his coffee and curls the croinut number I grabbed for him in his hand. "Who are you bringing?"

AMY DAWS

"Umm…I'm not sure yet," I reply awkwardly. *Seriously, where the fuck is Norah?*

Max hits me with a terrified look. "Kate said no singles allowed. Couples only. Apparently, she's writing some swinger erotic novel and wants to use the entire trip as a write-off. She mentioned making us put all our keys in a bowl."

"Shut up," I bark, jerking back. "That's fucked up, even for Kate."

"Yeah, I think she was joking about that part. But she seems dead serious about bringing a date. That girl is scary."

Suddenly, the bell on the front door chimes, and Norah walks in. She's bathed in sunlight and tugging at the black bandana covering her blond hair while buttoning her baker's coat over her ample breasts that I've felt the size of against my chest.

She halts mid-step when her eyes land on me. "Hi," she says woodenly.

"Hi," I reply with a frown because she has a weird look on her face. "How are you?" I add, clearing my throat because I realize I probably have a weird look on my face too.

"I'm good, Moser. How are you?" She glances at Max and gives him an awkward head nod.

"I'm great." I head nod too. It's strange.

"Great," she repeats and then shrugs weirdly. "Okay then, see you guys."

She scurries behind the counter and joins Rachael, who's just set down a fresh tray of croinuts to be frosted. I stare at Norah for far longer than is appropriate because now I know what her legs look like in a short dress, and I can't help but wonder what they would look like wrapped around me.

"What are you doing?" Max asks, interrupting my dirty thoughts.

"I'm hoping Norah will come with me to Aspen."

"As your date?"

"Obviously." I furrow my brows at him because I would have

thought that was obvious. "We got along great at her parents' thing Friday, so it seems like the perfect idea."

Max's eyes widen. "So that whole fake date thing you guys planned went well?"

"It went…good," I reply, turning my attention back to Norah as she finishes washing her hands and prepares to glaze the steaming sheet pan in front of her. She looks so excited. It's adorable. "Parts of the night were weird, but it was mostly awesome. Norah can be really fun when she wants to be."

"I told you I thought she could be fun when forced." Max is frowning at me when I turn to look at him again. He lifts his chin and side-eyes me. "You like her."

I scoff and take a sip of my coffee. "Duh, she's hot as hell and can bake. She's the perfect woman."

Max's eyes narrow. "I mean *like* like her. You're looking at her differently now. I wondered about this."

I pin him with a look. "I'm looking at her because she's glazing my croinut and I'm starving." And I know what her lips taste like and how her ass feels beneath my hands and against my dick.

Fuck.

"Yeah, okay," Max says with a knowing laugh. "Look, man, you do you. I thought it was crazy when you told me what you guys were doing this past weekend, but I'm just her franchise manager, not her love coach."

"You'd be a horrible love coach," I say. "You're shit with relationships. A great father, yes. A great husband…no way."

Max scowls at me before gesturing over to the donut counter. "So, would you invite Norah as a fake date or a real date?"

"What's the difference really?" I waggle my brows suggestively, and he barks out a laugh.

"I think Norah could name quite a few." He pins me with a look that says, *don't go there, Moser.*

I exhale heavily. He's right. Fake relationship or not, Norah isn't the type of girl to blur boundaries. Although, I would never have expected her to take me to her parents' thing this past weekend. And I damn well didn't see that kiss coming. So perhaps Norah could surprise me. That is, if she still wants me.

Shaking that thought out of my mind because the ball's still in Norah's court, I refocus my thoughts on Max. "Who are you going to take to the orgy party in Aspen?"

"Do you think it'd be crazy for me to take McKenna?"

His eyes are wide and hopeful as I fix him with a withering stare. "Your ex-wife's best friend? Yes, Max, I think it'd be a *horrible* idea for you to take her."

He sighs. "They're not friends anymore."

"Still…that is not a road you need to travel. Don't you have that Aspen friends-with-benefits girl you could call?"

He nods. "Yeah, and Everly is with her mom this weekend, so I think I'm available, but I should double-check."

Max pulls his phone out, most likely to text his ex and make sure she won't need him at all this weekend. It's been eight years since their divorce, and they co-parent their ten-year-old really well. I can't figure out if it's because they're both really mature or because Everly's mom ended up being a lesbian and the two of them went through a lot of shit to get to this point.

Regardless, Max gets Everly three out of four weekends a month and one weeknight every week. It's tricky for him to have a social life because the man is involved in almost every business deal in Boulder, but he always makes time for Everly.

Suddenly, Rachael is at our table with two croinuts in hand. "Hey, boys," she says with a smile. "Here you go…today's flavor is Morello cherry with toasted almond cream."

"I don't know what any of that is, but I don't care," Max says with a hungry look in his eye. "God, look at that. It's a work of art."

Rachael winks at his praise. "This is actually one of my new recipes."

"You and Norah are a dream team," Max says with a genuine

smile. "Are you going to be comfortable here all on your own when Norah's world implodes with more business and less baking?"

"If I could keep that girl out of the kitchen, I would…but fat chance that will ever happen."

Out of the corner of my eye, I see something move, and when I look over, it's Norah. Her blue eyes are wide, and she's waving me over and gesturing for me to follow her to the back exit.

"I'm…going to hit the restroom," I say, but Max and Rachael barely notice my words or my exit.

I make my way down the hallway, past the bathrooms, and out the rear exit. The warm air hits me, and my eyes find Norah standing there, waiting.

"Hey," I say casually and straighten my glasses, feeling oddly nervous for some reason.

"Hey." She wrings her hands in front of her, looking crazy shy. "How are you?"

She nods. "I'm okay…you?"

"Great." I hook my thumb back to the door. "I got a fresh croinut in there waiting for me, so my day is looking up."

She smiles and chews her lip nervously. "Look, are you still game for this fake relationship idea? If you want out of it, you can say so now. I would totally understand."

My brows furrow. "Norah, I wasn't high on champagne or a delayed, teenage rebellion Friday night like you were. I was dead serious when I said we could help each other out for the next few weeks. It's not just me doing you a favor anymore. This is mutually beneficial."

She exhales heavily. "Good…because my mother has been blowing up my phone all weekend to host a dinner with the Hawthornes, and I've been ghosting her, which means she's going to come storming in here any second now."

I smile knowingly and hit her with a coy tone. "Norah, are you asking me to be your fake boyfriend?"

She cringes, squeezing her eyes shut, and nods. "As pathetic as that sounds, yes."

I step toward her and wrap my arm around her shoulders, trying to loosen her up. The faint smell of vanilla and cherry hits my nose, and I get a strong urge to lean in and give her a big sniff. "This is going to be fun."

She groans and rubs her forehead over her Led Zeppelin bandana. "I have some stipulations, though."

I release her and cross my arms over my chest. "It would shock me if you didn't."

"So first of all, no one can know this is a lie. Max doesn't know, does he?"

I cringe. "Sorry, he's one of my closest guy friends, and I sort of told him all about the fake date plan before the party."

"Oh my God," she groans and scrubs her hands over her face. "I had a business meeting with him and he knew the whole time? He must think I'm so pathetic."

"No, he doesn't," I snap. "He thinks you're a boss bitch who puts work way above personal life. Plus, you're his franchise client, so there's client confidentiality or something."

She pops out her hip and hits me with a look. "Have you told anybody else?"

"No, I haven't. Scout's honor." I hold up three fingers and smile like a dope.

It works because the smile she shoots back to me lights up her whole stressed-out face. "Okay," she acquiesces at last. "Rachael knows too, but she's a steel trap. I'm not worried about her leaking it."

I can't help but laugh. "Norah, relax. We're not performing a high-stakes crime here. We're just a couple of friends being extra friendly for a while."

Her lips thin. "Just promise it won't get weird between us."

"Why would it get weird?"

"I don't know, Dean. I've never faked having a boyfriend

before." She turns and begins pacing. She tugs on the back of her bandana. "I don't know where to begin with all of this."

"Well, I have our first official outing as boyfriend and girlfriend."

She nearly trips over her feet.

"Aspen, this weekend."

Her eyes turn to saucers. "I can't go to Aspen. I have to work."

"On what?"

"On the press kits that are going out to all the media outlets for the opening of Rise and Shine-Denver. I have to write up press releases and do interviews. My list is a mile long."

I shrug casually. "It's nearly a five-hour drive…you can do it in the car."

"Dean."

"Norah."

"Faking it for a dinner and a wedding is one thing. Faking it in front of all your friends for an entire weekend is a whole other batch of nuts. I can't do this."

"Right, because why on earth would you ever want to do something that resembled fun?"

"What are you talking about? This is much more complicated than a fun trip."

I step forward and grab Norah's shoulders, willing her to take a deep breath. The girl is a ticking time bomb. She needs to relax, or she's going to blow.

"We can still follow your stupid rules, Norah. I'll even sleep on the floor in our room in Aspen. We'll be fine. Plus, you can tell your mother about our plans this weekend and get out of whatever matchmaking bullshit she's trying to pull with Douche Kayak. Not to mention, Kate will kill me if I don't bring a nice date, so I need you."

She groans and presses her head into my chest. "Dean, this feels like a bad idea."

"It only feels like that because you need a vacation." I wrap my arm around her and guide her back toward the bakery. "Now, let's go tell everyone the good news."

Norah stops and looks up at me. "Kate was pretty upset about my Team Dean admission last week. What if she hates the thought of you with me?"

I smile. "She only fights with people she likes."

CHAPTER 7

Norah

Dean's car pulls up outside of the bakery on Friday at noon. My week has been such a whirlwind that I haven't had time to agonize over this weekend road trip. Now that he's here, it's too late to turn back.

Monday after our alley chat, Dean and I both changed our Facebook statuses from single to *in a relationship*. We figured that'd be the easiest way to get the message out without having to text everyone individually. Dean forced me to kiss his cheek while he took a selfie. He posted it on his Instagram with hashtag bae—a bit over the top, but I had to laugh. He's having way more fun with this than I am.

Max was the first one we told in person. He laughed…hard. It was really unprofessional. Then Rachael came over and joined him, and the two of them proceeded to critique our horrible acting for the better part of the morning. Needless to say, Dean and I have some work to do to make this more believable when we're in Aspen.

When my mother saw my new relationship status, she texted and asked if my account had been hacked. When I told her no, it was real, she sent me several crying emojis. *Jesus, Elaine. Dramatic much?*

And of course, Rachael has been sending me GIFs of someone sitting back and eating popcorn all week long.

Probably the most challenging faking-it moment was when my mom's book club showed up at the bakery on Wednesday. They all fired questions at me about how Dean and I met. That was the easy part because Dean and I decided to keep that story pretty honest. So, I told them he'd been coming into the bakery and asking me out for months, and I finally said yes. Easy peasy.

The hard part was the fact that my mother was *dead silent* the entire time I chatted with all her friends. In fact, she's been giving me the silent treatment all week.

Why didn't I come up with the idea of a fake boyfriend ages ago?

Aside from that, it's been okay. Dean's the one with a more active social life, so this change of status must be affecting his day-to-day life more than mine. However, he hasn't complained. He's been coming into the bakery and working like everything is normal. He passed me a sweet note on a napkin over the counter that said I looked prettier than the croinut of the day. The cheeseball.

Now, I'm leaving work early to go to Aspen for a lover's getaway and to see if we can pull this off for a whole weekend. It all feels a bit dirty to be lying to Dean's friends, but at the same time, it's kind of exciting. This is the most scandalous thing I've done in years. Probably ever!

Rachael walks over to where I'm standing at the register and elbows me in the ribs. "He drives a Range Rover."

"Don't judge him too harshly for that," I reply, unbuttoning my baker's smock. "He's made my mother stop speaking to me for five blissful days, so he deserves free croinuts for life."

"Don't forget you're doing him a favor too," she says, side-eyeing me. "I don't remember the last time you left the bakery early for a weekend."

"I know." I groan and shake my head. "You sure you're going to be okay without me?"

"Zander and I got this!" She waves her hand. "You have business stuff to do anyway so it's not like you were really going to be here."

She's right. These days, I work upstairs in my apartment while Rachael runs the bakery. I'd be lost without her.

Dean strides in looking crazy hot in gray shorts and a fitted dark Henley. His beard has grown out a bit since my parents' party, and his dark hair flops over his forehead in an appealing way that makes me want to run my fingers through it.

I exhale and pull off my smock, revealing the outfit Rachael laid out for me: frayed white denim shorts and a heather green tank that makes my boobs look giant. Luckily, she let me put an unbuttoned plaid shirt over it, so I don't feel like I'm trying too hard.

"Hey, sugar butt, you ready for a road trip?" Dean asks, sidling up to the counter and pulling his Ray-Bans off to reveal his brown-sugar eyes.

Rachael barks out a laugh at his endearment that we argued about via text message all week. Dean said if he wasn't allowed some pet names, he wasn't going to look like a good boyfriend. I submitted when he told me it would drive my mother insane.

Rachael points at Dean. "You better be good to her this weekend, Dean Moser. I know where you live."

"You do?" he asks, his brows lifting.

She nods. "I got your address from Max…which means I can light your shit on fire if I hear you've done my girl dirty."

Dean's face falls. "Jesus…arson threats? I think you skipped a couple of steps there, Rachael."

She pins him with a stern look, and he holds up his hands in surrender. "I'll be the perfect gentleman."

I roll my suitcase around the counter to join him, and he walks over to take it from me. His eyes flash to my chest before swerving down to my bag. "Is this everything?"

"I sure hope so," I reply with a nervous grin. I was so busy trying to get some of my press stuff out of the way this morning that I had a packing emergency, and Rachael had to come rescue me. She ended up taking over, so I'm not entirely sure what she shoved in there. But she had the itinerary Dean sent over, so I hope she got everything.

"Let's get out of town then."

I grab the box of fresh croinuts I made for the weekend, and we load up quickly. Sliding into the passenger seat, I crack open my laptop and am already deep into my work before we leave Boulder city limits. I need to make good use of this drive if I'm going to screw off with Dean and his friends for a whole weekend. When is the last time I screwed off for a day, let alone a weekend?

The drive is quiet for the first couple of hours as I make my way through my long to-do list that Max gave me. When I look up and pop out my earbuds, Dean is listening to a podcast about birthmarks. *Definitely not yacht rock.* This is an even stranger choice, but I'm drawn into it, despite the mountain of emails I still need to reply to.

"This is so weird," I state, finally succumbing to my interest.

"I know. It's awesome," Dean replies, staring forward and listening intently with an awestruck look on his face.

"Why do we care about this so much?"

He shakes his head slowly. "I have no idea."

When we're about an hour away from Aspen, I close my laptop to take in the mountainous view. We used to come here to ski a lot in the winter, so I've been on this drive a million times, but nothing compares to entire mountainsides covered with aspens changing colors in the fall. It's impressive how I dream of living in Paris, but Colorado still manages to take my breath away even after all these years.

"So, are you done working finally?" Dean asks, his hand draped casually over the top of the steering wheel as he glances at me curiously.

I press my hands to the top of my laptop. "No, but I can catch up later."

"Good, because I think we need to revisit and revise some of your rules." Dean glances at me and waggles his eyebrows in an ominous way.

"What did you have in mind?"

"Well, Kate and Lynsey are like sharks, and if they smell blood in the water, they will attack. So…we need to tweak those PDA restrictions you have. I need to be able to touch you freely if we're going to sell this."

My chest tightens at the thought of Dean's hands on me. I still have a funny swirling in my stomach every time I think of that kiss we shared before. It was…surprising. I expected it to be rash and completely void of chemistry because all I cared about was pissing off my mother, but Dean took over that kiss and well…

It was hot.

Probably the hottest kiss I've ever experienced.

Which makes the idea of him fondling me in front of his friends *really* nerve-wracking. My voice is quiet when I ask, "What did you have in mind exactly?"

He glances out of the corner of his eye and, without asking, reaches across the console and places his big warm hand on my bare thigh just above my knee. "Something like this."

My entire leg erupts in goose bumps that I'm sure he notices but doesn't say anything. His fingers skate lightly over my skin as he settles into the embrace that seems simple but causes a riot of electricity to shoot straight up my thigh to the area between my legs.

He teases the frayed hem of my shorts with his pinkie. "Think this is okay?"

I swallow the lump in my throat and nod. "It's fine."

"You could hold my hand while I'm doing it too," he offers with a shrug.

I quickly wipe my palms off on my plaid shirt and then rest my hands on top of his like it's not causing me to feel hot all over my body.

He beams casually. "See? This is nice, right?"

I nod woodenly.

"And don't be surprised if I pat your ass once in a while. That's totally something I'd do to a girl I was serious with."

God, this is going to be harder than I thought.

"Also, kissing," Dean adds, wrapping his hand farther around my leg and squeezing. "I think we've established we're good at the kissing, so we should just keep doing that whenever it makes sense."

I pin him with a look. "I don't think we need to kiss."

"Why not?"

"Because…it's…weird to kiss in front of people. Tons of couples don't go that far in front of people."

"I'm not like most people, Norah. I'd be affectionate if I had a girlfriend like you."

"Like me," I repeat and chew my lip nervously. "What does that mean?"

Dean exhales heavily and pulls his hand from my leg as we approach a curve up a large mountain. "You're beautiful, you're successful, you're kind. You have killer legs. You're super uptight, which makes you a challenge, and I love a challenge. So yeah, I'm pretty sure if this were a real relationship, I wouldn't be able to keep my hands off you."

My body shivers at the assault of the casual compliments Dean just threw my way. How is he so cool with all of this? I wish I had an ounce of his confidence.

His voice cuts into my thoughts when he adds, "Frankly, I think we should pull over and have sex right now because, with the limited oxygen at this elevation, the sexual tension in this car is *stifling*."

Dean glances over with a teasing smirk and now I feel like I'm doing a good impression of that flapping bass fish on the wall that my mother mastered last weekend. "You're kidding, right?"

He shrugs. "I don't think it sounds like a bad idea."

"It sounds like a horrible idea because we're not really in a relationship," I bark and can feel a faint sheen of sweat collecting on my upper lip. I reach forward and open the vent to blow air on my face.

"And we have to be in a real relationship to have sex?" he asks, pinning me with a serious look.

"Um, it'd be preferred."

"People have casual sex all the time, Norah."

"Not me," I reply and instantly think of Barrett. We totally had casual sex after we broke up and then never spoke again because it was awkward afterward, and we both regretted it. I do not want to suffer through that with Dean.

I glance over at him and can't help but deflate a bit because he is seriously attractive. His square bearded jaw and strong sculpted pecs beneath that shirt could be worth a little awkwardness. But this cannot happen. We're business partners, and we have to get through a wedding in a couple of weeks. Sex would make everything more complicated.

Plus, I don't think he's serious. He's never serious.

I look away from him and stare forward with my hands resting safely in my lap. "We can't have sex. No way. We're two friends helping each other out and nothing more. Don't make this weird."

He sighs heavily. "Whatever you say, boss."

My anxious lip sweat has finally subsided by the time we pull up to a large brick-pillared private entrance a good thirty miles outside of Aspen. Dean said Max's house was nice. However, he failed to mention it's a freaking mansion that we have to drive over a stream to get to.

I'm speechless as we get out of the car, and I stare up at the giant home and its flagstone walkway flanked with aspens that lead to ornate double doors with carvings of lions on the front.

"Was that a bridge or a moat we drove over?" I ask Dean, and then suddenly, the front doors swing open, and Kate is standing there in all her wild, red-haired glory.

"Holy shit, Lynsey, he wasn't lying!" she hollers as she stares at me with her jaw dropped.

Lynsey emerges in the doorway beside her with a drink and thrusts her free hand into the air. "You owe me twenty bucks."

Kate shakes her head and marches out, stopping in front of me with narrowed eyes. "How much is he paying you for this?"

"Paying me for what?" I ask, genuinely confused.

"Paying you to be his fake date for the weekend?" Kate asks knowingly and turns to thrust her pointer finger in Dean's face.

Flames. My entire body is engulfed in flames. The lip sweat has also returned, and I might have some ass sweat happening like a winner. My voice is a stammering mess when I reply, "I-I'm not his fake date. I'm his girlfriend." I sound like a robot. Like a stupid, moronic, painfully sweaty robot. "I brought croinuts."

I thrust them into Kate's hands as Dean drops our bags and reaches around me from behind. His hands clasp around my waist in that delicious way that would normally make me feel small and feminine, but right now, it's making me feel hot and sweaty. I probably stink.

"Kate, I promise you, no money was exchanged in this transaction." He leans in and kisses the inside of my neck, and I want to barf because I feel a drizzle of sweat sliding downward.

"You two are really together?" Kate asks, shaking her head from side to side.

I shrug because actually saying the lie out loud feels worse than letting it be implied. Kate digs into her pocket and holds up a twenty-dollar bill.

Lynsey scurries over and takes the cash and the croinuts from her hands, smiling happily at Dean and me. "I could have called this over a year ago."

I frown at that bizarre remark, but then Dean clears his

throat. "Can one of you show me where we're sleeping so I can dump our bags?"

"I can do that," Lynsey peals.

"I'll give Norah the tour since this is her first time here." Kate wraps her arm around mine and waves Lynsey and Dean off with the bags. "People with this kind of money don't do tours. But I'm a cheap ass and genuinely love gawking at other people's worldly possessions."

She remains holding on to my arm as she walks me inside and describes the property like a realtor. The interior has a rustic hunting lodge feel with natural stone walls throughout most of the space and exposed mahogany beams on the vaulted ceilings. It feels like the entire property was created inside a cave except for the giant windows offering sweeping views of the aspen-filled mountains.

We head outside next, and Kate informs me the estate is thirty acres of picturesque scenery in the valley of Snowmass Mountain. There's a horse barn and equestrian pastures far off in the distance that Max rents out to locals. She points to the stream we came over (not a moat) and then ends the tour by the swimming pool and hot tub flanked with flagstones and pillars with fire shooting out the top of them.

"This looks more like a resort than a vacation home," I state, looking into the house that's glowing now that the sun has set. Everyone has congregated by the large stone bar located right in the center with the perfect view of the lit-up pool area.

Kate sighs heavily. "And it's only one of the many properties Max owns. Can you imagine?"

My brows lift. "I've been working with him for over a year and I had no idea he had this kind of money."

"Well, it's family money but in fairness, Max works like a dog. We can't all be lucky enough to get inheritances like Max and Dean. Some of us have to start our own businesses, right?"

"Right," I reply politely and return her offer of a high five as I inwardly process the Dean comment.

I didn't realize Dean received an inheritance. I'm actually not entirely sure how much money Dean has or what he does with his money. I know he dresses well and drives a nice car. And he clearly had enough cash flow to invest in my business. But that's the extent of my knowledge.

I let those wandering thoughts go as Kate leads me back inside and reintroduces me to everyone. First there's Kate's fiancé, Miles, who's the epitome of tall, dark, and handsome with crazy light blue eyes that stare at his fiancée like he wants to eat her every time she comes into a room. Then there's Lynsey and her husband, Josh, who's a doctor. He's the quiet type but Kate murmurs in my ear that they haven't had a weekend away from their one-year-old in ages and she wouldn't be surprised if they make baby number two on this trip. The friendly ginger-bearded guy who owns the tire shop in Boulder is Sam. Sam and Miles are apparently best friends and Kate introduces me to his fiancée, Maggie, who happens to also be Miles's little sister.

"Funny story about these two"—Kate barks out a laugh and points her finger into Sam's chest—"he started screwing his best friend's little sister behind *all* of our backs…especially Miles."

My eyes go wide and I expect the room to go dead quiet with awkwardness, but it doesn't. Maggie rolls her eyes and tucks herself up under Sam's massive arm while he leisurely takes a drink of his beer bottle. Everyone else is smiling and laughing like Kate tells this story all the time.

"But luckily, Sam fell for Mags hook, line, and sinker and now they are going to have an awesome winter wonderland wedding… so all is right in the tire shop."

Maggie flashes her ring as a sign of admission. "That is if Kate will finally give up the spotlight for a weekend."

Kate mock gasps. "Are you calling me an attention whore, Maggie?"

"Where would I ever get that idea, Kate?" Maggie laughs.

"Maybe because you've morphed into a bridezilla for the past month?" Lynsey chirps, taking a sip of her colorful cocktail.

Kate, Lynsey, and Maggie all begin to playfully argue and Dean gestures for me to come to the end of the bar where he's mixing a drink. I make my way over and notice he's already freshly showered and changed for the evening. He's sporting a pale blue button-down with the sleeves rolled up, revealing muscular forearms and an expensive-looking watch. His bottom half is covered in a pair of jeans that make his butt look ridiculously good.

"Doing okay there, sugar bottom?" he asks and my eyes flick up to his face, horrified that he might have caught me looking at his bottom.

"I'd be better with one of those." I point down as he squeezes a lime into his rocks glass. He hands his drink over without pause and I take a fortifying sip while staring at the three couples all lovingly wrapped up in each other's arms with drinks in hand. "I can see why you wanted a fake girlfriend this weekend. This group is intense. They're kind of disgustingly in love, aren't they?"

Dean shrugs and takes a sip of his freshly made cocktail. "Give it time and they'll all be fighting over the best divorce attorney in Boulder."

My lower lip sticks out at that remark. "Cynical much?"

"Aren't you too?" he asks, turning to face me with those chocolatey eyes of his. "You're anti-relationship as well, I thought. That's why we're business partners for the next few weeks." He clinks his glass to mine in solidarity.

"I'm not anti-relationship for everyone…just me I guess," I state and take an uncertain sip.

Suddenly, Max emerges from the kitchen. He has a gorgeous strawberry blond trailing him.

"Dean, Norah…you made it!" He reaches out and shakes Dean's hand and offers me a smile that borders on sympathetic. "You surviving okay so far?"

"This is a very dynamic group." I plaster on a smile.

Max laughs. "Yes, it is. This is Henley, by the way. She's a friend of mine who lives here in Aspen."

We shake hands and Kate begins shouting for our attention. I turn to see she's kneeling on top of her barstool. "Okay, everybody…as I'm sure you all saw on my itinerary, tonight we're splitting up. I've made reservations for the guys at a great little brewery and pizza place and the ladies are dining here in the palace."

Max shakes his head and takes a drink.

"So, let's go to our rooms, put on our slutty tops and meet back down here in an hour. Guys, make sure if you go to a strip club tonight, you dust off the glitter before you come back into Max's mansion. His live-in maid is on vacation—I wish I was joking."

Max rolls his eyes. "She's my house manager. This place is huge and I'm not here enough to handle it."

"We got it, Christian Grey. You're super humble." Kate waves him off and Miles lifts her down from the barstool as everybody breaks away to their prospective rooms.

Max exhales heavily and turns to Dean. "Is she going to be like this all weekend?"

"Worse, Max. Much, much worse." Dean throws his arm around my shoulders, drenching me in his appealing manly scent as he begins leading me away. "Allow me to show you to our room so you can get ready, sugar bottom."

"Does the sugar thing really have to stick?"

He frowns down at me. "You're a baker…I thought you'd love that endearment."

"I think you can do better, Moser."

"Whatever you say, boss."

Our bedroom is on the main level at the end of a long hallway that leads out to a lit-up veranda with tons of outdoor seating. There are some caterers outside that appear to be setting up for the girls' dinner. Dean opens the door around the corner and steps back to let me walk in first.

As soon as I see our room for the weekend, the butterflies erupt in my belly again. There's a giant four-poster bed that looks like a slice of beige heaven. The carpet is lush and bouncy beneath my feet and when I turn, I mosey over to check out the attached bathroom.

My jaw drops when I see floor-to-ceiling windows right next to a lush soaker tub overlooking stunning mountains. Beside the tub is a shower that looks straight out of a billionaire's magazine…if that is a thing. The tub is lovely with jets and the whole shebang, but the glass shower has double heads, back massagers, and a steamer.

Holy shit, I'm never going to want to leave this bathroom.

Out of nowhere, my mind does this weird segue into some sort of carnal cavewoman and the thoughts that echo in my head are horrifying:

Sex.

Shower sex.

Tub sex.

Dean naked.

Me naked with Dean.

Dean's ass that looks really good in those jeans pressed up against the glass window for all those aspens to see.

Dean's big, warm hands cupping my breasts as he presses me to—

"Norah." Dean says my name and I jump, my hands flying to my chest as I try to stop my heart from lurching from my body. "Did you hear me?"

"No, what?" I stutter and struggle to breathe because the bathroom suddenly feels ten times smaller now that he's in here with me.

"I said I'd take the couch." He straightens his glasses and frowns at me like he's debating if I need CPR.

"Oh…um…okay." I dip my head and scurry out of the bathroom, taking in big gulps of air.

I spot my suitcase on the sofa beneath the large bay window and make my way over to it like a lifeline. If I can focus on my bag, Dean can't see my red cheeks, and I'll have time to stop thinking about sex or showers or naked bodies.

Damn him. Why did he have to bring up sex in the car? I was doing just fine until he opened his big, stupid, flirtatious mouth.

With shaky hands, I unzip my suitcase, and the second I peel open the flap, my entire body seizes in panic. I gasp and slam it closed as fast as humanly possible.

"What's the matter?" Dean asks, his footsteps heavy as he rushes over to stand beside me. He stares at my suitcase that I'm white-knuckled and holding shut right now.

"Nothing!" I turn to sit on it.

Dean frowns at me, a laugh teasing the edges of his mouth. "Not nothing. What was in there? A mouse or something?"

I level him with a look. "A mouse, Dean? How the hell would a mouse get in my suitcase?"

He laughs. "I don't know. You're clearly freaked out about something in there, so just tell me what it is."

I shake my head from side to side.

"Norah."

"No."

"Norah," he says my name again and steps closer to me, wafting me with his freshly showered body and that deliciously seductive cologne. "I'm going to find out one way or another."

"It's none of your business," I state woodenly and feel my cheeks heat.

"Bullshit," Dean says with a sardonic grin and before I realize what's happening he bends over, grabs my wrist, and yanks my entire body up over his shoulder.

"Dean, stop it!" I cry out as his hands cup the backs of my bare thighs. "Put me down!"

"Not until I see what you're hiding in there." He turns and walks me toward the bed.

"I told you it's none of your business!" I kick my legs in a feeble attempt to break free. He just laughs and holds on tighter.

"You're my girlfriend…you're my business."

I growl as I bite my lip to prevent myself from yelling the truth of our situation and outing us to whoever is probably sleeping above us. Dean tosses me onto the bed like I weigh nothing and then turns to head back toward my suitcase.

I scramble off the pillowy-soft mattress and jump on his back just as he reaches my bag. Before I can stop him, he flips it open, and I die a thousand deaths when the pink object comes into full view for both of us to see.

"Holy shit," Dean says, his voice full of awe as he reaches down and picks up my pretty in pink bullet that, hours ago, was stashed safely away in my bathroom drawer.

I slide off his back and shove his stunned body away from my bag to snatch my vibrator out of his hand. "I'm mortified. Are you happy now?" I turn and tuck it away in a zippered pocket inside my suitcase. Rachael could have at least put it in its matching pink travel bag.

She is so getting dumpster duty next week.

Dean stares at me, his bearded jaw dropped as he struggles for words for the first time in his life. "Norah, that was a vibrator."

"No shit, Captain Obvious."

He runs a hand through his dark hair and hits me with a dis-believing look. "Norah, if you were so hot for an orgasm that you needed to pack a sex toy for the weekend, we seriously need to revisit this no sex policy you have."

"I didn't pack it," I snap, pushing back my hair and scrubbing my hand over my forehead. "Rachael did because I was working and struggling with what to wear, so she came in and took over because she's a monstrous human being who will be dead very soon."

Dean hits me with a flat look. "Seriously?"

"Yes! God, I'm not that desperate for an orgasm."

"But that is your toy?" he replies, watching me expectantly.

"Not that it's any of your business, but yes." I drop onto the couch and cover my face in humiliation.

After a moment of silence, the cushion dips beside me, and I can feel Dean's heat on my side. "I'm going to ask you a serious question, Norah, and I want you to reply honestly."

I pull my hands away from my face to look at him, my hands clenching into fists because I'm certain there's a horrible joke coming my way.

His eyes rove over my face before he tilts his chin and says, "When was the last time you were properly fucked?"

My entire body erupts with pins and needles, and I look forward, the heat of my blush rushing to the surface of my skin. "Dean, we are not talking about this."

"Why not?" he laughs.

"Because this is embarrassing." I cover my cheeks with my hands, and my insides clench with feelings I don't want to own up to right now.

He nudges me with his elbow. "It's not embarrassing. It's something friends talk about."

"You're on your way to a no-friend zone if you keep pushing me on this."

Dean rolls his eyes, not the least bit taken aback by my scathing tone. "It's been a month for me, which is actually a bit of a dry spell."

I huff out an incredulous noise. "It's been a year for me, so I don't remotely feel sorry for you."

"Jesus Christ, a year?" Dean barks and begins pacing in front of me. He takes his glasses off and pinches the bridge of his nose. "You haven't been fucked in a year? That's criminal. It's wrong! It's…I mean, look at you."

"Oh my God, shut up," I snap back and stand to face him, crossing my arms over my chest. "I can't sleep with random people I pick up at a bar. I need to halfway know the person before I can have sex with them. And clearly, I've been a little busy with work, which shouldn't come as a surprise to you."

Dean shakes his head like I'm a sad, sick puppy in need of

life-saving surgery, and he's the vet who's going to give it to me. He steps closer, his hands cupping my arms as he gazes at me. "Look, I was kind of joking in the car before, but now I'm serious, Norah. We need to have sex. We're both single, and we're both uninterested in a long-term thing. We're both using each other for the next few weeks, so why not take it a step further and make the most of this situation? I mean…are you not even remotely attracted to me?"

I bark out a really un-sexy laugh and shake his hands off me. "Do you know a single woman in all of Colorado who isn't attracted to you?"

He licks his lips and crosses his arms over his chest, causing his shirt to tighten around his sculpted arms. "The jury is still out on you. I've made my attraction to you very clear for a long time now. But I can't get a read on you. Are you just uptight or are you genuinely not interested in changing this fake relationship into a friends-with-benefits arrangement?"

"I'm not uptight," I volley back, hating how he calls me out every time I don't fall to my knees and do what he says. "I don't think it's wise for us to blur the lines. I have two bakeries to run right now, and my life is only going to get busier once the franchise options open. My mother is breathing down my neck for grandchildren I'll never give her. My father is making me feel guilty for upsetting her. I don't have time to pee, let alone have sex." I point at my suitcase and stomp my foot. "That pink vibrator gets the job done in less time than my twenty-minute croinut recipe, so excuse me for preferring efficiency."

Dean's stunned as he blinks back at me. "That's the saddest thing I've ever heard, Norah."

My hands ball into tight fists. "Choose your next words carefully, Moser, or you'll be sleeping outside with the sprinklers tonight."

"I'm sorry! I'm sorry!" He steps back and lifts his hands up in surrender. "If pinkie in there is all you need, more power to you. I just thought you could use a little more fun in your life."

"I have fun," I mumble and cross my arms over my chest to pout.

He lifts his brows and offers me a wry smile. "Well, just know the offer is out there. I can accomplish a lot in twenty minutes."

He shoots me a dirty wink, and my nostrils flare as I point at the door. "Just get out so I can get ready for the night, please."

He laughs and turns to leave while I head into the bathroom for a cold shower. Very, very cold.

CHAPTER 8

Norah

"You guys," Lynsey slurs, her eyes hooded as she clutches her tropical drink to her chest, and we all sit around the enormous outdoor firepit. "I'm terrified that sex isn't as good for Josh anymore."

"What?" we all coo back soothingly.

"Why would you say that?" Kate asks, pinning her friend with a serious look that is at complete odds with her drunkenness.

Lynsey cringes and points at her groin. "A baby came out of here…a big baby."

"A beautiful baby," Maggie trills with her sweet, perky voice. She's the youngest of this group, and her innocence is kind of adorable.

"The most beautifulest baby ever." Lynsey takes another drink. "But…a human being was extracted from that small orifice."

"So, what?" Kate slaps her hand on her thigh and leans forward so the fire illuminates her face. "What's the problem?"

"The problem is that I'm worried when Josh and I have sex it's like a hot dog down a hallway down there."

Kate erupts into a full-on belly laugh while I glance nervously over to Henley, who's an outsider like me. We both look around, not sure if we join Kate in the laughter or give sympathetic eyes to Lynsey. It's a sticky situation.

The catered dinner on the veranda was beautiful and civilized. We drank wine and chatted about the upcoming wedding and honeymoon Miles and Kate are going on afterward. Lynsey even had Miles fill out this adorable little quiz about Kate that showed how much he knows her. It was really sweet.

Now we've moved to the fancy firepit and downgraded to ice buckets of whatever drinks Kate found in Max's fridge, and the conversation has taken a turn for the worst if we're using the phrase "hot dog down a hallway."

"Why are you laughing, Kate? I'm being serious!" Lynsey whines, setting her drink down and crossing her arms into a pout.

Kate attempts to regain control of herself and reaches into the ice bucket for another drink. "Let me ask you a serious question, Lyns." She cracks a White Claw. "Have you been having G-spot orgasms with Josh since you had Julianna? Not just clitoral orgasms…but the inside magic tunnel Os."

"Yes, those are my favorite," Lynsey replies back quickly.

Kate gestures with her can knowingly. "Then there you have it. Women with big vaginas would never have G-spot stimulation…that's just science. Trust me, I write erotica for a living…I'm basically a doctor of boning."

"Can you not say things like that?" Maggie murmurs and sips her beer with a disgusted look on her face that makes me giggle. "You're marrying my brother, and this is going to give me nightmares."

"Do you do Kegels?" Henley asks, breaking the outsider silence pact I thought we had. Up until this moment, the whole evening was feeling like a dinner theater. Now if Henley is going to participate in the conversation, I suppose I should too. Her blue eyes flit toward the fire. "My older sister has had three kids so she's been doing Kegels for years. She says her sex life is great."

Lynsey exhales and nods. "I was doing them for a while, but I quit. I'll start them back up."

"Smart." Kate taps her temple. "I've heard good things about Kegels. I, on the other hand, am really hoping for a C-section situation for our future children so I can keep it all high and tight down yonder. I'm not a fan of cardio, and Kegels seem dangerously close to cardio."

"This is the strangest conversation I've ever had with you two," Maggie says, shaking her head as she glances back and forth between Kate and Lynsey. "And that's coming from someone who heard you two talk about how it doesn't matter if you shave your crotches because every time a man enters a woman's vagina, he's won the lottery."

"It's true!" Kate and Lynsey shout in unison, and it causes all of us to burst out laughing.

God, these girls are fun. Crazy and completely unfiltered. But fun.

"So…Norah," Kate says with a flourish and turns her terrifying eyes to me. "You've been quiet this evening."

I take a sip of my drink and shrug. "I'm just enjoying the show."

"Well, it's your turn now to spill the tea. You and Dean in a relationship. Gosh, I still can't believe it."

I shrug and offer a weak smile. "He's a persistent guy." Which became very evident when he propositioned me for sex again in our room earlier tonight. Thank goodness I never saw him before he left tonight because I have no clue how I'm going to act around him.

"Have you guys done the nasty yet?" Kate asks, waggling her brows at me.

"No," I reply honestly because it's the first thing that pops into my mind. Seriously, these girls are relentless. I had no idea this weekend was going to be consumed with so much sex talk. I should have seen it coming, though, because this is a bachelorette party for a bride who writes sexy books for a living. I clear my throat and add coolly, "We're taking it slow."

Kate and Lynsey look dumbfounded.

"Dean Moser is taking it slow with a girl?" Lynsey asks, clearly not buying it. "He must have serious feelings for you."

I flush, wondering if I've revealed too much, so I decide to hit them with more honesty. "Well, the slow thing is my idea. I'm not really into relationships. No offense to you guys who all seem blissfully happy, but I don't think I'll ever get married."

"Then you're a perfect match for Dean." Lynsey hiccups and then covers her mouth like she said too much.

"Why do you say that?" I find myself asking.

She glances at Kate nervously. "Just that…well, his parents weren't exactly picture-perfect when he was a kid. And he took their divorce really hard."

"Interesting," I reply with a frown. "I got the impression he was glad they split up." Lynsey and Kate exchange a weird look, and then Maggie's voice interrupts me before I can pry further.

"Why don't you want to get married? Did your parents have a messy divorce too?" Maggie asks, her brows furrowed with genuine interest, not judgment.

I shrug and sigh heavily because it's the million-dollar question I get from everybody. "I just worry I'll have to give up my dreams. My mother was a huge sales rep for Mary Kay cosmetics before she had me. She was one of those ladies who was so successful they gave her a pink Cadillac."

"Oh yeah, I've seen those. I want one!" Lynsey laughs.

"Right! It's amazing. She was a big deal and a top rep nationally. I've seen the awards she's earned tucked away in her closet. It's impressive and she made women feel good and earned a crazy-amazing living doing it. But once she had me, she gave it all up. I don't want that for myself. I have big goals for my bakery, and if I get married, I'm scared those goals will change. Marriage almost always leads to babies, and I can't do what I want to do with a kid."

Lynsey leans forward and frowns at me. "Lots of married couples choose to never have kids. And lots of women don't give up careers for their children. I'm a perfect example of finding a balance…even if I have a wide-set vagina now."

Everyone bursts out laughing because she said it so seriously, like she wasn't trying to be funny, which just makes it that much funnier.

When we all recover, I hit her with a meaningful look. "I know it's possible, but gosh, you and Josh are such an amazing partnership. You literally share a medical practice. That's a unicorn kind of guy you found there."

"Max said Dean's an investor in your franchise, right?" Henley states out of nowhere, turning all of our attention to her. "Isn't that kind of a partnership?"

My brows furrow. "Well, he's really a silent investor."

"That sounds even better," she replies with a bitter laugh. "To find a man who believes in you so fully he doesn't try to force his opinion on your business. Does it get much more unicorn than that?"

Everyone goes quiet for a moment as we process the sort of monumental truth Henley just dropped out of nowhere.

"Dean basically offered to be my baby daddy too," Lynsey adds with wide, sweet eyes. "When things were weird with Josh and me, he was willing to change his whole life to help me out. He's a total unicorn."

Kate nods. "Yeah, he may be a mountain manwhore, but even under his whorish ways, he's got magic in the horn of his."

Everyone nods in agreement, but my mind wanders back to our talk in the bedroom earlier tonight. I don't know if it's the firelight or the wine flowing in my veins, but I'm starting to ask myself why I was resisting Dean's idea so much? Yes, obviously, I'm busy. But if it's not a real relationship, how much more time could hooking up occupy? And clearly, Dean is a good guy, so I could do a lot worse as far as casual sex goes. And if there was a chance I could see him naked in that sexy shower, I don't know if I could live with myself if I didn't take it.

My body shivers when I remember what he said. *"When was the last time you were properly fucked?"*

Suddenly, Kate raises her glass, and I'm snapped out of my internal reverie. "A toast! To unicorn dicks…may they be much *much* bigger…than a hot dog."

We all laugh heartily, but Lynsey gasps as she squints at her watch. "Oh my God, I lost track of time."

"Why does it matter what time it is?" Kate asks, still holding her drink up mid-toast.

Lynsey smiles and glances toward the house that has a few more lights on than it did before. "I have a surprise for you, Kate, and it's so very *you*!"

"What do you mean?" Kate asks, lowering her drink. "There was nothing else on the itinerary for tonight."

Lynsey smiles. "Come inside, ladies. This is going to be fun!"

CHAPTER 9

Dean

"This is a bachelor party. We gotta take this dude to a strip club," Max slurs at the table we're all seated around inside the brewery Kate booked a reservation at.

Miles, Sam, Josh, Max, and I have done three beer flights each and are about five pizzas in and feeling like a million bucks. Onto the next stop.

I slap my hand on the table. "I'll hit the ATM."

Miles gets an uncomfortable look on his face. "Do we really have to go?" he asks with his voice rising at the end. "'Cuz if I'm going to be honest, you guys, I hate strip clubs. I always feel awkward 'cuz I don't know what to do with my hands. You're not supposed to touch the strippers but they are literally in your lap...so what...I just...hold my hands up like I'm under arrest?"

"We'll get you a police stripper," Max drawls, waggling his eyebrows excitedly. "Or a dominatrix who can tie your hands behind your back."

Miles groans and looks over to Sam for a rescue. Sam's deep voice says, "Why see strippers when my girl is hotter than all of them and will strip for me for free?"

Miles's head jerks back in horror, and he leans forward, thrusting his finger in Sam's face. "Bro, you can't say stuff like that…we talked about this, remember? I know you're fucking my sister, but I can't *know* you're fucking my sister. You guys are saving yourselves for marriage in my mind. Scratch that…you're not even going to have sex when you're married. If you have a kid, it's going to be an immaculate conception."

Sam bows his head in shame. "Sorry, man. It slipped."

"You can't use the word slipped around me anymore. Everything you say sounds dirty now and I'm going to vomit up all that gross IPA beer that Dean made us drink."

"You get used to the hops," I exclaim and shake my head in frustration. This crew cannot appreciate the delicacies of a good IPA.

"So, what? We're just…going back to the house?" Max groans like someone just kicked his puppy.

"No, we're going back to your mansion," Miles corrects, holding his fist out to Max for a bump. "Thanks for hooking us up, by the way. I know Kate is a lot, but fucking hell, I love her."

Max smiles. "Someone has to."

It's nearing midnight by the time the chauffeured van pulls up to the house to drop us off. The inside is lit up like a Christmas tree so the girls are clearly still awake. I'm actually kind of nervous to see Norah since I basically propositioned her in our room mere hours ago and we haven't spoken since.

But fuck, I couldn't help myself.

Thinking of Norah using that pink vibrator on her pink pussy made my dick rock-hard in my tight-ass jeans. God, how often does she use that thing? Does she watch porn while she does it? Is there someone she thinks about? These are the millions of dirty thoughts that have been racing through my mind after every sip of beer I had tonight.

And fuck me, why does she think a toy is better than the real thing? Who are the guys she's fucked who have let her become satisfied with a battery-operated device? They deserve to have the shit kicked out of them and their brains wiped because they clearly didn't realize the stunning woman they had in bed needed to be worshipped.

And I would worship Norah.

I'd worship her so much she'd forget about how busy she is, and how many goals she has to accomplish, and how early she has to get up to open the bakery. Her brain would be ruined by epic orgasm after epic orgasm…as it should be. I'd be willing to use that fucking pink thing on her if that's what she wanted. It would be better than sex to watch her cheeks go red, watch her squirm and grip the comforter, hear her frustrated noises.

Goddammit, I'm getting hard all over again.

I need to chill the fuck out because Norah is probably getting ready to inform me that I'm sleeping on the patio furniture for the shit I said to her earlier tonight. Part of me knows I deserve it, but the other part of me gets off on pushing her. I want to see her fall apart, lose control, feel something beyond stress. It would be a fearsome sight to behold.

We make our way toward the formal dining room where we hear the girls. When we turn the corner and see everything on the table, I think I'm being fucking punk'd.

The ornate, traditional, very classy dining room table is covered with erotic sex toys.

All sorts of crazy looking shit.

Vibrators like the one in Norah's bag, anal beads, butt plugs, dildos. Giant dildos that make me grimace. There's a section of what looks like massagers, but I'm pretty sure they aren't for your back. There's a whole display of creams and oils and cock rings and lube and fuck, I don't even want to know what else.

Jesus fuck, how long were we gone?

"The boys are back!" Kate squeals, rushing over to a stunned Miles and throwing herself into his arms. She's clearly feeling no pain.

The other girls all find their men, pulling them over to the table and pointing out things they apparently bought tonight because this was a sex-toy party.

I didn't know that was a thing.

Also, what are the fucking odds that Norah and I get in a fight about her vibrator mere hours before she's thrust into the kinkiest party known to man? I glance around for my fake girlfriend and my heart skips a beat when I see her walking down the hallway from the kitchen toward me.

I didn't get to see her before I left.

If I would have…I probably wouldn't have left.

She looks…*insanely hot.*

She's barefoot and wearing a sexy pair of black velvet leggings that hug her sculpted legs beautifully. Her top is a sheer black piece with a plunging neckline that looks like a soft breeze could blow it right off her tits and reveal the equally sexy green bra underneath. Her blond hair is curled and messy around her face.

She's clearly been partying with the girls tonight because her makeup is slightly smudged, but that smoky look makes her look even hotter. *I am so fucking screwed.*

I continue gawking at her body because fucking hell, she hides all of that all the time and I just…I knew she was hot but I didn't know she was this hot. I inwardly growl at the view of her creamy cleavage on full display. I'd kill to sink my teeth into her right fucking now.

Norah's eyes find mine and light up—the blueness of them intensified by the dark eyeliner I've never seen her wear. Her dark lips spread into a wide smile as she rushes over to where I'm stuck onto the floorboards, trying to remember to breathe.

"You're back!" she squeals, setting her drink on the table before standing on her tiptoes and wrapping her arms around my neck.

I shake off my stupor and grip her lower back to crush her to my body, barely resisting the urge to squeeze her supple ass. "I thought we were fighting," I murmur into her ear and inhale deeply. She smells sweet, like cake and vanilla and distinctly Norah. It's cock-twitching.

"Why would we be fighting?" She pulls back and blinks glazed eyes at me.

My shoulders lift. "Well, you kind of kicked me out of our room earlier."

She rolls her eyes. "That was before."

"Before what?"

"Before the sex-toy party I just attended." She leans in and whispers in my ear. "I put a minty oil on my pussy and I feel like my entire body is on the verge of an orgasm."

"Shut the fuck up," I bark, pulling away to look her in the eyes. "Are you messing with me, Norah?"

"Dean"—she pins me with a look, her eye-shadowed lids appearing heavy—"would I mess with you?"

My hands tighten around her waist hopefully. "You don't really have a sense of humor so I'd say no."

"Jerk!" She giggles, shaking my shoulders playfully. "If you don't believe me, go ahead and sniff between my legs. It smells like Listerine." She hiccups and then covers her mouth guiltily.

"Nooo, you're drunk," I groan and feel myself dying a little inside.

"I'm not drunk." She pulls me in close and cups my jaw, sliding her fingers through my beard as she slurs, "I'm horny and I want to rewrite our rules."

"Fuuuuuck," I growl into my fist and contemplate sleeping outside with the sprinklers.

This is just my fucking luck. Norah finally admits to wanting to have sex and she's too wasted to take her up on it. I look down at her, willing her to be sober because I have wanted this moment to happen for longer than I care to admit. I want to make her scream so loud the fucking horses in those stables over a football field away can hear her.

Her hooded eyes blink up at me.

She's drunk.

I don't do drunk.

I never do drunk.

I exhale the ache in my chest. "Let me take you to bed."

Norah thrusts her fist into the air. "It's about damn time, Moser."

I wave good night to everybody and my dick yells at me the entire time I assist a stumbling, drunken Norah to our bedroom. This is going to be the longest goddamn night of my life.

"Where's your suitcase?" I ask, steadying Norah as she sways on her feet in the middle of the bedroom.

"In the bathroom, why?" She hiccups, blinking her heavily mascaraed eyes slowly.

"Do you think you can find your pajamas?"

She grimaces. "What for? Won't they just get in the way of our fake sexing?"

She wiggles her hips in what I'm certain she thinks is seductive so I press my lips together and try not to laugh at her. Drunken Norah is adorable and relaxed and...I need her to go put some pajamas on and go to bed so she can stop tempting me.

"First of all...fake sexing is not a thing. Just go change, okay?"

"Whatever you say, boss." She giggles and turns to make her way into the bathroom.

I quickly dig into my suitcase for lounge pants and a T-shirt. The less skin exposed, the better for both of us. I grab some extra blankets and pillows out of the closet and make the sofa into a bed for me. I take my glasses off and sit down to wait for her to emerge, slowly reciting the ten golden rules of stock investing to get my mind out of the gutter. Avoid herd mentality, make informed decisions, invest in business you understand—

My list is interrupted when Norah emerges. The bright bathroom light bathes her in backlight so I can't totally see what she's wearing, but whatever it is...is not enough. "Norah, what the fuck are you wearing?" I ask, standing up and jamming a hand through my hair.

"It's pajamas," she says, swaying her hips to move the sad excuse for fabric that's so see-through, I can see the outline of her body. "But really, it's Rachael's idea of a joke…like the vibrator. She somehow found the sluttiest, most revealing clothes I own… and that's all that's in my suitcase. I should have known letting her help pack was a bad idea. She's a sand-bagging sonofabitch."

Norah steps farther into the room and the lamp beside the bed casts a warm glow on her, and now I can fully appreciate Rachael's joke. I tear my gaze away and look at the ceiling because the pajamas are completely sheer. Like her top she had on earlier, but this time, there's no colorful bra underneath. All she has on now is a pair of pale pink panties with tiny fabric flower blooms along the edges and a tank top with matching flowers along the bottom hem. It's loose and flowy and might be modest, except for the fact that I can see her pink-nippled breasts perfectly through the transparent fabric.

"So much better than a stripper," I murmur under my breath as I stare at the crown molding in the ceiling.

"What did you say?"

"Nothing." I tug my shirt off and offer it to her. "Put this on."

She staggers in my peripheral and her hand flies out to catch herself against my abs. I grab her arms and make sure she's okay. She's thoughtfully chewing on her lip as her fingers dig into my stomach. She doesn't attempt to hide the fact that she's checking me out.

"You weren't lying about the six-pack."

My abs tighten with a silent laugh. "I've had to increase my workouts because of your damn croinuts."

"That might be the sweetest thing you've said to me." She smiles and looks at me, blinking slowly through hooded eyes, then lifts her hands up like a toddler waiting to be dressed. When I pull the shirt down over her head, she reaches up and presses her lips to mine.

I taste her for a moment, drinking in her soft, full lips that

I've honestly fucking missed this entire week, but then force my-self to pull back. "Norah…"

"It's fake sexing time, Dean."

"Still not a thing," I murmur as she lifts her chin to kiss me again. "Norah, you're wasted. We can discuss this in the morning."

Her chin drops and she eyes me with confusion. "I think we're past the discussion phase of the business deal and it's time to have fake sex."

I shake my head regretfully, my dick screaming obscenities at me because I know what she's wearing under my shirt. "Not tonight."

"You're a tease," she cries, pushing me in the stomach with both hands and failing to move me an inch. She pins me with an accusing glower. "You just…offer your twenty-minute dick up to me earlier with your stupid, *When was the last time you were properly fucked?* voice and now you're taking it away! I should have known you were full of shit and messing with me. You're probably not even attracted to me. You just like to fuck with me all these years at the bakery for some sick twisted pleasure you get out of messing with a high-strung woman. And for the record Deano, I know I'm high-strung, okay? You try being raised by Elaine Donahue and learn how to let go of control…it's not easy, bitch. I've worked hard to become the person I am today and you will not make me feel like a fool—"

I slam my lips against her mouth to shut her the fuck up. She yelps her surprise but then softens against me, all those warm, luscious curves molding into my naked chest like a mem-ory-foam pillow. My tongue demands entry because I hate ev-erything she just said. Good God, is she insane? Does she not see how wild she makes me? Does she not know how hot she is, even in her drunken, slurred state? Even in her neurotic, measure three times, control freak state of mind? I'd have fucked her six ways to Sunday by now if she would have given me the opening.

But not like this.

Not like this.

No matter how fucking bad I want it.

I pull away, dragging ragged breaths into my lungs as I struggle to get enough oxygen. It's not the elevation that's the issue. It's Norah. She stares back at me, confused and uncertain, so for good measure, I grab her hand and press it firmly against my cock. Her eyes widen and her fingers twitch against my hardened flesh. "Tell me I'm not attracted to you one more time, Norah, and I will fucking spank your ass the second you're sober, right before I fuck it."

She inhales a shaky breath, her eyes like lava as they bore into mine. "Can I get that in writing?" A flash of a smile teases her lips.

Goddamn, I'm a saint. I kiss her on the forehead. "We'll discuss it in the morning, boss."

She giggles and slowly extracts her hand from my groin. My erection is painfully obvious in these cotton pants, and she won't stop looking at it, which only makes it worse. She swallows and says, "We'll only discuss our sex arrangement if you sleep with me tonight."

I frown at that remark. "What? I just said—"

"Sleep, not have sex, Mr. Killjoy."

I huff out an incredulous laugh. "You want me to sleep with you?"

"Yes, or no deal tomorrow. Those are my terms." She lifts her sleepy eyes to me and smiles knowingly.

I shake my head at her. "Always fucking negotiating."

She squeals excitedly and bounces over to the bed seeming less drunk than a bit ago. *But still not sober,* I remind my aching cock. She pulls back the covers and I can't help but admire her in my white T-shirt. Other women have worn my shirts before. Most without asking. But none have looked as good in them as Norah.

I turn off the lights and join her in the bed. The bright

moonlight streaming into the room illuminates her body as she faces away from me in the bed.

Being in bed with her is strange.

I mean, it's not uncommon for me to spend the night with a woman. But it is unheard of for me to spend the night with a woman I haven't had sex with. I haven't slept in the same bed as Kate or Lynsey, and they are my two closest friends.

I groan heavily and try to clear my mind of any sexual thoughts so I can actually get some sleep.

"You smell good," Norah says without turning over to look at me.

"You can smell me from your side of the bed?" I ask, rolling onto my back and propping my hand behind my head.

"Your T-shirt," she says, and I hear her inhale deeply.

"Ah," I reply, not knowing what else to say. "You smell pretty good too."

She turns over to look at me with an amused expression on her face. "Are you wearing my slutty pajama top? I'm not too drunk to miss that, am I?"

My chest shakes with silent laughter. "I mean…in general. Every time I've been close to you. You always smell sweet, like something I want to bite."

"Promises, promises." She giggles and I realize that this is the first time I've experienced flirting Norah. I like her…a lot.

After a moment of silence, her voice whispers, "Hey Dean."

My eyes pop open. "Hey Norah."

"What if I told you that minty oil is still making me unbelievably horny?"

I take a deep breath in and pray to the saint of no sex. That's a thing, right? "I'd say just try to go to sleep and forget about it."

"Or…" Her voice trails off so I turn my head to look at her. Her eyes are bright and twinkling in the darkness. "Or since you think I'm too drunk to have sex with, you could watch me use my pink vibrator right here in this bed."

I did not see that coming.

"Are you fucking with me, Donahue?"

She shakes her head. "I think this is the perfect solution to a very obvious problem."

"Um…okay." *Look, I never claimed sainthood, alright!*

Norah scurries into the bathroom faster than a fucking ninja. She returns to bed in five seconds flat and is smiling like a kid on Christmas morning. She scoots under the covers and lays on her back, her hands clutching the device to her chest nervously.

She chews her lip for a long moment and then looks over to me. "I'd feel better if you were doing it too."

"I'm afraid I forgot to pack my pink vibrator," I croak, assuming she's going to chicken out and I'm going to have to take an ice-cold shower right the fuck now.

She reaches over and shoves me with her hand. "I mean…you know…you take care of yourself while I take care of myself."

Once again, *I did not see that coming.*

I nod my agreement like a caveman, because I've lost all intelligent vocabulary on account of all the blood rushing to my already stone-hard dick. This woman is seriously going to kill me.

She nods subtly and both of us move our hands beneath the covers. I slip my hand inside my pants and fist my cock gently because I'm already on the verge of blowing it, and she hasn't turned her damn vibrator on yet. Suddenly, the light buzz of her toy echoes in the room and she exhales a trembling breath as her hand begins to move beneath the covers. Her eyes close as she rolls her head into the pillow and arches beneath the covers. I glance down and see a tiny thrusting action coming from where her hand is moving.

I pump myself slowly, biting my lip and imagining the feel of her skin touching mine. Of her breath hot on my ear as I push into her wet, slick heat. It's intense and it's all concealed under this massive blanket. The only thing that makes what we're doing obvious is the rustling of fabric and the buzzing of her toy. We're like two fucking teenagers, alone in the dark, too embarrassed to actually watch what we're doing.

But I'm not a teenager.

I'm a grown fucking man.

"I want to see you," I husk, my voice raw with desire. "I want to see what you're doing to yourself."

Her blue eyes flutter open as she turns to look at me, her eyes glancing down to the tent I'm pitching and then looking to me nervously. She nods her agreement and pulls her hand out from beneath the covers. Sitting up in the bed, she reaches behind her and pulls my shirt off her body and then lies back down, the blanket still covering her lower half.

"I want to see you too." She repeats my words back to me, and it takes every muscle in my body not to let go of my cock, roll on top of her, and fuck her senseless.

But it's better this way. It's naughtier and more forbidden. It might be the hottest fucking thing I've ever done with a girl.

I kick the blankets off both of us and push my loungers down. The weight of my erection causes my strained cock to flop onto my belly.

"Holy shit," she croaks, chewing her lip excitedly as she stares at me. "How do you wear those tight pants all the time with that anaconda?"

My stomach tightens with laughter. "I get them tailored all the way up to my balls so there's just enough room." I grab myself and stroke once, head nodding to her hands. "Keep going, boss. This is getting good."

She smiles shyly and lies back, flicking on her vibrator again before slipping it under the thin fabric of her panties. She's moving quicker now, wasting no time as she ramps herself back to where she left off.

My eyes drift to her nipples, rock-hard little pink buds straining against the sheer fabric. *I will bite those nipples tomorrow*, I lament and speed up my hand as I notice her breaths increasing and her little noises getting louder and louder. She struggles between closing her eyes and riding her pleasure to watching me as I sit up on my elbow and pump myself like it's my last dying wish.

"I'm close," she cries, her back off the bed now as she moans a deep sound. She wiggles the vibrator along her clit in quick, swift motions, her forearms tight with the effort.

"Look at me when you come, sugar tits," I command, my voice leaving no room for argument. "I need to see you fully let go."

Her wide, wanting eyes lift to meet mine and I wince as I try to hold off. I'm close too, so fucking close. But I can't blow it before her. I need to see her lose herself just once…I need to cement the image of her writhing in pleasure into my brain forever.

"Oh God, Dean!" she cries out, her voice high-pitched and loud as her free hand fists the sheet and her legs begin to shake. Her lips part as she utters this long, weird noise that's not exactly human sounding. She finally looks away and drops onto her back, her chest heaving as she struggles through the aftershocks of her orgasm.

My name on her lips when she loses herself might be the hottest thing I've ever seen in my life. For years I've thought Norah was gorgeous from a distance. This perfect, untouchable, unbreakable snow globe. But seeing this other side to her…this sexually awakened essence beneath all the lists and organizing and business plans… it's incredible. And it's no wonder I couldn't say no to her tonight.

I'm gripping my dick like a vise and the second I relax my hand, all the blood rushes to the tip and I'm jacking cum all over my belly and chest.

"Fuuuck, Norah," I cry out as I fall onto my back, my entire body spring loaded as my cock pulses out the aftermath, dripping down my shaft and onto my groin. Jesus, I've completely lost myself next to this woman.

"Oh my God." Norah's voice is awestruck and I look over to see her staring openmouthed at the whole scene of me jacking all over myself like a teen who doesn't know the trajectory of a good orgasm. She looks at me, smiles her innocent smile and says, "This is going to be so much fun."

CHAPTER 10

Norah

"We're riding bikes down a mountain?" I ask dubiously over a cup of coffee as I sit at the breakfast counter in the fancy mansion kitchen watching Barb, a woman apparently hired to cook for us, butcher the omelets.

"Yep!" Lynsey beams from her seat next to me. "We take a big chair lift thing up to the top, rent our bikes and gear there, and then ride downhill. It's a bunny hill type of route so not too treacherous. I have prizes for whoever comes in first."

"That sounds fun?" I say it like a question because I'm not a super active person. I'm the *walk through the mall in air conditioning* type. Doing anything on a mountain besides skiing seems way too adventurous for me. I didn't think Kate was super outdoorsy either, so I'm surprised this is our activity for the day. The itinerary said we were riding bikes but I was expecting the ones you can rent to ride around Aspen and go shopping.

Barb ruins her fourth omelet, splashing raw egg all over the gas burners and I can't take it anymore. I push back from my stool and move around the counter to stand beside her at the stove. "Do you mind if I take over?"

The woman's wide, worried eyes blink back at me. "Could you? I'm a fill-in for the guy who was supposed to be here and omelets are my kryptonite. If you can do better I'll be your sous and we can split the payment."

I press my hand to her shoulder. "I don't want money. This is fun for me. We've got this."

I grab an apron stashed in the catering box, and Barb and I find a rhythm in the kitchen as the rest of the group begins to trickle in looking almost as satisfied as I feel.

"Norah's making the omelets?" Kate cheers excitedly. "That's sweet! As payment I shall give you one of the eighteen sex toys I went home with last night."

Barb quirks a shocked brow that everyone ignores as they regale the events from last night. Our evening was apparently a lot more exciting than the guys'. But I'm barely listening to what everyone is saying because my mind is re-living what happened to me later on.

I masturbated in front of Dean Moser. Good God!

I woke up this morning hoping I'd dreamed it, but when I saw my pink vibrator sitting on the nightstand in the bright morning light, the entire act came back in full clarity. And the worst part— it wasn't just the alcohol that made me do it. Or that stupid minty oil the sex toy woman told me would make my vagina feel silky.

It was Dean. And the physical reaction my body has whenever he's around me. I've been denying it for too long and last night, I just snapped.

He was still sound asleep when I woke up this morning so I figured I could either watch him sleep like a loser, or come out to the kitchen and avoid him like a winner.

"Good morning, everyone," Dean's voice booms, and I freeze after flipping the final omelet and focus intently on the sizzle.

I see him out of the corner of my eye moving toward me. Oh my God, what's he going to say? *Please God don't let him make a joke about my sex toy in front of everyone. Barb will think so much less of me!*

He snakes his hands around my waist as I freeze in place,

holding a spatula in front of a hot flame. His manly scent engulfs me as he presses his hard body into my back and nuzzles my neck with his bearded jaw. "Good morning, sugar tits."

I growl-smirk while turning around to glare at him. "I told you what would happen if you called me that."

"Promises, promises," he jokes and leans in to drop a chaste kiss to my lips, his hand lingering on my hip and dipping to fondle my ass in front of everybody.

I can't stop smiling as I turn back to the stove and place the last omelet onto the large serving dish. Dean snatches a piece of bacon off the tray Barb just finished plating and I swat at his hand. "Go sit at the table and wait, you animal."

He winks at me and makes his way over to an open seat. When I finally tear my eyes off him, I discover Kate is staring at me with the biggest smile on her face I've ever seen. She presses her lips together, caught in a rare moment of silence and turns to join everyone getting ready to eat.

Breakfast goes semi-smoothly but we all have to rush back to our rooms to get ready for our excursion. Dean already showered and dressed so once again, I'm dressing alone and wondering what the fuck is going on between us. Was that display in the kitchen just for his friends? Was last night a one-time thing? Is he embarrassed we did that? Will we do more of it?

My mind is reeling by the time I join everyone in the big van that's taking us to the chair lifts. Dean is beside me in the van and he's quiet as he rests his hand on my thigh the entire journey. I open my mouth several times to say something but I stop myself. Now is not the time to figure out the inner-workings of our fake relationship.

We arrive at the Snowton Bike Park chair lifts, which are these giant pods that can hold up to six people or three people and three bikes. Since we're renting bikes at the top of the mountain, Dean and I squeeze into a pod with Max, Henley, Sam, and Maggie. It's a quiet ride and the beautiful view of the changing aspens is ruined by the flashes of bikers I watch going over these enormous jumps.

"What is this, the X-Games?" I croak, my hot breath fogging up the glass as I stare down at my future death.

"We're not doing the jumps trails," Dean replies casually and squeezes my leg.

My palms begin to sweat and I scooch away from him because my entire body gets clammy. The thing is, I'm not an athletic person. I can ski, kind of. I can play volleyball, a little. I can swim pretty well but only because my body has this strange natural buoyance that makes treading water shockingly effortless. But bike sports…so not my thing.

I manage to keep my inner freak-out to myself, hoping that once I'm suited up in my bike gear and see the trail we're taking, it won't be so bad. Lynsey called it a bunny route, right? If I can ski a bunny hill, surely I can bike a bunny route.

Kate, Miles, Lynsey, Josh, Sam, Maggie, Max, Henley, and Dean are all lined up in that order, suited with helmets, gloves, and funny looking shorts with butt pads that Rachael did not have the foresight to pack for me.

Lynsey's voice calls out, "Okay, this is a timed couples race and there will be prizes."

"What?" Dean's posture perks up as he straightens his bicycle helmet. "You didn't tell me it was a race. I would have stretched."

I cut Dean a *WTF face* while Lynsey rolls her eyes and continues, "There's a sweet prize for the winning couple and let me tell you…you want this prize, guys. I want this prize."

"Yeah!" Max calls out, clapping his hands. "Let's do this."

"Since we're all taking the same trail, couples will be spread out with five minutes between each heat. Kate and Miles…you're first. Dean and Norah…you guys will be last. We'll meet at the bar at the bottom of the hill and the trail guys will write down our finished times for us to reveal at the festivities tonight."

"Woohoo!" Kate squeals excitedly. "I don't even like sports but this is going to be fun."

Fun? Why does she think this is going to be fun? Nothing about this seems fun.

"Let's go," Miles bellows and he and Kate shove off, leaving a trail of dust behind.

Dean hops off his bike and begins to stretch. My eyes widen. "Are you being funny right now?"

"Funny about what?" he asks, extending his arm over his head.

"About the stretching. This a bunny trail, right?"

"Yeah, so?"

"So, you're warming up like we're on the Amazing Race or something."

Dean stops what he's doing and walks over to where I'm standing, trembling over my bike. "Hey Norah, now might be a bad time to tell you I'm crazy competitive."

"What?" I exclaim, my entire body erupting in sweat.

Dean grimaces and swipes his finger along my upper lip. "We can't lose this race. I want that prize."

"You don't even know what the prize is," I shout, my voice venturing on shrill.

Dean's shoulders lift. "I don't care. We can do this. I believe in you." He kisses me chastely on the lips and adds, "Plus, Kate is a horrible gloater if she wins. We have to crush her."

The other couples take off one by one, and I get this strange feeling I might never see them again. I should have made eggs Florentine for their final meal instead of omelets. If that's their last memory of me, it's going to be kind of basic.

Dean holds his fist out to me when it's our turn and I shake my head nervously at him, gripping my handle bars so tightly, my forearms are already aching. The trail guy waves for us to go and before I can smarten up and abandon this ship, I push forward and begin my descent down this so-called bunny hill.

"Bunny hill my ass!" I scream as I turn off the emergency exit ramp on the trail the guide informed us of during our orientation session. He told us it was meant for the weak and after what I've experienced so far…I am so very weak!

A small brewery with bike racks stationed outside comes into sight and I make a beeline for it, stumbling off my bike as I try to hop off while it's still moving. I let it crash to the ground as I un-buckle my helmet and toss it into the nearby woods.

My heart is permanently lodged in my throat as it clears way to make room for my lungs that are going to explode. I place my hand over my chest and turn as I see Dean approaching on his bike, looking totally chill.

I point an accusing finger toward the trail we just departed. "That was not a bunny hill!" I exhale heavily and move to the fenced off vantage point that overlooks the mountain and the trail we were just on. It looks like this emergency exit is only half-way down the entire trail and I didn't make it this far by choice.

It was by force.

I was forced into this.

By Dean, the Devil.

"Norah, what's going on?" Dean asks as he places his bike into the rack and unclips his helmet. "We're going to lose the race."

I hold my finger up to silence him. "Your fault," I bark out, pacing back and forth in my jogging shorts and wincing at my ass that feels like I sat directly on top of a pointy aspen tree. "You never warned me this trip would be this active. What the hell kind of shit are you trying to pull?"

Dean watches me pace in front of him, rubbing my ass cheeks and crying out in pain. "I didn't realize the trail would be that fast. I'm shocked we're the only ones who stopped at the halfway point." He looks back at the few random people sitting outside on the patio drinking beer like it's just a casual Saturday.

"And all that bullshit cheering you did," I snap, ripping my gloves off and throwing them to the ground next to my bike. "*Doing great, sugar! Keep up the pace, sugar! We can catch 'em, sugar!* Could you not hear me screaming?"

"No," he exclaims, his eyes wide in shock. "You were in front of me so I couldn't hear a thing. Norah, God, if you were that scared, you should have stopped."

"I wanted to but that trainer guy freaked me out about using the front brake and flipping over the handlebars."

Dean clenches his teeth and nods. "Yeah, that can be dangerous."

"We're taking the lift down," I state, pointing at the area behind the brewery where riders can go up or down the mountain. "I'm going to have PTSD from all this!"

Dean begins to approach me like I'm a snake who might strike. "Let's get you a drink and maybe an edible or something."

"I don't want drugs," I groan and then fall into his arms as he wraps around me to rub my back soothingly. "I want a time machine so I can go back and stay in the kitchen with Barb at the mansion." Dean's chest begins shaking and I jerk up to look at him. "You better not be laughing."

He purses his lips and shakes his head with a mock frown before lowering his lips to mine in a long, lingering kiss that relaxes me almost instantly. It's surprising and nice, and I'm a little confused by it because we still haven't talked about what we're doing together exactly, but I go with it because it feels good. And because I need it after the journey I just had.

He pulls back and threads his fingers through mine in a waffle hold. "C'mon, sugar butt, let me buy you a drink. I'll text the others and tell them to go back without us. We can take a cab home."

It takes two beers out on the patio before I can finally enjoy the mountainous view and stop resenting it. I sigh heavily and move my gaze to Dean, who looks like he's posing for some outdoor adventurist magazine. He's as cool as a cucumber, sitting in an Adirondack chair, wearing his white athletic tee and Ray-Bans, drinking a beer, and running a hand through his dark hair like he doesn't have a care in the world. My eyes lower to his tight black bicycle shorts. Normally, guys in shorts like that are not something that draws my attention…but Dean's thighs are ridiculously muscular. And the bulge he's rocking beneath that stretchy fabric, *the bulge that I saw in the flesh last night,* is doing really embarrassing things to my body now that I'm no longer screaming in terror.

I self-consciously finger-comb my hair because I probably look like I'm coming down from a manic episode. Which isn't far from the truth. I take another drink and smile sheepishly at him. "My throat has finally stopped hurting from all the screaming."

Dean grimaces. "I really am sorry. I have a competitive streak and completely missed the fact that you were freaking out."

"It's fine." I wave him off. "I was trying to play it cool."

Dean pulls off his sunglasses and gazes at me with those caramel brown eyes that I can finally appreciate again, now that rage has cleared from my vision. "Why were you trying to play it cool?"

I pause for a second, chewing my lip before deciding to hit him with the thoughts that have been racing through my mind all day. "I wasn't sure what last night meant exactly."

"What do you want it to mean?" he asks, staring at me with a grave look that makes me squirm in my seat.

I shift my gaze and look out at the mountains again. "I don't know…I was waiting for you to say something. You've been acting all touchy-feely with me all day but I didn't know if that was an act for your friends or because of what we did last night."

I turn back to see Dean watching me, concern marring his features. "Do you regret last night?" he asks seriously.

"No," I reply quickly, my eyes wide. "I mean, I was tipsy but I knew what I was doing." I pause, wiping the condensation on my beer glass with my fingers before nervously adding, "And I thought it was kind of fun."

Dean's shoulders seem to relax as he takes in my reply. "I'm really glad to hear that. I've been stressed out all day at the idea that I might have taken advantage of you."

"Taken advantage of me?" I shake my head and huff out a self-deprecating laugh. "It was my idea. I practically threw myself at you."

"I know, but still. I have a hard rule about fooling around with someone when they've been drinking. What we did last night was not expected and not something I'd normally say yes to. So, I'm not proud."

I recoil at that last remark, and horrifyingly my eyes start to sting as his words evoke a shameful response deep inside of me. He's not proud? Was what we did really that embarrassing for him? God, and I just confessed how much I enjoyed it. *Holy shit, this is humiliating.*

Dean notices my mood change and his jaw drops in horror. "I didn't mean it like that, Norah. I just meant…fuck."

I stand from my seat, desperate to get away from his watchful eyes when suddenly, his warm hand snakes around my elbow and he pulls me back to him, yanking me onto his lap. He cups my cheek and pushes stray hairs out of my face as I attempt to plaster on a cool expression.

"I didn't mean that the way it came out."

"It's fine," I reply stiffly, my posture ramrod straight in his arms as I look away and take in a cleansing breath.

"It's not fine." He turns my face back to him, rubbing his thumb along my cheekbone that has a hot tear streak running down. He struggles with what to say next before finally offering, "That comment goes back to my parents. It has nothing to do with you and what we did. What we did was hot. And I'm glad we did it, but only because you are too. No regrets, right?"

He stares into my eyes with worry, like he's still not convinced what we did was wrong. But it's not what we did that he's worried about. It's how I feel about it now, in the light of day that has him so freaked out.

"I already said I don't regret it, Dean," I reply, relaxing into his lap and touching the frown line between his eyebrows. "What's your deal? Why are you so worried? What does this have to do with your parents?"

Dean grimaces like he doesn't want to talk about this but then sighs when I continue watching him expectantly. He releases my cheek and sits back and takes a long sip of his beer before he finally cracks. "They used to get drunk and fight all the time in front of me. I was just a kid but I can vividly remember them coming home late and screaming horrible things at each other, about each other. They even said horrible things about me."

"Like what?" I ask, my eyes fixed on Dean as he appears to be struggling with this truth. "What would they say about you?"

"The biggest highlight my dad used to say was that my mom got pregnant to trap him because he came from money and she should have had the abortion like he wanted. He screamed it at her like he didn't know I was in the house. But I was always in the house. And it was bad enough they fought like that… but then I'd have to listen to them"—he swallows and I watch his Adam's apple slide up and down his neck—"make up. It was fucked up. I couldn't believe they'd want to be intimate with each other after saying those horrible things. But they were so drunk, I don't think they knew what they were saying or doing."

"Jesus, Dean," I croak because I don't know what else to say. "That's awful."

"Yeah, it was…and it's why I don't mess around with girls if they're drunk. I saw how hollow and depressed my mom was the day after their fights…like she couldn't look herself in the mirror. It killed me. Even if she was a consenting adult, those nights completely trashed her confidence. She still dates fucking ass-holes like my dad. She's a magnet for them, I swear."

My heart clenches at Dean's tough words about his parents. He hinted at their dysfunction at my parents' party, but I didn't imagine it to be this bad. My parents were always the type to argue in hushed whispers and even then, my dad would usually end up giving in to my mom and it would be over. Screaming at each other isn't something I can picture.

Honestly, hearing about Dean's parents makes me feel guilty for complaining to him about mine. How did he even give me the time of day with this fake-dating scheme? How did he not laugh in my face and call me a spoiled brat who doesn't know what real problems are?

"Do you have much of a relationship with your parents now?" I ask, hoping things have improved since they divorced.

"Yeah, we're okay." He shrugs. "We used to be closer when my grandpa was still around. My dad's dad kind of forced us all to have these family dinners on Friday nights even though my parents had split up. I think it was his way of making sure my parents were getting along in front of me. But he passed away when I was eighteen and now I pretty much only see my parents for holidays and odd dinners…separately, of course, which is better."

I chew the inside of my cheek. "That's kind of sad."

He wrinkles his nose. "It's fine…I'm only telling you all this so you understand that last night…that was me losing control. That's never happened to me before with a woman. So, if I've been quiet with you today, it's because I liked what we did last night, but I feel guilty. I don't want you to feel like I took advantage of the situation. And I really don't want Rachael to burn down my house," he deadpans and I can't help but laugh.

I cup his bearded jaw in my hand and pin him with a serious look. "I promise I was of sound mind and body and I genuinely enjoyed last night."

"Thank fuck for that." After a sigh of relief, a smirk toys at the edge of his lips as he stares at my mouth. "Because watching you last night was probably one of the sexiest things I've witnessed, and I watch a lot of porn."

My lips part in shock and I cover my cheeks to hide the blush that weird compliment elicits. He can't be serious, right? Dean has slept with a lot of girls…probably more than I want to know. How is it possible that what we did last night could rank that high?

I stare at him, looking for any glimpse that he's teasing me but he's gazing back at me with wide, fierce eyes that don't seem to be hiding anything. Maybe I'm naïve but, I believe what he's saying. And I'm highly mortified for being flattered.

"It's kind of hard to believe it was all my idea," I croak, pulling my hands down from my cheeks and owning my shame.

"You're telling me," he barks out a laugh and squeezes my leg before leaning in to speak in hushed tones. "I haven't been able to stop replaying the image of you with that pink vibrator all fucking day and these damn bicycle shorts hide nothing."

I bite my lip and glance at his lap in awe. God, this is so crazy. It's madness. It's entirely unlike me to hook up with a mountain manwhore on a couples' trip to Aspen and then want to keep hooking up with him.

But I can't help it.

I feel this insane sense of power over making a gorgeous, crazy-confident man like Dean lose control of himself in public. Maybe it's because I haven't had sex in ages, maybe it's because my stress level is through the roof and this weekend off is what I've needed to get some clarity, but…I'm not done with Dean.

I'm far from done with Dean.

This thing we're doing here…it needs to continue.

I shoot him a smile and take a deep breath before saying the words I won't be able to take back. "Well then, why are we still on this stupid mountain when there are loads of other things we could be doing?"

Dean quirks a brow and returns my smile, dazzling me with his handsomeness as he slides his hand up under my shirt, and teases my lower back. "I want to be clear here. Does this mean we're officially fuck buddies?"

"Yes," I reply with a crisp nod and move off his lap, glancing at his groin as he leans forward to cover himself.

"With no strings?" he adds pointedly while gazing at me.

"No strings." I prop my hands on my hips and hit him with a look. "This is just a small addendum to our business transaction."

"Not everything is business, Norah." He chuckles softly and stands, holding his jacket in front of him. "And there's nothing *small* about what's happening inside my shorts."

I bite my lip and smile. "We both know what we want and don't want, which is a relationship, so we can totally handle this fake sexing arrangement."

Dean shakes his head. "You're really trying to make that a thing, aren't you?"

I agree proudly. "Friends with benefits and fuck buddies are so overused. Fake sexing…it has originality to it. Pizazz," I add, dancing my fingers between us.

"Like a croinut," he offers with a wink that makes my smile grow.

"Maybe even better than a croinut."

CHAPTER 11

Dean

Y ou know that feeling when you have a boner all afternoon and you have to tuck it up into the waistband of your bike shorts to hide it from the world?

No?

I didn't either…until Norah and I reached the bottom of the mountain…*and ran into my fucking friends.*

Devastation, travesty. Pain!

Horrible, awful, indescribable pain is what my body suffers the entire happy hour nonsense we are forced to sit through with Kate and everyone else. They all look totally chill like they're on vacation without a care in the world.

I, on the other hand, have a very big care in the world: my fucking lap rocket that won't go down.

It must be the damsel in distress look Norah currently rocks that makes all the blood rush to my cock because I can't stop staring at her as she visits with the girls. Her cheeks are pink from being out in the sun, and her blond hair is frizzy as it sticks out from under her Boston bandana. I love her assortment of grunge rock headwear. It's a sexy contrast to her angelic features, and it's completely original. Norah could be a generic cute little blond I'd hit on at any given bar, but she's more than that. She wears giant, unflattering baker's shirts and classic rock bandanas. She's rarely aware of what's going on in a room because she's usually in her head analyzing something. And when she's not analyzing something, her thoughts are laser-focused on her work and her to-do list.

I'm going to have a blast forcing her to let go these next couple of weeks.

The sun is beginning to set by the time we leave the mountain, and I sense the nerves in Norah's body language. She's like a coiled spring preparing to snap, and I want to be there when she finally releases all that pent-up tension.

By the time we reach the house, I can barely keep my hands off her. We're moving down the hallway straight for our bedroom when Kate's voice calls out behind us.

"Norah, come outside! We have ladies here to do manis and pedis."

Norah's eyes widen as she turns and glances at my situation. "I kind of need to shower," she replies weakly over my shoulder.

"Shower after," Kate yells back. "Come on."

She offers me a sympathetic shrug. "I do need my toes done."

I groan and fall against the hallway wall. "You're fucking killing me, boss."

She smiles coyly. "Just think of it as foreplay."

"Isn't that what we did last night?"

"Nah, that was just good ole masturbation." She stands on her tiptoes and kisses me on the cheek before whispering, "This will make tonight that much more fun."

She takes off to meet the girls, and I make my way into our en suite to take an ice-cold shower and try not to think about how much better this would be if Norah was with me. I stare at my strained cock that doesn't want to limp away and offer it a quick apology.

Fucking hell, what is with me? The suspense of tonight has me hornier than a teenager who's discovered Pornhub for the first time, which makes no sense because I've had a lot of sex. I've fucked plenty of women. Why does Norah have me so keyed up?

Maybe Kate and Lynsey were right, and those girls I was picking up at the bars bored me. I certainly never popped boners in public for any of them.

Or maybe the stakes are higher because I dropped a crazy truth bomb on her at that mountainside brewery, and that's so unlike me. Talking about my parents is not something I do. Ever. Kate and Lynsey don't even know as much as Norah does.

My parents are a subject I avoid because the relationship I have with them is strained at best. My dad moved to Denver for work years ago and is with a new woman every six months, and my mom still asks me constantly who my dad is seeing. It's exhausting. One would have thought a divorce would make it possible for them to move on, but they both seem stuck in an endless loop of dysfunction.

Yet another reason I never want to get serious with anyone. Getting serious means you're permanently fucked in the head. And who wants that baggage? Honestly, my situation with Norah is a win-win. I get to have repeat sex with someone I genuinely like, and we both get to go our separate ways when this is over. It's the perfect situation for me.

I finish showering and dress for what Kate referred to as "game night" tonight. I have no clue what the hell game night will be, but knowing Kate, it won't be fucking Monopoly.

CHAPTER 12

Norah

Oh my poor, poor ass, I cry to myself as I slowly walk down the hallway to join everyone. The pain wasn't bad when I got my pedicure. It wasn't horrible when I took my shower. But when I started to apply my makeup and put on my burgundy sweater dress and thigh-high, nude suede boots, my ass felt like it had been the victim of a wicked tumble down some stairs.

I find everyone in the large living room. A wood fire is crackling, and a giant charcuterie spread, complete with champagne, is on the coffee table. Dean smiles as I approach, gesturing for me to sit beside him on the couch. He is seriously hot in his jeans and dark green shirt, but my attention is distracted when I have to sit beside him…on my *poor, poor ass.*

Gritting my teeth, I gently lower myself next to him, and he instantly wraps his arm around me, drenching me in his spicy cologne. "You look gorgeous, sugar butt."

"Don't say butt," I croak, my voice catching in my throat as I lean back on his arm and try not to cry.

"Why not?" He frowns and adjusts his glasses as he looks me up and down curiously.

I rub my lips together slowly and stare forward with my hands splayed out on my thighs. "My ass feels like it was whipped by my KitchenAid mixer on high, and I'm suddenly very sorry for my croinut dough." Dean trembles beside me, and I look over to see he's laughing. "Don't laugh, you asshole!"

"I can't help it!"

"This is your fault!" I exclaim and shove him in the chest. "You could have told me to buy some stupid butt-pad shorts."

"We didn't ride that long," he replies, failing miserably to hide his amusement. "I didn't think you'd get saddle sore from one downhill ride."

"I'm going to kill you," I grumble and cross my arms over my chest. I attempt to cross my legs but wince when a shooting pain bolts up my left ass cheek.

"It's really that bad?"

"Yes," I pout.

He tightens his grip around me as his other hand reaches over to caress my bare thigh. "I'll just have to take your mind off it then."

Butterflies.

Glorious, delicious, wispy butterflies take flight in my belly, effectively erasing my ass pain.

Dean's smiling eyes sparkle and lock on my lips as he leans in closer. His shirt brings out the little flecks of green in them I've never noticed before.

"Would it help if I rub your ass later?"

"Only if you do it with IcyHot," I murmur and then smile when he laughs again. I'm seriously enjoying the image of a laughing Dean. It could get addictive.

His hand moves up my thigh, and I gasp, anticipating his higher touch later. I tilt my head, hoping he's going to kiss me because that would definitely help with the pain.

"What's up, party people?" Kate's voice chimes in, tearing my focus away from Dean's very soft lips. Kate's standing in front of the fire looking adorable in a little red dress with her curly red hair wild around her shoulders. She clutches several envelopes in her hand and asks, "Who's ready for game night?"

Everyone groans, and she scowls at us before continuing. "Okay, so, as some of you know, I'm launching this new swingers book series, and it's all going to be based on the swinger lifestyle. I'm still learning a lot, but I have this idea to open a club in my series that's based around a Swinger Scavenger Hunt where couples have to participate in the game before they get busy. This is why I needed you all to bring a date this weekend."

Everyone looks around nervously, clearly worried that this trip is turning into something none of us prepared for.

"Relax, you freaks. No one here is swinging."

"Fucking right, we're not," Miles states seriously and hits Kate with a possessive look that leaves no room for interpretation.

Kate winks at him, clearly not the least bit put off by his alpha male moment. "This is just a fun scavenger hunt that you'll do with your partner…it's a little sexy…so you could call it foreplay maybe, but hey, what you all do after the game is completely up to you." She hits Max with a guilty look. "You have a cleaning crew, right Max?"

Max's jaw drops. "Yes…why?"

"No reason!" Kate chimes brightly and then continues. "Okay, so…rumor is, in the 70s, swingers used to display gnomes on their front lawns to indicate they were open for swinging to their neighbors. Fun, right? What we all thought of as Grandma's innocent little lawn decoration can actually be a sign of fluid sexers! Ha! Okay…so, every couple will get a custom scavenger hunt sheet. You need to read the clues, collect your gnomes, complete each gnome challenge, and report back here. I've staggered and altered all the clues so none of you can follow each other and cheat. And since Norah and Dean didn't complete the trail today, we decided to shift that big prize Lynsey teased earlier for this challenge. Which means, the first couple to find their five gnomes, wins."

"It's a couples' massage back in Boulder," Lynsey blurts out excitedly and turns to look at her husband, Josh. "I shouldn't win because I organized the prize, but screw it, we have a one-year-old, and we need this, right babe?"

Josh laughs. "Whatever you say, Jones."

Everyone breaks, and I turn serious eyes to Dean. "I don't have a one-year-old, but I have an ass that feels like it was Mike Tyson's punching bag, so I need that massage, Dean."

"Okay," he says, pinching his lips together to fight back a smile, but it's completely ineffectual. "Now who's the competitive one?"

"Look, I'm sorry for sucking on that mountain, but I'm going to make it up to you because this is way more my style."

"Swinging is your style?"

I reach over and poke him in the ribs. "Scavenger hunts, Dean. Focus here. I was the master of scavenger hunts at the Methodist church camp I attended when I was a kid. I don't know what Kate's challenges are going to be exactly, but I think we have a real shot at this."

Dean nods. "Then let's do it."

Kate passes out the envelopes, and everyone retreats to their prospective corners to begin. With shaky hands, I pull out the paper and begin to read. "Find the gnome that gets wet like clockwork. Complete the challenge hidden under the gnome and receive a bonus point."

I look at Dean, and his brow is furrowed in concentration. "Gets wet once in a while? Like from a shower? Or the pool?"

"Those don't run on a clock," I reply, chewing my lip nervously, and then my eyes widen. "A sprinkler!" I look around nervously to see if anyone overheard me.

Everyone seems to be deep in thought on their own questions, so I waffle my fingers through Dean's and pull him through the living room. "Let's go read this in our bedroom so we can think," I state a bit obnoxiously for all to hear.

Dean laughs behind me, and I shoot him a glare. Fucking amateur. Half the battle with scavenger hunts is maintaining a good poker face, so you don't inspire the pack to speed up.

We bypass our bedroom door and dart out the side entrance onto the veranda. Cool autumn air whips around my exposed thighs, and I shake away the chill. "There's got to be a sprinkler system out here…we need to find it, and we'll find the gnome."

Dean and I spread out, walking around the perfectly manicured lawn and looking for any sign of a sprinkler system. My heart is racing at the thrill of a competition I can actually enjoy. I really should read one of Kate's books. If she puts this much time and attention into her research, I'm sure they're great.

"Found a gnome!" Dean hollers.

I shush him and rush over to where he's standing by a big landscaped berm full of mums. I grab the clay gnome and look underneath it. "Find a dark corner and make out for three full minutes. Set a timer so you don't cheat! Honor system is intact."

Dean doesn't miss a beat as he grabs my hand and pulls me across the patio to a stone cut out on the side of the house. My heels scrape against the flagstone pavers as he twirls me around to face him in the dark alcove. His tall frame is illuminated by the lights behind him as he sets the gnome down on the ground and fiddles with his phone to start a timer.

"You ready?" he asks, looking at me and shoving his phone in his pocket so his hands are free.

My chest rises and falls as I bite my lip and nod while silently praying he can't hear how hard my heart is thumping inside my chest. The mixture of the competition excitement and the anticipation for what I know is coming later tonight collides and creates a heavy fog of desire in my lower belly.

My voice is raspy when I answer, "Ready."

He steps closer, his warm body blanketing me as he braces a hand against the stone by my head and backs me against the wall. His eyes lock with mine, a whisper of a smile dancing in his gaze as he dips his head to my level. "Go," he utters before he brushes his lips gently against mine.

He tastes like red wine, and that, coupled with the scent of his spicy cologne, has my toes curling in their boots. I splay my hands out on his chest and tilt my head as his lips move slowly, almost lazily, with no offer of tongue. My brows furrow as I wait for him to turn up the heat like he did in our bedroom last night. I may have been drunk, but I remember every single second of that kiss he planted on me.

It was a great kiss.

This is a whisper of what I know Dean is capable of. What's he waiting for?

My lips quiver impatiently as I snake my hands up behind his neck and pull him closer. I've been through enough these past few days, and my stress level with the new bakery and franchise opening and especially my mother has me operating at a level ten. Which means I don't want an appetizer or a sample platter kiss. I want a four-course meal of the man who's been flirting endlessly with me for ages and who hours ago agreed to have sex with me.

My chest heaves as I crush my breasts against his hard body and thrust my tongue deep into his mouth. I turn us around so now he's pressed against the wall and I'm in control of the kiss.

It's been a year. A whole freaking year since a man has kissed me, and I need more. I've earned more.

Dean must get the memo because his hands grip tightly around my waist and a thrill shoots through my core as they rove up my back, and his tongue meets mine thrust for thrust—tasting, teasing, and demanding full reciprocation. My nipples tighten when his palms brush the sides of my breasts, and I can't help but let out a little moan of hope.

I comb my fingers through his hair and fall deeper into this feverish moment as he grabs my leg and pulls it onto his hip, causing my hemline to ride up as he thrusts his groin between my thighs. The thin fabric of my silk panties offers no protection against the rough texture of his denim, and the friction is delirious. My pelvis develops a mind of its own, and I feel myself grinding against him in small, thrusting motions.

Good God, I'm losing my mind right now. Rachael was right.

My battery-operated toys are no match for some genuine hip action.

Dean's other hand drops, and he grabs my ass and pulls me up around his waist, but a stabbing pain has me crying out and jerking my leg out of his grasp.

"My ass!" I gasp and press my forehead against Dean's chest as I flinch against the onslaught of pain. "Anywhere but my ass!"

"Fuck," Dean growls, tucking my hair behind my ears so he can see my face. "I'm so sorry, Norah. I completely forgot."

Tears prick my eyes from the intensity of the horror that just befell me. "Oh my God, that hurt like a bitch."

"Shit, I really am sorry. Are you okay?" He crooks his hand under my chin so he can look at me, concern etching his handsome features.

I nod. "I'm okay. It hurt…but it was kind of a good hurt… like a deep tissue massage from a really big guy named Sven."

Dean's chest vibrates with laughter. "Want me to do it again?"

"God, no!" I pull out of his touch. "Are you a sadist?"

He laughs and steps toward me, his body bowing over mine as he cradles my cheeks gently in his hands. "I'm kidding. Come here."

He lowers his mouth and kisses me deeply again, putting me right back into the moment and forgetting all about the horrid pain in my derriere. His tongue swirls with mine as lust begins to squeeze my insides. His right hand skates up my ribs as he gently caresses my breast.

"How about here…can I touch you here?" He bites his lip and watches his hand squeeze my C cup before his thumb glides over the top of my still hard nipple.

I nod my head and exhale a shaky breath. "Yes, you can touch me there."

He turns me around in one quick motion, his hands sliding up my body to cup both of my breasts as he kneads them possessively. "Do you like my hands on you, sugar tits?"

I nod slowly, feeling totally drugged out with arousal and the view of his hands on me. "Yes."

One hand moves downward to tease my clit over my dress. "Do you want to say fuck this scavenger hunt and let me take you to bed?" he asks, his voice hot and gruff in my ear.

My head turns to look up at him. "God, yes!"

He smiles and kisses me on the cheek. "Good, because I never set a timer."

In a breath, Dean steps back and grabs the gnome while yanking me by the arm out of the dark alcove and back toward the door we came through earlier. My body feels like a live wire that could go off at any second. I can't remember any man's touch lighting me up the way Dean's does. Granted, there haven't been that many men in my life, but I think there might be some serious perks to having sex with a mountain manwhore. Dean clearly knows how to touch a woman—confident and sensual while still surprisingly intimate. I wonder if he's like this with all the women he's been with?

Bad segue. Very bad segue. Just stay in the moment, Norah. Don't think about Dean's other conquests. This is just sex...sex that you need in your life.

As soon as we make it to our bedroom door, Kate emerges from her own darkened corner. "Done with the hunt already?" she asks, pinning us both with a pointed look as she glances at the gnome in Dean's hands.

We pause awkwardly, looking at each other for a quick excuse. "We just...need to brainstorm," I mumble at the same time Dean says something about flashlights.

Flashlights? What the hell?

Kate smiles victoriously. "I think this series is going to be a best seller!"

Dean rolls his eyes and wrenches open the door, calling out good night as he places the gnome in front of our room and unapologetically slams the door in Kate's face. He spins me into his body, his lips finding mine again as his hands work their way up the skirt of my dress. "Please tell me Rachael packed you more naughty lingerie."

I smile and silently remind myself to give Rachael a raise on Monday as Dean peels my dress over my head to reveal the matching pale pink bustier and panties.

"Fuck," Dean growls reverently as he stares at my body on full display for him like he's trying to memorize it. Moisture pools between my legs as a hungry look casts over his features. "Did Rachael buy all this stuff for you, or is this from your personal collection?"

"It's mine." I cover my stomach nervously. "But admittedly, I would have packed more modestly for this weekend...because, well...I didn't expect *this* to happen."

Dean's dark, liquid eyes hit me with a curious glint. "All this sexy underwear deserves to be worn, Norah."

"I do wear it," I reply crisply while stabbing a finger into his meaty chest. "It's a feminine power thing."

Dean bites his lip and grabs my hand, combing our fingers together between us. "What does that mean exactly?"

"It's something I read years ago." I tilt my head to watch his reaction. "Experts said wearing a Superman T-shirt under your clothes made wearers feel more confident and powerful in business. I figured if a Superman shirt gave men big-dick energy, sexy lingerie could do the same for women. I've been wearing stuff like this ever since."

Dean blinks slowly as his brows pinch together. "Are you trying to tell me you're in stuff like this under that baker's parka you wear?"

"Pretty much." I glance down to play with the vertical ribbing along my rib cage. "I have drawers full of this stuff. You don't want to know how much I've spent over the years. But hey, that big-dick energy has grown my business immensely, so it clearly works."

Dean stares at me with a sort of fond look on his face and then shakes his head dismissively. "Had I known you had this going on under that tarp you wear, I would have tried a lot harder."

I bark out a laugh. "If that was you taking it easy, I don't want to know what trying hard would have looked like."

"Now you'll never have to find out." He flings off his glasses and steps closer, dipping his head to kiss the mounds of cleavage created by my push-up bra. His voice is deep and gravelly as he murmurs, "You taste as good as you look, sugar."

I roll my eyes. "I bet you say that to all the girls."

My breath catches when he grabs my breasts greedily in his hands and pins me with a look. "I've never meant it more than right now."

My lips form a thin line as I nod to his chest. "Your turn."

His brows furrow. "My turn?"

"I'm in my underwear…so you should be too."

He shakes his head like I'm some silly puppy in need of training. "Norah, you're not controlling this tonight."

"Say what?"

"You control every other aspect of your life. Let me have this."

He steps forward, pinning me in place with his chocolatey eyes, and reaches behind me, unfastening the several clasps of my longline bra. I gasp when the air hits my bare nipples, but Dean doesn't look at them. Instead, he continues watching my face as he skates his fingers up my belly and slowly circles each of my breasts one at a time.

My hands clench into fists as I silently will him to just fucking bend me over the couch or something already. Do I need to remind him it's been a year?

"It's hard, isn't it?" he croaks, his breath hot on my ear as he nuzzles it.

"What?" I question, my head falling back at the heady sensation of his whiskers on my flesh.

"Letting go."

I sway in my heeled boots. "Dean," I moan when he finally grazes my hardened nub and rolls it firmly between his fingers.

"What do you want, sugar?" he asks, leaning in and pressing his lips to my throat in long, sensual kisses.

"I want sex," I state honestly. "Now. It's been too long. We need to hurry this along."

Dean tsks and moves his lips to the other side of my neck, paying special attention to my shoulder as he murmurs, "I want to savor this, Norah. Let me get to know your body first."

He backs me up and slowly lays me on the bed, careful of my tender ass as he pulls off my boots and his lips explore my body—my mouth, my neck, my shoulders, my breasts. Definitely my breasts.

I didn't think it was possible to orgasm from nipple stimulation alone, but the combination of his lips and that trim beard on my body is doing crazy things to my libido.

He finally returns to my lips, and I grab his face and wrap my legs around his hips to pull him on top of me. I need to feel his weight against me. I want to touch his dick and see if he's…

"Not yet," he says, moving to my side and propping himself on his elbow as he caresses his fingers along my stomach. "I need to see if you're ready."

I hit him with an unamused look. "Take your pants off and find out."

Dean smiles, pressing his face into the blanket as his entirely-clothed body shakes with laughter. "You're so bossy."

"It's the lingerie," I reply and curl into him while reaching for the button on his jeans.

"You're not in charge right now." He grabs my hand and stills it. "Lie back again."

I suck in a deep breath while he slowly drags his fingers along my hip bone and teases the hem of my panties. He watches me hungrily as I writhe on the bed in anticipation. When he finally steals his fingers inside the fabric and gives my center one gentle swipe, I practically preen like a cat.

"You're fucking soaked." He growls an approving noise.

"I could have told you that." I level him with a look, my arousal-drunk eyes blinking slowly at him before I gasp and arch off the bed.

Dean plunged a thick, long finger inside me without warning, and oh my God, this is where I die.

"And so tight," he says reverently.

I groan, my hips greedily thrusting up into his touch, begging for more. "A year, Dean."

"We're going to make up for that tonight," he says, and I hear the rustle of the bed as he moves down to stand between my legs.

His erection is straining against his jeans as he peels my panties off, dropping them to the floor to expose my bare center to his watchful eyes. His fingers trail slowly up my legs as he kneels and blows a cool breeze over my center.

"Holy shit," I cry out, bucking up toward him in surprise. Have I ever been this turned on in my entire life?

The answer is no. A resounding NO.

"I'm going to taste you now, Norah," Dean says, and I have to close my eyes because I can't watch. It's all too much.

He spreads my thighs with his large, warm hands as his mouth descends onto my sex. He flattens his tongue along my clit before pulsating it against me and causing a riot of heat to shoot through my limbs, all the way down to the tips of my toes that are now curling into his shoulders.

The build is instant. Way too instant. Is premature orgasm a thing for women? Because…

"Oh, my God!" I scream when Dean tilts his head and sucks with animalistic intensity.

But apparently, he knows what he's doing because something inside me snaps, and my entire body erupts as hard pulses of aftershock shoot through me, causing my stomach to tighten as I cover my face in embarrassment.

That…was quick.

I feel Dean's huff of laughter against my inner thigh, and I glance down at him. "Something funny down there?"

He shakes his head. "Nothing funny at all." He stands and begins unbuttoning his shirt. "You should lose control more often. It looks good on you."

I melt into the mattress as Dean begins to disrobe. "I need a minute," I state, unsure I'll be able to handle the image of Dean naked so soon after a mind-shattering orgasm.

"No breaks," he clips, pulling his shirt off his shoulders.

"Why no breaks?"

"You're letting go, Norah. Don't take over."

My eyes wander from Dean's face to his tanned shoulders. They're broad and smooth and curved with the perfect amount of muscle. Not too big, but nowhere near small. His abs are outlined more distinctly with each harsh breath, and the line of his hip bones point right to his erection, something that should be sculpted someday.

When he undoes his jeans and reveals his erection, giving it room to breathe, I gape. Yes, I saw it last night, but standing there with it pointing at me, throbbing with need, I really appreciate the sight of it more.

It's a good-looking dick.

It'd be a Main-Event, front and center croinut for sure.

If I were willing to share…which, I'm not.

Dean extracts a condom from his jeans and rolls it on with a deft ease I don't really want to think about right now. The bed dips as he crawls up between my legs.

"How's your ass?" he asks, staring at my lips with hunger.

"Closed for business," I deadpan.

His body shakes on top of me with his silent laughter. "I wasn't asking for anal, sugar…just making sure you're feeling good."

My brows lift. "I just orgasmed on your face in less than a minute. I think it's safe to say I'm feeling alright."

He smiles and dips his head to kiss me. It's sweet and intimate, surprising since this is only a casual thing, but it feels right. I rake my nails along his back and kiss him with fervor while wrapping my legs around his waist and sliding them along his hips. The skin-on-skin sensation feels so incredibly good. I've missed how a man's body molds against mine. I've missed being desired and turned on.

Desperation courses through me, and I thrust my damp sex against him as his erection squeezes between our two flush bodies. He breaks our kiss, his breath stuttered as he says, "I'm going to orgasm in less than a minute too if we don't do this."

I nod, my eyes wide as I glance down and watch him center his tip between my folds. He watches me for a moment before slowly pushing himself inside me.

It's tight. Way too tight. A year's worth of stress causing extra tightness. But thankfully, my slick, wet heat makes his entry possible, and when he's buried as deep as I can take him, my fingers dig into his biceps as I groan out a long, "Ohhh my Godddd."

"Fuck," he growls as his head drops onto my shoulder while our bodies adjust to the sensation overload. He pulls back and gasps for breath, his lips parted as he adds, "Fuck, you feel incredible."

"You too," I croak, grinding upward and silently begging him to move so I find some relief.

He takes the hint and pulls back, propping himself up on his hands before slowly thrusting inside me. My head flattens to the pillow, and I hear myself whimpering with breathless excitement. Everything right now is sensation overload. My hormones have completely taken over my body, and at any second, I'm going to start making animal noises.

"That's it, sugar…just let go." Dean's voice is raw and full of need as he begins moving at a quicker pace, his eyes blazing down on me the entire time. "You're so beautiful when you let go. It's impossible to look away."

I blink up at him; the intensity in his voice isn't something I'm used to hearing. Dean's usually playful or sexual, or purposely over the top. He lives his life teasing others. But the sincerity he's displaying right now is a new look for him, and it intensifies my arousal. Our eyes lock for a brief second, and something deeper than the sexual nature of what we're doing ignites. Almost like Dean sees me more than anyone has ever seen me before. It's unnerving.

But I'm quickly distracted when Dean hoists my leg onto his shoulder and thrusts deeper than before, stroking a spot I don't think has ever been stroked before.

"Oh my God," I cry, feeling every thrust, every noise, every growl of pleasure in the room as a pressure builds deep inside me. It's intense and overpowering, like a roller coaster descending at a hundred miles an hour that I couldn't stop even if I wanted to.

"Let go for me, Norah," Dean hisses, his jaw taut as he fights against losing his own control. "I need to watch you come."

That's apparently all it takes because the next thing I know, I'm screaming his name and shattering violently as he continues moving inside, not missing a beat as my inner muscles clamp down around him, making it tighter between us than it was before.

"Fuuuck," Dean groans as he shakily struggles to continue thrusting.

Suddenly, he stills on top of me, and his eyes slam shut. He expels several stuttered breaths as if he's trying to get control of himself. But clearly, he fails because the next thing I know, he's undulating between my legs, and I can't help but watch him with great fascination. Dean's normally so composed and at ease in his own skin. The image of him losing himself and climaxing is something I'd like to see again and again.

Seconds later, he collapses on me and buries his head into my neck, his breath hot on my collarbone as his muscular body trembles over me. I lift my hands to stroke the back of his head and neck soothingly as I watch his back rise and fall in rapid succession.

I can't help but smile.

That was literally the best sex I've ever had.

Granted, I haven't had a lot of sex. And the memories of the sexual encounters I have had are fuzzy at best. But surely that had to be good for him too, right? I mean, I know he's had a lot more partners than I have. But coming that quickly and that powerfully and being this spent afterward is a good sign, right?

Dean's weight becomes heavy on top of me, and paranoia starts to seep into my fluttering mind. Is it possible that was just run-of-the-mill, average sex, and he came quickly because he couldn't be bothered to go longer with me? Why isn't he speaking?

"Are you alive?" I ask, shaking his shoulders to make sure he hasn't fallen asleep from boring sex while his dick still twitches inside me.

"Barely," Dean croaks before breathing deep and rolling off me.

The cool air hits my skin, and I grab a sheet to cover up, feeling strangely self-conscious now. "How was it?" I blurt, not attempting to play it cool.

Dean lies on his back and closes his eyes. "How was what?"

"How was what?" I give an indignant huff. "Oh, I'm talking about the charcuterie from earlier tonight, of course."

Dean turns and eyes me sleepily. "What are you talking about?"

I sit up on my elbow and pin him with a look. "I'm asking how the sex was, you idiot."

"Oh…that." Dean looks at the ceiling casually. "It was good."

My body instantly deflates. Good.

Good, not great.

Good, not perfect.

Just…good.

Disappointment flutters in my belly. If someone called my croinuts good, I wouldn't sleep until I changed the recipe nineteen times and made myself sick sampling all of them. Good is a three-star review from a food critic. Good is below average.

I nod awkwardly and bite my lip. "Then I guess I have work to do."

"Come again?" Dean asks, lifting his brows at me.

I sit up in bed and run my hands through my hair. "There's no point in having fake sex if it's just good. I don't do things to be good. I do them to be great. If sex isn't something I'm great at, then I need to figure out what the hell I'm doing wrong."

"Norah…" Dean starts, but I ignore him as I hop off the bed, dragging the sheet with me.

"I'm taking a shower. I need to think."

"Norah." Dean repeats, but I quickly walk away from him, ignoring the silly knot of rejection forming in my throat.

I stand in front of the mirror and slather some toothpaste on my brush. I can't look at myself as I brush my teeth. Why did I agree to this whole situation in the first place? I was doing fine on my own. Yes, I wasn't having sex, and yes, my mother was up my ass and practically arranging a marriage for me, but I was good. I was running a successful business. I didn't need a fake boyfriend to deal with my family issues. I certainly didn't need fake *mediocre* sex to add to my to-do list. Why am I putting myself through this? I have enough going on in my life, and now I have to figure out how to up my sex game? *Stupid, Norah! So, so stupid!*

Suddenly, Dean's warm body heat presses up behind me. I see his naked reflection in the mirror. "Sugar tits."

"Don't shooga tiiis me," I mumble around a mouthful of foam.

He tilts his head and hits me with a playful smirk. "I didn't mean what I said."

I huff and spit into the sink, wiping the dribble on my chin with the back of my hand before replying, "You seem to mis-speak a lot when it comes to me."

Dean's jaw goes tight. "That's because I'm an egotistical dick."

"Clearly."

"And because if I told you that was the best sex I'd ever had, I lose all my man cards." His brows pinch together as he continues to stare at me in the mirror.

I shake my head and rinse my toothbrush. "It wasn't the best you ever had. Don't patronize me."

"It was top three for sure," he says, wrapping his arms around my waist and resting his head on my shoulder. "But only because you were in the moment, and I've never seen you like that…it was disarming. I lost it way earlier than I meant to, and I'm not used to coming that quickly."

I blink back my confusion. "You premature ejaculated?"

His body shakes against my back as he laughs. "I wouldn't call that premature…just…I didn't give you that twenty-minute dick I promised you, and I'm disappointed in myself."

The darkness that had overcome me slowly starts to wash away with his confession of losing control so quickly in bed. My lips part with a slow smile that spreads across my face. "So…good really is good?"

Dean exhales heavily. "In this case, good is great. Good is mind-blowing. Good is *seriously good.* But now you're psycho-analyzing and sucking all the fun out of it. You need to chill the fuck out."

I turn on my heel and face him. "I want to be good at fake sexing."

Dean fights back a smile. "First of all…it's established that you are good. Too good. Second of all, there was nothing fake about what we just did in there."

"You don't know that," I reply smugly and cross my arms over my chest, embracing this sense of power I have surging through me all of a sudden. "I could be a great actress for all you know. You don't know me that well, Dean."

He narrows his chocolatey eyes with a smile that gives me butterflies. "There's no way you were faking, sugar butt."

I shrug. "Maybe, maybe not."

He quirks a brow. "Maybe we need a repeat in the shower for confirmation, and I'll make good on my twenty-minute-dick promise."

The corners of my mouth twitch as I try not to smirk. "I suppose I could fake it again…you clearly need the practice."

Suddenly, Dean grabs my sheet and yanks it off my body. "Where's the damn IcyHot? Because you need a serious spanking."

Dean

Norah Donahue could be a big problem for me. I shower the next morning after just giving Norah her…what…sixth orgasm in the span of twelve hours? Shit, I've lost count. We did it in the bed, the shower, on the bathroom counter, and once more a few minutes ago.

This morning was kind of a sneak attack for the beautiful Norah. I woke up early smelling her with my dick rock-hard, and the fact that I rarely get to wake up next to the women I'm sleeping with meant I could make good use of my morning wood.

And good use I did.

I started off spooning her from behind and rolling her nipples softly as she slept. God, she has exquisite breasts. Soft and full, and the perfect handful. And her ass as she swirled it against my cock was fucking life-changing. She let out these little moans of pleasure before she finally woke up and grabbed my massive erection behind her. I rolled over and tossed on a condom before coming back behind her and pulling her leg up onto my hip to push deep inside her.

It was sleepy sex full of hoarse, morning voice cries and

complete relaxation as I thrust slowly inside her, rubbing her clit leisurely to a slow-burning orgasm. The sensation of her smooth back snug against my front as the sun rose over the mountains gave me my own mind-blowing orgasm.

It was after I pulled out of her and she fell back asleep that I got this eerie feeling I've never had with another woman—the worry that I might never get enough of her.

Like I said…*big problem.*

I dress quietly and creep out of the bedroom to let her sleep. We don't have to hit the road for another couple of hours, and after the bang session we had last night, the woman deserves some rest.

I find Kate and Lynsey in the kitchen nook, sipping coffees and nibbling on the croinuts Norah brought.

Kate hits me with a knowing look. "Well, look what the cat dragged in."

I roll my eyes and help myself to a coffee. "Good morning, ladies."

"Good morning, Dean," Lynsey says, shooting me a naughty smile. "We missed you during the rest of the game last night. Were you spending some alone time with your *girlfriend*?" she asks in a sing-song voice.

I shake my head and sit beside Lynsey and opposite Kate. "Just wanted to get away from the obvious looks you two kept shooting us all night."

Kate presses her hand to her chest looking offended while shifting her voice into a horrible British accent. "Tis not our fault we're mesmerized to see our Dean with a worthy partner suitable for our delicate tastes."

"Indeed," Lynsey quips, donning her own horrible accent but sounding a lot more like Audrey Hepburn in *My Fair Lady*. "She's a proper lady if you ask me."

I groan while the girls giggle, and Lynsey adds, "This is certainly an upgrade from Lala."

"Norah is not an upgrade," Kate corrects, her eyes wide as she looks at me. "She's an entirely different jet. Girls like Lala are budget airline types. Norah is a private jet all on her own. Seriously, Dean, she's amazing. I want to date her."

I shift uncomfortably, hating that I'm lying to my friends. But honestly, after adding sex to this agreement with Norah, what we're doing is pretty much dating. Just because we both know it has an end date doesn't make it any less so.

"Norah told us you guys were taking it slow," Lynsey says, elbowing me in the arm knowingly. "I guess a lovers' getaway to Aspen took you two to a new level, huh?"

"We're not at a new level," I reply with a frown, worry creeping inside me.

"Any couple who can have a sex marathon like you two did last night are certainly hitting a new level," Kate snorts, causing Lynsey to choke on her coffee.

The girls laugh as they wipe up their liquid mess and return to picking at their croinuts while a nervous sensation settles in my gut. Are Norah and I at a new level? I mean, clearly sex is a new level but is this insatiable feeling I have when it comes to her something I need to worry about? Because, let's face it, when I watched Norah orgasm with that vibrator, my fingers, my tongue, and my cock, I knew she was different from other girls. In the best way.

But I should be careful because I don't want Norah to think I want more than casual sex. Maybe after I drive her home today, I'll avoid any future plan discussions so it's clear I'm not looking into the future. And I'll avoid the bakery on Monday too. That'll be a good test to make sure I can listen to my mind over my cock.

CHAPTER 13

Norah

"Today's flavor of the day is a new creation and the best one our girl has ever come up with if you want my opinion!" Rachael's voice chirps in the background as I crouch over a fresh tray of croinuts that just came out of the fryer. "It's a light cinnamon and sugar coating with a stripe of decadent Valrhona dark chocolate on the top. Inside is a super airy champagne cream filling that tastes like a party in your mouth. Seriously, skip the donuts. Today's croinut is worth the wait."

"That sounds great," the customer replies, and I hear the machine click as three numbers are pulled from it.

Rachael proceeds to ring them up and make their coffees while I gently squeeze the pastry bag with a rounded tip full of the chocolatey topping. Damn, this flavor of the day is a work of art, if I do say so myself. I need to add it to my Denver menu because it will be a hit there, for sure. They might even be good for the morning show segment Max has lined up for me.

Plus, they taste better than sex.

Well, maybe not better. But they were certainly inspired by sex. Sex I haven't been able to stop thinking about since Dean dropped me off at my apartment last night.

I blow the butterflies out of my belly as images of the weekend replay in my mind for the hundredth time. Seriously, I don't know if it was because I haven't had sex in so long, or because Dean and I were making good on our little tiff we had in the bathroom, but we went at it like rabbits the rest of our time in Aspen.

It was kind of insane.

It felt like Dean was on a mission to make good on his twenty-minute-dick promise, and I was making up for lost time. Who knows? But I sincerely hope there's a repeat soon of whatever madness that was because I am already dreaming about round five. Or is it six? Does the Friday night masturbation session count?

A thousand times yes.

I grin as I top the batch of croinuts off with shavings of white chocolate to give it a bubbly champagne finish and then set them aside as Rachael approaches. "Girl, you need to be *inspired* more often. This flavor is one of your top three bests. Look at our croinut count!" She points at the back of the machine that gives us our printout so we know how many to make. "Zander looks stressed out making dough in the kitchen. It's hilarious."

"You should go help him," I state while shifting to the next tray.

"Zander's fine. You need to finish your Aspen story. What happened when you guys finally emerged from the bedroom?"

I sigh in merry remembrance and set down the frosting as she begins to plate the finished croinuts for the customers and glances at me excitedly. "Well, Dean was already out there with everyone because I'd passed out after we…well…ya know."

"Oh, I know," Rachael says, nodding with greedy eyes.

"And it was kind of embarrassing because all his friends clearly knew what we were doing since we bailed on the scavenger hunt early. God, the way Kate looked at me made me feel like I'd just lost my virginity."

"Born again virgin maybe," Rachael chirps. "You have got to be hurting, considering you went from famine to feast in the span of twelve hours. I'm actually surprised you're not walking funny this morning. Is he more of a donut hole than a donut?"

"What?" I ask dumbly, and then her euphemism hits me like a ton of obvious donuts that has me scrunching my eyes closed with laughter. "Oh my God, stop. Too far!"

She laughs and shakes her head. "I get it. He looks like he'd pack an average donut hole."

"No! He's not an average donut hole," I state defensively and then lower my voice and lean in close. "In fact, he's…well above average. He's a Main-Event croinut, okay?"

She hoots with laughter, and I can't help but laugh along with her. This is so, so embarrassing. But also so, so fun. I've been neglecting this part of my life for so long, and it feels good to gossip with a friend about something other than work.

I lick my lips and lean in close to add softly, "And I am a bit sore, which makes it impossible to stop thinking about it. God, I feel like such a kid." I adjust my Journey bandana on my head and shoot wide eyes at her. "I'm thirty years old for goodness' sake. I shouldn't be this sex-crazed. What is wrong with me?"

"You're finally living a little, girl," Rachael replies and sticks her tongue out at me playfully. "You've had your head down and focused on the bakery for so long you forgot what it's like to let your hormones rule you for a hot minute. Just embrace that feeling. It's fun. And it's clearly helping you in more ways than one." She points at the sex-inspired croinuts, and I can't help but giggle.

"That's very true," I reply smugly as I prepare to start on the next batch.

"So, what now?" Rachael asks, grabbing her mug of coffee on the back counter and taking a sip.

I drop the hot croinuts into the cinnamon-sugar mix. "I don't know exactly. I'm assuming he'll be coming into the bakery today because it's Monday, and he always comes in on Mondays, so I'm going to feel him out when he gets here."

"No, no, no, no, no," Rachael exclaims, her dark eyes accusing.

"You do not wait until he decides when you do it again. You want more donut hole, right? It was good, and you'd like seconds?"

"I'd like seconds of his very sizeable *croinut*, yes."

Rachael's dimples pierce into her cheeks as she smiles at me. "Then you call him right now. Take the croinut by the balls 'cuz you need all the sex you can get, honey," she booms, her voice carrying out to the entire bakery.

"Oh my God, lower your voice," I hiss and grab the tray of finished croinuts off the counter and shove them at her. "I thought our euphemisms were working quite well!"

"Sorry, I got carried away." She gets a guilty look in her eyes and glances at the customers.

I relax. "Just go deliver these before they get cold, please."

She takes the tray from my hands. "Okay…I'm just saying this *croinut* you're working with has an expiration date, so if I were you, I would watch my timer very closely and try to get in a lot of batches before that bell dings." She shoots me a dirty wink and slinks off to deliver the goods.

However, her parting words leave a lasting impression because anxiety creeps inside me. I don't want to wait until Dean comes into the bakery. What if he doesn't come in today? Maybe he's going to do that guy thing and wait three days so he looks aloof and cool. I'm zero aloof and cool. I have zero chill. I managed not to be horribly awkward yesterday morning in the car ride home with him, but if this is all fake, then there's no need to play it cool. How can I make the most of this arrangement while I have it?

Rachael returns, and it's like she can read my mind. "Just call him and invite him over tonight for dinner. No man would turn down a well-cooked meal by you. He'll know what you want."

I bite my lip and nod. "You don't think I'll look desperate?"

Rachael quirks a brow. "I repeat, no man will turn down a *well-cooked meal,* especially the no-feelings-attached kind of dining."

I nod knowingly. "Okay, here…take over."

I hand her the chocolate frosting and wipe my hands on my baker's coat before pulling my phone out of my pocket. Rachael is watching like a hawk, and I can't handle that sort of pressure, so I head toward the back alley. I prop the phone on my shoulder and begin picking up some stray trash while the line trills.

"Hello?" Dean's deep voice reverberates into the line, and my stomach clenches with unease.

"Hey, Dean?"

"Hey, sugar butt." I can hear the laughter in his voice.

"Are you coming into the bakery today?"

"Should I be coming into the bakery today?"

"Oh well…that's up to you, I was just wondering…"

"Yes?"

"I was wondering if you were going to have dinner tonight?" I ask a little too fast and cringe with thankfulness that he can't see me right now. I begin to pace, hoping it will quell my nerves.

"I eat dinner most nights, Norah."

"Right…of course." I scratch the bandana on my forehead nervously. "It's just…I had these two really nice cuts of salmon, and I was thinking about making them."

"That sounds nice."

"Do you want some?"

"Of your salmon?"

"Yeah…I, um…thought you could come over, and I could cook for us."

The line goes quiet for a second before Dean replies, "Norah, is this a booty call?"

My eyes widen, and I cough out, "No…a booty call? No. I just…I had the salmon."

"So I've heard."

I exhale heavily. "Forget it, okay?"

"Norah…"

"What?"

"I'd love to come over and have some salmon."

Ugh, I hate my life. "If it's an inconvenience, I can eat the salmon myself."

"Oh, can you?" he asks with a teasing tone in his voice.

My lips thin as I sarcastically respond. "Yes…if you recall from our trip, I'm well equipped to consume on my own."

Dean's deep chuckle vibrates through the line, making the hairs on my arms stand as I recall how it feels when he laughs into my neck. "I'd really hate to see you eat alone."

"I'm going to kill you."

"No, you're not," he replies smugly. "But hey…I'm good with hooking up tonight, but I have a better idea."

"What?"

"You come over to my place and let me cook for you."

"What? But…the salmon," I stutter, not really liking the idea of being out of my own space.

"You cooked last time. It's my turn."

My brows wrinkle at the loss of control, but I hear myself grumble back, "Okay then."

"Okay then. I'll see you tonight."

"See you tonight."

"And Norah?"

"What?"

"This will get easier."

I sigh heavily. "You could make it easier by torturing me less, you know."

"But where's the fun in that?"

We say our goodbyes, and I drop onto the bench, and a million nervous butterflies leave my belly. Dean was spot-on: I totally just made my first booty call. And I sucked at it. Not only did I suck at it but I also lost all the control I was subtly trying to claim.

However, if letting Dean take charge this weekend inspired a whole new croinut flavor, maybe letting him cook for me can inspire a whole new pastry. The creative side of my brain alights with that exciting possibility because let's face it, my creative brain has been shoved to the backburner for far too long while I've been focusing on the Denver location and the franchise plans.

Now might be the perfect time for creative Norah to come out and play.

CHAPTER 14

Norah

Dean's townhouse is on the edge of Boulder, a little off the beaten path for a guy who loves the nightlife so much, but as I pull up, I can see the appeal. The homes look brand new with great views and a really nice bike path just across the street. Based on the people milling around, it seems like a community of young twenty and thirty-somethings. I never gave much thought to where I lived after moving out of my parents' place when I opened up the bakery. I knew if I was getting up before the sun rose to prep dough, I needed as much convenience as possible.

I ring the doorbell and straighten out my slouchy pastel pink sweater that I threw on over a simple white V-neck tee and ripped skinny jeans. Rachael said since this was technically a third date, I should dress casually. She then added that since this was a casual sex situation, fire engine red lingerie underneath was a must. Thankfully, I have drawers full of this stuff so that was the easiest choice I made for the night. However, now that I'm standing outside Dean's house visualizing sex again, I'm starting to feel highly *une*asy.

Dean opens the door, and his scent immediately hits me, causing me to bite my lip to hide my pleased smirk. God, he always smells so good. It's hard to resist the urge to press my nose into his chest every time he's near. His cologne probably costs more than my car payment, though.

He props his arm on the doorframe, offering me an easy smile as he stands barefoot in a pair of jeans and an untucked button-down, looking all tall, dark, and Boulder. He's trimmed his beard to a five o'clock shadow again, and I have to admit, I prefer him this way.

I thrust the Tupperware into his hands that I brought and swipe at the sweat collecting on my upper lip. "It's a seven-layer strawberry cream cake."

"I already made dessert," Dean replies, narrowing his eyes at me. "I told you I was cooking tonight, Norah."

"You can save it for later then. I'm a baker, Dean. I rarely show up anywhere without something."

Dean tilts his head and adjusts his glasses while his penetrating gaze takes a slow inspection of my body. "I'm glad you ditched the baker's coat and classic rock bandana because you look good enough to eat." He winks before stepping back and gesturing for me to come in. As I walk past him, he leans down and whispers in my ear, "And I'm not just saying that because you're probably wearing sexy lingerie underneath those clothes."

"Um...thank you?" I chirp while biting my lip and trying my best to ignore the flurry of butterflies that once again take flight in my belly at the feel of his hot breath on my neck.

As I walk through the entryway and enter the living room, the swirling in my stomach stops when I see the image before me. "I thought you were rich," I blurt out, pointing at the floor.

"What?" Dean laughs and strides past me toward the attached kitchen.

I point at the seating. "What kind of rich guy has beanbags for furniture?"

"Those are surprisingly comfortable." He pulls two beers out of the refrigerator and uses a bottle opener before returning to where I'm standing. "Come on, try one out."

He passes me the beer, and I take a sip, wincing at the bitter taste of the IPA. "Refreshing."

He pins me with a seductive look. "Now have a drink while sitting on my beanbag."

I bark out a laugh. "Not when you say it like that."

"How did I say it?" His eyes dance with mirth as he watches me with a delighted smirk.

My nose wrinkles, and I curl away from him. "Like you just asked me to sit and spin or something."

Dean lets out a deep, genuine laugh that brings those butterflies back fast and furious. "It's just a beanbag chair, Norah. Not a sex swing."

He takes a drink, and my eyes fixate on his Adam's apple as it slides down his thick neck. "Do you have a sex swing?"

"No." He nearly spits out his beer. "Do you?"

"That's a firm no," I retort and shiver at the thought. "My kink-iness ends at lingerie and pink vibrators."

"Works for me." He waggles his eyebrows and takes another sip before gesturing back to the chairs. "C'mon, Norah, squish around in the beanbag chair. It'll be fun."

"Sitting is fun?" I roll my eyes before turning to lower myself onto the noisy seat. I look at him, completely unimpressed. "It... feels like a beanbag chair."

"I know, right?" Dean replies excitedly and flops down next to me. He takes a sip of his beer before frowning at me. "What gave you the impression I was rich?"

"Oh, I don't know...maybe the fancy clothes you wear and the car you drive...and that pesky half a million you invested in my bakery."

Dean rolls his eyes "The clothes and car are kind of like your lingerie obsession. You wear sexy lingerie to feel powerful, and I wear nice clothes and drive a nice car to feel successful. I actually agree with you. You get out what you put into the universe."

"Okay..." I take another drink, my brows still furrowed. "And the bakery?"

He shrugs casually. "That's business."

"So…you're not rich?"

He lifts his shoulders. "I'm comfortable."

"Why are you being so cryptic?"

"Why are you being so nosy?" He laughs. "Are *you* rich?"

"Um…I was starting to feel pretty *comfortable,* but now I'm pretty poor because I've re-invested a lot of my money back into my business. It doesn't mean I can't afford a decent couch, though."

Dean sighs heavily and runs a hand through his dark hair, pushing the loose strands off his forehead. "I'm not home very much, so I don't really see any point at dropping loads of money on furniture."

"Why aren't you home very much? Where do you go?"

"Your bakery, my co-working space…wherever." He shrugs dismissively. "I used to hang out at Kate and Lynsey's a lot when they lived in this complex, but that's obviously changed now. And I keep hoping someday I am going to move somewhere more exciting than Boulder. Having a bunch of shit would just tie me down."

My lips purse at that surprising remark. "Where would you want to move to?"

"I'm not sure yet…I'm waiting for inspiration to strike." He winks playfully at me. "And when I *am* home, I'm usually upstairs in my bedroom because my bed is *very* comfortable." He waggles his brows suggestively. "Want to see?"

A flush runs up my cheeks, and that nervous sweat threatens to return. My voice is thick when I reply, "Maybe we should eat first." I rub my sweaty palms on my jeans and play with one of the frayed holes. "I'm kind of excited to see the culinary delights you've crafted for us tonight."

He shoots me a boyish smile and lifts his brows. "Oh Norah… you're in for a treat."

He heaves himself out of the beanbag chair and offers me

AMY DAWS

his hand. When he yanks me up, our bodies brush against each other, and a flurry of desire rushes through me at the contact. Dean drapes his arm around my shoulders and guides me to the wooden stool at his breakfast bar. As I sit down and glance into the kitchen, my eyes widen in horror.

Dean's kitchen is…a disaster. A horrible, dirty-dishes-and-food-everywhere, filthy disaster.

"Is that cream of mushroom?" I ask, pointing at the opened tin can sitting out beside an empty can of green beans.

"Yep! This is my mom's recipe." He winks and hunches over to peer into the oven.

"What recipe?" I ask, anxiety creeping inside me as I wonder what he's about to pull out of there. I can smell it, but I can't place it.

"I made you"—he pauses as he grabs a glass casserole dish with a pot holder and spins around to face me—"tater tot casserole."

"What?" I stare down at the strange dish and try not to laugh.

"Tater tot casserole," he replies excitedly and sets it on the counter, shoving several dishes out of the way to make room. "Ground beef, green beans, and cream of mushroom with tots and cheese on top. It's the best."

"You don't eat tater tot casserole," I reply with an accusing frown and point at his body. "You can't look like that and eat stuff like this. It's scientifically impossible."

He narrows his eyes at me. "You can't make baked goods like this"—he points at my Tupperware dessert that I spent ninety minutes making and is now lost in the mess that is Dean's kitchen—"and look the way you look."

I shake my head. "I'm not sporting a six-pack."

"You're perfect," he says, taking a nibble of a crispy tater tot. "And we can have cheat days. It's about moderation."

I sigh as he proceeds to dish the food into bowls…not plates. Bowls that he probably uses for cereal. He truly is a bachelor. This

162

is a side of Dean Moser I could have lived without seeing. He places a bowl in front of me and gasps dramatically. "I almost forgot." He turns around and finds something in a bag buried below a few other bags on his counter and retrieves a sprig of…

"Mint? Are you actually garnishing tater tot casserole with… mint?" I am horrified.

"Presentation is one of the five senses, right?" He blinks back at me with wide-eyed innocence that would be annoying if he wasn't so sexy. He brings it to his nose and sniffs. "Plus, it smells good. Double whammy."

I cover my face with my hands. "I feel like I've entered some sort of alternate universe."

He laughs and moves around the counter to sit on the barstool beside me with his own mint garnished bowl. I point at the mess in the kitchen. "You're not going to clean any of that up?"

He wrinkles his nose. "Maybe later. Eat now, it'll get cold."

I shake my head while taking a bite and…well…actually…it's really good. It's comfort food, so of course it's good. And I'm not opposed to comfort food. Not at all. I love a good pot roast with some chutney potatoes and a nice spring salad mix.

This meal here, though, it's not what I expected from Dean. He's polished and poised. He puts off a metrosexual vibe as a young urban professional in Colorado. A guy who is well-versed in the art of charcuterie boards isn't the kind of guy I'd expect to serve tater tot casserole in cereal bowls.

However, he's also not the kind of guy I'd expect to go on a fake date with a newish friend just to help her out of a jam. Maybe there's more than meets the eye with Dean.

"You said this was your mom's recipe?" I ask, trying to dig a little deeper into the mystery man beside me.

"Yes, she made this all the time growing up." He takes a drink of his beer. "It was cheap and easy."

"Cheap?" I ask, furrowing my brow. "Were you guys on a budget?"

Dean finishes his bite before replying, "Not really, but my mom grew up poor—like trailer park poor—so I think those habits sort of stuck. My dad always hated it because he grew up with money and enjoyed spending it, which always drove my grandpa nuts."

"Is this your grandpa that passed away when you were eighteen?"

"Yes. My dad's dad. He was actually pretty incredible. He sold men's clothing for years and was crazy smart with his money. And very frugal. Everything my dad was not. The whole situation is pretty ironic because when my grandfather passed away, he left his inheritance to me instead of my dad." He laughs bitterly.

"Yikes," I reply with a cringe. "Why did he do that?"

"Because my dad is a functioning alcoholic and terrible with money. And because my grandpa loved my mom, even after the divorce. He knew the prenup she signed left her with nothing. My grandpa figured that if I had the money, she'd at least be taken care of."

I nod thoughtfully as I process all of this. "So, was it your grandpa's inheritance that got you interested in investing? Did you major in finance at college?"

Dean shakes his head. "I never went to college actually. The money my grandpa left me was a decent amount, but college would have burned through a lot of it. I knew if I wanted to take care of myself and my mom long-term, I needed to be smart with that money, and going to college doesn't really guarantee you a high-paying job. My grandpa was always great at investing and had taught me a lot with my own small investments, but I still had so much to learn. So, after he died, I gave myself one year to figure it all out. I read tons of finance and technical books about algorithms and trading. I subscribed to the *Wall Street Journal* to stay in the loop as I tested trading strategies with a small percentage of my inheritance. I read everything I could get my hands on and when that year was up, I took a risk and dumped it all in the stock market and have been able to live off that for over a decade now. It turned out really well."

"Holy shit," I croak, openmouthed. "That's ballsy."

Dean shrugs. "I just went with my gut. My grandpa always told me my gut knows what my head hasn't figured out yet."

My brows lift as I take in all this new information. Dean is so not just the Boulder mountain manwhore he appears to be. He's...kind of incredible. "Where does Max come into this picture? You do a lot of business with him, right?"

Dean pushes his bowl away and turns to face me. "Max read some article I was featured in for a finance magazine years ago about high-earning investors under thirty. He saw I lived in Boulder so he looked me up for a meeting. At that point, I was still only doing investments for myself, but I had a reputation out there, and Max was interested in hiring me to do some investing for him. It worked out well because I was ready for a new challenge. Once I made him a good chunk, he started referring some of his friends to me. Now, I have six clients I manage under my own hedge fund."

"Jesus," I reply and shake my head in disbelief. "This is all so foreign to me. I just use my dad's contacts for all my financial stuff. Nate's dad is actually my accountant, so I guess Nate will be my guy eventually too."

Dean's jaw goes taut. "Well, if you ever want me to take a look at your finances, let me know."

"That sounds dirty." I giggle, and then a thought hits me. "Did you say you take care of your mom?"

"Yes, I take care of her, but I feel like I've been doing a lot of talking, Norah. It's your turn." Dean straightens his glasses as he peers pointedly at me. "When did you realize you wanted to be a baker for the rest of your life?"

I reach for my beer and take a sip before I reply. "I suppose it was when I was a teenager and sold my first dozen cookies for twenty bucks." I laugh, and a fondness creeps up in my chest when I recall the moment. "I sold them to my dad, but I guess that was all it took. I got the itch to start my own cookie business as a teenager, and the moment I realized I could make real money doing something I loved, I was hooked. After that, it was culinary school or bust."

"And was owning your own bakery and expanding into a franchise what you were hoping for back then?"

"The franchise thing never occurred to me in the early days," I reply honestly. "I thought having my own bakery was a big enough deal, but once national food critics arrived, I thought… man, I've made something that could be bigger than me. It motivated me not to just bake but to also have a brand and a concept… that's when the take-a-number machine idea came in. Everything needs a gimmick, you know? I mean, I'm no Starbucks, but what I'm doing is working. My baked goods can be appreciated by more than just my parents now."

Dean shoots me a knowing smirk. "Your parents really aren't that bad, you know."

"I know," I groan and run my hand through my long bob. "Their hearts are in the right place. They are just so traditional, and it's hard for them to wrap their minds around me wanting a different life than what they have."

Dean reaches out and tucks a stray hair behind my ear. "There's nothing wrong with knowing what you want."

I shiver beneath his touch, and the room goes eerily quiet as his words hang in the air. When it comes to business, I've always known what I wanted. First, it was to simply bake and eventually own my own bakery. After that, it was to perfect my croinut recipe and open a franchise for them. Now I'm gearing up to open a second location. Business goals have always been easy for me to make. Personal life goals, on the other hand, have taken the back burner.

But not now.

Right now, I'm here in a fake relationship with an attractive man I can have casual sex with, just what I need. So, what the hell am I waiting for?

I lift my eyes, and the heated look Dean's throwing at me indicates we're on the same page. I lean into his touch and stare at his lips as I voice the words that have been on the tip of my tongue since he opened the door tonight. "Right now, I want you."

CHAPTER 15

Dean

My body tenses at the obvious need in her voice. It's sensual and raw, and it takes everything in me not to slide my fingers into her short wavy hair and grip it at the roots before devouring her mouth with mine. I press my elbow on the counter and lean in to whisper against her lips, "You want me to fuck you, sugar?"

"Yes," she replies breathily and licks her plump upper lip as her eyes hood in a way that makes my cock press snugly against the back of my zipper. She inhales sharply, and adds, "But only after we clean your kitchen because sitting among this mess is slowly killing me inside."

I pull back, completely ripped out of my sexual trance as laughter breaks free from my chest. "I'm actually impressed you held out this long."

She shakes her head knowingly. "I knew you did this to torture me." Narrowing flirty eyes on me, she stands and saunters into the kitchen with our bowls. I follow with the rest of the dishes and can't help but chuckle silently to myself because she is spot-on.

I get a thrill out of pushing this woman's buttons. When things aren't perfect, she gets all twitchy and red because she loves to control things. Making lists, checking things off that list one by one. It's fucking adorable, and it makes the minutes when she's laughing and completely in the moment all that much sweeter. Too sweet actually.

So much for avoiding Norah today. I was all set to listen to my mind over my cock, but then she had to go and surprise me by making the first move and it was impossible for me to say no to her.

Big problem.

But this is casual. Our terms are clear. This is going to be fine. Maybe the more I have her, the less I'll want her. That's how it usually goes for me with women, and Norah will be no different.

"You need to hand wash Teflon pans," she says as she begins filling the sink with soapy water while I toss the garbage and load the other dishes in the dishwasher.

"I'm not really a fan of high-maintenance dishes. If it doesn't live through the dishwasher, we just weren't meant to be."

"Typical guy." She shakes her head as she plunges her hands into the soapy water and starts scrubbing.

I finish wiping off the countertops and stand beside her, towering a solid foot over her when we're both barefoot. "I can't believe you brought a dessert tonight. I had really fancy Jell-O and Reddi-wip all ready to go in the fridge."

Norah hunches over the sink and shakes with laughter. "Jell-O is not a dessert."

"It is with Cool Whip on top," I state, turning around to press my ass to the counter and crossing my arms to pin her with a glare. "Is what you brought really that much better?"

I reach over and grab the round container and pry the top off. My lips part when I see she's brought a gorgeous round cake that is so perfect, it belongs in a cookbook. It has alternating layers of white cake, strawberries, and pink cream. The top is a thick mound of white whipped topping that I'm certain didn't come from a can. And dead center is a spray of artfully sliced strawberries arranged into the shape of a flower.

"Okay, you win." I groan appreciatively and swipe my finger along the edge to taste the cream. "You seriously win."

"I should hope so." Norah laughs and then sets the final pan in the sink to dry. She dries off her hands and turns to face me with a teasing look on her face. "I mean…it's no tater tot casserole, but I was short on time."

I hit her with a silent look of warning. "Norah Donahue, are you mocking my casserole?"

"I wouldn't dream of it," she exclaims, and a rosiness crawls up her cheeks as she fails to hide her smirk. "It's obvious you slaved away at those tater tots. Did you peel the potatoes yourself?"

She's patronizing and smug, and I fucking love it. "I didn't realize you were such a food snob." I dip my finger into the cake and help myself to another sample.

She presses her lips together. "I make you filet mignon, and all you can muster up is a casserole. I bet you didn't even make it. I bet you had your mother make it, and you just staged this mess to make it look like you actually put some effort into tonight."

Her sass hits me right in the nuts, and without pause, I dig my finger into the fluffy white topping of her cake and swipe it across her nose.

Her blue eyes fly wide. "Did you seriously just—"

I do it again, this time hitting her lips and cheek. The smear looks like the outline of a seahorse.

"Dean," she squeals and wipes the dollop of topping off her cheek. "I spent time on this!" She puts her finger in her mouth, and my eyes zero in on her lips as she sucks it off.

There's that zipper again.

"You were being a snob," I state firmly and take another lick. Damn, this is good.

"Takes one to know one," she snaps and takes the cake from my hands, holding it behind her with one hand as she presses her other to my chest to hold me back. "Stop picking at my dessert. You don't deserve it."

"Aw, don't be like that." My hands clench around her waist, and she bites her lip excitedly, clearly not opposed to the close contact as I pull her flush against my body. I dip my head down and lick the topping off her nose. "It tastes too good not to be sampled."

She squeaks and struggles to hold on to the cake behind her as I press my whipped-cream-covered lips to hers. *Fucking hell, my zipper is going to break soon.*

She breaks our kiss, a little breathless as she says, "Fine then…you should just have it all." She pulls back just enough to bring the cake in front of her and shoves the entire thing in my face.

The room goes black and all I can hear are the sounds of cake flopping onto the floor and Norah's giggles echoing in my kitchen. With pursed lips, I remove my cake-covered glasses and eye her with disdain. "I hope you're happy because now we're going to have to eat my shitty Jell-O."

She covers her mouth, and her giggles turn to full-on belly laughs. "My cake is too good for you anyway."

I flick my tongue out to lick a dangling strawberry off my chin and nod. "Truer words have never been spoken." In a flash, I reach out and grab her by the waist, hoisting her away from the cake mess on the floor and up onto the counter in one fluid motion. She smiles and grabs the towel she used earlier to wipe my face off and hers. When we're both relatively cleaned up, I pin her with a look and add, "But you signed up for this, right?"

It's a loaded question I hope she reads the subtext to because I'm suddenly feeling the need to reconfirm this arrangement. We're back in Boulder and back to our real lives. Can a woman as sexy and fun as Norah really only want casual sex?

She bites her lip and moves her hands down my chest before wrapping her legs around my waist. "I signed up for fake sex with my fake boyfriend, so what are we waiting for?"

Her eyes dip hungrily to my lips, and in one fell swoop, our mouths collide, and we're a mess of sticky whipped cream residue, tongues, and hot air as we make out like it's been weeks since we last touched each other instead of hours. We break apart, and I hurriedly attempt to unbutton my dress shirt as Norah rips off her cardigan and tosses it onto the floor. She then peels off her white tee to reveal a red lace bra that shows her nipples through the sheer fabric and a deep, animalistic groan vibrates through my chest.

I got to know Norah's body quite intimately in Aspen when I kissed every part of her on the bed and when she let me suds her up in the shower. She's narrow but curvy with an ass and tits that were made for rap videos. And she has a heart-shaped birthmark on her hip that I now know is called a "café au lait" birthmark because of that stupid podcast we listened to together. But staring at her as she sits on my kitchen counter, lips raw, chest heaving, and denim-clad legs spread open for me…I feel like the luckiest son of a bitch in the world.

I step between her legs and dip my head to suck one of her nipples into my mouth through the fabric. The texture of it, along with the softness of her skin, tastes like the perfect mix of naughty and nice. Goddammit, she feels so good—soft and supple and sweet. Maybe the sweetness is leftover whipped cream, but either way, I need to taste more of her.

I pull back, my dick throbbing as I anticipate my tongue on her clit again. I try to rid her of her jeans, but Norah clearly has other ideas. She slips off the counter and turns us around so I'm pressed against the countertop. Her hands move to my fly, and she frees me in a matter of seconds. Before I realize what's happening, she's on her knees, and my eyes are fixated on her in shock as she wraps her large lips around my girth and pulls me to the back of her throat. She sucks and licks and makes these little noises in the back of her throat like she's appreciating a slice of her delicious cake instead of blowing my rock-hard cock.

This is definitely a first. Don't get me wrong, I've had blow jobs before. Plenty of them. But never from someone as sweet and innocent as Norah. Fuck, I need to cement this memory to my brain for future spank bank material because...It. Is. Everything.

I comb my fingers through her hair and rock my hips into her, my abs contracting with every thrust. This seems to excite her more as she sucks harder, pulling me deeper down her throat, and I have to bite my lip and stare at the ceiling to stop myself from blowing my load too soon.

When I can't take another second of it, I pull out of her mouth and yank her to her feet. Her jaw is dropped in confusion, and I could climax at the sight of her mussed hair and raw lips.

"I need to be inside you." I grunt and turn her around and flatten her on my kitchen counter. I can't look at her anymore. If I stare at her face, I'm going to fucking come in two seconds just like the first time we fucked.

In a quick maneuver, I pull a condom out of my wallet and roll it onto my wet cock before reaching around to help her get her jeans off. I pause to relish in the dainty red lace thong I tell myself she wore just for me.

I dip my hand inside her and cup her mound while sliding my finger along her slit. "You're fucking soaked," I growl into her ear, turning my nose into her hair to inhale her scent.

"I know," she groans, undulating her hips against my fingers, practically begging me to touch her deeper.

I thrust a finger into her core and bite my lip at her tightness. God, she's so fucking snug. So fucking wet. So fucking perfect. I need to be inside her.

I pull my hand out and hold her red panties to the side before crouching down to position my tip at her entrance.

Without pause, I push into her.

Hard.

"Dean." She cries out my name and splays her hands on the counter as she tries to find something to hold on to.

"Norah," I croak and collapse over her back, my hot breath on her shoulder blade. "Fuuuck," I huff because my dick is going to blow any second, and I need to take a minute to get some fucking control.

She wiggles back into me and moans, begging me to move, so I man up and do what men do when they're balls deep in the most beautiful woman they've ever seen.

I think about my grandma or the S&P index or the sticky mess on the floor or anything and everything that isn't how fucking great Norah's pussy feels around my cock.

Once I've regained some control, I stand and pull out of her before plunging back in. "Fuck, you feel so good, Norah."

"Oh God," she moans and presses her forehead against the cool granite. I plunge back in and she gasps, her creamy back arching beneath my hand where I'm holding her thong to the side as it strokes over my slickened cock with every retreat.

It's fucking glorious.

The next few moments are an animalistic blur of grunts and thrusts and cries. A haze of sweat-slickened backs and tight grips on hips. Norah's loud and raspy voice fills my ears as she calls my name over and over. She climaxes around me within the first two minutes, but I don't give her a second to recover. I just keep moving in and out, in and out, every stroke of her channel on my cock causing my muscles to tense more and more.

She comes again when I reach around and thumb her clit. The image of her writhing against my counter makes me feel like a fucking champion. The sight of her losing her mind tips me over the edge too, and I no longer care about giving her a twenty-minute dick.

I can't help myself. This sex is good. Too good. And as I moan and flinch and empty myself inside her wet, slick heat, gripping her hips like a fucking lifeline, that urge I had before of never being able to get enough of her returns like a thundering stampede.

"Oh my God, Dean," Norah groans as she extracts herself from my grip and turns her wide, sex-filled eyes to me. "Please, feel free to bend me over any surface we come upon in the near future…'cuz that…was some stress-relief sex, right there."

I force an uneasy smile as I pull the condom off, knotting it before depositing it in the trash. "We went to all that effort to clean up, so it seemed like a good idea."

She readjusts her red thong. "You know what would taste really good right now?"

If she says my cock, I'm going to have to break all my rules and marry this girl.

"My seven-layer strawberry cream cake," she growls and then steps over the mess on the floor to begin rifling through my cupboards. "What kind of baking ingredients do you have in this bachelor pad?"

"Prepare to be underwhelmed." I tilt my head to fully appreciate the image of her in red lingerie digging around in my kitchen. It's not a bad look. I could almost get used to it.

I shake that thought out of my head. "How about we get dressed and go out for some ice cream?"

She turns her wide blue eyes at me. "Now you're talking."

CHAPTER 16

Dean

I stride into Rise and Shine Bakery the next morning with my laptop in hand, ready to work. I'm meeting a client later, so I'm dressed in gray slacks, a bright green blazer, and a striped button-down. I feel good. Really good. Possibly because I had great sex last night...twice. Once before ice cream and once after ice cream.

But mostly I feel good because Norah and I are amazingly on the same page. She didn't sleep over last night because she had early bakery deliveries this morning. And as we sat in her car and licked our cones, we established that sleepovers weren't a great idea since this was a casual thing anyway. I thought Norah was going to bust out a yellow legal pad and make another list of rules since we haven't written anything down for this new arrangement, but she held back. Maybe I'm wearing her down a bit after all. That food fight we had last night definitely seemed to relax her.

"Dean, I already took a number for you," Kate calls out, waving me over to the booth she's sitting at.

"That's what she said," I reply with a laugh and then turn to find Norah staring at me from behind the counter. She's dressed in her classic white baker's coat and another one of her Heart bandanas. She doesn't seem to like my joke.

Smiling broadly, I walk over to the end of the counter where she's standing. "Morning, sugar lips."

She narrows her eyes at me. "Is that how boyfriends talk in their girlfriends' establishments?" Her lips twitch as she fights back a smile. She's not pissed. Not even a little. She's just seriously cute.

"Never." I shake my head slowly. "I don't know who said that… it was some guy behind me. You want me to kick his ass?"

"Yes, please." She stops the charade and smiles while she sets about arranging the last of her tray of donuts in the glass case. "You're here early this morning."

"Kate wanted to work together today, plus I have a client coming after a while." I prop myself on the counter and waggle my brows at her. "And I missed you, of course."

"More like you missed my baked goods." She turns and begins filling a cup of coffee for me. She shoots me a flirty side glance and adds, "Croinut flavor today is strawberry cream."

I press my hand to my chest. "You really do love me, don't you?"

She bursts out in an awkward laugh, and I immediately regret my casual comment when her cheeks flame red, and she begins dabbing at her upper lip with the back of her hand. She then turns to hand me a coffee cup while blurting out, "Boyfriends get free coffee."

"Seriously?" I reply while glancing down at the steaming cup in my hands like it's my savior because it's rescuing me from needing to explain my last comment. "Had I known this little rule, I would have made you my girlfriend ages ago." I point at the coffee cup. "This is a great financial investment."

She rolls her eyes. "Stop flirting with me and join your friend over there. She's been mumbling over her computer for an hour. I think she needs some help with her swinger book."

I guffaw and grip the strap of my laptop bag. "Okay, but I should probably give my girlfriend some sugar before I eat her sugar." I pucker my lips and lean over her counter expectantly.

"You are so lame." She giggles and pauses when she sees I'm genuinely waiting for a kiss. Finally, she huffs out a noise and leans over the counter. It's a quick, soft kiss, but it's enough to remind me how good she always tastes.

When I head over to join Kate, she's staring at me like the cat that got the cream. "You guys are seriously so cute."

"I get free coffee now." I smile and slide into the booth while pulling out my laptop. It takes a moment to realize I can't stop smiling. Almost like I'm a lovesick puppy, which is ridiculous. I clear my throat and try to shake the euphoria out of my brain that I get whenever I'm around Norah. *It's just the good sex…that's all this is. Good sex makes a guy loopy.*

"Lynsey and I died watching the two of you together in Aspen. You were so cute," Kate says, abandoning her laptop and perching her elbows on the table to waggle her brows at me. "And now here…how you just walked in and casually kissed her over the counter. Why have you been holding so strongly to your mountain manwhore ways when you are so clearly excellent boyfriend material?"

I pause and take a sip of my coffee. "I guess I just hadn't met the right girl." *Who would agree to have casual, stringless sex with me.*

Kate shakes her head. "Gah, I still can't believe Norah agreed to go out with you in the first place. I had no idea all these years of you coming in here, taking a number, and eating loads of her baked goods, when I know you are obsessive about your fitness, was you playing the long game with her. It's impressive, Dean. I tip my hat to you."

I watch Norah as she emerges from the back kitchen with a fresh batch of croinuts. "I didn't realize I was playing a game, but I guess it's working out for the best."

"Would Norah be into a weekly game night?" Kate asks excitedly while taking a sip of her coffee. "Lynsey and I were thinking the eight of us could do something every Friday night. Board games, card games, we could go bowling sometimes. You two, me and Miles, Lyns and Josh, and Maggie and Sam. Now that you're finally wife'd up, we can do coupley stuff like this."

"I am not wife'd up," I retort, feeling tension build in my neck as Kate continues on the subject of Norah and me. I take a sip of my coffee and add, "Don't forget this is all still new."

"It didn't look new in Aspen," Kate replies with a smile. "You two looked like you were made for each other. She softens your bullshit ways. And you bring her out of her shell. It's really cute."

"Let's chill it on the couple stuff, okay?" I grumble and open my laptop to check the market for the eighth time today. "I'm not the one getting married in less than two weeks. You are."

Kate groans knowingly and then begins venting about some issue with her florist. I tune it out and turn to watch Norah frost things like it's my favorite category on Pornhub. She looks happy too. Smiling more than usual while she's working.

It's just good sex. Sex makes people happy. That's what Kate sees. Nothing more.

The bell on the door dings behind me, and a chill runs up my spine. I turn around to see that it's Norah's mother, Elaine, striding into the bakery. She's dressed in activewear, and her silver hair looks extra spikey as she makes her way toward Norah with laser focus.

Last night, Norah told me her mother hadn't spoken to her since we became a couple and apparently going a week without talking is unusual in Norah's world. You would have thought I was some sort of drug dealer for her to be so resistant to the idea of Norah being in a relationship with me, but Norah said it has to do more with her embarrassing the family in front of all her friends that night at the party. Either way, Elaine Donahue is clearly good with mind games because I could tell the lack of contact was bothering Norah.

I wonder what Elaine's business is today?

Norah's blue eyes are wide as Elaine steps to the side of the counter and begins talking softly with her. When Norah glances over at me for the briefest of seconds, I'm on my feet and making my way over to them. Fake boyfriend or not, I'm going to be supportive.

"Mrs. Donahue, so nice to see you again," I say casually as I prop myself on the counter and grab a sample of the croinut from the sample tray. Strawberry cream might be my new favorite.

"Oh…you're here," Elaine says crisply, her eyes looking me up and down like she's judging my entire outfit. I get the impression that Mr. Donahue is more of a brown, oversized suit wearer, so I'm sure my style choices aren't her cup of tea.

"Dean," I state my name as a reminder. "I'm here a lot."

"Yes, Dean. Nice to see you again," she grinds out, clearly not pleased to see me in the slightest as she turns her attention back to Norah. Man, I connected with Norah's dad in seconds, but Ice Queen here is going to take some serious thawing.

"My mom just invited me out for dinner with her and the Hawthornes," Norah says through a pasted-on smile.

"Oh, how nice…which night? I'll clear my schedule." I smile warmly to Elaine, who's not melting a single drop.

"Oh Norah, this is just a couple old families getting together. No need to bore Dean with all our reminiscing." Elaine smiles crisply at me and turns away from me like I'm dismissed.

Norah sucks in a breath. "But Mom, Dean is my boyfriend. We spend most nights together, and he gets very sad when we're apart."

My chest shakes with silent laughter over Norah's dramatic flourish. "What can I say? I'm a needy guy, Elaine."

Elaine's perfectly plucked brows furrow as she snorts through flared nostrils. "I suppose I could call and see if they can make room for one more."

"I'm sure they'll be able to manage," Norah replies.

Elaine takes a step back from the counter and nods stiffly. "Fine then. Dinner is at seven on Saturday night at Jill's

Restaurant in the St. Julien hotel. It will be me and your father, Jim and Carol, and of course Nathaniel. He's really looking forward to seeing you again, pumpkin. You two rushed off from our anniversary party so quickly he hardly got a word in with you."

"I'm afraid that was my fault, Mrs. Donahue," I interject, detesting Elaine's scornful eyes on Norah. "It's really hard for me to share your daughter these days." I wink at Norah, who looks like she's fighting back a laugh, before turning my attention back to Elaine.

"Well…please do try to control yourself on Saturday." Her lips twitch with annoyance. "I must be going."

She turns and hustles out of the bakery, and I find Norah smiling at me. "As far as fake boyfriends go…you don't suck."

CHAPTER 17

Norah

Saturday night, Dean buzzes my apartment door at six thirty sharp. I straighten out my gray shift dress before hustling down the steps to meet him outside. The cool September night air hits my bare legs as I tighten my black suede jacket around my shoulders.

"Hello, beautiful," Dean says while propped against his SUV like he's posing for a catalog ad for Range Rover. He's dressed in dark slacks and a white button-down with charcoal piping along the seams. It's a little less flare than his usual style, but with his dark-framed glasses and freshly trimmed beard, he's hot as ever.

I self-consciously finger-comb my short blond curls, suddenly feeling like a slob next to Dean. "I didn't have Rachael's help tonight."

"You don't need it." Dean opens the passenger door for me. "You look stunning. Stop fidgeting."

I slide into the car and hit him with dubious eyes. "This is my normal demeanor when preparing for an evening with my mother. Don't tell me you've forgotten."

Dean laughs, eyeing my legs with a dirty look before closing the door and walking around the car to the driver's seat. His car smells like him: expensive, manly and new. I could get used to it

He heads down the road toward the restaurant and begins rambling to me about a big meeting he had with one of his clients earlier today. Talking about our jobs has sort of become a new normal for us the past several days. Either via text or one of the several times we've seen each other. It's been kind of nice. Normally, Rachael is my sounding board for all things business, but Dean actually has really good business insights and has been extremely helpful with all the Denver bakery preparations. I'm useless when it comes to his hedge fund issues, but he seems to just appreciate that I'm willing to listen. If I didn't know any better, I'd say this is how a real relationship feels. Especially considering we haven't gone a single evening without seeing each other since our food fight night. We're still sticking with the no-sleeping-over rule, but we're definitely not giving each other a lot of space.

Last night he invited me over to rectify the fact that I had never seen the movie *Good Will Hunting*. However, we were only a few minutes into the movie before I was naked on Dean's beanbag chair with his face between my thighs and his name screaming from my lips. By the time he was done, all I could hear was Matt Damon's voice in the background asking, "How do you like them apples?"

I can say with absolute certainty that I liked those apples very, very much.

The point is, I'm feeling good about this fake relationship situation. I'm finally finding some much-needed balance in my life between work and play. I'm hoping I can apply this newfound freedom in my life without requiring a fake friends-with-benefits boyfriend.

However, for now I'm making myself live in the moment. I don't need to worry about how Dean and I are going to go back to being friends after this or how we're going to deal with our official breakup when the time comes. I'm just going to enjoy this while I have it.

We pull up to the St. Julien hotel and make our way through the lobby to Jill's. It's a dark and luxurious restaurant with a French bistro feel to it. White linen tablecloths and elegant glassware on every table. The food is excellent, and it's a place people like my father and Nate's father would take clients to.

The hostess ushers us over to the table where my parents and Jim and Carol are already seated, despite the fact that we're five minutes early.

"Pumpkin!" my dad bellows as he sees Dean and me approach. He stands up and walks over from the far side of the table to greet me. He looks me up and down before leaning in to kiss my cheek. "You look radiant, Norah. Have you been out in the sun a lot this week?"

I pull away and laugh. "No, can't say that I have."

"Huh, you look different. Glowing almost. Isn't my daughter glowing, Jim?" My dad turns to Nate's dad, who rises from his seat across from the one my father vacated.

"She looks healthy," Jim says, combing his gray mustache and dipping his head toward me. "Nice to see you again, Norah."

"Nice to see you, Jim." I look at my mother and Carol seated in the middle of the rectangular table with glasses of red wine in hand. "Hi, Mom. Carol. You all remember Dean?"

"Hello everyone." Dean reaches across me to shake Jim's hand while my father claps him on the back and asks, "Well, what libations are we having tonight?"

"Whiskey tonight, son. I tried that IPA beer you recommended, and I just can't do it."

"You have to try it a few times. It grows on you."

"It feels like it's growing legs in my stomach." My dad grimaces in remembrance.

Dean laughs and takes the seat next to my mother, which might be safer than sitting across from her because he at least doesn't have to look directly into her eyes too much. I take the chair next to Dean at the end of the table, leaving the space beside me open for Nate.

My palms are sweating so much that I grab the black linen napkin at my seat to wipe them off.

"Norah, why are you so sweaty?" my mother hisses quietly while Dean and my dad continue to lean back in their chairs and talk alcohol behind her.

"It's hot in here," I retort, and fan my face. "Don't you think it's hot, Carol?"

"I'm actually a little cold," she replies and I want to roll my eyes. Sand-bagging sonofa—

I notice Dean's shoulders shaking with silent laughter as he places his hand on top of mine. "Try to relax, pumpkin." He winks playfully at me.

"Don't," I warn with narrowed eyes. "I gave you sugar lips under direct protest. Pumpkin was not a part of our agreement."

"Rules were made to be broken, Norah." Dean smiles and sits back in his chair to continue chatting with my father. I hate how easy this is for him.

"Did you all start the party without me?" Nate's voice echoes behind me and I turn around to see him approaching.

He's dressed in a gray suit that hugs him perfectly. His pocket square is bright green and I'd swear he's taking a page out of Dean's fashion book.

Nate says his hellos to our parents and then comes to stand beside me. "Nice to see you again, old friend."

He holds his hands out wide and…well, I guess we're hugging. I stand and accept the embrace, noticing his smell isn't nearly as enticing as Dean's. When I pull away, I gesture to Dean and state awkwardly, "The boyfriend."

Nate laughs like I'm an adorable little child who is just learning to speak for the first time. "Ah yes. Nice to see you again. Dane, was it?"

"Dean," Dean corrects with a pained smile.

"I didn't know you were going to be here tonight," Nate replies while the two forcefully shake hands before sitting down across from each other.

"Where she goes, I go," Dean says, taking my hand again to give it a squeeze.

"You're the ole ball and chain in this relationship, huh?"

Dean presses his lips together and opens his mouth to reply, but a waitress appears just in the nick of time. "I see we have some newcomers here now. Can I get you guys some drinks?" She glances from her notepad, and her eyes go wide. "Dean?"

My head snaps from the waitress to Dean, whose eyes are equally wide. "Lala."

"What are you doing here?" she asks, rubbing her outlined lips together as she shoves her pad and paper into the black apron around her waist. I take a second to quickly look her up and down. Whoever this girl is, she's extremely young. I'd be surprised if she was over twenty. She's gorgeous, though. Petite with a unique super-short buzzed haircut. How does she know Dean?

Dean shifts uncomfortably, dropping my hand to adjust his glasses. "I'm…out to eat, I guess. I didn't know you worked here."

"New job," she says with a lift of her shoulders. "I had to quit my job at the salon after I burned my hair at Lynsey's tiki bar. They didn't really want a haircut like this at their front desk."

"I see." Dean glances nervously at me. "Well, it was nice to see you again."

His dismissive tone doesn't go over very well, and she turns her emerald laser eyes on me. "Who are you?"

"Um…I'm Norah," I reply stiffly and feel my mouth going dry for some ridiculous reason. "I'm sorry, did you say you burned your hair at Lynsey's tiki bar? Dean's friend, Lynsey?"

"Drinks," Dean says with a forced smile and stands from his seat. "I'll go to the bar. I feel like going to the bar. What can I get you, pal?"

Nate furrows his brow at Dean and points at the waitress before Dean snaps his finger. "You look like a whiskey guy. Norah, I know what you like. We'll be right back."

Dean moves behind me and wraps his arm around Lala

before ushering her away from the table. She looks confused and glances back at us over her shoulder as Dean hurries her away from us.

"Does that girl have cancer?" Carol asks Nate.

"I think she said she burned her hair." Nate looks at me curiously. "Do you know, Norah?"

My mother's eyes bore in on me so I sit up and smile. "What are you all going to order? I'm starving!"

I open my menu and pretend to study it as I watch Dean stand at the bar with Lala. They're speaking close together in hushed tones, and the way he places his hand on her shoulder makes me feel like they are more than just acquaintances.

Jealousy spikes hard and fast in my belly, and I hate myself for it. This is all fake. None of what Dean and I have is real. So why would it bother me if this is a girl Dean used to date?

Dean returns to the table and avoids eye contact with me as he opens his menu. A second later, a different waiter comes over with our drinks and sets about taking everyone's food orders. When he's gone, I take a sip of my wine and open my mouth to say something to Dean when Nate interrupts.

"Norah, do you remember how I used to sneak into your house all the time when we were teenagers?"

"What?" my mother mock gasps and presses her hand to her chest. "You didn't! I would have known."

"It was stupid," I mutter around my glass and wave my mother off. "We didn't do anything wild or crazy. We just watched movies and ate way too many cookies."

Nate laughs freely. "Yes, sneaking into your house was pretty much our only form of entertainment for years. There were a few exciting nights when you would come downstairs, Elaine. We would hear you coming, and I'd hide in the furnace room."

"I can't believe this!" my mom chants dramatically. "Jeffrey, did you have any idea this was going on?"

"Not a clue," Dad says with a laugh and takes a sip of the

amber liquid in his rocks glass. "Jim, your son was clearly out of control."

"Oh yes," Jim says with a scoff. "I was highly worried about him and his bad-boy ways…especially with that French horn he wouldn't go anywhere without."

Carol interjects on her son's behalf. "That French horn got our son a music scholarship, thank you very much." She pats Nate's arm affectionately, and Nate rolls his eyes and shoots me a wink.

"You played French horn in college?" Dean asks, leaning over to drape his arm on the back of my chair. This is the first time he's said a word since ushering that girl away, and I'm watching his every move like a hawk.

"For the first two years," Nate replies sheepishly. "I realized it wasn't exactly helping me with the ladies so I quit and spent time at the campus gym instead."

"You look incredible," my mother says, eyeing him appreciatively as she swirls her wine. The entire act annoys the shit out of me because she's barely looked at Dean this entire evening. "What kind of workout regime do you do? I'm looking to change mine up a bit. My aqua aerobics isn't challenging me enough."

"I do a lot of boot camps," Nate says with a nod and puffs his chest out a bit. "Kickboxing, taekwondo. Extreme weight lifting. Anything with a little rough contact…I'm into it." He smiles at me again, and I swear he flexes his arm in his dress shirt. "How about you, Norah? Do you like a little rough contact?"

My cheeks flame with how awkward that question is. I dab at my upper lip and murmur, "Um…I give my croinut dough a good beating some days, I guess."

Nate laughs a little too loudly and shakes his head admirably. "Still adorable as ever."

"I'm a runner," Dean interjects, tilting his head and eyeing Nate with a look that doesn't seem all that friendly. "I like my life so I don't feel the need to take out any aggression on inanimate objects."

My lips part in surprise at the obvious challenge in Dean's tone to Nate. What is he trying to do right now?

"Who says they're inanimate?" Nate waggles his brows suggestively and I can't help but frown because…*ew, it has a sexual assault tone to it.* "Oh man, that reminds me…Norah, do you remember when we were kids and we tried to leapfrog over those electrical boxes on the side of the road and I biffed it and landed on my chest?"

I can't help but burst out laughing because the image of Nate eating shit explodes in my mind. "Oh my God, I had totally forgotten about that! You couldn't catch your breath and I nearly peed my pants from laughing so hard."

Nate and I both keel over laughing, and my mother's scolding voice echoes in my ear, "Norah! That doesn't sound funny at all. That sounds dangerous. What were you two doing near electrical boxes?"

"I don't know," I reply with a laugh and a shrug. "We were dumb kids, I guess. And man, that day must have given me brain damage because I always laugh when people get hurt. It's so messed up."

"Probably why we were so close," Nate replies, draping his arm over the back of my chair on the other side. "I was always hurting myself. I was such a klutz."

"Well." I pat him playfully on the arm. "You clearly grew into your own skin. I bet you could clear that electric box easily now."

"We should try it out later."

"In this dress and heels? I'll be the one eating dirt this time!"

Nate and I continue laughing for a moment and I glance over at Dean who looks decidedly annoyed. Maybe it was one of those stories where you had to be there?

"Nathaniel, have you found a place to live yet?" my mom chimes in just as the food is placed in front of us.

"I'm afraid not. There are not a lot of options in the higher price-point I'm looking for."

"What a pity," Mom replies. "You should talk to Dan Scott, he has some beautiful properties and some very affluent clients."

While they begin discussing Dan Scott's properties, I nudge Dean and pull his gaze away from his steak. "You okay?"

He furrows his brow and digs into his food. "Yeah, why wouldn't I be?"

"I don't know, you seem tense."

"I'm fine," he clips back coolly.

I take a quick bite and ask quietly, "Who was that earlier?"

"Who was who?" he asks, still avoiding eye contact with me.

My brows lift. "The uh, waitress girl." I keep my voice low so the others can't hear us.

Dean purses his lips and shakes his head. "Just someone I used to know."

"Used to know?" I ask, leaning in to gain his eye contact. "As in biblically?"

Dean's face sours as he turns to look down the table to see if anyone is listening. "Norah, this isn't the place."

I pause because his lack of an answer is an answer. I can't help but ask, "How old is she?"

Dean hits me with a warning look. "It doesn't matter. Why are we talking about this?"

"Just curious," I reply and rub my lips together. "I didn't know that was your type. Did she graduate from high school yet?" My voice edges louder.

"Stop," Dean snaps, and we lock eyes for a long, heated moment that's heavy and charged with sexual energy, wildly confusing me.

Nate clears his throat, and I see he's watching our entire exchange with rapt fascination. "Everything okay here?"

Dean hits him with a glower. "Everything is fine, Nate." Dean's tone is sharp on the T as it echoes out over the table. "Better focus on your own plate there…ours are plenty full."

Nate's blue eyes narrow, and he glances over to me with a strange twinkle in his eye. "Norah, remember the time you gave me your first cookie?"

My brow furrows. "My first cookie? What do you mean? I'm pretty sure my parents were my cookie guinea pigs for years before I ever made outsiders sample anything."

Nate laughs smugly. "No…this cookie was an extra special one. It was really late at night, the summer before we were both going to leave for college. And you told me you didn't want to go to college without having this particular cookie tested?"

Pins and needles. My entire body erupts into pins and needles as realization dawns.

I take a sharp breath and glance over at Dean, who seems like he's picked up on the analogy as well. I glance at my mother and Carol who are deep into a gossip session, thank God, and my father and Jim are too deep into their whiskeys to care what we're talking about at the other end of the table.

I force my hands to stop trembling as I turn my eyes to Nate. "I'd rather not talk about that particular recipe, Nate. This surely isn't the time nor place. In fact, I don't think there's ever a time and place we need to talk about that cookie."

"Oh c'mon, Norah." Nate huffs out a laugh and reaches out to hold my hand. Although, he doesn't just hold it, he twines his fingers between mine in an intimate waffle hold. "It was a good cookie. And it was special. It means a lot to me that you—"

"That's enough," Dean says, leaning across the table to wrench my hand from his. He glowers menacingly at Nate. "One more word and you and I are going outside."

"Whoa, whoa, whoa," Nate says, holding his hands back defensively. "We're just talking about cookies, man. Norah's a baker. This is what she's passionate about. I'm surprised you don't know more about her passions."

Dean flattens his hands on the table and eyes Nate fiercely. "I know a hell of a lot more than you ever could about the woman sitting between us. So just quit with the walk down memory lane, okay? You're coming off a bit desperate, and you're probably making your French horn jealous."

"I think going outside sounds like a great idea." Nate's nostrils flare as his hands turn to fists on the table.

Dean's chair scrapes against the floor, and I quickly stand and wrap my arm around his. "Bakery emergency! I'm so sorry, but we have to go!"

"What?" my mom tuts, completely oblivious to the showdown these two are in the middle of. "What kind of emergency could happen at a bakery?"

I flop my hands out wildly. "A small fire. It's out, everything's okay…but I need to check the damage."

"Oh no, Norah," my dad exclaims, concern etching his features. "Maybe I should come with you."

"No, Dad," I say, holding my hand up. "Please, finish your dinner. It's a small fire that's already been put out." I pin Nate with a look that cannot be misinterpreted and then squeeze Dean's arm tightly again for good measure. "And I have Dean, so I'll be just fine."

"Are you sure?" he asks, looking uneasy.

"I'm sure. Thank you for dinner. Sorry we have to run." Dean's body is as stiff as a board as I attempt to pull him away from a smug grinning Nate who, up until this moment, I thought was a decent guy—an old friend I have genuine memories with. But what kind of person brings up taking a girl's virginity in front of her boyfriend and parents at a restaurant? God, what a pig!

When we step outside, Dean yanks his arm out of my hands and stomps to the car, leaving me behind in the cold wind. My heels clack against the pavement as I try to catch up. When I reach his car, he's holding the passenger door open for me to get in, and without a word, I tuck myself in, anxiety bubbling all the way up my throat.

The moment he slips behind the wheel, I rush out, "Dean, I'm—"

He holds his finger up. "Not now."

I frown, disarmed. I've never seen Dean upset. Not even with his friends or anyone. He's usually Mr. Happy and Chill and Trouble-Free. I sit quietly as he pulls out of his parking stall and makes his way to my apartment. I assume he's going to shove me out of the car while it's still moving, but he doesn't. He parks, gets out, opens my door, and follows me all the way into my apartment.

We walk into my kitchen, and he helps himself to a bottle of water in the fridge, his jaw muscle ticking angrily as he leans against my kitchen counter, still fuming like he was at the restaurant.

I take off my jacket and lean against the counter opposite him. My voice is quiet when I say, "Hey so…fight's over now. I think you won."

"Fuck that guy," Dean growls, shoving a hand through his hair. "Fuck him and fuck his French horn."

My brows lift as I huff out a little laugh. "Jeez, what'd his French horn ever do to you?"

"This isn't funny, Norah," Dean snaps, shooting fiery eyes at me. "He was talking about taking your virginity in that restaurant, wasn't he? All that bullshit about tasting your cookie before college? I'm pretty good at reading subtext, so I knew exactly what he was saying."

My face flushes with embarrassment. "Yes. I have no clue why he brought it up. That was so weird."

"You gave it to that douchebag?" Dean seethes, pointing at the door like Nate is on the other side of it. "Why him? Of all fucking people?"

"I was young?"

"And drunk?"

"No, I wasn't drunk," I snap back. "I was seventeen, and he was going away to college in California. I was getting ready to start culinary school, and I felt weird that I hadn't had sex yet. Neither of us had…it wasn't about a connection or a relationship.

I didn't have feelings for him. It was just something I wanted to do."

Dean licks his lips and shakes his head. "It was a box you needed to check off one of your precious lists, wasn't it?"

Anger spikes in my belly. "Don't mock me. I was a kid, and I had sex…that's it. I didn't know he was going to bring it up over a decade later in front of a judgmental dick like you."

Dean shoves himself off the counter and paces in front of me, squeezing the half-empty water bottle in his hands like it's Nate's neck. "I should have waited out in the parking lot for him to come out so I could kick his ass."

"And hit inanimate objects like Nate?" I reply with a laugh, trying and failing to lighten the mood. "Dean, you don't need to kick his ass."

"The hell I don't," he snaps, turning on his heel to pin me with wide, wild eyes. "It was bad enough he threw it in your face, but he has some fucking nerve talking about that in front of me. You and I are together. I'm your goddamned boyfriend!"

"Fake."

"What?"

"Fake boyfriend," I correct softly, watching him deflate a bit as his face twists in a strange swirl of anger and confusion. I step forward to elaborate. "Meaning this is all fake, so you shouldn't care what some guy says about me."

"I don't have it in me not to fucking care…" Dean sets the water bottle down on the counter, his hands curling into fists at his sides. "Why the fuck wouldn't I care? I'm sleeping with you. You're my friend. I care about you. I should have keyed that fucker's car. I bet it was that pretentious Bentley I saw in the parking lot. You should give me his parents' address. A thirty-year-old man still living at home with Mom and Dad deserves to have his car fucked with."

"Dean, you're hardly one to talk. You drive a Range Rover." I huff out a soft laugh and walk over to him, pressing my hands to his chest that's still tense with rage. He looks away from me, his jaw muscle ticking as he takes his glasses off and pinches the bridge of his nose. I cup his whiskered jaw and make him look at me. "Look, I appreciate the friendly offer of vandalism, but I don't care about any of this. Nate is…Nate. He was always kind of awkward when we were kids."

Dean tilts his head and narrows his eyes at me. "Clearly not too awkward for you to let him fuck you. You must have been desperate back then."

"Ouch," I croak, pulling myself away from him like I've been burned. "That was harsh."

Dean cringes at my shift in mood. "Look, I'm sorry, but this whole night was bullshit, Norah. I was blindsided back there."

"By what?"

"You could have told me you slept with him."

"So what if I slept with him?" I bark, crossing my arms over my chest. "What difference does it make?"

"I'm playing the part of your boyfriend to keep you away from a guy your mom thinks is perfect for you because you told me you don't want to be with him. But in fact, you have been with him. *Biblically*!" he mocks, throwing my earlier word back in my face. "I'm trying to figure out what the hell you needed me for."

"Just because I slept with him back then doesn't mean I want him now," I snap, stomping my foot and clenching my own fists because Dean is acting like a jealous boyfriend. This entire fight is ridiculous because one, he's not a real boyfriend, and two, there's nothing to be jealous of. "You know I have no interest in being in a relationship and that's clearly all Nate is interested in."

"Oh, that's right. You're not interested in any sort of real relationship because you're going to leave this life behind for Paris, someday, right?"

"Maybe," I exclaim, feeling my own rage bubbling up inside me. This issue isn't even about me. This is a cock-measuring competition and nothing more. Dean's just mad Nate touched his toy first. "Why does any of this matter? I didn't know we were supposed to share past hookups! If so, I'd love to hear more about buzz-cut Barbie back there. You sure like 'em young, huh, Dean? No wonder it was so easy for you to fake it with me. I'm nowhere near your type, so there was no chance of you catching any actual feelings."

"Lala isn't my type…she was a mistake."

"Ya think?"

His eyes snap to mine. "I don't need to be judged by you right now. You apparently like douchebags with no table manners. I don't know why you're bothering with me when you so clearly want to give Douche Mower more of your cookies."

"Shut up. I do not want to give Nate any of my cookies."

"You flirt with him like you do. I'm surprised you didn't ask him to take a number so he could be next in line after me."

"I was not flirting," I exclaim and shove my hands through my hair. "I was caught up in memories, that's it. My cookies have been well taken care of recently, so why the hell would I want to dip them in someone else's milk?"

The room goes silent as we both stare daggers at each other, and when my lips twitch, that's all it takes, I burst out laughing at the ridiculousness of what I just said to Dean. He shakes his head and fights back his own smile.

"Oh, my God." I giggle, shaking my head and covering my cheeks. "If someone heard me yelling about giving someone my cookies, I'd never be able to show my face in Boulder ever again."

Dean's face relaxes as he laughs along with me. "The dipping in milk part was especially inspired."

"I thought so." I exhale all the tension away. "For a fake couple, we sure did a great job at having a real fight."

Dean's smile falls, and he pins me with a look. It's a dark, needy look that fits right in with the roller coaster of emotions we are experiencing. His Adam's apple slides down his neck as he swallows and pushes himself off the counter. "We should probably fake make up then," Dean says, his voice deep and husky as his eyes dip to my lips.

"Seriously?" I reply with a huff, my arms folding and unfolding nervously in front of me.

He slowly moves toward me and stops when he's a foot away. Pushing a strand of my hair away from my face, he says, "The only thing that makes a good fight worth it is a good fuck afterward."

His words hit me right in the libido, and my insides squeeze with desire. "If you say so."

He tilts his head as his eyes rove hungrily over my face. "We can add it to your list of rules if you want."

Without another word, he dips his head and crushes my lips forcefully with his. It's harsh and unapologetic, full of anger and passion and need and…something else. Something I can't quite label.

I wrap my hands around his neck and whimper into his mouth because I had no idea that fighting could be foreplay. I had no idea that beneath all our harsh words was a simmering of desperate desire and an urgency to connect on a more carnal level.

Our tongues dance as we make our way toward my bedroom, leaving a trail of clothes behind us. Dean's hands are rough on me, like he needs to touch me everywhere all at once and even then it's not enough. The intensity is amazing. After all that frustration and miscommunication and confusion…this is the only thing that makes sense right now. He and I. Our bodies colliding.

"Dean," I cry out his name when we're both naked, and he's tossed me on top of my duvet.

He finds his trousers in the doorway and pulls out a condom. He grunts impatiently as he rolls it on, his jaw taut with need. When he sees me lying there, naked with my chest heaving in anticipation, he shakes his head slowly, and says, "Fuck Norah, you're so beautiful."

The intensity in his gaze has me swooning, but before I can reply, he comes over me, holds my wrists against the bed, and slams deep inside. No prep, no swipe, no glance to see if I'm ready. He just knew I was ready. And God, was I ever. I couldn't have been more ready. The soaked panties that were tossed somewhere in the kitchen were proof I'd been ready for a while.

What happens next isn't a sweet, slow sexual encounter. Dean doesn't take his time with my body and kiss every inch of it.

We fuck. Hard. Fast. And loud. Very, very loud.

Our foreheads press together as we climax at the same time, our gasps of release intermingling with one another. When our eyes connect, for a moment, a very brief moment, I let myself fantasize that Dean is my real boyfriend, and we had a real fight tonight. And what we just did was real makeup sex.

Not fake.

And the thing that makes all those fantasies feel like a reality…is the fact that Dean gets rid of his condom, crawls back into my bed, wraps my naked body in his arms, and kisses me softly before saying into my hair, "I'm sleeping here tonight…got a problem with that, sugar lips?"

"Fine by me," I croak into his chest and bite my lip nervously as our breaths synch with one another.

He kisses my forehead and murmurs, "I'm sorry for getting upset tonight."

I quietly gasp and reply, "I'm sorry too."

He grunts a sound of approval, and in seconds, his breathing becomes deep and heavy as he falls asleep, still holding on to me, still breathing in my hair, still nuzzled into my cheek. It feels real. The fight, the makeup, the holding…it all feels real.

That's okay, right? Because it was Dean who said rules were meant to be broken.

CHAPTER 18

Dean

The morning light pours in through the bedroom's frosted sliding doors, waking me way earlier than my body is ready for. When I come to, I'm spooning Norah like this is something I do on a regular basis.

It's not.

In fact, I can't remember the last time I spooned a woman, and now I've done it with Norah twice in only a week. Steeling myself, I press my nose into the back of her neck and inhale her sweet vanilla scent. It's enough to get me hard if I wasn't already sporting morning wood. I could so easily slip inside her right now, no condom, no barrier…just her flesh with mine. God, I bet she'd feel incredible bare. I wouldn't have a chance at a twenty-minute dick without a condom.

Fuck, I need to get control of my thoughts or I'm going to climax in her damn sheets. I gently pull my arm off Norah, careful not to wake her. It's barely seven a.m. on a Sunday, which means it's the one day Norah's bakery is closed, and she gets to sleep in, so the last thing I want to do is fuck that up because I demanded to sleep over last night.

Fuck.

I make my way into her attached bathroom and relieve

myself, trying to shake off this hangover. I barely had a sip of the drink I ordered last night, so this isn't an alcohol hangover.

It's a Norah hangover.

Last night was a lot. Too much. I was mentally prepared for Norah's mom, but Douche Whacker coming in hot…I did not see that coming.

Fucking Nate aka Captain Douchebag aka The Idiot still stupid enough to be bragging about the girl whose virginity he took when they were kids. Who fucking does that?

I knew as soon as he shook my hand that this dinner wasn't going to be about two friends catching up. He was letting Norah know straight up that he was available and interested. Fucking prick.

Every time I tried to talk last night, he'd interrupt me with an insipid *'Norah, remember when'* story that wasn't even interesting. I have better *'Norah, remember when'* stories from only knowing her a few years than that idiot does from knowing her most of their lives. He's fucking pathetic. He's still living at home with his parents and trying to put the moves on a woman with a boyfriend…nice moves, bro.

And that talk about Norah's cookie. He was baiting me. No doubt about it. He wanted me to lose my temper in front of her parents so they wouldn't approve of me. Then he can swoop in with his family connection and all their history and help Norah's mother pick out the monogram for their bathroom towels.

I played right into his hand too. I'm glad Norah got me out of there before I made too big of a fool of myself in front of her parents. None of this is real, but I actually like Norah's dad. I don't need him thinking I'm some idiot hot head who can't keep my cool.

Why couldn't I keep my cool? God, the way Norah and I were fighting last night and how hard we made up afterward…it reminds me of something…

My parents.

Fuck.

Chills crawl up my spine at that disturbing thought. When I glance at myself in the mirror, I hate what I see reflecting back at me:

My father.

I quietly step out of Norah's bathroom, suddenly very anxious to get out of here. To get away from Norah, away from her bed, her smell, her presence.

I pause at the foot of her bed, watching her for a moment as she sleeps. She looks so peaceful. And innocent. She looks young and trouble-free. She doesn't deserve my mind-fuck thoughts right now.

I quietly creep out of her bedroom and retrieve my clothes off the floor. It's a trail all the way to the kitchen, but when I'm dressed, I know I can't leave without saying something. I need to come up with an excuse.

I search through the kitchen drawers and find a yellow legal pad. When I flip one page over, a familiar list comes into sight:

NO PDA

FRIENDSHIP HOLD

NO STARING

NO BOSSING

NO BUSINESS TALK

NO KISSING

My how things have changed.

We started off so innocently. Now, we're having sex, holding hands every which way, and sleeping over. And hell, I never stopped the staring thing. Dammit, this is messy.

I scrawl a note, telling Norah I had a tux fitting this morning, and I'll call her later. As I drive back to my place, my mind races with thoughts. Thoughts about Norah and me together and if this is something I could see doing beyond this fake situation. Beyond Kate's wedding. The idea makes me highly uncomfortable but the idea of all of this being over in less than a week isn't much better.

There was a reason I'd been dating women like Lala. They were easily dispensable. They didn't have anything I was interested in long-term, so when it was over, I literally never thought about them again.

But Norah...she's...the perfect woman. Mature, natural, sweet-natured, motivated, genuine. A little anal-retentive and naïve, but that's the icing on top. Plus, she's the best sex I've ever had by a long shot. She's too good for me. There's a reason I don't date women like Norah.

As I pull into my garage, my phone rings in the passenger seat beside me, and I see it's my mother calling. I haven't talked to her in a few weeks, so I swipe to answer. "Hello?"

"You're up early," my mom's voice croaks through the phone line. "I was just going to leave you a message."

"Yeah...I...couldn't sleep," I murmur, running a hand through my hair.

"Well, it's nice to hear your voice. How are you?" she asks, and I hear the flick of her cigarette lighter in the background.

"I'm good...are you on your way to work?"

"Yep...gas stations do not close on Sundays no matter how badly I want them to."

"I suppose not."

She takes a long drag and asks, "How's that little girlfriend I see you posting pictures of all over the internet?"

"It was one picture, Mom."

"Whatever...she's your girlfriend, though, right?"

"Yes."

She huffs a knowing tone. "You must be hiding her from me."

"What?" I snap, irritation prickling my scalp. "I'm not hiding her from you. Why would you say that?"

"Because I've never met a single one of your girlfriends."

"That's because I never have any," I reply flatly. The line goes quiet, and I can hear her sniffle. "Mom? What is it?"

She clears her throat. "Nothing...I just..."

"What?"

"Well, I just hope you're not too ashamed of me to introduce us someday," she croaks and takes another drag.

"Why would I be ashamed of you?"

"Because I work at a gas station, and I don't have some fancy job with a fancy office."

"Jesus Christ, Mom," I growl and take my glasses off to scrub my eyes. It's way too early for her fucking mind games. "I would never be ashamed of you."

"Well…I don't make much money, and I don't dress very well. And you know I'd be living in a dump if you weren't paying my rent, so I'm sure you're not excited to show some new girl off to the likes of me."

"I don't care about any of that, Mom." I clench my teeth while squeezing the wheel of the car. She always does this. She always throws herself a pity party and villainizes me.

"Your father cares about that stuff," she huffs incredulously. "And I hate to remind you, but you have his genetics."

My teeth crack at that remark because it gets thrown in my face a lot. "Mom, I have never hidden you from anyone because I've never gotten serious with anyone. This relationship stuff is all new to me."

"So, this girl must be special then. Which is why I feel hurt that you haven't told me about her yet. What does she do? What's she like? Who's her family? You say you're not like your father, but this is exactly what he would do. Hide me from his work friends and only take me out to places he wouldn't know anybody."

"Mom, stop this," I bark, my anger flaring up fast and furious. "You're being ridiculous."

"And you're mean just like him too."

"Mom, I am not mean," I state, biting my tongue so I don't lose my temper on her because it only makes things like this worse. "I'm telling you I'm not my father. Now, did you call for a reason or just to tell me what an awful person I am?"

She sighs heavily. "My car needs new tires."

I shake my head and roll my eyes. "Fine. I'll swap cars with you at work this week and take it into Tire Depot."

"Thanks, sweetie." She releases a little laugh. "You're a good kid, you know? I just don't want your father's genes to spoil you, that's why I say these things. You be sure to treat that girl you're with right, okay? Don't screw with her mind like your dad did to me for years. If you're not serious about her...you cut her loose before she winds up pregnant and brokenhearted like I did."

My eyes close as I exhale the vile words she just said to me. "Got it, Mom."

"Love is for suckers."

"So you keep telling me."

"You'll take care of my tires?"

"I'll take care of your tires."

"Okay, love you."

"Love you too." I hang up and sigh.

Love is for suckers is probably tattooed on my mother somewhere. I know for damn sure it's tattooed in my brain. I've heard it too many times for it not to be.

Which is why Norah and I can never be more than what we are right now. I'm not good enough for her to be more than a fake boyfriend. Not now...not ever.

CHAPTER 19

Norah

"Is purple my color?" I call out to Rachael through the dressing room curtain.

"How am I supposed to know if you won't come out and let me see?" Rachael calls back, and I swear I hear her hiccup.

"Enjoying that complimentary champagne?"

"Yes!" She giggles. "You should take me shopping more often. I didn't know this place existed."

"It's just around the corner from our bakery."

"Well, I never come this way," she replies with a laugh. "And if you won't show me, maybe you should show Dean. Send him a little preview of what he'll get to take off Saturday night."

"That's actually not a bad idea." I turn to give myself a good angle in the boutique mirror and take a quick pic of myself.

Me: Is this dress fancy enough for the tire queen of Boulder's wedding? You said it's an outdoor reception, right?

Dean: Yes, it's outside. And that will work.

I pause at his clipped reply.

Me: Okay…that's it? No flirty comeback? No dirty texts? I can keep shopping. Rachael is with me and she's enjoying the free champagne more than Kate enjoys the free coffee at Tire Depot.

Dean: The dress looks good. Go with it.

Me: OK...

I chew my lip nervously before sending another text.

Me: You want to come over tonight? I'm sure there's another movie out there I haven't seen, and we could *not* watch it together.

My text hangs in the universe, and I immediately wish I could take it back. Dean has been distant the past couple of days. He came into the bakery Monday morning like he usually does, but he had a client with him, so he didn't flirt or do any of the fake boyfriend things he normally does. Now it's Tuesday evening, and we have no plans to see each other, which is unusual. I'm trying not to read too much into it, but considering we went from seeing each other every night to a few short and sweet texts after he slept over Saturday night is causing a knot to form in my stomach.

My heart leaps when my phone chimes back with his reply.

Dean: Actually, I have to go out of town for a couple of days.

Me: Oh, really? Where?

Dean: My dad needs help with his house in Denver. A pipe burst in his bathroom, and I guess it's a mess.

Me: Oh, okay. When will you get back?

Dean: Friday, but I have the rehearsal dinner that night.

Me: Oh, is that something I should go to?

Dean: Nah, I won't bore you with that.

Me: I don't mind. Your friends are fun.

Dean: It's cool. I'll see you at the wedding at 5, okay? You'll have to drive yourself because they want to do bridal party pictures before the ceremony.

Me: Oh...okay.

Dean: See you Saturday.

I step out of the dressing room and hit Rachael with a look. "It doesn't seem like he cares what I wear."

"Say what?" Rachael scoffs and takes a sip of her champagne from her spot on the beige chaise lounge by the dressing rooms. "That boy is Mr. Fashion Forward. I would have thought he'd want you to match his tux at the very least."

"I guess not." I sigh and flop down beside her. "His texts were weird too…it feels like something's up."

"What would be up?"

"I don't know. But he said he's going out of town for a few days and won't see me until the wedding. Isn't that weird when our fake-dating thing is supposed to be ending that day? It feels like he's over it." My heart sinks, and I turn my wide eyes to Rachael. "God, what if he's over it? What if he's over me? What if I snored in my sleep Saturday night, and he's completely disgusted by me now?"

"Oh my God, don't be a dramatic Karen," Rachael replies, waving me off like a fly. "You slept with him in Aspen, and he came back for more snoring. He's just busy. Plus, you said the sex Saturday night was the best you've had. You said it was better than a soufflé."

"It was for me…maybe it wasn't for him."

"That's not how sex works." She pins me with her chocolatey brown gaze. "You get out what you put into it, and if you said it was better than a soufflé, then it was just as sweet for him, honey. He's probably genuinely busy. It was a little crazy that you two were seeing each other every night last week. Even real couples don't do that."

"It just…felt right." My brow furrows as an embarrassing thought crosses my mind. "And this is going to sound crazy, but…I miss him."

Rachael's lips part as she inspects my face like she's counting my pores. "Do you have feelings for him, Norah?"

"Obviously," I huff defensively and cross my arms over my chest.

"I mean more than sexual. More than friendship." She grabs

my arm so I'm forced to look at her. "Has Miss All Work and No Play finally cracked?"

"I don't know, okay?" I exclaim and stand to get some space between Rachael and me. It's like she's in my mind, and I don't know what my mind is thinking, and it's all a bit overwhelming. "I can't figure out what's going on with me. How do I even know what I'm feeling? What are feelings? Feelings are stupid. I do not like feelings. How does one even interpret feelings?"

Rachael sets her champagne flute down and follows me to the three-way mirror. "Okay, relax…just tell me this: You said you missed him. Do you think you miss him like you'd miss a salty chip? Or miss him like a piece of really good chocolate?"

"What is that supposed to mean?" I ask, completely confused by her thought process.

"Well, if you miss him like a salty snack, it's a quick fix. One pretzel nugget or Cheez-It and you're satisfied. But if someone told you that you could never eat sweets again…how would you feel?"

"Devastated."

She pins me with a look, and it hits me.

"Oh my God, I have real feelings for Dean!" I twirl and hold my hands up like the room is closing in on me. "How did I get real feelings for Dean? How did he become a sweet to me?"

"I don't know, girl." Rachael laughs knowingly. "White boys aren't my type."

"Especially Dean," I exclaim and pin her with a look. "He's arrogant and stubborn and pushy. He thinks he knows everything. I have goals and a plan. I don't want a real boyfriend. How on earth did this happen?"

Rachael crosses her arms and hits me with a smug grin. "You stopped working for once and let yourself have some fun."

"Well, that was stupid," I reply with a huff. "I immediately regret that decision."

"No, you don't," Rachael says and points her finger at me.

"You've been happier in the bakery these past couple of weeks then you have been in ages."

"No, I haven't."

"Yes, you have. You're coming up with new recipes, you're not micromanaging the Denver construction anymore. You didn't lose your shit on Zander when you saw the dumpster mess last Friday, and it was his turn to clean up back there. You just cheerily picked it up yourself…and you hummed while you did it."

"I don't remember humming."

"There was definite humming," she volleys back. "And let me tell you, classic power ballads hummed loudly without a backup band are not nearly as impressive even with those back-alley acoustics."

"Oh my God, this is terrible." I stomp over to my dressing room, throw back the curtain, and sit down on the bench. "This is not what Dean signed up for. He's not into me like that. If he knows I have real feelings, he's going to lose his mind. What am I going to do?"

"I'll tell you what you're going to do." Rachael walks over to squat in front of me and places her hands on my thighs. "You're going to look hot as hell for that wedding."

I roll my eyes and hear her growl as she squeezes my legs to make me look at her. "You're going to look hot at that wedding, and you're going to go there and have fun. Don't say anything to Dean about your feelings. Just…remind him why you two couldn't stay apart for an entire week. Be yourself! You can be kind of adorable when you're not bossing everyone around."

My lips curl with disgust. "Thank you, I think?"

"You're welcome," she chirps back with a smirk. "Seriously, just go enjoy the night. Have fun and see how he is with you. Weddings are a great place for couples to evaluate their relationship. If you get good vibes from him, you'll know when to talk about these sugary-sweet feelings you've developed."

I nod as I take in those relatively easy instructions. "I think I can handle that."

Rachael stands up and places her hands on her hips. "Now please God, take that basic dress off. We need to find you a real dress. If you only have one more night with this man, it needs to be the best night of your life." My smile is wobbly as she closes the curtain and calls out to the attendant who helped us earlier.

One more night with Dean doesn't feel like it could be enough. But if he's pulling away, I'm not sure I have much choice in the matter. I have to hope I can prove to him I'm more than a fake girlfriend. That what we have is far from fake.

CHAPTER 20

Dean

I can't help but laugh as Kate attempts to stuff her layers upon layers of tulle wedding dress through the hoop of a tire swing.

"Sam, Dean…little help here," Miles pleads as he awkwardly attempts to shove his fiancée through the ring of rubber.

Sam and I give each other a wary look before going over to help manhandle the bride. The tire swing is hanging from a dilapidated rope on a tree in a wooded area near where the ceremony is set to start soon. The ceremony and the reception are both at this outdoor wedding venue tucked inside Boulder Canyon. It's rustic with scenic mountain views that Kate couldn't care less about because…there's a tire swing in our midst.

"I hope someone is recording this," Miles's sister, Maggie, deadpans to Lynsey, and the two burst into giggles.

"The picture will be worth it," Kate bellows just as I get hold of the back of her dress and tug it through the hole. "I'm in!" She drops her strappy-heeled feet into the grass and twirls herself to the photographer with a satisfied sigh. "Okay…Miles…give the man your sexy smolder."

"I can't just smolder on demand," Miles mumbles with a pout while moving to stand behind Kate.

Kate huffs out a noise and tips her head up. "Fine, give me a kiss then."

The two of them press their lips together while the rest of us stand back and let the photographer do his thing. We've been taking pictures out in the woods for nearly three hours now, and I have no idea how Kate isn't exhausted.

She looks beautiful, though. I was surprised to see she went with a traditional wedding dress—big, poofy skirt and all. Her red hair is pinned up on top of her head, and she looks like a Disney princess. For the romance author who writes erotic novels in a tire shop, I expected something very different.

Although, if you look at the bridal party, I guess that's Kate's version of flair. We're all a mismatch, wearing different dresses and suits in various fall colors. The groom looks sharp in his fitted navy-blue tux with a black bow tie while his best man, Sam, is wearing a tan trim suit with a blue Windsor. Miles's sister, Maggie, is in a flowy burgundy dress, and I ended up finding a dark plum-colored velvet tux jacket I paired with a slim black tie and trousers.

Lynsey sidles up next to me in her olive-green bridesmaid dress and nudges my shoulder. "You having fun, Dean?"

"Oh yeah, a blast. I love weird wedding pictures." I shoot Lynsey a playful wink.

She smiles as we watch the two for a moment. "They look happy."

"That they do," I reply, tilting my head as Miles begins to push Kate in the swing.

"I'm really happy you're with Norah," Lynsey says, turning her focus back to me.

"Oh?" I remove my glasses to clean them with my pocket square, trying to play it cool.

Lynsey tsks softly. "Yeah, I worried that today would be hard for you after you professed your feelings to Kate not that long ago."

"Um, it was like two years ago," I correct, feeling my shoulders tense with discomfort. "And I think we all knew I wasn't serious. I dated you too, if you recall. Boundary issues, I think you like to say I have?"

Lynsey shrugs and hits me with a somber expression. "I know…but the truth is, I worried that you were hooking up with all those random girls this past year because you were still hung up on Kate or maybe too scared to put yourself out there again. I mean, to be best friends with two girls who couldn't love you the way you wanted to be loved has to mess with a guy's head."

"What the hell are you babbling about?" My entire body tenses at her pointed words. I put my glasses back on and shoot her a murderous look. "Don't psychoanalyze me, Lynsey. I'm not paying for a session here."

"Chill out." She holds her hands up. "I'm just saying I'm glad you put yourself out there with Norah. She's awesome."

"I know she's awesome." I clench my jaw, annoyance prickling my spine.

She touches my arm and adds, "And I totally saw it coming. The way you talked about Norah when I was pregnant with Julianna…I could tell there were real feelings there beneath all that macho man stuff you like to project. I mean…you quit going to your co-working office down the street to spend more time in her bakery. And you waited and watched for just the right moment to ask her out. Ugh! If that's not an adorable meet-cute, I don't know what is."

I cut her an exasperated look. "Lynsey…seriously."

"What?"

"Why are we talking about me right now?"

She shrugs and smiles. "This was just a roundabout way of me telling you that I'm really happy for you."

"Okay, great," I reply, wishing I had a beer in my hand right now.

"Is Norah here yet?"

"I don't know, why?"

"You haven't heard from her? You guys haven't been texting today?"

"No, why would we be texting?" I ask, my brows furrowed.

"Because you're in a relationship, and that's what people in a relationship do. They check in on each other. I've texted Josh twenty times in the last hour."

I roll my eyes. "That's because he's chasing around the flower girl, and you're worried she's going to ruin her dress."

"She just needs to make it down the aisle and then I don't care what she does to that dress." Lynsey adjusts her own dress and looks behind us. "I hope Josh is okay with her by himself. There's a lot of nature out here for Jules to make a mess in."

Just then the event organizer calls over to us. "Would someone please get the bride out of that tire swing? It's time for you all to take your places."

The extraction process goes a lot easier, and everyone sighs with relief to see there are no tire smudges on Kate's white dress. The organizer whisks Kate down a hidden path to avoid the guests while the rest of us make our way to where everyone is being seated.

As I follow the group, I nearly trip mid-stride when I see Norah delicately walking in her strappy heels over to the white chairs all lined up at the outdoor altar.

My eyes do a double take because she's…breathtaking.

She's wearing a slim black dress that hits below her knees with a slit up to the middle of her thigh. The bodice is a low-cut V-neck with scalloped lace trim over her flesh. Is that part of the dress or some of her sexy lingerie peeking out of the top? I shake that thought away before it gets out of control.

Her blond hair is curled softly, barely brushing her collarbone, and a small section is pinned back by a black feather, showing off her fresh and dewy face. Natural, just like her.

Fucking hell, tonight is going to be harder than I thought.

"Oh my God, is that Norah?" Lynsey gasps from beside me.

I clear my throat and manage a nod because I can't form any coherent words right now. My heart is in my throat, and my dick is threatening to burst through my slacks just before I have to walk down the aisle. I can't tear my gaze away from her as she checks in with Kate's brother. He loops his arm in hers and ushers her to a seat on the bride's side.

We make our way over to where Norah was, and I swear I can smell her scent. Is that possible? We're outside. Surely her scent wouldn't linger here. Does the human brain have some sort of memory trigger where you can access someone's scent when you're stupidly desperate for it?

Because I am stupidly desperate for it. And desperate for her.

I've missed Norah this week. I've missed her more than I've ever missed any human in my entire life. I've never missed my parents, they pretty much suck. If I don't see or hear from them, that's a good thing. I've missed Kate and Lynsey lately since they've been busy with their own lives, but I prefer them in small doses, so it hasn't been as intense of a feeling.

But Norah…I have been aching for her all damn week. I would close my eyes and picture her face without even trying. Then at my house all I could do was picture her next to me, in my bed, naked on my beanbag chair. Her cake-covered face in my kitchen. My entire townhouse was hammering me with annoying memories of the seriously short time we spent together. And that's the kicker.

It's only been a couple of weeks. Who misses someone they've only been with for a couple of weeks? What the fuck is wrong with me that I had to force myself to hide from her because I couldn't stop thinking about her? I hated lying to her about being out of town but it was survival mode. I had to find some space to get control of myself and make our last night as a fake couple somewhat bearable.

However, seeing her right now, in that little black dress with those big blue eyes…my control is fleeting.

CHAPTER 21

Norah

The sun is beginning to set as Dean walks with Miles's sister down the aisle to an acoustic guitar playing "Baby I Love Your Way" by Peter Frampton. As great as the guitar sounds and as pretty as Maggie is with her dark hair and light blue eyes, I can't tear my eyes from Dean.

That man can wear a suit.

A nearly black-purple velvet tuxedo jacket is not something many men can pull off...but Dean does it and does it well. He's trimmed his beard down to just the whiskers again, and his dark-rimmed glasses complete his unique style. He's seriously the most handsome man here today. Maybe the most handsome man I've ever seen. I can't believe it's been a week since I've seen him. It feels like longer and shorter all at the same time.

He takes his place next to Lynsey as Josh lowers Julianna down to the ground to begin her own march as the flower girl. She toddles down a white-lined aisle in a fluffy flower-girl dress. Her short brown hair is curled and a little wild as she walks and trips several times, forgetting all about the autumn leaves she's supposed to be dropping. She finally reaches her mommy and squeals with delight as Lynsey bends over to scoop her up.

Julianna's smile disappears when she notices Dean standing

beside them. She frowns at his jacket, and her chubby little finger reaches out to touch the alluring texture. Dean smiles fondly at her and Lynsey, and when he reaches up and gives her his finger to squeeze, I feel something strange clench in my body as a little knot forms in my throat.

The music changes, and the minister tells everyone to rise as Kate makes her way down the aisle. Tears run freely down her cheeks, and I turn to see Miles's reaction to his bride-to-be. Miles looks stoic and happy, and when I shift my smiling eyes to Dean, I inhale sharply.

I assumed his eyes would be fixed on his best friend walking down the aisle, but they're not. They are locked on mine, and the intense cocoa smoldering behind his dark-rimmed glasses causes my entire body to flush.

Dean has watched me in the bakery many times before. He's made my dreaded lip sweat creep up without trying. It's why I had to make a rule for him not to look at me too much when we started this fake-dating situation in the first place.

But this isn't just him watching me.

He's…consuming me.

And the look in his eyes is not causing lip sweat. It's causing all the blood in my veins to boil with need.

I force myself to look away when Kate meets Miles, and the two take each other's hands for the ceremony to start. They look so perfect up there…his dark to her bright. I didn't spend a lot of time with the two of them, but after watching them in Aspen and here, it's clear how much they love each other.

Marriage has never been something I've pictured for myself. Even when I was young, I could never see myself in a wedding dress and choosing to be with one person forever. But as the two of them recite their vows and the entire crowd of a hundred and fifty people laugh along with them when Miles mentions only knowing Kate by her pen name for the first several weeks they were together, maybe there is a perfect person out there for everyone. If Kate and Miles can get past that kind of a hurdle, maybe there could be a man out there who could give me wings instead of roots.

When the ceremony ends, I follow the crowd as we make our way to a large outdoor pavilion nestled among the trees and a nearby creek. It's stunning inside with tented white fabric draped along the ceiling and chandeliers with Edison bulbs mixed with the outdoor lighting. The décor is an eclectic, rustic mix of fall colors with pops of plum and burgundy throughout.

I can't help but laugh when I notice the cake topper features a little groom with a toolbox and grease all over his face standing next to a bride with her leg propped up on a tire. Very Kate and Miles.

"Norah, you're by us," Lynsey's husband, Josh, waves me over with a polite smile as he feeds Julianna goldfish crackers in her high chair beside him.

I make my way over to them and glance at the beautiful knotty wood table covered in burgundy mums and candle-lit Mason jars. "I was walking around aimlessly, wondering if there was a seating chart somewhere."

"You got stuck at the kids' table, I'm afraid," Josh replies with a huff.

"Nothing wrong with the kids' table." I sit down on the other side of Julianna and smile brightly at her. "Hi there, cutie. You did a great job as a flower girl."

"Donut," she calls out clearly, and my eyes widen.

"She remembers me!" I lean down to talk to Julianna some more. "Have you tried my croinuts yet? Next time you come in with your mommy or daddy, you'll need to have some patience and take a number."

She stares back at me like she has no idea what the hell I'm saying but then reaches toward me, and demands, "Out, out."

"It looks like she wants out?" I ask, glancing over at Josh.

Josh nods. "If you hold her, I'll go grab us a bottle of wine."

"Um…I'm not really experienced with kids." I offer her my finger to stave her off.

"You'll be fine," Josh says as he stands while looking around for the bar. "I was an overprotective freak when she was little, but now they pretty much bounce when they're dropped." He leans in with intense eyes. "We just need to make it twenty more minutes until the grandma babysitter rescue wagon arrives."

Josh takes off like he finally has his first taste of freedom. Julianna squeals impatiently and reaches toward me. She seems determined, so I slip my hands under her arms and attempt to get her out of the high chair. Her foot seems to be stuck on something, and her dress is too poofy for me to see what exactly it's stuck on. She gets a good grip on my hair, causing a curtain over my eyes, so I can't see anything when suddenly a familiar voice echoes, "Need a hand there?"

I look through my mussed hair to see Dean standing over me looking…well, a lot better than I do, I'm sure. "Yes, please. She seems adamant to get out of this, and Josh apparently needed booze in a bad way."

Dean chuckles and bends over to assist, wafting his scent all over me in the process. It's hard to focus. But there's a baby in our hands, so focus is probably important.

Finally, Julianna is free as she crawls into my lap and grabs her sippy cup off the table. She tucks it into her mouth and lies against my chest, clearly pleased with the seat upgrade.

Dean lowers himself onto the open seat beside me. "She looks comfortable."

"The jury's still out on my comfort level," I huff out incredulously and attempt to straighten my hair while holding tightly to the small child on my lap.

Dean watches me for a moment with a slight twinkle in his eyes that gives me butterflies. "Good groomsmanning up there," I blurt out dumbly. This feels awkward. Why does it feel awkward? He's seen me naked for goodness' sake.

He shakes his head, clearing whatever thoughts he had a second ago. "Technically, I was a bridesman not a groomsman."

"Sure, sure," I reply knowingly. "Well, you look really nice."

"You look"—he blows air out his lips as he looks me up and down—"too good. This wasn't the dress you sent me a picture of."

"Rachael got a hold of me." I smile at him and chew my lip nervously under his rapt perusal. "How was your dad?"

"My dad?"

"Yeah, your dad's water damage or something?"

"Oh, that." He looks away and props his arms on the table. "It's fine. All good now."

I nod slowly. "That's good. It's been a while since I've seen you."

"A week," he replies instantly like he, too, has counted the days. The muscle in his jaw ticks as he watches everyone finding their tables, eating hors d'oeuvres, and grabbing drinks.

"You okay there?" I ask, tilting my head and noticing his hands are clenched into fists. He looks uncomfortable, which is unusual because Dean is usually Mr. Cool and Casual everywhere he goes.

"I'm good." He clears his throat and sits back in his seat. "I was just thinking we should probably talk about our breakup at some point."

"Our breakup?"

"Yeah...this is our last fake date, and we haven't really discussed what we're going to do."

My lips twitch as Julianna turns to lay her head against my chest as she continues sucking on her sippy cup. "What did you want to do?" I ask hoarsely. It's been a week since we've seen each other, and the first thing he wants to talk about is our fake breakup. My hands feel clammy as I clutch the baby to my chest.

Dean shrugs dismissively. "I don't think we have to do it here in front of everyone. If we did, I think Lynsey would interject and try to counsel us back together before we'd even get out the door."

"Oh yeah, that's not good." I force a laugh, but my mouth must be sucking on about eighty cotton balls at the moment.

"A quiet breakup should be fine. We can change our relationship statuses tomorrow online and let people figure it out like they did when we were first together."

"Okay…sure," I reply, suddenly wanting to pass off Julianna and storm off. He's being so cold, so distant…so…mean. My heart begins to hammer in my chest as my temper rises. I clench my teeth and narrow my eyes at him. "I'm sorry, but should I even be here?"

"What do you mean?" Dean asks as he mindlessly plays with the burlap table runner in front of him.

A strange noise bubbles in my throat, and I see Julianna blinking, like she's going to fall asleep in my lap any second now. I take her cup that's falling from her hands and set it on the table in front of me. "Maybe I should leave early, and you can tell everyone I dumped you right here."

Dean finally turns to face me, his brooding eyes searching mine. "Norah, what's your problem?"

My lips pull into a sneer as I protectively clutch a sleeping Julianna to me, like I'm holding on to my own bare heart. "My problem is that I was looking forward to tonight. I played nice with your friends for the past two weeks. I went shopping and got a new dress. You know I don't go out much, and I thought… silly me, maybe we could actually have fun tonight," I whisper yell so I don't alarm Julianna.

"We can have fun," Dean balks, shrugging his shoulders casually.

"No, we can't because I haven't seen you in a week and sixty seconds into our first conversation, you're talking about dumping me. I'm afraid I don't see the option for fun anywhere in sight."

Just then, Josh returns with an open bottle of red and a smile. "I have booze!"

"Sorry, I have to go." I stand awkwardly because I've never had a kid fall asleep in my arms before yet manage to pass off the sleeping flower girl to her father before grabbing my purse.

"Norah." Dean says my name, but I can't bring myself to look at him due to the really annoying knot of rejection forming in my throat. I make my way through all the wedding guests, praying like hell I don't look as awful as I feel.

"Norah!" Dean is right behind me as I exit the glow of the reception hall and head down the gravel path toward the cars. The sun is nearly gone, and the chill in the air now matches the vibe I was getting from Dean.

A warm hand wraps around my arm and turns me around. "Come back in with me."

"No," I snap, yanking my arm out of his grip, a twinge of anger roiling in my belly. "What's the point?"

Dean falters, his eyes blinking nervously behind his glasses. "Because we had a deal."

I huff out an incredulous laugh. "Well, the deal was supposed to be fun, and this is officially not fun."

"What do you want from me, Norah?" he asks and shoves his fingers through his hair, leaving it disheveled. "Tell me what to do here."

Standing before me, he looks…dejected, as though he's in pain. His eyes seem full of sorrow and confusion as they search mine for answers. I want to grab his face and tell him right here, right now that we should stay together. That we shouldn't plan our fake relationship breakup. But he's not ready for that. He's forgotten what we're like together. He's forgotten we're good for each other. I need to remind him. I need to show him how much fun we are together.

I inhale a shaky breath and steel myself to sound cool because this is probably the last chance I'll have with him. "Maybe you can take a dose of your own medicine and live in the moment with me tonight. Have a little *fun*." I poke him in the chest, and he rubs the spot like I used a knife to stab him. "It used to be you pushing me to have fun, remember?"

His brows lift, and the corners of his mouth twitch with mirth. "Oh, I remember."

I step a little closer and crane my neck to look up at him. "We should probably fake kiss because everyone is watching us fake fight right now."

He doesn't turn to confirm the fact, which is good because it was a total lie. Instead, the humor disappears from his face, and his brows furrow as he cups my cheeks and crushes his lips to mine.

I thought it would be a playful kiss. Something light and silly...good for a show. But it's anything but a show.

It's fierce and possessive with a need so intense, tears prick the back of my eyes. When he finally releases me, we're both gasping for breath, and his voice is thick when he says, "I missed you this week."

My brows lift as that comment causes serious tummy flipping action. I chew my raw lip and attempt to come off as casual. "Did you fake miss me or real miss me?"

"Real," he recalls, pain creasing his features with that admission.

"Okay then," I huff, my heart thumping with hope that I scarcely allowed myself to have before.

"Okay then."

I pull back for some fresh air, staring into his dark eyes. I want to confess everything to him right here, right now. Can he see how badly I want to be with him? How much I want to make this more? I clear those thoughts out of my head because I don't need to plan right now. I need to be in the moment.

A smile teases my lips as I grab his hand and pull him back toward the reception. "Let's go have some fun."

Kate and Miles know how to throw a party. We drink, we eat, we laugh. Between Miles's fellow mechanics doing beer chugging competitions by the creek and a few of Kate's smutty romance author friends singing karaoke, I manage to have the best time I've ever had at a wedding.

And I forgot how much I love to dance with Dean. The two of us dance like no one is watching when, in fact, everyone is watching. There are at least a dozen people who drunkenly stumble up to us and slur, "You two are next."

And instead of it completely freaking either of us out, we just laugh and roll with it because it feels good. On the surface, I suppose we are faking, but deep down, we're as real as it gets. The more fun I have with Dean, the more I don't know if Dean and I were ever truly faking it these past few weeks. You can't fake chemistry like this, right?

Dean even drives my car from the reception hall to his place like we're a real couple. And when we park, he opens my door, grabs my hand in a waffle hold, and pulls me into his house.

The second we're inside, his lips are on mine, tasting, teasing, and stirring me into a frenzy of desire. My purse thuds as it drops to the floor, the sound of him undoing the zipper of my dress as he kisses my shoulders is the best aphrodisiac of my life.

I shimmy out of the dress and move in to kiss him again, but he stops me, holding me by my shoulders as he reverently stares at my black lace lingerie set. He swallows slowly before picking me up, wrapping my legs tightly around his waist, and carries me upstairs to his bed.

My lingerie and his clothes end up on his bedroom floor. When we're both completely naked, he lays me down in his bed that smells like him and kisses me everywhere. He whispers my name against my skin, over and over, like he's trying to commit this moment to memory.

So am I.

It was a great night after our little spat, which says a lot about us as a couple. We could hear each other in the moment, voice our concerns, and move past it. To this.

"I'm on the pill," I croak, sitting up to stop his hand as he kneels between my legs and prepares to unwrap a condom.

He pauses and looks at me seriously. "Okay?"

I shrug nervously. "We could…go without…if you want. I trust you. Do you trust me?"

He takes a deep breath and bites his lip, nodding once like it hurt him to admit it.

"Okay then…no condom," I confirm and reach out to take the rubber from his hands and toss it to the floor.

Dean slowly moves over me, his bare tip gliding against my wet slit as he groans a needful sound and positions himself at my entrance. "Are you sure?"

I cradle his face in my hands, pull his glasses off, and set them on the nightstand so I can see his eyes more clearly. "I'm sure."

He stares directly into my eyes as he slowly pushes inside me. So slow, so tender, so sweet. The lack of a barrier is something we both have to adjust to…it feels different. Exposed. Bare. Honest.

"Dean," I gasp, my hips undulating beneath him with need for more.

"Norah," he says, pulling back and thrusting slowly inside again. "You feel so good."

"Oh God," I cry, my hands wrapping around his body as my fingers dig into his back. He feels so good up against me. Like he fits. Like we fit. It's a bizarre feeling because for years I've only cared about my work and the bakeries and being successful. I never wanted to be tied down to anyone because I wanted to take over the world. Dean makes me feel like I want to stay in this moment with him, forever. It's too much. It's all too much.

"I'm close," I exclaim, my thoughts racing along with the sensations in my body.

His grip tightens on my hip as he stares into my eyes. "I've never done this with anyone before."

"Me neither." I grip his nape and hold on for dear life.

He thrusts again. "Only you, Norah."

I nod my agreement.

"Only you," he repeats before both of our bodies seize with a frenzied need to chase this climb we're both experiencing.

He crushes his mouth to mine as my hips pump up to meet him thrust for thrust. Our breaths are a tangled mix of hunger and passionate desire. The sensation is so intense it doesn't take long for us to shatter and explode into the dark abyss.

Everything about this moment feels right...natural...*real.* So real, I never want it to stop.

CHAPTER 22

Dean

A light snore wakes me, and as my eyes begin to open, I feel a soft grin tug on my lips as I recall the fact that Norah is in my bed, in my arms…snoring. I relish the weight and heat of her body sprawled over mine. She's using my chest as her pillow, and the warmth of her breath causes goose bumps to pepper all the way down to my toes, awakening my already growing cock.

I lightly run my hand down her back, caressing her soft skin, hating the fact that this is my last morning with her.

Nuzzling my nose into her hair, she begins to stir on top of me. "Are you awake?" she croaks, squirming and making my dick pulse.

"Just woke up," I reply, forcing myself to stop sniffing her like a fucking caveman. "How're you feeling?"

She groans into my chest. "Awesome. And maybe a little sore."

I can't help but smile. "We did go a week without it."

She lifts her head to prop her chin on me. "That's a record for us."

My brow furrows as that comment forces reality into this bed. There will be no more records for us to set because this is it. This is the end.

I bring my hand to her face and brush my fingers along her cheekbone, trying to commit her features to memory; I'm going to miss it. I'm going to miss her. I miss her already, and she's literally naked on top of me.

The corner of her mouth twitches into a grin. "What are you thinking about right now?"

"You're the perfect woman."

Her face splits into a wide smile. "You're such a suck-up."

"It's true," I admit honestly and push my hands through her hair. "You deserve to know it."

I pin her with a serious look because I want her to believe me. I want her to hear me and know she can have anyone she wants...if that's what she wants. But I'd be lying if I didn't admit that I'd be okay with her living her life as a nun because the idea of another man seeing her like this guts me.

Her forehead creases between her brows as she pulls away to sit crisscross and face me. She tucks the white sheet to her chest and replies, "You're...pretty incredible too."

I shake my head slowly. "No really, I'm not."

"You are too." She laughs and pokes my leg that's sticking out of the blanket. Her cheeks flush a ruddy color as she adds, "Actually, I was going to see if you maybe wanted to come with me to my TV interview in Denver on Saturday."

"That morning show thing Max hooked you up with?"

A nervous look flits across her face. "Yeah. They said I could bring a guest, and I thought it would be a good thing for a boyfriend to attend."

"Boyfriend?" I lift my brows curiously and sit up, propping myself up on the headboard. "But...our deal is over. Do you feel like you need a fake boyfriend for this TV thing or something?"

"No...I don't need one. I want one."

"I don't understand."

She runs a hand through her hair. "I thought you could come as my real boyfriend...not fake. The grand opening for the

Denver location is that afternoon so we could make a weekend out of it. I have a pretty sweet Airbnb for the month since I'm going to be spending so much time getting Denver up and running. You could come check it out, and we could go to the opening together."

"As a real couple?" I ask, my body clenching with fear that I'm about to ruin everything.

"Yes, real," she replies with a laugh, and her eyes blink hesitantly. "I'm suggesting we not break up. We just…see how this goes for a while. We clearly enjoy each other's company, right?" She looks at me with wide, innocent eyes that are painful to look at.

"I thought you didn't want a real boyfriend," I state through clenched teeth as an ominous feeling creeps over my body.

Norah shrugs, and a shy smile flits over her face. "I thought so too…but the past few weeks have made me realize there's more to life than work and growing my empire. It felt good to have a partner…and not just any partner…*you*." She glances at me with wide, hopeful eyes. "You've kind of opened my mind to other possibilities, Dean. I mean hell, last night when people kept telling us we were going to get married next…I didn't totally recoil at that idea, which is a huge development for me."

"You can't be serious," I snap, reaching over and grabbing my glasses off the nightstand. This is a complete one-eighty from the girl I got to know a few weeks ago who swore off men for bakeries. What the hell is going on here?

"I'm not saying I want to marry you," she huffs with a laugh. "I'm just saying my priorities have shifted a bit. God, I even had baby eyes for like a split second when I saw you hold Julianna's little hand during that wedding. I mean, clearly, I'm not serious about that, but even the glimmer of that thought has never happened to me before. It feels meaningful for me."

"Well, congratulations," I bark, my tone scathing.

She flinches as if I slapped her. "What does that mean?"

I lick my lips and slide my jaw from side to side. "I'm glad you've had this epiphany and want a completely different life, but that doesn't change anything for me."

"It doesn't?"

"No. Jesus, Norah," I huff, scrubbing my hand over my forehead with clear agitation. "I only agreed to this fake relationship because I thought you and I were on the same page. At what point did you flip the fucking script?"

She folds in on herself, her shoulders hunched. "I don't know."

"You don't know?" I throw my legs off the side of the bed and grab my boxer briefs up off the floor. I pull them on and turn to hit her with a menacing glower. "Was it all bullshit?"

"Was what bullshit?"

"You acting like you didn't want a relationship. Telling me you wanted bakeries, not babies. Your mother drama. Your Paris dreams. Were you just using me to make Douche Mixer Nate jealous or something?"

"Nate? What?" She slides off the bed and wraps the sheet tightly around her body. "Nate has nothing to do with this."

"Okay, well, I guess I don't know what to believe from you anymore."

"Why would you say that?" she asks, hitting me with puppy dog eyes that completely gut me.

"Because I feel betrayed," I snap, my voice rising so loudly it rattles the light fixture above us. "You claimed you were Team No Relationship. No marriage. No kids. Miss Fake Sexing is a Thing and now you want a real boyfriend? This isn't what I signed up for. This is messy."

"This isn't messy…you and I aren't messy. Last night wasn't just casual sex, Dean. You made love to me." Her voice quivers at the end, causing me to look at her just as her chin begins to tremble.

"Oh please," I scoff and run a tense hand through my hair

while trying to ignore the emotions she's projecting so she won't get mixed signals. I need to be very clear right now. "That wasn't making love."

"I disagree," she snaps, stomping her foot on the hardwood floor. "I might not be as experienced as you are, but I know what I felt. That wasn't just sex. The look in your eyes—"

"Is the look in every man's eye when they go bareback for the first time," I growl, my temper boiling over to a place I'm not proud of. To a place that feels raw and exposed and everything I never want to show anyone.

Norah gasps at my guttural words hanging in the room like a thick, dirty fog that can't be cleared. I can't take them back, no matter how much I want to. With trembling hands, she bends down and grabs her bra and panties from the floor. She stomps into my bathroom and shuts herself inside with a loud thud.

I begin pacing and jam my hands through my hair because I hate myself right now. I hate hurting her like this because she doesn't deserve it. Maybe my mother was right, and I am my fucking father. And if that's the case, it's better that Norah knows now, not after a real breakup that crushes her completely. This is what's best for both of us.

Norah emerges from the bathroom in her underwear, and I move toward her slowly, feeling a desperate need to de-escalate this. "I'm sorry for that comment, Norah. That was mean. You caught me by surprise."

"How did I catch you by surprise? You're not that stupid, Dean," she cries, her red-rimmed eyes killing me inside. She shakes her head and pins me with an accusatory glare. "All this time together you manipulated me to have more fun…to let go… to change the core of who I am. And silly me, I thought you were having fun too. I thought what we had was unique and *real*, not fake. Then when I decide I like letting go and I might want more, you accuse me of coming out of nowhere with this? Go to hell!"

"Norah, stop." My face crumples, and I desperately want to

reach out and pull her into my arms and take this pain away from her, from both of us. She's right. We have been more than casual. But if I admit that right now, I'm sending her more mixed signals. This can't happen. "I'm just not a long-term kind of guy."

Her head jerks back. "Yet you professed your love to Kate and you volunteered to be Lynsey's baby daddy."

"Because they're my friends. I'm safe with them." Can't she see that they are different? That she is different?

"And you're not safe with me?"

"Fuck no," I roar, and my chest expands and contracts like I have to manually tell my heart to keep beating. "I've never felt more unsafe with any woman in my entire life."

The room goes silent as my words do what they need to do, and the world spins all around me.

"Then I guess this is goodbye," Norah croaks, her eyes welling with tears.

She moves to leave, and I shift, blocking her path, my body subconsciously willing her to stay while my head knows what's best. "This isn't how we were supposed to end. It was a business deal, remember?"

"It stopped being a business deal the minute we started having sex, don't you think?"

I close my eyes, shards of regret slicing through every inch of my body. I can't believe I did this. I ruined us. I really am my father's son. "Norah, I still want to be your friend."

She nods, and an errant tear slides down her face. "Sure, that sounds good. We can be silent friends. Sort of like you're a silent investor. It's hard to tell if they exist without looking at the paperwork."

With those parting words, Norah steps past me and heads downstairs and out of my house, leaving deafening silence in her wake.

CHAPTER 23

Norah

My apartment doorbell buzzes, but it's the hallway bell and not the street bell. I peel my face away from the Netflix marathon I'm currently in the middle of and wonder who the heck came up my apartment steps without being buzzed up?

I throw myself off the couch and make my way down the hall to peek through the peephole. The sight on the other side causes my entire body to convulse violently.

"Norah, open up, I know you're home," the terrifying voice muffles through the thick wooden door.

I hold my breath and splay my hands out on the door and duck in case the person can magically see me through the peephole.

"Norah Renee Donahue, open this door right now, or I swear I'll make up for all those years I never spanked you."

"Harsh words, Elaine," I mumble before unchaining my door and opening it to reveal my mother in all her perfect, active-wearing glory. I bet Elaine has never gone a night without a perfect eight hours of sleep.

She blinks and looks me up and down like I'm a foreign object. "Why aren't you downstairs opening the bakery? You do realize it's Monday, not Sunday, right?"

"I know it's Monday, Mother." I roll my eyes and do my best to ignore the flashback of yesterday. "Rachael and Zander opened for me."

"Why?"

"Because I had some calls to make." I fiddle awkwardly with the wood on the doorframe and try to avoid her eyes in case they turn me into stone.

"I don't understand." She points at my baggy T-shirt I've been wearing for over twenty-four hours. "It's nine thirty on a Monday morning, your second bakery opens on Saturday, and you're up here lounging in your pajamas?"

"I'm surprised you remembered it's opening," I pout.

"Oh hush, I've had the open house invite on my calendar for weeks." She pushes past me and makes her way down my hallway into my kitchen. "Norah," she gasps, looking at the mess all over the counter. "What on earth?"

"What?" I ask sleepily, crossing my arms over my chest like a sullen teenager.

"Why does your kitchen look like you've been robbed?"

I shove a hand through my greasy bed hair. "I was baking."

"It doesn't smell like you've been baking."

"I baked yesterday...just haven't had a chance to clean up yet."

My mother's face twists up in disgust. "What did you make?"

"Cookie dough. I'd offer you some, but I ate it already."

My mother nearly starts her own convulsions now. "What is going on here? This isn't like you, not at all." She moves into my kitchen and rolls her sleeves up before filling the sink with water. "Is this because of that boyfriend of yours? I do not care for him, Norah. Look at the influence he's having on you. These pans are going to have to soak."

"He's not my boyfriend anymore," I state flatly, dropping onto a barstool because my body feels heavy on my feet. "We broke up."

She stops scrubbing and gapes at me. "You broke up?"

I nod slowly. "Indeed, we did. So now that that's over, you can go back to your matchmaking schemes."

My mother stares at me like I've grown a second head. "You never let me set you up, so why would you suggest I try now?"

"Maybe things have changed." I shrug and force a fake smile.

"Is this one of your insipid jokes, Norah?" my mother snaps while dropping several dirty bowls into the dirty water. "Are you trying to distract me with the hope of setting you up before you tell me something truly horrible like you're moving away or something?"

"Mom." I steel myself to say what I need to in order to get over Dean. "I'd actually like you to set me up."

Her eyes flare, and a hopeful smile spreads across her face. "With Nathaniel?"

"Not Nathaniel," I groan, and my body shivers with repulsion.

"Why not?"

"He's horrible, Mom."

"Horrible how?"

I decide to hit her with the truth. If I'm going to give Elaine the freedom to embrace her matchmaking skills, she needs to be okay with some oversharing. "Well, when Nate and I were younger, we sort of messed around before we both went off to school."

"Okay..." she says, nodding like she's hip on my lingo, which is kind of amusing.

"And apparently, Nate thought it would be cool to bring that up at dinner the other night...in front of Dean."

My mom's nose wrinkles. "That's obscene."

"I know. And Dean was not cool with it. It's why we left in such a hurry. There was no fire at the bakery. I was trying to put out a different kind of fire."

My mother sighs and shakes her head. "I feel sorry for Nathaniel."

"I'm sorry, what?" I nearly screech. I'm having this nice heart-to-heart with my mother, and then she totally comes out of left field with that. "How on earth could you feel sorry for Nate? He was a pig that night, Mom."

"I know, and I'm not excusing his behavior." She stops with the dishes and wipes her hands off before she continues. "Carol told me he wasn't doing very well in California. Apparently, he hated his job, and then the woman he was with cheated on him with one of his colleagues. Jim was all set to sell the firm to an outside buyer, but Nathaniel told them he was moving home, and well, they kind of changed their plans to help give him a boost. It's kind of sad. It's why I pushed you so hard to give him a chance. Maybe he could use a friend instead."

"Well, it's not going to be me," I state through clenched teeth.

"Norah…"

"What? He was horrible at that dinner, Mom. At your party, he was smug and patronizing. I don't care if he was heartbroken or not."

"Well, you can't blame the man for losing his mind a little bit in front of you…you're…*you*." She folds the dish towel perfectly as she gets a matter-of-fact look on her face.

"What is that supposed to mean?" I ask, feeling strange at that remark because it's not something I've ever heard from my mother.

She shakes her head and waves her hand. "Well…Carol and I have always wanted you and Nate together, so I'm sure she was bragging about you to him like I was bragging about him to you. I'm sure after all his unpleasantness in California, he thought he'd come back home and reconnect with you. Then you show up with Dean, who looks like he belongs in Hollywood a lot more than Nathaniel ever did, and he kind of lost his mind, I suspect. You'd be a hard girl to miss out on, Norah. You're quite the catch."

"I am?" I croak as her words hit me like a ton of bricks. I've never heard my mother speak about me like this…*ever*.

"Obviously," she spouts with annoyance as she helps herself to a cup of coffee that I made earlier. "You're successful and independent. You're beautiful with very little effort, and frankly, I'm envious of that. Plus, you're creative *and* business savvy, a lethal combination. Not to mention, you're opening a second bakery and launching a franchise. I underestimated all the hard work you've been doing. Dean made me see the light with everything he said about you at our anniversary party. You've done what others only dream of, pumpkin."

Holy croinuts, I've entered the Twilight Zone.

Elaine Donahue has actually been listening. Apparently, fake-dating Dean has had some positive effects after all. My mother almost sounds proud of me. And maybe a tiny bit envious?

My voice is thick in my throat when I ask a question that's been on my mind a lot recently. "Mom, what made you stop working for Mary Kay?"

She holds her mug tightly and hits me with a curious look. "I had you, of course." She says it crisply like there's no other possible answer.

"I know, but you could have done both." I run my hands nervously along my thighs, terrified this will change the direction of our conversation, but I need to understand this secretive part of my mother's past, so I keep pressing. "Women work and have children. And you were pretty incredible at your job from what I can tell. I've always wondered why you quit and didn't try to do it all."

"Oh, pumpkin." She gets a thoughtful look in her eye and then carries her coffee over to the stool beside me. "Honestly, I planned on doing it all. I loved that pink Cadillac." She laughs softly as she sits down. "But we struggled to get pregnant, and when you go through something like that, it's only natural for your priorities to shift."

My lips part. "You never told me you struggled with infertility."

She waves me off and blows on her coffee. "It wasn't something people talked about back then, but yes, we struggled for years to have you and for years after you were born to try to have another. I always wanted three kids, but it was never in the cards. Once the doctor told us there was nothing more to be done, that was it. I knew where I needed to be."

"Where did you need to be?" I ask, trying to get over the fact that this is a deeply personal thing my mother has been holding inside her my entire life.

"With you of course." She smiles affectionately and reaches out to tuck a strand of my messy hair behind my ear. "I loved teaching you to sew and bake and put on makeup. We got to do all the fun mother-daughter activities you see in those fifties movies."

"You could have done that with a job, don't you think?" I question, feeling almost guilty that my existence took her away from something she loved.

"Probably, but your father made good money, and once I had you, I didn't care about my work anymore. I didn't want to be on the road selling makeup. I wanted to be home with you."

I blink back my shock and feel a strange warmth inside my chest over finally seeing how much my mother loves me to give up something she cared so much about. "Do you ever regret it?"

"Quitting my job? Heavens no." She swats me lightly on the leg. "I loved what I did, but it didn't feed my soul. Not the way baking does for you. I knew I had created a monster the minute you started asking for cookbooks for Christmas." She laughs and gently touches my cheek.

I huff at that remark. "You made a cookie monster."

She snorts at my lame joke, which causes both of us to burst into girlie giggles. It's hard to make the ice queen laugh so I'll definitely cherish this moment. When we both collect ourselves again, I ask her a question that's been niggling in my mind ever since I asked Dean not to break up with me. "Do you think I'm strong enough to do it all?"

"What? Open all these bakeries?" She arches a knowing brow. "Without a doubt. You have been training for this most of your life, and you had a great teacher."

I smile and shake my head before correcting her line of thought. "Not just the bakeries but maybe…have a family or a husband." *Or at least a boyfriend.*

"Is that what you want?" She pins me with a look venturing on hope but trying to be pragmatic at the same time.

"I'm not sure yet. I'm just pondering," I reply, chewing my lip thoughtfully. "I sort of feel like I've been so hyper-focused on the bakery that I've missed out on some fun experiences."

"You can do anything you set your mind to, Norah." Her lips twitch with a pleased smile before her eyes soften on me. She reaches over and caresses my arm affectionately. "I admit I've been pushing to set you up for so long because I didn't want you to have any regrets in life. Business is a wonderful accomplishment, but being a mother…it's my greatest joy in life. But just because it's my great joy doesn't mean it has to be yours. I've underestimated you for far too long, Norah. It's clear to me you truly know your own mind, and I'm sorry it took me so long to see that."

"It's okay." I shrug her off as a weird knot forms in my throat over her praise.

"It's not okay." She squeezes my hand so I'm forced to look at her serious face when she adds, "I'm proud of you and all you're doing, and I can't wait to see your bakeries popping up all over the nation. You're incredible. And you did it all on your own."

She shakes her head in amazement, and tears well in my eyes. Flashbacks of my mom and me in the kitchen together flood my mind. "I couldn't have done it without you inspiring me," I croak, the tears spilling freely as I swipe them away. "My favorite memories as a kid are you and me baking together."

Her lips purse, and her chin trembles. "Mine too, pumpkin." She smiles and sniffles loudly, clearing her throat almost aggressively because Elaine Donahue does not get emotional. "And I must admit something to you that I've been hiding for several years now."

"What?" I huff, wiping my nose on the back of my hand.

She side-eyes me nervously. "Those weekly boxes of croinuts I buy for your father's office every week?"

"Yeah?"

She rubs her lips together and shakes her head. "Sometimes I never deliver them."

"What do you mean?" I ask, my voice rising in pitch.

"Some weeks, I keep the entire box for myself and hide them in the freezer from your father. They are sinfully addictive, Norah. That burnt vanilla, smoked caramel flavor you made one day last month…I have dreams about it."

My belly shakes with unconcealed laughter. "Mom! You've been shame-eating croinuts behind my back?"

"I have." She giggles along with me, and new tears form in her eyes from laughing. "I'm not proud."

"You should be proud." I sit back and see my mother in a whole new light now. "It's kind of savage."

We both laugh for a good long while, letting the moment fully soak in. For once, a visit from my mother isn't leaving me a stressed-out ball of nerves. I could get used to this.

"I'm really glad you came over this morning, Mom," I say with a contented sigh I haven't felt in ages.

"Me too." My mother smiles affectionately and adds, "And no matter what you decide to do with your life, you are always enough. You don't need to have babies or get married to make me happy. I want you to do what inspires you. But I will be slightly disappointed if you never make it to Paris someday."

"What? Why?" This is the first time my mother has acknowledged my travel dreams.

She shrugs and gets a faraway look in her eyes. "To be independent enough to pick up and travel the world is something I kind of regret not doing when I was younger. The longer you wait to do things, the harder it is."

"You and Dad should go to Paris, Mom." I waggle my brows excitedly at her. "It could be a perfect fortieth wedding anniversary trip. And probably easier than planning another party."

She laughs and hits me with a sweet smile. "Maybe you'll be able to show us around."

"Maybe." A strange sense of urgency pushes that plan into action. One thing my experience with Dean has taught me—I have enjoyed being a little selfish and letting loose these past few weeks. And taking a break from work hasn't had any disastrous effects on my goals. So really, what have I been waiting for?

My mom's hand squeezes mine again, pulling me out of my inner musings. "I just want you to be happy. If you're happy, I'll want for nothing."

"Yeah right." I narrow my eyes at her.

"I'll *try* to want for nothing," she amends with a guilty look. "Does that work?"

I nod. "You have a deal, Mom."

We shake hands, and I almost start crying all over again when Elaine pulls me up off my chair and wraps her arms around me. The hug is only awkward for a few seconds before I sink against her shoulder and smile. My relationship with my mother has never felt more real than at this moment.

CHAPTER 24

Dean

When I was little, I had one of those creepy jack-in-the-box toys that was a hit or miss when the damn thing would pop out. And today, as I head to Rise and Shine Bakery for a last-minute investor meeting Max called me about, I'm a lot like how that stupid toy made me feel. Coiled, tight, and unsure of what's going to spring out at me when I walk in the door.

I've had investor meetings with Max and Norah at the bakery before. It's common for them to keep me updated on the progress of the Denver location, and with the grand opening coming up, maybe this is a run-of-the-mill meeting. But the last-minute call is highly suspicious, especially because it's been four days since Norah and I ended things, or rather, I ended things with Norah. And that hurt look in her eyes has been haunting me every damn minute.

I'm a fucking asshole.

It's no wonder everything became messy. I wasn't my normal detached self with Norah. The Dean that Norah had was completely different than the Dean I give to women like Lala. With Norah, I let my guard down too much. I spent the fucking night with her for shit's sake, multiple times. And I laughed with her…a lot. I never laughed with those random hookups. I gave them the

Dean fuckboy façade, a foolproof way to get me laid with as little attachment as possible. It wasn't fun with them like it was with Norah. It was just what I did when I wanted to get laid.

But Norah is grown up and her own person. She's motivated and has her own life. She wasn't one of the flings I struggled to have conversations with. I could talk to Norah all day long. I'm not surprised she caught feelings. I caught them too.

I was just surprised she wanted to act on those feelings. I didn't expect that. That sex we had…it was out of this world amazing…the best I ever had…but the last time wasn't making love for me. It was goodbye.

But not goodbye forever. Just goodbye to this fake arrangement. I still want to be a part of Norah's life. I still want to come into her bakery and flirt with her until she gets those flushed cheeks. I want to go to her grand opening and cheer on her success. The woman is a machine; she is unstoppable. I want a front row seat for that show.

But I can't let her care about me as more than a friend. I can't ruin her the way my dad ruined my mom. Norah has way too many dreams to accomplish without me dragging her down and fucking up her priorities.

So at today's meeting, I'm going to remind her that I'm here as a friend and a supporter. I'm invested in not only her business but also her future. She's the best investment I've ever made.

As I enter the bakery, the familiar bell dings above my head. I see Max at a corner booth by the window. He waves me over, and I grip my laptop bag and move toward him while glancing at the counter to search for Norah. Rachael is standing with a fresh tray of croinuts she's currently ignoring to shoot me a dirty look.

"Hey, Max," I croak, clearing my throat and trying to drown the tension in my chest.

"Hi, Dean," Max says and shifts uncomfortably in his seat.

"Everything okay?" I ask as I slide into the booth across from him.

He nods crisply. "It should be. Let's wait for Norah." He looks past me, and his face spreads into a smile. "There she is."

I sense her before I see her, and when I turn around, it's like a sucker punch right to the guts. She's dressed in a jean jacket with a yellow tank top underneath and leggings. Her hair is styled and not concealed under one of her classic rock bandanas. She looks…great. Completely unaffected by what happened between us and ready for this meeting. Maybe we can move past this after all.

"Hi guys," she says politely as she drags a seat over from the nearby empty table. She lowers herself onto it and clasps her hands on the table, barely ghosting her eyes at me. "Thanks for making this last-minute meeting work, Dean."

My name on her lips sends a memory of the two of us naked in bed together, and I straighten my glasses and force the memory away. "Anytime. What's going on? Everything okay with the grand opening? Is there a construction issue?"

"No construction issues. The grand opening is right on schedule. It should be a good turnout there," she says to the table.

"That's good," I reply, willing her to look up and show me those eyes so I can stop remembering them with tears. "So, what's the meeting today for exactly?"

Norah looks over at Max and gives him a wobbly smile. "Max, you know the technical stuff we discussed, so I'll let you take it from here."

"Technical stuff?" I frown as Max pulls out a large manila envelope and opens it in front of me.

"Yes, well…it's not that technical, Dean. Basically, Norah would like to buy out your investment in Rise and Shine-Denver."

"What?" I snap, my head jerking back like I've just been punched. "What are you talking about?"

Max shoots me a painfully polite smile. "Norah and I met yesterday, and we went through some of her options, and she feels it's important for her to be the sole owner of her second location."

"She doesn't have the capital for that," I bark, irritation spiking in my belly at this preposterous idea.

"I'm selling my apartment," she states firmly, and I glance over to see her staring at me with emotionless eyes. "It's not quite worth your full investment, but my accountant thinks I can swing a loan for the rest."

"Your accountant?" I growl, losing all manner of professionalism. "Let me guess…Douche Convertible?"

She blinks rapidly. "Nate, you mean? Yes, we had a meeting yesterday, and he thinks this is something I'm able to do."

I scoff at the idea that she met with that asshole after what happened at dinner last week. How the hell has she not fired him for the shit he said? I lick my lips and pin her with a look. "So, you're not going to have a Boulder residence at all anymore?" I ask, my tone acidic.

"It's really none of your business," Norah quips, and her entire demeanor is giving me serious Elaine Donahue vibes.

"This is a joke." I redirect my anger to Max. "Why are you okay with this, Max? She needed my investment to help launch her franchise."

"We're delaying the franchise plans for now."

"What?" I exclaim and yank my glasses off to gape at him. "What the hell are you doing, Max? You're her franchise director. You should be consulting her better than this."

"Norah is my client, and I'm acting in the best interest of my client. She's still proceeding with the franchise plan…just delaying it for…reasons."

"What kind of reasons?"

"I'm going to Paris if you must know," Norah bites, her voice wavering as she tilts her head and pins me with a fierce look like she's going to claw my face out. "Once the Denver location is up and running, I'm going to take some time and stay with my friend from culinary school and do a little traveling. I want to have some fun and come back fully inspired before I launch."

"But why now?" I groan, running a hand through my hair. "You've been working on this franchise for over a year. You've been dreaming about it for even longer. This is everything you wanted, and it's ready. Why delay now? Because of me? Because of what happened between us?" I ask, not able to hold up the pretenses of a business meeting any longer.

"This isn't about you, Dean," she volleys back, her nostrils flaring. "I've made a pros and cons list over all of this, and I have a solid plan. And now that I don't need working capital for the franchise right away, I can own the bakery outright with no partner."

"But I'm a silent partner."

"Not silent enough." She turns her gaze to stare out the window, looking stiff and hard and nothing like the warm, ball-busting Norah I've grown to know these past couple of years.

I reach out to touch her hand, and she recoils like I've burned her. "You can't do this, Norah."

"Actually, she can." Max winces and pushes the original contract I signed over to me. "It was a part of the agreement that she could buy you out at any time as long as it's a fair offer both parties agree upon. You initialed here."

I don't bother looking at the contract because I don't care what she's offering. "I *know* she can do this, but she shouldn't. There was a reason she sought outside investment. The interest rate she'll pay on a loan to buy me out has to be through the roof."

"It's terrible," she huffs out a laugh.

"Then don't do it." My tone is venturing on begging, but I can't help myself. The idea of not being a part of Norah's life in this way kills me.

She shakes her head and pins me with emotionless eyes. "I learned the hard way not to mix business with pleasure once. I won't do that again."

She stands. "Max, I'll let you iron out the final terms."

"Norah," I call out, but she ignores me as she walks away without a second glance.

I turn to Max and shake my head. "This is fucked up, Max."

"It's what she wants, Dean."

"She doesn't know what she wants."

"Don't be a dick," Max snaps, his eyes narrowing at me. "I realize something must have happened between you two and your stupid arrangement, which I could have told you was a bad idea…but the truth is, she has more business sense in her little finger than every client you have in your hedge fund. Buying you out and owning two bakeries is a lot, but she has a great product and a plan for more great products. She can handle this."

"I know she can handle this, but I hate she's delaying her franchise plans. You know she's ready."

Max shakes his head. "If she wants to travel for inspiration, it's better she does it now than before she starts opening up all over the States. This isn't a bad idea. There's no rush for her franchise. She can have her croinut and eat it too." He shoves the contract in front of me and clicks his pen. "Just sign her offer here. It's a good offer. You're an investment man, and this is a great return on investment. It's a win-win."

"No offer will be good enough." I growl and shove the papers back at him.

"Dean," Max seethes, his voice taking on a harsh tone I rarely hear from him. "Just make this easy on me, please. I have to interview nannies after this because Everly's mom just informed me she has to work overseas this winter, and I seriously don't need to be chasing you down right now."

My brows furrow at that admission. "You need a nanny? Isn't Everly old enough to be home alone?"

"No way," Max scoffs. "You know my crazy hours. I kill myself to clear out the days she's not with her mom, so having her every day and night will be a huge adjustment, and I'll need help. A lot of help. And the owner of this nanny agency is not making this process easy. That woman wears on my last nerve."

"I'm sorry, Max," I reply lamely because this is so not my area of expertise.

"It's not your problem." He waves me off and pushes the contract toward me again. "Just take this off my list, please?"

"I can't do that." I slide out of the booth, my entire body suddenly feeling very weak at everything changing all around me. I went from having it all to having nothing in the blink of an eye, and this isn't what I want. Not by a long shot. "Norah was a good investment, and that's the one I want. End of story."

"Dean, come on." Max holds his hands out helplessly. "You have to at least negotiate with me. Give me a counteroffer I can discuss with her. You owe her that much."

I glare at him and resist the urge to punch him in the nose but instead reply, "I need to think about it."

Max purses his lips. "Just try to hurry. She wanted this buttoned up before the opening in two days."

"Things like this can't be rushed, Max." I turn and walk out, knowing that I don't want to lose my investment in Norah's bakery. If I lose that, I lose her, and I'm not ready to lose her.

CHAPTER 25

Norah

My phone trills as I send off an email confirming my television interview timeslot for Saturday morning. I see it's Nate's name on the caller ID and begrudgingly answer, "Hello?"

"Hey, how did your meeting go today?"

I sigh heavily. "Okay, Max says he's countering, though."

"I'm not surprised," Nate huffs.

"It's annoying, but hopefully he comes back to Max with something soon. I want this over."

"You sound stressed," Nate says and clears his voice before stammering, "Do you w-want to maybe meet for a drink?"

My spine straightens at that request. "Nate, we talked about this."

"I know, I know," he replies, and I can hear him ruffling papers in the background. "But I kept my promise to you, Norah, and our meeting yesterday was strictly business."

"Which is what you deserve after that crap you said at my parents' dinner," I state through clenched teeth. "You're lucky I kept you as my accountant at all. If I wasn't on such a tight deadline with this bakery investment buyout, I would have looked for a new accountant."

"I know. God, I get it," he whines, sounding flustered. "Which is why I want a chance to explain myself, Norah. Explain why I was so horrible. And apologize again."

"Nate, it's not necessary," I reply and then hear the voice of my mother telling me she feels sorry for the guy, and he could use a friend right now. *Ugh...stupid mom voice!*

"Please, Norah? One drink and then you can leave if you want. You and I have a lot of history, and I feel like shit knowing you think I'm such an asshole after all these years."

"Douche purse," I correct.

"What?"

"I think you're a douche purse, or wagon, or canoe, or whatever random object I can tag onto the end of douche." I cringe when I realize I'm talking like Dean.

Nate expels a weak laugh before he asks again. "One drink? And then I promise you can go back to the douche phrases as much as you want."

I agree to meet Nate at Pearl Street Pub, a casual dive bar located up the road from my bakery. It's close and convenient, and frankly, after all the big life decisions I've made in the past forty-eight hours, a drink sounds really good. Plus, I need to celebrate that I'm going to Paris. *I'm actually going to Paris!*

I'm not moving to Paris, but honestly, who moves to Paris without at least visiting it first? No one. And frankly, I have a friend there who practically screamed over FaceTime when I asked her if I could stay with her for a few months, so this is something I should have done ages ago.

My plan is to start in Paris for a few weeks and then spend time in Italy and Switzerland. Um, hello...swiss chocolate! Maybe I'll go to Spain for some tapas and England for some high tea. The sky's the limit. But I plan to keep things open with the overall goal to basically take a food tour of Europe and come back to

America weighing four hundred pounds. It will be worth it. I'll feed my face and my creative soul, and when I return, I'll launch my franchise, full steam ahead.

And who would have thought that the woman to inspire this crazy idea would be Elaine Donahue? Knock me over with a feather.

I stride into Pearl Street Pub and glance around the dark, dingy bar before I spot Nate at the bar in a black suit, clearly having come straight from the office. I tug my jean jacket around my shoulders like a coat of armor and make my way to him.

"Norah," he says and stands to offer me a hug.

I accept because…well, I'm weak. "Hey Nate, how are you?"

"I'm good." He holds the stool out next to him. "What are you drinking?"

I sit up straight when I say, "Champagne if they have it."

The bartender rolls his eyes at my request but brings me over a glass of champagne. I look at it with a smile because I could be drinking bubbly in Paris in a month if all goes well with the Denver bakery.

"Cheers," Nate says and clinks his glass with mine, shooting me a sheepish smile. "Congrats on your second location."

"Thank you," I reply and take a tentative sip because I'm certain it's horribly cheap. It is…but I'm too excited to care.

"It's a huge accomplishment." Nate nods enthusiastically. "And then going to Paris too? Damn, you're living the dream, Norah."

I laugh shyly. "I'm trying to have some fun. I've focused on my goals for so long, I kind of forgot to refill the creative tank in my head, you know?"

"I'm an accountant, so I don't have any idea what you're talking about," he says with a laugh. "But it sounds amazing."

"I hope so." I roll my glass in my hands, and Nate's eyes bore into me.

"I have to tell you again, Norah, how incredibly sorry I am

about that dinner," he rushes out like he could barely hold the words in a second longer.

I take a deep, cleansing breath. "I get it, Nate, but it's not something you can apologize your way out of. It was so inappropriate, especially because I had a boyfriend at the time." I quickly take another sip while trying to ignore the sting of reality that I'm not stating out loud: *My boyfriend was fake.* Very fake. So fake that the idea of us not being fake anymore sent him running for the hills.

But the reality is, nothing about what Dean and I had felt fake to me, which was likely the problem all along. He was living in reality, and I was living in a fantasy.

Nate sets his beer down and pins me with a grave look. "I hope my actions aren't why you and Dean broke up."

"It's not," I state through clenched teeth, still smarting over the fact that Nate knew about my breakup at our business meeting because my mother told his mother. My mom and I may have had a great heart-to-heart, but Elaine Donahue is still painfully on brand.

"There are no secrets between our mothers, I'm afraid," Nate says with a shrug. "And that's part of why I lost my mind at that dinner. You have to understand that my mom has been talking to me about you since the moment I told her I was moving back to Boulder. She told me how successful your bakery was and how you were more beautiful than when we were kids, which I couldn't believe because you were the prettiest girl in our high school."

"I was not," I huff, shaking off that weird compliment.

"You were, Norah. You were stunning and hyper-focused, knowing exactly what you were going to do with your life. I was this French-horn-toting loser you were way too kind to."

"Nate, you weren't that bad."

"Oh my God, I was," he replies with wide eyes. "I was horribly awkward, and you were so nice to me. I couldn't believe you wanted to even…"

"Don't finish that sentence."

He holds his hands up. "I wasn't going to…I promise."

"And please don't mention cookies."

"I won't." He laughs bitterly and stares at his beer. "But I'm telling you all this to make you understand when I showed up to your parents' party and saw you looking more beautiful than I could have imagined *and* you were successful *and* you had a boyfriend…I just…I don't know, I got carried away. I was trying to show off in front of Dean because he looks like a guy who's never struggled with women a day in his life."

"Yeah," I confirm, hating how the mention of Dean's name makes my eyes sting. I've ignored the pain for days, hoping it'll get better, but after seeing him this morning, I realized it's going to be impossible to forget about him. He's unforgettable. "You really didn't need to worry about Dean."

Nate rolls his eyes. "Dean is everything I wish I was."

"Nate," I scoff, shaking my head at his self-deprecation. "You're doing amazing. You're all grown up now and taking over your dad's firm. You're not the same kid you were in high school. Not by a mile, but even if you were, I didn't mind that kid."

"Yeah, I guess." He sullenly takes a drink of his beer, and the slumped posture of this tall, handsome man is painful to look at. "Wish my ex could have seen that."

I reach out and touch Nate's arm. "I think your ex sounds like a bitch."

Nate laughs and gives me a glimpse of the kid I used to play checkers with who didn't have a care in the world. "She kind of was a bitch."

"Then good riddance." I hold my drink out, and we clink again.

"Good riddance." He points at my nearly empty glass. "You want one more, or do you need to get going?"

He waits on bated breath for my answer, and I can't help but see a bit of myself in him. A few weeks ago, I was the awkward, overworked, stressed-out control freak who couldn't manage a social calendar if my life depended on it. But now, I'm changed. I want more. Perhaps Nate is the best drinking companion I can hope for right about now.

I nod and smile. "Let's drink."

Dean

I need IPA.

I need loud music.

I need sticky floors.

I need my clothes not to smell like Norah fucking Donahue and her baked goods.

I throw my arm over Lala's shoulder as we meander down Pearl Street in search of our next bar. It's dark out already, and we've been drinking since five o'clock because Lala turned twenty-one, and I ripped up a contract that my friend Max told me I was under direct obligation to sign.

Fucking Max. What a traitor. I should trade some of his best stocks tonight in retribution for the pain he is causing me.

I won't. But I should.

"Let's go to a dive bar," Lala sings as she points at Pearl Street Pub.

I nod slowly, thinking that's just the sort of stink I need in my life. However, this is Miles's and Sam's favorite place, so I murmur, "Just make sure Kate and Lynsey and that whole crew aren't inside, okay?"

"What?" Lala giggles and pulls me through the door.

I cringe and glance around nervously because the very last fucking thing I need in my life are my two sister wives seeing me out with Lala when they don't have a clue that Norah and I are over. I haven't been returning any of their texts, nor have I updated my fucking social media because, well, I've been busy ripping up half-million-dollar contracts and stuff.

"I don't see them!" Lala squeals as she rushes over to the end of the bar to order drinks.

My gaze follows her, and my eyes squint when I see the back of some very familiar blond hair. It's familiar because I've had my hands wrapped in it several times while driving inside her. My gaze slides over to the guy sitting next to the familiar hair, and I might upchuck the four IPAs I consumed at the last bar.

"Fucking Douche Printer," I grumble quietly as Nate's gaze lands on me.

He frowns and straightens his posture like a peacock trying to show off his stupid feathers. At the same time, the familiar hair turns her head and laughs at something he said, giving me a full view of her stunning profile.

My fucking sugar lips is out with Nate…laughing.

And the hits just keep on coming.

I beeline over to where they're sitting, passing Lala without a second glance, and stop right between Norah and Nate. "Well, hello, you two."

Norah stiffens and turns to look at me, her blue eyes blinking nervously at me. God, she looks good. I saw her this morning, but I swear she's gotten prettier. My eyes drop to see their legs are dangerously close to one another, looking all cozy and happy, like they're having the best night ever.

Must be rough.

"Fancy seeing you guys here." I nod to them and straighten my glasses, noticing Norah has a glass of champagne. "Out celebrating?"

Nate turns in his stool to face me and cocks his head to the side. "It's really none of your business," he says with disdain.

Coming out swinging, Nate. Good for you, buckaroo.

I laugh and shake my head, turning back to Norah. "Well, I ripped up that stupid contract your douche accountant here helped you with, so I can't possibly imagine what you could have to celebrate." I gasp and cover my mouth. "Or are you two out on a date? Did Douche French horn finally get his second chance with you, sugar tits?"

"Dean," Norah growls, finally gracing me with her voice. "Go away. You're clearly drunk."

"And you're clearly too smart and beautiful to be going out with this Douche Beer," I slur and point at Nate. "Seriously, Norah. What the fuck are you doing? You went from not wanting to date anyone to picking the lowest guy on the totem pole?"

"Why do you care?" she snaps, her nostrils flaring as she glares at me.

"Because you're changing into a completely different person, and it seems like you're throwing your life away."

"How am I throwing my life away?" she exclaims, hitting me with wide, wavering eyes. "You're the one who encouraged me to change, remember? You're the one who told me to live a little and have some fun outside of work. What's so wrong with what I'm doing with my life?"

My head jerks forward as I step closer to her, inhaling her sweet scent all over again. "You're throwing away solid investors like me, you're delaying your franchise launch that's going to be amazing, you're selling your fucking apartment, and you're dating a sycophant who brags about plucking girls' cherries."

Nate stands up, closing in on my profile as he grinds out, "Walk away, Dean."

Just then, Lala comes stumbling over with two draft beers, slopping them all over the floor as she sidles up next to me. "An IPA for you, Deano, and a Busch Light for me."

I cringe and begrudgingly take the beer as Norah's eyes slide to Lala and turn into fiery pits of hell. Norah huffs out a sardonic laugh and shakes her head. Without a word, she pulls on Nate's arm to lower him onto his stool and turns away from me.

"Want to play darts?" Lala asks, taking a drink and shaking her hips to the dull bar music.

I stare at Norah's back, dumbfounded that she just turned her back on me like I was nothing. Like I'm nobody. Like I'm not worth fighting for, and what we had didn't matter. How can she be so cold?

I reach out and tap her shoulder. "Norah, we need to talk." My eyes are hooded as memories of being a kid and my parents completely ignoring me flood back in fast and hard.

"No, thank you," Norah says, shaking off my grasp.

"Norah," I growl, and then Nate's back in my face again. "This guy." I shake my head and laugh. "What's up, California Ken? Got something to say to me?"

"You need to leave, Dean."

"You need to leave."

"I was here first, bud."

"I need to talk to her."

"She clearly doesn't want to talk to you."

"Don't you fucking talk to me like you know her." I push him to the side so I can take his seat, and he grabs my arm and whirls me around, causing me to drop my beer.

The glass shatters and Norah turns around, her eyes wide, her lips parted. "Dean, stop it!"

"I didn't do that. Your fucking new boyfriend here did."

"Dean," Norah growls and stands up, setting her champagne down before grabbing me by the hand and yanking me toward the front door, leaving Nate and Lala behind.

Her grip on my hand is a friendship hold, not a waffle hold. I didn't even know what the fuck those stupid terms were until this woman came into my life. And now, that's all she wants from me…a friendship hold. The churning in my belly has me regretting all those beers I had tonight.

She pulls me outside into the darkness, and the blue lights from the interior beer signs illuminate her angelic face. *God, she's pretty.*

"What are you trying to do, Dean?"

"I'm trying to talk to you."

"Why?"

"'Cuz I need to know what's going on with you."

"You don't need to know, Dean. It's none of your business."

"It is my business because you and I are friends."

She flinches at that term and closes her eyes tightly as she shakes her head. "We were friends…maybe…although honestly, that's not true because friends don't treat each other the way you treated me in your house on Sunday morning."

Her words hit me right in the guts, and I groan while running a hand through my hair. "Norah, I'm sorry about that. You have no idea how sorry I am."

"Sorry doesn't mean anything, Dean, because I fell for you, and you rejected me. I can't stay friends with a guy who rejected me. I'm not like Kate and Lynsey. I can't get over it and stay friends."

"You're nothing like Kate and Lynsey," I groan, my head pounding at that realization. "You're…special."

"Don't."

"Don't what?"

"Don't give me the *you're special speech* after you showed up here with Lala. It's all hot air with you. It's all that stupid flirting you did with me in the bakery, back when I was Luke Danes and you were Lorelai Gilmore."

"Wait…I thought I was Luke."

"No, I'm the bakery owner, I'm Luke."

"Why do I have to be the girl?"

"Because you're the colorful, plucky patron who blows in like a freaking storm. You mess everything up, and you leave a wake of destruction behind you."

"What about you, Norah?" I snap, irritated that I'm taking all the blame here. "You said all that shit to me in my house and totally blindsided me with talk of marriage and babies."

"I was speaking hypothetically," she cries loudly, throwing

her arms out dramatically. "I wasn't telling you I wanted to marry you. God, we hadn't been together that long. I was speaking candidly to a *friend* about the fact that my priorities have changed, and I'm open to more now."

I nod slowly, my eyes narrowing. "So, because of that, you're letting your mother play matchmaker? You're gonna be out there dating guys like Douche Curb? Am I going to start seeing you on Pearl Street every night now?"

"I guess so." She shrugs helplessly. "I liked having a boyfriend, fake or real…so the idea of sharing my life with someone doesn't sound so bad. You have Lala, so why can't I find someone too?"

I scowl, anger bubbling up inside me. "So, because you want a serious relationship, you have to cut me out of your business and your life?"

She nods and makes a noise in her throat. "That's the way the croinut crumbles, Dean."

"No…no. This isn't fucking fair, Norah." I take a couple of steps away from her to get some air, some perspective. "We promised each other we could do this. We had an agreement, and you broke that agreement."

"And you ripped up my contract today, so I guess we're both shitty at business," she seethes.

My jaw clenches with frustration. "I hate this. I hate that you're here with him. You deserve better than him, Norah."

"I wanted you." Her voice cracks and breaks my heart into a million tiny pieces as her eyes turn red around the edges.

My voice is hollow and emotionless when I reply flatly, "I'm not good for you."

She steps toward me, her lips trembling, lips I've kissed countless times, lips I want to kiss again as she asks, "Why do you think you're not good for me?"

"Because I'll hurt you." I force myself to look her in the eyes, and it's painful. Like looking at the fucking sun.

She draws in a long breath through her nose. "Why will you hurt me?"

The muscle in my jaw tics incessantly as I swallow the knot in my throat, unwilling to utter the dark truths I know about myself. It's better she doesn't know. It's better she forgets about me and thinks of me as an asshole for the rest of her life. It'll be easier for both of us.

When she realizes I'm not going to answer, she rubs her lips together and takes a step toward the bar door. "I'm going back inside with Nate because at least he can apologize and mean it."

She turns to walk away, and my voice is guttural when I whisper, "I do mean it."

CHAPTER 26

Dean

"**D**ean! Are you in there? Dean!" A loud pounding on my front door causes the ringing in my head to start again.

"Dean, open up!" More pounding…and maybe some kicking.

"I have a spare key, one second."

I roll my eyes and shake my head as my two best friends have a conversation in front of my house about who deserves my spare key, and why don't they both have spare keys, and whoever lives the closest should have the spare key because of emergencies, and since Kate spends all her time at Tire Depot, she thinks she's considered closer even though she doesn't live at Tire Depot, and by the time they get my front door open and step into my living room, I'm wishing I had a chain on my door.

"What the hell?" Kate exclaims, finding me flopped in one of my beanbag chairs in the living room. "He's alive."

Lynsey follows Kate and blinks back her shock. "We thought you were dead."

I roll my eyes and shake my head. "Why do you two go to death? You're so dramatic."

"Because I haven't heard from you since Kate's wedding," Lynsey says, her voice rising in in pitch. "One second, we're doing the Macarena, and then next, you and Norah take off and you ghost me for six straight days. Why haven't you answered my texts?"

"Haven't felt like talking." I shrug and squint up at Kate. "Aren't you supposed to be on your honeymoon?"

She rolls her eyes. "We're waiting until it's cold as balls for a honeymoon, remember? I told you we're doing Hawaii in February."

"Oh yeah."

Kate's eyes lower to the floor beside me. "What is that?"

I make a move to shove the evidence behind me, having forgotten it was there, but Kate's quick like a fucking ninja. She grabs the two boxes off the floor and shows them to Lynsey, who gasps like she's on a telenovela.

"Are those…gas station donuts?" Lynsey screeches like she's just found heroin.

"So what if they are?" I groan, pulling my glasses off and rubbing my eyes. It's way too early in the morning for a dose of these two.

"Dean!" they both peal in unison.

Lynsey flops into the empty chair beside me and touches my arm. "Did you and Norah break up?"

I jerk my head back and blink at her. "What makes you assume that?"

Kate kicks my beanbag and answers for her. "Because you're mowing down shitty donuts like a fucking caged animal when Norah makes the couture of pastries. Jesus. Tire Depot serves better stuff than this."

"What happened?" Lynsey asks with a gentle tone that is way too motherly.

I stare at my television, and mumble, "Nothing."

"Did you two break up?" she asks again, clearly not giving up.

"No." I scoff and roll my eyes. "Not really."

"So, you're still together then?" I glance over and see Lynsey smiling hopefully at me.

"No, actually."

"We don't have all day, Dean," Kate snaps, standing in front of me with a murderous gaze. "Start talking or I'm going to start pouring out your IPA beers in the fridge."

I hit them with the truth. "Norah and I are no longer together because we were not technically a couple. It was all a lie."

"A lie? What do you mean?" Lynsey's wide brown eyes are blinking at me like an innocent little Bambie.

"Norah needed a date for her parents' anniversary party. I needed an approved date for your wedding. Neither of us were interested in a relationship, so we used each other for fake dates."

"But you guys banged in Aspen," Kate blurts out.

I shrug. "It transitioned into something more than just fake dating."

"Like friends with benefits?" Lynsey asks.

I flinch. "Something like that."

"Been there. It's always messy." Kate sits on the floor in front of me. "But I don't get it…you and Norah weren't fake."

"Yes, we were."

"No, you weren't."

"Yes, we were."

"Dean," Kate snaps, pinning me with her blue eyes. "I have a PhD in erotic romance, and you two were not faking a thing. You weren't even faking orgasms. We could hear you guys in Aspen."

I press my lips together. "That last part is true…the rest. All fake."

"Bullshit," Kate counters, shaking her head at me. "You two were the real deal. I'd even say you were in love."

"You don't know what you're talking about." I spit the words out through gritted teeth, hating she's saying everything I've denied for days now.

"No, you don't know what you're talking about," Lynsey

volleys back, her voice rising at the end. "God, Dean, you are so annoying sometimes."

"What the hell did I do to you?"

"You let Norah get away when you're clearly in love with her."

"I'm not in love with her, and I didn't let her get away," I growl and heave myself off my beanbag chair to get some fucking space from these two crazy women in my house. "Norah pushed me away. She's buying out my investment in her bakery so she can get as much space between us as humanly possible."

"Seriously?" Kate asks, looking astonished from her spot on the floor. "Damn, that girl goes big. I'm impressed."

I shake my head in disgust. "She wants nothing to do with me anymore. She said she wants a real boyfriend and a real life with open possibilities. She's going to France to stay with a friend for who knows how fucking long."

"So, go with her. Be with her," Lynsey exclaims, and her hopeful naiveté makes me want to smother my face in a pillow.

My voice is resigned when I reply, "No fucking way, Lynsey. I'd ruin her."

The room goes quiet as Kate and Lynsey gape at me for a long moment.

"Why would you say that, Dean?" Lynsey asks, her voice grave.

I pin her with a look. "You've met my parents, Lynsey."

Her chin juts out, and she shoots a knowing look at Kate. "He's more messed up than we thought."

"Shit, you're right," Kate confirms, standing up and walking closer like she's going to examine me. "I really thought setting him up with someone nice would fix him. Can you do therapy on him, Lyns?"

"Doubtful. He's too far gone."

"Guys, stop talking about me like I'm some charity case. I'm getting really tired of it."

Kate tsks. "You pretty much are."

"Jesus," I groan and turn to walk into the kitchen and grab myself a beer. Who cares that it's only ten o'clock in the morning? "Is it time for you guys to leave yet?"

"We aren't going until we fix this," Kate says matter-of-factly.

"There's nothing to fix." I stand at the counter that I can't look at without thinking about Norah. "I can't be Norah's boyfriend, even if she still wanted me. I said some fucked-up shit to her, and I messed with her mind because selfishly, it felt good to be with her. I let my guard down and ignored all the signs that feelings were involved, which makes me a selfish prick because I knew our fake arrangement was ending." I huff out a self-deprecating laugh. "God...I would have done my father proud."

"You are not your father, you big dumb idiot," Lynsey bellows and holds her hand out to Kate for help out of the beanbag chair. Once Kate's yanked her up, Lynsey stomps over to me with her hands on her hips. God, she really is a mom now. "Dean, you are the warmest, most generous guy I know...I mean, my husband is great, but he's a solid fifty percent dickhead, and I still love him like crazy. You have a much lower dick ratio than Josh, so you certainly deserve love too."

Kate laughs knowingly. "She's not lying, Dean. And you tolerate your mother like a fucking saint. I would have bagged off on her years ago if I were you."

"She's my mom," I state defensively through clenched teeth.

"I know, but give yourself some credit. She's a toxic relationship for you, yet you grin and bear it, treating her with so much unconditional love and respect. You are amazing."

"I feel sorry for her. I mean, Jesus, look what blind love did to her. She's so bitter she can't hold down a functional relationship. If I turned into that or, God forbid, I turned Norah into that...I'd never be able to forgive myself." The image of Norah turning into my mother slices through me like a knife.

"Dean," Lynsey groans, pain evident in her voice. "You are not your mother or your father. You are your own person. Just as Kate and I are our own persons. Do you look at the two of us and think our marriages are going to fail?"

"No," I huff honestly. "You guys found unicorns or whatever. Kate, you love Miles's macho alpha male, jealous bullshit, and Lynsey, you're the perfect antidote for Dr. Dick's psycho intensity."

"And you pulled Norah out of her shell more than I've ever seen her," Kate states sincerely as she pins me with a serious look. "I've seen Norah at Rise and Shine Bakery for years, and she's never looked as happy as she did when she was with you. You two were in your own little world. It was adorable. And she really cut loose with us girls in Aspen. I mean, when she put that mint oil on her vajayjay, I swear to God, I almost peed my pants."

"I did pee my pants," Lynsey confirms with a giggle. "Having a baby totally messed up my bladder control. But the wet pants were worth it because we had so much fun with Norah."

I shake my head sadly because I knew she would fit in with my friends without even trying. But it doesn't silence that voice in my head that says, "But what if I hurt her?"

"It might happen," Kate says urgently as she walks over and grabs my arm so I look at her. "Both Lynsey and I have had moments where our relationships looked like they were doomed. But have you forgotten that you were the guy helping us put it all back together?"

I cringe as I think back to that stupid carburetor Kate, Lynsey, and I drove up into the mountains to find for Miles when Kate had screwed up royally with him. And hell, I took a punch to the face from Dr. Dick on Lynsey's behalf, so I guess it's easier for me to help them with their problems than it is for me to accept their help with my own.

"We'll help you through all the bumps, Dean," Kate adds, pinning me with so much sincerity I almost can't believe it's her. "Because every day you give your heart to someone, there's a chance you won't get it back. But every time they give you their heart in return…it makes the risk totally worth the reward. We all take risks with love every day."

"God, that was beautiful." Lynsey sighs.

"I'm a writer," Kate says firmly.

I shake my head at her ridiculousness. "What if it's too late? She's doing everything she can to stay away from me. She's going to fucking Paris for a few months."

"Then go with her. Or wait for her. Or do long distance. But don't let her go and meet a hot, sexy Parisian man and come home with a guy who has a bigger baguette than yours."

"God, did you have to paint that visual?" Lynsey cringes with her nose wrinkled.

"Yes. I told you, I'm a writer," she deadpans.

"So, what can I do then?" I ask, trying to redirect their focus because I'm starting to feel something intense in my gut that might have been there all along, but I ignored it because I didn't realize what it was every time I looked at Norah. Grandpa always said your gut knows what your head hasn't figured out yet.

"Her grand opening is tomorrow, right?" Kate asks, turning away and beginning to pace in my kitchen.

"Yeah, and she has a TV interview in the morning she wanted me to go with her to until I fucked everything up."

Kate rubs her hands together conspiratorially. "In a romance novel, that's the perfect moment for an epic grand gesture. Who's ready to plot?"

CHAPTER 27

Norah

"Okay, the chamber of commerce people are going to be here for the ribbon cutting any minute. Places everyone," I call out to the staff we've hired to help for the grand opening today.

It's nearing four o'clock, and our grand opening celebration is from four until six, starting with a ribbon cutting, a short welcome speech by me, and then free croinuts for the first hundred people who walk in the door.

"Oh my God, Norah, the line of people is wrapped around the building now! There has to be over a hundred out there."

"I told you to stop updating me about the line, Rachael," I exclaim and begin to fan my face to stop the crazy lip sweat that's forming. "I'm sweating like a pig here. I knew Denver was going to be bigger than Boulder, but I didn't know it would be like this."

"The sweat is giving you a nice sheen because you look beautiful, girl," Rachael says, appraising my white pantsuit. "This is what you wore for your TV segment earlier, right? How did that go? We were too busy here to watch."

"It was amazing," I squeal excitedly, forgetting all manner of professionalism on a day like today. "I made fresh croinuts on camera. And the hosts and I had great chemistry. The producer said they are sending a TV crew out to film the ribbon cutting to air on their five o'clock news."

"Holy shit, a morning segment and an evening news segment? That's incredible," Rachael exclaims, looking as excited as I am.

"I know." I exhale and try to collect myself. "How's the staff doing? Everything ready to go, you think?"

"Yep, Zander is cracking the whip. The first fifty croinuts are ready, and the next are on the fly."

"Okay, but we're still—"

"Having everyone take a number for the full experience. We got it, boss!"

I huff out a laugh and hit Rachael with a meaningful look because she's become so much more than my right-hand lately. She's become my closest friend through the whole Dean fiasco. "I could not do any of this without you. I'm sorry I've been so up and down lately."

"Don't apologize for living your life." She waves me off as she heads back toward the kitchen to help out. "You worked hard to enjoy today, so try to relax. Go have some coffee."

"Good idea," I call back as she disappears. My heels clunk on the freshly waxed black and white tiles as I make my way behind the counter to pour myself a drink. I need it after the mania of today.

The TV interview did go great this morning, but what I didn't tell Rachael was that I had a stupid girly dream last night that Dean would show up at my segment and just…be in the audience watching. In my dream, his presence was his apology, and he walked up to me in the middle of filming and told me he loved me.

Then I woke up and realized it was all a dream. I live in reality, and the reality is, Dean doesn't want me. Fake dating each other was a harebrained idea, and I should have known it would end in heartbreak.

But even with the pain I feel in my chest every time I think of him, I can't help but be grateful this heartbreak inspired some changes in my life. Changes I'm crazy excited about. Rachael is taking over Boulder while I get Denver up and running. The manager I hired here seems charged and ready to take over once I head to Paris. Things are going to be okay.

"Hey, Norah," Max's voice calls out from the front door, and I swerve over to see him striding toward me. He does a wide gesture around the space, stepping out of the way of one of our workers doing a last-minute wipe down of the tables. "Wow… this looks amazing."

"I know, right?" I reply with a smile and make my way around the counter to join him. "It really came together. It's got the Boulder feel but with a more commercial, edgy punch. Should be a good dummy for the franchise portfolio."

"Definitely," he says with a smile as his eyes widen. "Did you see that line outside?"

He hooks his thumb behind him making me cringe and force myself to avoid the windows. "I quit looking outside an hour ago. The bigger the line gets, the more my heart tries to crawl into my throat. It's in survival mode right now."

Max laughs at that. "Well, you have about forty of your personal guests all waiting outside in that roped-off area, and the chamber people said they are ready when you are, so I can escort you out whenever you say the word."

He has a peculiar look in his eye, and I know why. "Dean didn't sign the contract, did he?" I clench my teeth and shake my head in frustration. "He had to ruin this day, didn't he? I wanted to cut that ribbon and tell that crowd out there that this place is mine. This concept, this idea is all mine and that I didn't need him…or anybody else to…ugh! It doesn't matter. Today is a good day, and I'm not going to let him spoil it."

Max pulls a cream envelope out from behind his back. "Actually, he signed it."

My lips part as pins and needles erupt over my entire body. "He did?"

"Yep. With your original terms and everything."

With shaky hands, I take the envelope and glance at the contract, hating the fact that my chin is trembling. I frown at Dean's familiar handwriting and hate that this moment isn't making me jump for joy. Tears form in my eyes, and I do my best to push them away. "I don't know why I'm sad right now."

Max hits me with a sympathetic smile. "Maybe because Dean's a good guy."

"I know he is." And that's the part that kills me inside.

Max huffs out a noise and hits me with an all-business look. "Congratulations, Norah Donahue, you are now the proud owner of two Rise and Shine Bakeries."

I smile, but it doesn't feel as sincere as it should. "Thanks, Max. Tell the chamber people I'm right behind you."

He takes the contract and gives me a tight nod before I steel myself to walk outside and live in the moment, no matter the emotions warring inside my heart.

Dean

Norah steps out the front door of Rise and Shine-Denver, and the small crowd of people gathered in the roped-off area applaud, along with the hundred people lined up around the block for a croinut. I duck behind the large speaker and notice that Norah's face falls when she spots the giant stage setup with rock-concert-level equipment right in the middle of the blocked-off street.

She points out the setup to Max, and he waves her off as he introduces her to the chamber people. They have a small microphone with a tiny amp that makes the professional equipment

I'm hiding behind look obscene as they do their little welcome speech.

I spot Norah's parents front and center along with Nate and his parents, plus Kate and Lynsey, and Miles and Josh, who's got a squealing Julianna on his shoulders practically frothing at the mouth for her next sugar fix.

My eyes drift back to Norah as she listens to the chamber person rattle on about her business. She looks stunning in that white suit. It's sexy but professional and gives me vibes of those stupid baker's ponchos she normally wears but a million times better. She's smiling and nervous, still trying to figure out what the hell the setup is behind all her guests who are seemingly here for her. My gut twists because I know this crazy plan Kate, Lynsey, and I dreamed up could go epically awesome or epically horrible.

Norah takes the microphone and welcomes everyone to Rise and Shine Bakery. She tells them about her recipe and the different flavors she will have to offer. Today's flavor is caramel apple with a flaked dark chocolate finish. She says a lot of the things she said during her morning show feature that I watched with rapt fascination.

God, she's incredible.

It was at that moment I knew I had to sign her stupid buyout contract. Even if it was unnecessary for her to buy me out, she deserves to own this success all on her own if that's what she wants.

Finally, the crowd applauds as Norah cuts the ribbon and laughs along with everyone as she holds up the giant scissors. There's a TV crew and a photographer nearby, snapping photos like crazy, but before she steps back to let everyone inside to enjoy the party, Max reaches for the microphone, much to Norah's confusion.

"Thank you all for being here today," Max says, yelling into the mic so I can hear him from my location. "And I promise we're going to let you eat very soon, but first, we have a special surprise for you that even Norah doesn't know about."

Norah's face is fucking adorable as she attempts to look amused and not totally fucking freaking out. But I know Norah, she had a list of everything that needed to be done today, and whatever is happening was not on the list, so she's losing her shit.

Max smiles and continues, "A mutual friend of ours was able to pull some strings to make this treat happen…so, while you're inside getting your sweet treats and helping yourself to some complimentary champagne, please put your hands together to welcome the musical stylings of Foreigner!"

Norah's face contorts into this strange mix of anger and confusion. Honestly, it's not attractive, which attracts me to her even more. I step out from behind the speakers as the band all take their places. Their road crew got here an hour ago and busted ass to set up, bitching about our shitty stage quality while I profusely apologized and told them I did the best I could in only twenty-four hours. I made sure to repeat how glad I was they could be here. Even if I had to pad some lady's pocket at the city hall in order to rush a permit request for live music. *And, holy shit, Foreigner is playing at Norah's grand opening right now!*

The lead singer walks up to the mic, and says, "Who's hungry?"

The crowd of people in front of the ribbon and wrapped around the building all cheer so loudly, people from nearby streets begin walking over to see what's going on.

"Cool," the lead singer says. "Hey, can someone please take a number for us because we'd all love a caramel apple croinut after we're done here?"

Everyone cheers, and I see Norah making her way through the parted crowd, her face still the picture of confusion.

"We had a request for some of our power ballads, so I hope you all enjoy a little song we call, 'I Want To Know What Love Is.'"

By the time the band hits the chorus, Norah is front and

center, gaping at the band with tears in her eyes while everyone swarms around her to cheer the band on. I move to the edge of the stage and can't help but fixate on Norah as the passion she has for this music falls freely down her cheeks. She's mesmerized. Rachael begins jumping and dancing as the music picks up, and Norah laughs and half-heartedly joins her, still shaking her head in bewilderment.

Then it's as if she senses me watching because suddenly, she turns and finds me through the small crowd, standing down below the left side of the stage back behind the speakers. She wipes away her tears as she weaves through the crowd, passing by Kate and Lynsey. By the time she reaches me, my heart is in my chest.

She points beside her as colorful stage lights illuminate her silhouette. "That's Foreigner."

"I know," I reply with a laugh.

She blinks back and shakes her head. "They want a croinut."

"I know." My belly shakes with laughter. God, she's beautiful.

She runs a hand through her hair and glances back to them as they shift over to "Feels Like The First Time" next. "Do you know how this happened?"

I jam my hands into my slacks and step closer to her so she can hear me over the speakers. "They were supposed to have a show with Kansas tonight in Denver, but the lead singer of Kansas got sick so the concert was rescheduled. And Foreigner was just...I don't know...chilling at a bar somewhere? Max knows a guy who knows them."

"Max does?" she asks, her jaw dropped.

"Yeah, it's all kind of serendipitous how it came together, and I had to jump through a million hoops to block the road off and get a live music permit at the last minute. Plus, the band likes Fresca, which is not easy to find, but I found it." Norah blinks back at me, clearly still too stunned to fully comprehend everything I'm saying so I keep rambling to fill the silence. "And hey, they didn't have any bandanas, but they have T-shirts, and I bought you a bunch, so I figured maybe you can cut one that's the size of a bandana so you can wear it at the bakery if—"

"Dean," she cuts me off, blinking her wide, tear-streaked eyes at me. "I thought you were more of a yacht rock guy."

"What?"

"Nothing," she shakes her head quickly, visibly clearing her thoughts as she refocuses on me. "Why did you do all this?"

I swallow my pride and say the words I came here to say, "Because I want you back."

Norah's lips part, and she presses her hand to her chest like she might actually be gasping for air. "But you said—"

I cut her off, not wanting to hear her repeat the horrible things I said. She deserves the truth. "I said nothing because I was too scared to tell you I'm terrified I could hurt you the way my dad hurt my mother."

She bites her lip, her eyes bending with sympathy. "Dean, you're not your father."

"I know," I reply and take a step closer, my hand itching to touch hers but holding back because I still don't know what she's thinking. "But I have a dark passenger inside me, you know? That asshole can flare up sometimes and really fuck shit up. I know apologies are fucking bullshit, and the things I said to you can never be erased, but you have to know the truth, Norah, because I've been lying to myself for way too long."

"Lying about what exactly?" she asks, tilting her head like she's trying to read my mind.

"About my feelings for you. Even before you and I started fake dating…all that stupid flirting I did, the reason I invested in your franchise and came to work in your bakery all the time. Norah, my gut knew you were worth taking a risk on in more ways than just business. I'm so sorry it took my head this long to figure out I'm in love with you."

She inhales a sharp breath and steps back like she's going to bolt. "You don't mean that."

"I do mean that." I step forward and grab her hand with desperation laced in my voice. "And look, I know dropping the love bomb is a lot today and you're opening a new bakery and going to Paris, and God, I do not want to hold you back from that. But since you forced me to sell my investment back to you, I thought maybe we could do a new contract that says I can be your long-distance boyfriend and visit you in Paris and fight off any Parisians with big baguettes."

"What?" She shakes her head with a pinched smile of confusion, so I elaborate as tears fill her eyes.

"I just want to see you because I'm in love with you, and I miss you even right now as you stand in front of me," I rush out and add stupidly, "And I swear I will not hold you back from getting that fat ass in Paris that your mother would hate."

She laughs and then kind of groans, and then tears are coming down, and *fuck*, I can't tell if I'm winning or losing right now. With a deep breath, she steps into my arms and wraps her hands around my head. Burying her face in my neck, she wafts her perfect sweet, vanilla scent all over me. Her face wiggles against my collarbone, and I pull back slightly to ask, "Are you wiping your lip sweat off on my shirt?"

"Yes," she croaks into my neck with a laugh. "There's a camera crew filming us right now."

"Okay, cool, just checking." I pull back and see a smile that looks very promising. "And?"

"And I think I might love you too, but I might write a pros and cons list just to be sure," she says quietly and thoughtfully and so fucking on brand.

"I'm good with that." I press my forehead to hers and breathe in the sweetest relief I've ever felt in my entire life. "Is it cool if I kiss you now, or would you rather I not because of the cameras?"

She smiles up at me. "Let's give 'em a show."

CHAPTER 28

Norah

"**H**oly shit, if I knew you were getting a place this nice for your temporary Denver digs, I would have totally agreed to be your boyfriend last weekend."

"I'm going to kill you." I smile through my threat because I can't help it. Tonight was easily the best night of my life. And not just because Foreigner played at my bakery opening.

Okay, it's mostly because Foreigner played at my bakery opening. But it's also because Dean is here, in my new Denver pad, walking around like a boyfriend.

"How can you threaten murder on me?" Dean asks, slipping off his suit coat and making his way into my kitchen. "I had Foreigner play for the grand opening of your bakery. There were at least four news crews that showed up tonight because of that surprise performance. How many interviews did you do?"

"Five." I cringe as I drape my jacket over a nearby barstool and ditch my heels.

"And how many did you tell it was your boyfriend who pulled out all the stops for your big day?" Dean lowers his glasses and pins me with a look.

"Only one, but I was nervous. I wasn't prepared for any of this tonight, and you know I do better with prep."

Dean sighs and shakes his head. "You're just lucky I love you."

My face scrunches up at his words because I still can't get used to them. Tonight was unimaginably awesome. We danced, we drank champagne, and I gave tours of the bakery to my friends and family while having Dean beside me the entire time. Even my mother gave Dean a very nice hug when she saw him again, a very big step for the ice queen. Nate steered clear of us, which was definitely for the best. I might end up needing a new accountant by the end of all this, but we'll see how things progress over the next few months first.

And Kate and Lynsey...my God, you'd have thought they were attending Dean's and my wedding. They looked so happy watching us holding hands and visiting with customers that I felt like I kind of gained a couple of sisters all of the sudden. Josh even passed off sweet Julianna to me so I could walk her up to the machine to take a number for her and her dad to have a croinut. It was a perfect grand opening.

And speaking of croinuts, we closed down the night after making four hundred and seventy-two in only four hours. Not bad for a first day. In fact, it was pretty epic.

And I knew the minute Dean kissed me as Foreigner played behind us that I didn't need to make a pros and cons list to know I was in love with this man. The proof is in the croinut.

"I still can't believe Foreigner came in and had croinuts in my bakery!" I flop down on the long black sofa in the living room that connects to the kitchen and dining room. I swipe through the eighty photos I had Rachael take of me with the band. "This picture is so going on the wall in the bakery."

Dean ditches his shoes and socks and joins me on the couch to glance through the pictures with me. "It's really crazy how well everything worked out tonight."

"Thank goodness for Max." I shut my screen down to look at him.

"You mean, thank goodness for Dean," Dean corrects me,

looking offended. "It was my idea. Do you know how many palms I had to grease to get the permit and the equipment out there with only a twenty-four-hour notice? This whole thing wouldn't have happened without your boyfriend being awesome."

I quirk a knowing brow at him. "This whole thing wouldn't have had to happen if my boyfriend would have stayed my boyfriend."

Dean wilts slightly but then wraps his arms around me and pulls me into his chest. "Hey, we should try that makeup sex thing again. We were pretty good at that if I remember correctly."

I pull back and turn to face him. "I think we should talk first."

Dean winces and takes off his glasses to pinch the bridge of his nose before turning to give me his full attention. "Kate and Lynsey warned me this was something boyfriends had to do a lot."

"What else did Kate and Lynsey say?" I tilt my head and eye him curiously. "Seriously, I want to know. I mean…the band and you showing up and saying everything you said was…amazing. But I want to make sure this is real, Dean. That you're genuinely ready for this."

"I'm ready, sugar butt." Dean reaches out and grabs my hands, twining his fingers with mine in a way that sends goose bumps up my wrist. "I realized a lot of things this past week."

"Like the fact that Lala is way too young for you, and you were an asshole for going out with her again?" I pin him with an accusatory stare, and Dean cringes and nods his head.

"I didn't mean to be out with her," he groans, his voice laced with frustration. "I was drinking alone, drowning my sorrows, and she came into the bar. I was so drunk at that point that I didn't think about who I was with. I ditched her after you left… you have to believe that nothing happened between us."

"I believe you," I reply, the corner of my mouth quirking up with relief over the fact that trusting Dean has never been an issue for me.

"And you and Captain Douche Cookie?" His eyes turn dark as he asks the silent question.

I sigh, knowing this was coming. "It wasn't a romantic outing."

"You didn't give me that impression at the bar," he replies, his sulky lip sticking out adorably.

I reach out and tug on it. "You didn't deserve to know what I was doing because you didn't want me." I jut my chin at him defiantly.

"I always wanted you," Dean says, running his hand up and down my thigh as his eyes rove over every one of my features. "It just took me a minute to realize that all the shit my mom has said to me over the years about me being like my father and being bad for women has kind of stuck. I used to think it rolled right off my back, but clearly, it didn't. I'm planning to have a big talk with her about how her comments are affecting me. Her baggage can't be mine."

"I think that's great." I jerk my head in amazement at how mature and adult he sounds. Dean is normally the guy looking to have fun. Peter Pan syndrome through and through. This is certainly something he's given some serious thought to. "And you know, I'd love to meet your mom sometime if you're ready for that. Maybe it'll help to see you with a girlfriend."

Dean's eyes dance with affection. "She would actually love to meet you. And she's not so bad when she's not talking about my dad."

I squeeze his hand, feeling like we're already off to a great start. Dean pulls my hand up and kisses it tenderly before adding, "And I want you to know when I told you I felt unsafe with you, it's because the stakes are high here. I don't want to hurt you or for you to hurt me."

My chin trembles at the vulnerability in his voice. "I feel the same way."

He nods and squeezes my hand. "But Kate says love is worth taking a risk, and she has a self-proclaimed PhD in romance."

I huff out a laugh. "As long as she doesn't suggest swinging, she gives out solid advice."

Dean kisses my hand again and looks around. "So, you're selling your Boulder apartment for sure? Is that really necessary?"

I sigh and sit back to take in the place we're in. "I kind of want to find a place farther away from the bakery. I need better boundaries in my life, you know?"

Dean nods thoughtfully. "And…Paris?"

"Paris," I repeat with a grin.

He reaches over and tucks a stray hair behind my ear. "That will be awesome for you."

I turn my face into his hand to kiss his palm. "I'm thinking Denver should be settled in a month, and then I can probably book my flight." I narrow my eyes at him and add, "Do you really want to come out and visit me?"

"Fuck yes, I do," he replies with a frown and puffs his chest out like a caveman. "I'm not letting your sexy ass run the streets of Paris alone."

"Is that right?" I can't stop smiling.

"Yes," he growls and grabs my waist, pulling me onto his lap to straddle him. His eyes burn with possession as he adds, "I'll give you space to do your thing, but not too much."

"That sounds good." I splay my hands out on his chest and lean down to brush my lips against his, wondering how I could ever want space from this man. I pull back and murmur into his ear. "You might be sick of me in a month anyway."

"You might be sick of me," he volleys back, letting out a little groan as he tastes my neck and slips his hands under the back of my shirt.

I inhale his perfect scent as though it was made just for me. "I doubt that."

"I doubt that too."

He undoes the clasp of my bra with very little effort, and my nipples are hard as stone as my breasts point directly at what I want. I straighten on his lap as he pulls my top and bra off and growls when his eyes feast on my breasts. He tosses his glasses to the side before leaning in to suck each nipple into his mouth in long, luxurious kisses. His chin whiskers cause delicious prickles to alight all over my chest as I grab his head and pull him closer.

"Dean," I moan as my hips gyrate on his lap, my panties soaking with arousal as he continues worshipping my breasts, his hands clutching my sides possessively. "Dean," I cry out again and pull his face up to look at me before I say, "Make love to me."

"God, yes," he croaks, and suddenly, he stands, holding me around his waist as he makes his way down the hallway toward the bedroom.

Dean drops me onto the bed and makes quick work of his clothes and the rest of mine. He crawls over me and kisses me fiercely, possessively, his lips reacquainting themselves with mine as his silky erection slides between us.

"I need you inside me," I beg against his lips.

"One more kiss," he says, rubbing his nose against my cheek before finding my lips again. "God, I missed you," he growls as he pulls away and positions his tip between my legs.

"I missed you too," I groan out as he drives into me hard and fast, stilling inside me like he wants to lie here and live for a while.

My hands clutch his back as I will him to move, and he gets the message. He pumps in and out slow and steady, moving his mouth to kiss my neck and collarbone and any other part of my body he can reach while still remaining firmly connected down below.

Our cries of passion fill the room as we both succumb to the coiled tension inside us. When I shatter around him, I grip his back so hard I'm certain I'll leave bruises, and at the same time, he swells inside me and then shudders his own release.

We both heave for breaths together, and I can't help the contented smile that lifts the corners of my mouth.

Dean pulls back and looks at me, pressing a sweet kiss to my lips. "You happy, sugar lips?"

"Definitely," I reply, wrapping my legs tighter around him and wishing we could stay in this moment forever.

"Want to go again?"

"Definitely."

CHAPTER 29

Dean

A few months later

"**D**ean!" Norah's voice calls out from behind me, and I turn away from the luggage carousel to see her running toward me, full steam ahead. I drop my carry-on in time to catch her as she barrels into my chest, arms tight around my neck, legs snug around my hips.

She's like my own little spider monkey.

I band my arms around her waist and turn my freshly shaven face into her neck and hair to inhale deeply. Thank fuck Paris hasn't changed her scent. *God I've missed this smell.*

I've missed this woman.

It's been two months since she left Boulder, and I only had six weeks with her before she left. It wasn't enough. I didn't come close to getting sick of her. Not even when she talked me into staying with her in Denver when the bakery ended up requiring more of her time than she originally anticipated.

"Oh my God, I can't believe you're actually here!" she cries into my shoulder, her body shaking against mine.

I laugh and squeeze tighter before lowering her back to the ground. "Let me get a look at you," I say, pushing back the hair from her face that's grown out a lot since she left eight whole weeks ago. "You look well-traveled."

She smiles and wraps her arms around my waist, pulling me close. "Well, I am…I've been to six countries since I've arrived."

"And which city is your favorite?" I ask, pinning her with a look.

Her eyes warm as she reaches up and cups my face in her hand. "I'm going to have to go with Boulder."

"You are such a suck-up," I growl and dip my head to kiss her.

Holy fucking hell, it's been too long since I've felt these lips. Way too fucking long. It's amazing how easy it was to fall into a relationship with Norah.

I reach around her and grab her ass, giving it a hearty squeeze right in front of all the other people waiting for their luggage.

She squeals and swats me on the chest, effectively breaking our kiss. "What are you doing?"

"I'm seeing if that big ass you're working on is coming along nicely."

"Well, stop…there are people around."

"Don't care," I reply, dropping a kiss to her nose. "Besides, isn't this the city of love? Surely, a cheeky ass grab isn't that shocking."

We retrieve my luggage from customs and make our way out to the bank of taxis on the curb. Norah sits in the middle of the back seat, our bodies entwined as she talks a mile a minute, pointing out various landmarks as we make our way to her friend Chelle's pied-à-terre.

It's incredible being near Norah again. It's shocking how I've lived most of my adulthood avoiding relationships, and the minute I find myself in one, she bags off to Paris for three months. I wanted to come out and surprise her a month ago, but I held back. She and Chelle were doing some amazing backpacking, and as much as I missed her, I didn't want to be *that guy* who couldn't let his girlfriend off the leash for too long.

But now that I'm here, she's going to have to fight me off with a stick.

Norah bites her lip and shoots me a wicked smile. "I have a surprise for you."

"What?" I ask, waffling our fingers together as we pull down a residential street.

"Chelle is away for the full two weeks you're here. She found someone to cover for her at the restaurant, and she's staying with a friend in Belgium."

"You're kidding," I growl, dipping my head in to kiss her lips. "So, you're saying we have her place to ourselves for two whole weeks?"

"Yep," Norah chirps as I bite her neck and suck a little.

God, I seriously need to get her naked, fast.

The driver turns down several weird angled streets before stopping at a tall apartment building with tiny terraces and café-lined squares outside of it. After we grab my bags, I follow Norah inside the lobby of the building, and by the time the elevator door closes, my lips are on her again as she struggles to press the button for the fourth floor. When it chimes, indicating we've arrived, she grabs my shirt and drags me down the narrow hallway to the street-view apartment.

I barely see the flat before Norah and I are dropping bags and stripping off our clothes.

"Shower," I murmur as I pick her up and follow her finger in the right direction. "I smell like an airplane."

"Not to me," Norah cries, raking her hands through my hair as she kisses me fiercely.

The water takes an insane length of time to get hot, and the two of us stand awkwardly staring at each other before breaking into belly laughs. When it's finally hot, it's game on again as I step inside the small shower stall and press her up against the wall, wasting no time before pushing deep inside her.

"Oh God, Dean," she cries as the hot water pours on top of

us, and my dick gets reacquainted with its favorite place in the world.

"Fuck, Norah…I missed you."

"I missed you," she whimpers as I pull out and thrust back inside her, holding her up and rocking her against my hips in quick, rapid succession.

It takes less than three minutes for her to find her release, which is a fucking miracle because I explode seconds later, emptying myself as I press my wet face into her wet chest and let the sound of the water drown out my heavy breathing.

When I put her down, she has a coy smile on her lips that I know all too well. "What are you smiling about, sugar butt?"

"Nothing." She giggles as she grabs the shampoo and proceeds to lather up my scalp before adding, "I better get a twenty-minute dick before you leave in two weeks."

I pinch her sides, and she squeals with laughter, turning her hip into my dick and causing it to come back to life again. "If someone would participate in video sex more often, perhaps I would have been better prepared."

"Just wait until you hear how thin these walls are," she exclaims, hitting me with her wide, blue eyes. "Even my pretty in pink vibrator is on sabbatical."

"Thank fuck Chelle is gone, because this would have been a seriously awkward two weeks for her since I can't manage to keep my hands off you." I dip my head and kiss her while squeezing her ass in my hands. God, it feels good to be back in the same time zone again.

We finish showering, and Norah shows me her bedroom that used to be Chelle's office. It's small, but it has its own terrace, and Norah said she spends her mornings out there doing bookwork for the bakeries and organizing things back home.

After round two in her bedroom, Norah makes some croissant sandwiches and opens a bottle of wine that we enjoy on the terrace and take in the view of several people milling about shopping, eating, and having a drink in the middle of the day. At least three pastry shops are within eyesight, and as I glance over and connect eyes with Norah, I can't help but say, "Paris suits you."

"Yeah?"

I nod and take a sip of my wine. "You're glowing."

She narrows her eyes at me. "That might be the orgasms I just had."

A smug smile spreads across my face that likely has to do with my own orgasms as well. "Video chatting is nice, but it pales compared to seeing you in the flesh. You look so beautiful and very relaxed here."

"I feel it." She exhales heavily like she's drinking in that emotion. "I didn't realize how overwhelmed I was with both the opening of the second bakery and launching the franchise so soon after."

"It was a lot." I tilt my head and eye her thoughtfully. "Are you having any second thoughts about doing the franchise at all?"

"No," Norah exclaims, her eyes wide. "God, no. Actually, with how great the Denver location is doing, I'm more excited to get the franchise moving."

"You just needed a break first," I deduce.

"Exactly." She peers down at the courtyard of people sipping coffee and gets a faraway look in her eyes. "This has been totally rejuvenating for me, and now I'm kind of excited to go back home and kill it."

"Thank fuck, because I'm ready for you to come home," I grumble with a desperate tone to my voice that I don't care if she hears. "Life is boring without you."

Her shoulders scrunch up around her ears as she giggles. "I can't say Paris is boring, but it just got a *lot* more fun now that you're here." She pins me with a sincere look, and our gazes lock for a long, lingering moment, urging me to throw her over my shoulder and take her right back to bed.

But I'm here to see my girl in Paris, and that's what we're going to do. "So, talk to me about what we're doing for the next two weeks. Where are we headed? I know you have an itinerary hidden somewhere, so whip it out already."

"That sounds dirty," Norah squeals before ducking inside and grabbing her yellow legal pad. She returns and flops down in her seat, looking like she's getting ready to run a board meeting. "But you're right…I have it all mapped out."

"How very on brand of you." I wink at her.

"And I have some rules," she says, biting her lip nervously.

My brows furrow at that. "Rules?"

She nods and flips the page, squinting at her handwriting. "Yes… rules for a newly-in-love couple to make it through a two-week European vacation together."

"This should be good," I groan and straighten out my glasses in preparation.

"Number one, waffle hand-holding only. Number two, sex every night and morning."

"Mornings too?" I reply with a smirk. "My, aren't we demanding in Paris?"

She points her pen at me accusingly. "You got me addicted to morning sex in Aspen."

"Oh, so it's my fault," I huff with a laugh.

"Everything is your fault, Dean." She shoots me a mischievous wink. "Okay, number three, no going to bed angry. We talk it out until we can fuck it out."

"That's a Boulder rule too, so I already agree to that one."

Things became a little tense back home before Norah left on her trip. She was stressed about leaving the bakeries, and I was stressed about her leaving me, and…well…we had a fight. But it was okay, because my dark passenger stayed firmly in his place, and we were able to work through everything all in one night.

I'm learning how to be a good boyfriend one step at a time.

And honestly, talking with my mom about everything was a

big part of that. She felt horrible when I told her that the things she said made me feel unworthy of love. She even cried, which was a little manipulative on her part. I held strong and told her if she wanted to meet Norah and be a part of our lives, she needed to take accountability for the baggage she pushed off on me about Dad.

I am not my father.

I am not my father.

And strangely enough, the time we've spent with Norah's parents has given me a great example of what a long-lasting love can look like. Jeff is a man I strongly admire because he's selfless with his wife and madly in love with her and all her neurotic, overbearing tendencies. And as much as I would never *ever* say this to Norah, she reminds me of Elaine in a lot of ways. Which means I can learn a lot from watching Norah's dad. He's the kind of husband I want to be someday.

I exhale heavily at that thought because that's a new idea that's been creeping inside me ever since Norah left for Paris. Being her boyfriend has been incredible, but the more time we spend together, in person or even via video calls, the more I can see the appeal of putting a ring on her finger.

What can I say? I'm a man in love.

"Rule number four," Norah says, pulling me out of my internal reverie, "kisses constantly. This is France, and if you're not kissing, you're not living."

I lean over the small table between us and make good on that rule right away. The kiss ramps up into a deep, drugging embrace that makes me want to forget her itinerary and just spend two weeks in this apartment together. Have I mentioned I missed her?

When we pull apart, her upper lip has a nice sheen on it, and I smile proudly. "I like that rule."

"Last rule," she croaks, gazing into my eyes with a warmth I can feel in my bones. "Always say I love you."

"I love you." I state it softly and with a deeper feeling than I could have imagined having for another person. "I love you."

The End

More from the Wait With Me Boulder Crew:

Wait With Me—Kate & Miles

Next In Line—Maggie & Sam

One Moment Please—Lynsey & Dr. Dick

MORE BOOKS BY
AMY DAWS

The London Lovers Series:
Becoming Us: Finley's Story Part 1
A Broken Us: Finley's Story Part 2
London Bound: Leslie's Story
Not the One: Reyna's Story

A London Lovers/Harris Brothers Crossover Novel:
Strength: Vi Harris & Hayden's Story

The Harris Brothers Series:
Challenge: Camden's Story
Endurance: Tanner's Story
Keeper: Booker's Story
Surrender & Dominate: Gareth's Duet

Payback: A Harris Brother Spin-off Standalone
Blindsided: A Harris Brother Spin-off Standalone
Replay: A Harris Brother Spin-off Standalone
Sweeper: A Secret Harris Brother Standalone

The Wait With Me Series:
Wait With Me: A Tire Shop Rom-Com
Next in Line: A Bait Shop Rom-Com
One Moment Please: A Hospital Cafeteria Rom-Com
Take A Number: A Bakery Rom-Com
Last on the List: A Boss/Nanny Rom-Com

Pointe of Breaking: A College Dance Standalone by Amy Daws &
Sarah J. Pepper

Chasing Hope: A Mother's *True* Story of Loss, Heartbreak,
and the Miracle of Hope

For all retailer purchase links, visit:www.amydawsauthor.com

ACKNOWLEDGEMENTS

At last, Dean and Norah are complete! This was a slow burn book for me in the age of covid and I couldn't have completed it without my trusty team of helpers!

My beta readers, Beth, Jennifer, Franci, and Jane Ashley Converse. Man, you guys are so clutch for me! You all help me out in ways that are unique to you and our friendship. I am so, so thankful you all still tolerate me and my endless book update emails and needy verbal processing. My stories are better because of you!

My PA, Julia: Thank you so much for being my sounding board always and for reading whenever I need you to and your overall badassery. Thanks to my sister-in-law Megan for our boozy brainstorms. They are my favorite! And thanks to my editing and proofing eyes, Karen, Jenny, Lydia, and Julia. Squeaky clean books are so important, so thank you.

Last but certainly not least, I always love to thank my family. For starters, my dad, who distracted me from writing on my lakeside writing retreat this summer. I didn't get much done on my book, but sitting outside with you was more meaningful than words anyways. To my hubby who still occasionally takes his shirt off when I tell him to, thank you for dealing with me in all my neurotic ways. My eight-year-old, Lolo: You were a huge distraction being home with me this summer and I wouldn't trade it for a million words.

And to my special six angels in the sky…thank you for inspiring words and thoughts and feelings and perspective. You made me the mother I am today.

MORE ABOUT THE AUTHOR

 Amy Daws is an Amazon Top 25 bestselling author of the Harris Brothers Series and is most known for her punny, footy-playing, British playboys. The Harris Brothers and her London Lovers Series fuel her passion for all things London. When Amy's not writing, she's watching Gilmore Girls or singing karaoke in the living room with her daughter while Daddy awkward-smiles from a distance.

For more of Amy's work, visit: www.amydawsauthor.com or check out the links below.

www.facebook.com/amydawsauthor

www.twitter.com/amydawsauthor

instagram.com/amydawsauthor

Printed in Great Britain
by Amazon